DOUBLEDAY
Romance Library

LOVE IN THE WILDS

THE MARRIAGE CONTRACT

INNOCENT DECEPTION

NELSON DOUBLEDAY, Inc.
Garden City, New York

Printed in the United States of America

CONTENTS

❦

Love in the Wilds

Love in the Wilds

by SUZANNE ROBERTS

ONE

THE LAND had a dreamlike improbability about it; there seemed to be an ocean of grass, grass of a peculiar light green, the color of shallow tropic seas. It appeared to be endless in expanse, flecked everywhere with the fleeing figures of wild animals—thousands upon uncountable, incredible thousands. Beyond this there were low mountains, rocky outcrops like strange ships sailing a flat, inland sea.

Jennifer, peering out the window of the plane, could see zebras and gazelles grazing, while vultures flew above them in an effortless circle beneath the descending plane. The sky around them was serene and blue; now, she could make out the air terminal at Nairobi, a low, whitewashed building with palm trees all around it.

The plane came to a smooth landing and people began unfastening seat belts, gathering up belongings, saying goodbye to each other. It had taken three jets to get her here; she had lost track of the hours, due to long layovers in Morocco and Gabon. She had been tired, very tired, as she left New York to begin the first long leg of the trip, but now, she suddenly felt renewed, uplifted, and a growing sense of excitement began in her.

She had not anticipated the heat; it came upon her like a moist steambath, taking her breath for a second, making her feel dizzy. Then, with the others, she made her way down the steps of the big plane and walked across the expanse of cement glistening in the brilliant sunlight. She must look for Maggie; she should have wired from Morocco—the plane was terribly late—

"Jennifer? Jennifer Logan?"

Jenny turned quickly around. The woman was smiling, in her late fifties, perhaps, with friendly blue eyes peering over large sunglasses. She wore a white floppy hat and pants suit; she looked rather like one of the well-to-do ladies from New England, in town for a day's shopping.

"Aunt Margaret?"

"So," the older woman said, beginning to smile. "It is you! Yes; I should have known—I remember your eyes." She hugged Jennifer; there was the pleasant, cool scent of cologne. "I expect you're dead on your feet, poor darling. I've been hanging around here half the day, waiting for you."

They were walking through the terminal. It was large, not so big as those in New York, but very modern. People embraced each other, talking in a language Jenny didn't understand, but, unlike when she was in Morocco, she was certain it wasn't French.

"I'm terribly sorry," she said, allowing herself to be guided toward the baggage department. "The plane had some sort of mechanical problem and we had to wait for hours."

"Well, at least you're here, my dear, safe and sound." The brilliant blue eyes glanced at her again. "Are you all right? Perhaps you'd like a cool drink before we go to the reserve."

"That would be nice."

"Good. Go on in and order something—get a sandwich too, because my cook won't be in until morning; she's gone to help her daughter have a baby. I'll see to your baggage and get them in the jeep—you just go on in and find a table."

Jenny nodded and obediently went into a large, very pleasantly cool room where food and drinks were being served by white-coated waiters. She should have realized that her great-aunt would be very efficient. Maggie had raised Jenny's mother and her mother had been like that. She blinked her eyes in the near-darkness of the room and finally made her way to a window table with shaded green glass. From this vantage point, she could see the brown mountains and the waves of pale green grass beyond the airport.

Well, she'd done it. Made the decision, turned her life around, headed in a new and, she hoped, far better direction. A smiling waiter appeared almost instantly with a pitcher of fresh iced tea, poured a glass for Jennifer, and inquired in nearly perfect English about her order.

"Someone else is coming, thank you. I believe we're going to have a sandwich."

It surprised her a little that the menu, printed in three languages, contained things that were familiar—eggs, salads, fresh fruits in season, cold chicken. Perhaps it wouldn't all seem so strange after all. Perhaps she would be able to adjust at once, finding that the stories she'd heard of Africa—tales of dark places, weird voodoo rites, vicious animals, and poison darts—were all foolish.

Perhaps in no time at all, she would be able to erase every memory of Brendon Miles and the mistake she had very nearly made with him. She had managed, on the long, arduous flight over not to think of the life she was leaving behind her—her job at the advertising agency, her nice little apartment she'd waited nearly a year and a half to get, the pulsing, exciting pace of New York. But now, sitting there waiting for her great-aunt, the dreaded feelings—feelings that asked what on earth was she doing here, why had she made such a decision in such a brief time, was it too late to make a transatlantic call and get it all back again—began to come to her.

The surprising letter from Maggie had come just two weeks ago, with a warm invitation to come and spend some time in Africa "any time you please." Jennifer, who had spent many sleepless nights trying to make up her mind about Brendon Miles, had seen the letter as some sort of enchanted, heaven-sent messenger, offering her a quick way out of her problems. Staying in New York meant working for Brendon; it seemed unthinkable to quit, to go to work in some other place, have another boss, live in the same city as he did and never see him again. She had felt trapped, doomed, locked in a snowballing situation that drew her nearer and nearer to a sexual affair with him, an affair she did not really want.

Now, she was safe, safe from that, at least. She might miss her life, her job, her apartment, miss seeing him—but at least, she wouldn't end up like so many young girls—involved in a heartbreaking affair with her married boss.

Maggie hurried into the room, glanced around, and, seeing Jennifer, came over to the table, taking off her wide-brimmed hat. Her hair, like Jennifer's, was rich, dark auburn, without a trace of gray in it. There were fine lines around and under Maggie's blue eyes, however, but still, she seemed young and full of energy. It had been seven years since Jennifer had seen her last; Maggie and her husband had flown over for the sad funeral of Jenny's mother. Since that time, Maggie's husband had died—Jenny had sent a cable at the time, and now, she realized it seemed odd to see her aunt without Jack. They had been married nearly forty years when he died of a poison arrow meant for a leopard.

"I've had your luggage loaded in the jeep," her aunt said, sipping the cold tea. "You didn't bring much, did you? That was very clever of you."

"I'm afraid I left in rather a hurry." No need to tell all of it, not just now. If her aunt could recover so beautifully from losing her beloved husband, surely she, Jennifer, could quickly get over a man she shouldn't ever have wanted in the first place!

"I really didn't expect you to come, you know," Maggie said, her eyes studying Jennifer. She smiled, her hand reaching out for Jenny's. "But I'm awfully glad you did. Frankly, I've had my bad moments since I lost Jack. No," she said quickly, "please don't sympathize. We had thirty-nine perfect years together and I'll be darned if I'm going to give in to self-pity. Some women never find what I had with him."

"Some of us get sidetracked," Jenny said, and she saw something spark in her aunt's blue eyes, some kind of intelligent, quick reasoning. Surely she must have wondered at Jenny's quick decision to quit her job and come here, with only a brief cable to announce the time of her arrival.

Maggie patted her hand, then turned her attention to the menu.

"Try the cold chicken, dear; it's probably very good here. After today, you can start acquiring a taste for authentic African food."

"I'm sure I will."

"First we'll have our lunch, then, when I've got you back at the house and rested, we can talk. If you feel like it, that is."

So she did suspect there was a reason for the hasty exit, the retreat from New York, the strange turnabout and the cable, asking if Jenny might come to Kenya and stay "forever, maybe, if you could help me find a job, Aunt Margaret. . . ."

It was a powerful-sounding motor under the hood of that oversized, four-wheel-drive vehicle, and Maggie handled it as if she'd been born to it. In what seemed like no time at all they were on their way, breezing down the modern highway and finally, turning off on a narrow road that led to the bush country. Here, only five miles outside the city, Jennifer was introduced to the old, unchanging Africa. They were passing a hunting camp; dusty and seemingly deserted, a glinting mound of wire snares seemed to be everywhere, on both sides of the road. Jennifer, wearing a large-brimmed, borrowed hat

(Maggie had thoughtfully brought one along) looked at them without understanding.

"Damn!" It was Maggie, her mouth grim. "No matter how many game scouts tear those obscene, evil things down, the poachers always put them back up again!"

"What on earth are they?" Jenny had to nearly shout above the roar of the engine. "What are they for?"

"To kill, that's what." Maggie's tanned face was expressionless, but there was deep contempt in her voice. "Death by snare. Vicious, slow torture. The animal catches its neck or leg in a loop and tries to escape—the harder it pulls, the deeper the noose sinks into its flesh. I've seen some of them with their heads nearly torn off from the snares, or legs missing."

"But—how can—why do they allow—" A kind of slow horror was washing over Jenny. She had not bargained on cruelty, although of course, she should have expected it, in one form or another, in this still-primitive country.

"Oh, they're outlawed," Maggie said above the noise of the motor, "but that doesn't stop them. Some of them, the poachers, work for commercial syndicates. It isn't going to end until stupid, vain women stop buying coats made of skins, or handbags made of crocodile—even some perfumes have aphrodisiacs made out of pulverized rhino horn. Looks like we'll have to do another big sweep, and get all the snares we can. But they'll be back in a week or two. They always are."

"And you—the government, can't stop them?"

"Not for long. Poachers usually believe they have a God-given right to kill the game." Maggie glanced at Jennifer. "Sit tight now, we're coming to a sharp turn." She twisted the steering wheel as Jenny held her breath. They were going up a steep hill; to the right and left of them the pale grass flowed like a shimmering green curtain. "*Nyama ya mungu,*" Maggie said.

The road narrowed; Jenny put both hands on the seat and clutched it.

"What did you say?"

"There's a Swahili phrase which means 'meat of God.' The poachers think they have a divine right. Don't worry, you won't tumble out. I've never lost a passenger yet from this old crate!" Maggie shifted into high gear as they climbed the steep hill. "I've only got one rule about riding in this machine and that's that I don't drive at night anymore, because of the arrows."

"Did you say arrows?" Jennifer's voice was alarmed.

"In very thick bush, you can't see very well, so you can't duck. We're coming into that sort of terrain just now. The bloody poachers use them, of course, to kill game—the arrows are poisoned and when the poison is fresh, it'll kill a wild animal in thirty minutes." She stared straight ahead. "Jack died on our front porch. He'd managed to drive the jeep to the reserve and on to our house there, but there wasn't even time to call a doctor. It was dark, you see—he was just on his way home from Nairobi. I never go out at night anymore; it's the one rule I must insist you obey, Jenny."

Jenny nodded, still clutching the seat. Was she, she wondered, going to be afraid, always afraid of something terrible happening while she was here? She stared at the brilliant green grass as they drove onward. It might be good for her to feel fear, to worry about things like wire snares and poison arrows; fear might be a kind of purging for her, a release from a very different kind of trap—the one she'd nearly fallen into because of Brendon Miles.

They entered the reserve shortly before dusk. The large wooden gate was lifted to let the jeep pass through by a smiling black child who grinned in delight as Maggie handed him a small bag of candy bought in Nairobi.

"That's Massukuntna's grandson," she told Jenny. "You'll meet Massukuntna at the house, most likely. His wife is my cook, but as I told you, she's away until morning."

The old man, a tall, spare Shangaan elder, was waiting for them, squatting on the wide porch of the main house, smoking a long pipe. He stood up as Maggie pulled up, parking the jeep.

"He'll bring your things, Jenny." She waved as the old man approached them.

"No rain yet," he said, his eyes watching Jennifer, the newcomer. "Rain won't come for another two weeks. I had a dream that told me."

"Well, you haven't been wrong yet, Massukuntna. This is Jennifer Logan, my niece, child of my sister's daughter."

Jenny, suddenly feeling a bit shy, put out a friendly hand, but the old man didn't take it. Instead, he made a rather formal bow and began unloading her suitcases.

"We'll have a drink on the porch if you like," Maggie said. She led the way to the wide, screened door, and held it open. "It usually takes people around here a while to get friendly, but when they do, they love you for life. So don't be offended."

"I'm not."

They were inside the house, in the hallway. It was blessedly cool; fans from the inner rooms caught the air and sent it wafting throughout the entire, shaded house. Jennifer, following her aunt up the lovely, carved staircase, began to think of a cooling bath and the first solid night's rest she'd had since getting Maggie's invitation.

"Jack and I always called this the guest room," Maggie said, pushing open one of the bedroom doors. "Now, it can be your room, for as long as you want to stay." She was busy opening the windows, the deep closet, turning down the white-sheeted, double brass bed. Suddenly, her face was serious. "After you let me know you were coming, I told myself I ought to write to you or cable you or something—and tell you something about what you could expect. But I had the feeling that you were very anxious to get away from New York."

"Yes," Jenny said quietly, "I was."

The old man had brought the bags, setting them down just outside the door. Once again, he looked hard at Jenny, his eyes appraising and intelligent.

"Then it's good you came," Maggie said, "even though this place takes some getting used to."

That, Jenny was to learn, was putting it mildly. The big house had ten rooms, not including the spacious kitchen, and a porch that faced Lake Naivasha. Beyond, in the back, was the deep green forest and brush, and to the west lay the rain forest. The house was elevated somewhat, with the porch resting on imbedded poles, so that there was altogether a stunning view of the blue lake and the lush vegetation. Left alone in her bedroom, Jenny, wearing her bathrobe, leaned out the window and called to Maggie, who sat on the front porch, feet propped up on the porch railing.

"Aunt Maggie?"

Maggie put down her drink and squinted upward in the fading sunlight.

"I guess you found out, Jenny." She was close to smiling

"I can't find—there doesn't seem to be—"

"A bathtub?"

"Yes."

"Come on down and have your shower, dear."

"Down? Down there?" Jenny stared in surprise at the odd-looking contraption her aunt was pointing to. It was a sort of round, fenced-in structure with a cloth bag suspended overhead by rather frayed-looking ropes. "You mean I'm supposed to shower out there—in the *yard?*"

"Water's all ready for you, dear, nice and warm. You'll find some lovely French soap in the top drawer of the bureau. Bring a towel, dear, and shampoo—it's French too—I have it sent from the Ivory Coast." She grinned, finally. "Taking an outdoor shower always surprises my guests from the States, but you'll get used to it."

At first, Jenny felt ill-at-ease about taking off her robe, standing nude inside that rustic-fence enclosure, but then she realized the fence actually came up to her chin, or nearly so, and the only living things rude enough to stare were six or so monkeys who sat or lounged in a big tree nearby. Every time Jenny pulled the rope to pour warm water on herself, the creatures made a strange, screaming noise and a few of them, Jenny noted with amazement, even clapped their little hands.

Whether it was the hard-milled soap, the rich shampoo in the pretty bottle, or perhaps wildflowers growing nearby, she didn't know, but there was a lovely fragrance wafting around her as she showered, and the water was as soft as milk, flowing over her slender body. She began to feel better, much, much better, and finally, after rinsing her freshly washed, shoulder-length hair, she found herself laughing out loud at the antics of the little monkeys. One of them, flirting with her, showing off, swung from tree to nearby tree, scolding and chattering, turning his tiny, hairy head to see if Jenny was watching.

She toweled herself dry and, wrapping the soft towel around her head, got into her robe and stepped outside the confines of the makeshift shower. She looked toward the porch, but her aunt must have gone inside. The whole house seemed to glow with a soft light—candles—and it occurred to Jenny that there probably wasn't any electricity here at all. *Good,* she told herself, walking through the deepening shadows toward the house, *no lights, no phone, no radio or television—wonderful!* The world she had come from would surely dissolve into a kind of muted background, which was exactly what she wanted it to do!

Aunt Maggie said nothing that night to Jenny, nothing about why she had come so suddenly, and as the two women said goodnight an hour or so after Jenny's lovely shower, she still had asked no real questions. There would, thank God, be plenty of time for talk. Perhaps, Jenny thought, a good, honest talk with a kind and understanding woman was exactly what she needed; she had not spoken to anyone about her near-affair with Brendon, not even the other girls in the office, although she felt quite certain that they knew.

Her boss, at forty, had been attractive, there was no mistake about that. Stunned with grief at the sudden death of her youngish mother, Jennifer moved from the somewhat staid little town on the Miles River in Maryland to New York—and was almost instantly swept up in an atmosphere of intrigue and romance.

Perhaps, she was to realize much later, she had been looking for something, someone, to love, and unfortunately, Brendon had made himself all too available. What began with a kind of light bantering in the office developed into his inviting her to attend television shows with him ("Make lots of notes," he told her, and she believed him) because many of their advertising clients had spots on T.V. After that, it seemed only natural to allow her kind boss to buy her a very late supper, after a show's taping, and drive her to her small, Eastside apartment.

How could she have been so naive, so foolish? By the time he finally got around to kissing her, in his car, outside her apartment, she imagined herself to be in love with him. After that, she refused to attend the show tapings, refused the suppers, even the phone calls he'd make from a bar someplace in Manhattan. She had the usual symptoms—the burning desire to see what his wife looked like, the insane eagerness to believe his wife really was the wicked witch Brendon said she was, the dreams about making love, the conflict about wanting to quit her job and being afraid she'd be sorry—

But now, lying in that big, soft bed with the netting over it, with the silvery moonlight making blue-white puddles on the scrubbed wood floor, all of that seemed misty and almost dim to her, as if she had really put it away forever. Or as if it had not really been important and was very easily forgotten.

She slept a dreamless, exhausted sleep, finally opening her eyes at some sound. For a second, she did not know where she was; the room was silent, still bathed in the blue and silver light, and a moist breeze, forerunner of the monsoon season due any time, cooled the large bedroom. Jenny turned her head to look at the small traveling clock she'd remembered to bring along: quarter past two. She had been in bed and asleep since before ten.

The sound she heard was music. She listened, not at all sure that she wasn't dreaming, and deciding she wasn't, got out of bed, pushing back the clean-smelling mosquito netting to go to the open window. Then, she put her ear against the sturdy screen and listened once again.

It was definitely music, very raucous, the blaring, disco beat she'd learned to hate in New York. There had been lots of dates at the end of her stay there, men who took her dancing, young men who were supposed to erase her threatening feelings for Brendon Miles, but didn't. She had gotten mightily sick of that kind of music, and now, it came as a mild shock to hear it of all places, here, in this remote and peaceful place in Africa. Drums, native drums, wouldn't have surprised her; they would have been pleasing to hear, in fact, but this music—where could it be coming from?

It seemed to come and go, drifting in on the night wind, so she speculated that wherever it was, it was very likely some distance away. Finally, she crawled back into the comfortable bed, closed her eyes and once again, slept.

She awoke to a discreet tapping at the door, then a plump, smiling black woman came in.

"Good morning. I am Manguana; your auntie usually has her tea downstairs, but if you like, I can bring you a cup here, although I'm very busy with the children this morning."

"Oh no," Jenny said quickly; she wasn't used to the idea of having anyone do anything for her. "I'll get a cup myself, thank you, in the kitchen." She realized she had slept very well and felt surprisingly good, refreshed. "Aunt Maggie told me you were helping deliver a baby yesterday."

Manguana smiled. "A boy, very fat and handsome." She was, Jenny realized, quite old, and yet, her skin was satin-smooth and nearly unwrinkled. "I'll make you a nice honey cake for your second tea today. Massukuntna told me you are far too skinny."

"Massukuntna? Oh yes—your husband." Jenny smiled. "That would be lovely, thank you."

In the bathroom, Jenny took a good long look at herself in the old-fashioned, full-length mirror. Yes; she was a bit too thin, but thin in New York had somehow meant something different from what it apparently did here. In New York, she had always felt a certain pressure, as if she had been asked to run someplace, hurry up and run someplace. How long had it been since she'd really felt at ease with herself, with life, so that she could enjoy just sleeping or eating?

Too long. She stepped out of her nightgown and stretched, beginning to feel a lovely sense of anticipation. Her amber-colored hair and matching eyes were like her mother's, Laura's, but Jenny had never felt beautiful. It was her mother who had attracted men; they had sought her, loved her, wanted her—and she had married and divorced three of them before her death.

She found Maggie sitting on the porch behind a small table, typing, her glasses slightly down on her nose.

"There you are, Jenny. I hope you rested well—you look as if you took a magic beauty pill. I'd forgotten what lovely hair we Kenton women have. Red but not brassy. I see you've got a cup; have more tea, dear."

Jenny settled herself in a comfortable wicker rocker that faced the lake.

"Kenton women?"

"That was Mama's maiden name, dear. Your grandmother's too, of course. We've all got her hair, God rest her restless soul. Are you feeling better?"

"Much better, thank you. Manguana said she'll make me a honey cake. She thinks I'm far too skinny."

Maggie laughed, taking off her glasses. "She told me that, too, when I first came here with Jack. That was twenty-five years ago, when your mother married your father and I felt I could do as I pleased at last. Jack so wanted to take this job here—so off we came." She gazed out at the lake. "I've asked myself a thousand times if I'd do it over, if I'd come here again, knowing I'd lose him the way I did."

There was a small silence. "Would you, Aunt Maggie?" Jenny's voice was gentle. She had always been fascinated by love, the blinding, spellbinding love that sometimes happened between a man and a woman. She had seen her mother in love, or what passed for love, but it never had lasted. Her mother had always tired of the men, always had wanted out of the arrangement, finally. But Maggie—what Maggie and her man once had was very real and beautiful; Jenny could believe that because even now, her aunt's eyes shone when she spoke of the years with him.

"I'm not really sure, Jenny. He was happy here; he loved Africa and the people here—but mostly, I'd give anything to do it over again, do it all over and refuse to come here. I'd somehow convince him to keep on with his veterinary practice in Maryland. I guess," she said, going back to her typing, "that only happens at night. One gets a bit weary of sleeping in a half-warmed bed, you know." She looked at Jenny as if to dispel the sudden mood of gloom. "Look, why don't you type this for me, dear? I've always been rotten at typing, I'm afraid. I've written a letter to our office in Nairobi about the poachers' traps we saw coming down here, requesting they sweep the snares."

"I'd love to," Jenny told her. She took her aunt's place at the small typewriting table. "Oh, by the way, Aunt Maggie, I heard music last night, coming from the south, I think it was. What on earth was that?"

Instantly, Maggie's tanned face seemed to go pale; her blue eyes flashed what could only have been outrage.

"Music? This far away? Damn him—that man has no decency at all! There was Manguana's daughter, having her baby in the village, and I'll bet that music was even louder there! And the animals—anything could disturb them, make them upset or nervous—"

"But where was it coming from?"

Maggie, her mouth showing her anger, had opened a desk drawer and was holding a powerful-looking pair of binoculars up to her eyes. "From the lodge, my dear. From Damien Lear's infamous hunting lodge. One would think that when those rich idiots he lets stay there go off on their safaris, they'd want to get a good night's rest before doing their killing. But no—they're up at all hours, carousing and drinking and listening to that insane music!"

Jenny wisely asked no more questions about the mysterious Damien Lear that morning. Whoever, whatever, he was, Maggie very clearly despised him—and Jenny had never before seen her good-natured aunt dislike anybody!

The letter typing, along with a somewhat detailed report containing figures on the past month's budget for the reserve, took up all of the morning. Jenny took a moment to have more tea, along with Manguana's delicious honey cake (warm, sweet, filled with peanuts and thick honey), then she stood up, stretched, and walked with Maggie to the shelter house built for the monkeys.

"We fence in all the animals we can," Maggie told her as she strung up golden, ripe bananas onto a hanging rope. "The monkeys, of course, we can't very well contain. They come into the reserve, eat, chatter, look around and then go back to the bush, most of them. Some of them stay, though—like old Lovely here." She reached up and handed a banana to a bright-eyed little monkey who'd been watching them from her vantage point on a giant tree limb.

"Lovely?"

Maggie smiled. "It seemed like a proper name for her, since she's so sweet-natured. When you've been here awhile, Jenny, you'll find yourself changing your ideas about animals. You won't find a single one of them repulsive or ugly. It may amaze you to know that one actually comes to revere them, because they, like us, are God's, aren't they?"

The two women worked side by side, stringing the fruit onto the rope, pouring fresh lake water they carried in buckets into the watering troughs, putting fresh straw down for one very pregnant monkey who seemed content to sit and chew on grass instead of eating with the others.

"Aunt Maggie," Jenny asked finally, as they walked back toward the house together, "do you mind telling me why you dislike that man so?"

There was a small silence; only a tightening of Maggie's jaw told of her reaction to the name.

"He's a killer," she said finally, as they came in sight of the house. "That's why."

"A killer! I don't understand—"

"Jack didn't agree with me, but my husband was a saint and I'm not. We both knew Damien Lear from the time he first came here, and we knew when he bought that piece of land that it was to be used for the wrong purpose."

"For what purpose?"

"Money. Drinking and getting up at dawn to stumble out and kill animals. That's what those paying guests of his do, most of them. Not only that, he thinks we're all a bunch of bleeding hearts here at the reserve, that it goes against nature to look out for wild animals, protect them, the way we do. If you want to know what I think, Jenny, I think he's a totally embittered, horrible man who doesn't give a damn about anything—man or animal!"

"He sounds terrible," Jenny admitted. "I'm sorry if I got you all upset."

"I mean to send a note over there," Maggie muttered. "I'm going to let him know that if he doesn't turn down his bloody taped music, I'll see to it that a curse is put on him!"

"A curse! Aunt Maggie, you don't actually believe that sort of thing, do you?"

"No, and neither does he. But at least," her aunt said as they climbed the porch steps, "he'll know how riled up I am!"

There were children living on the reserve grounds with their parents, some twenty little ones in all. While their parents worked on the reserve, they usually played around the main house. This time they accompanied Jenny while she fed the animals and they napped while she spent the remainder of the day doing some bookkeeping chores for Maggie. At dusk, Jenny walked alone to the lake to watch a pack of cheetahs drink and nurse their young.

There was a feeling of peace beginning to filter into her, a sort of lovely magic that filled her with a sense of energy yet allowed her to sit content in absolute stillness as she watched the rain forest birds and animals at close range.

Even the oppressive heat this evening didn't change her happy mood.

"Things will be released when the rains come," Maggie said, sipping a glass of white wine with her soup. "When the time for the rain gets near like this, things get—pent up. It always happens." She looked at Jenny over the candlelight. Manguana had set a card table up for them, on the porch, with candles and wine Maggie said she'd been saving for company.

"I don't want to be that," Jenny told her. "I don't want to be company."

"Be whatever makes you feel best, my dear."

"What I'm trying to say is—Aunt Maggie—you told me I could stay on if I wanted to. Did you really mean that?"

"Of course. But I think it's far too soon for you to make up your mind to that. When the time is right, I'll take you on a bush tour. I want you to see a bit of what Damien Lear tries so hard to keep as it is. But you aren't ready for that sort of horror yet. We'll go before the rains come."

Slowly, Jenny put down her spoon. The soup was very filling, with herring and some sort of sweet-tasting meat and okra and eggs in it. She was used to eating very little.

"Horror?"

Maggie nodded. "Yes, horror. And Damien says it's survival of the fittest. Some of them die miserably. Last week we found a female waterbuck who'd gone to the lake to drink, full of fever. He claims that what we're doing here is nothing but zookeeping. But as I said, he's an angry, bitter man, in spite of what he pretends to be." She put down her wine glass. "I'm going to bed, Jennifer. No more of this morbid talk, if you don't mind. Speaking of Damien Lear this late in the day might very well give me nightmares!" She leaned over and gently kissed Jenny's smooth cheek. "Sleep well."

"Goodnight, Aunt Maggie."

But this night, Jenny could not sleep no matter how hard she tried. Finally, she realized that *trying* to sleep was foolish, so she put on her robe and padded barefoot down the freshly scrubbed wooden stairs and out to the porch.

The night sky was stunningly beautiful, filled with gray and silver rain clouds, rolling, boiling, moving across the high face of the moon, seeming to change color from silver to purple and blue, coming lower and lower, like some mysterious, mystical bag filled with endless water about to dump itself on the dry forest. She understood that feeling of release her aunt had talked about, the sudden feeling of freedom when the rains finally came.

And as she watched that silver-streaked sky, they began, the slow droplets of water. At first, Jenny thought it was only some night bug on the leaves of the orchids that grew wild all around the porch, but then another came, and another, making a little sound, a quick, steady little tune. A bird screamed from somewhere in the rain forest nearby, flying swiftly toward the clouds, as if it couldn't wait for the blessed, cooling water to fall upon it but must go and meet it on its way down.

Jenny stepped from the high porch to the yard as if she were in a trance; Massukuntna had been wrong this time, mistaken this time, for he had said it would come in two weeks. But here it was; here it came, heavier now, beginning with an earnestness that soaked her hair and her thin nightgown and made cool mud of the dirt under her bare feet. She stood in the yard with her face upraised, loving the feel of its softness on her face, on her body, like a lover's caress—soothing and yet exciting . . .

A new time had begun then, in this part of the world. A time of renewal, of strength, a time when the weary trees and thirsty lakes could replenish themselves. From their shelter house, the monkeys screeched out in excitement and beyond, in the rain forest, she could see the great trees moving as animals moved in them with a sense of joy and urgency.

Suddenly, a window opened and Maggie's scolding voice called to Jenny:

"Jennifer! Do you want to get the chills?"

Jenny took a deep breath. "All right—I'm coming in!"

But on the porch step, she turned to listen. There was no music coming from Damien Lear's lodge tonight. Either he had taken Maggie's message seriously or else even such a man as he was enchanted by the unexpected flow from the skies, coming so much sooner than expected.

And surely, Jenny thought, smiling her thanks as her aunt put a huge dry towel around her shoulders, surely that was a very good sign, this early rain, as if, like the thirsty trees in the forest, she too could be renewed, changed, given new joy and strength.

TWO

No MATTER how early in the morning Jennifer got up, dressed, quickly washed up and hurried downstairs, her aunt was always already there, calmly sitting at her desk in the study, usually with a finished tea tray nearby.

"Good morning," Maggie would say sweetly, "did you oversleep this morning, dear?"

Usually, it would barely be light outside. And now that the rainy season had come, it was darkish all day long, but that didn't mean the chores lessened in any way. On the contrary, there seemed to be more to do now than ever, since keeping the young animals dry was very important.

There was, as Maggie said, so much to lose, so much to save, by helping them. Within that first week there, Jennifer had watched in awe as a lioness, regal, haughty, usually amused-looking when tourists were frightened of her, gave birth to three fat cubs. The following day, a baby elephant was born and promptly named Peanuts by Jenny and the children who usually went with her when she did the feeding.

So gradually, she was unwinding, getting used to and actually becoming a part of this strange, secluded life. Some people, but not all of them on the reserve, spoke English, so sign language or a friendly smile or gesture in some cases served to make new friends for Jenny. The children took to her at once and after the feedings outside, she began teaching them little games to play indoors. They taught her games too; she found herself laughing once again.

Afternoons were spent typing for Maggie—reports were endless, copied in triplicate always, sent to parks and other reserves, with bills for food, accounts of money spent, papers to government officials for their stamp of approval, letters to park directors, scientists, veterinarians, rangers, game scouts. She wrote up documented complaints concerning poachers and sent notes to tribal elders from the bush country, asking them to tea.

It was on the day of such an anticipated visit from an elder that Jenny had tea on the screened-in porch. Maggie, with the visiting elder, had gone off to attend to the repairing of a fence knocked down by an angry cheetah, a spoiled old female who had wandered onto the reserve several months before, bleeding badly from the cruelty of a poacher; her tail had been cut off, to be sold and used as a fly whisk.

"Manguana, I haven't heard that music coming from Mr. Lear's lodge lately."

"Your auntie put a stop to it," Manguana said. "The doctor sent a letter of apology, but your auntie tore it up."

Manguana, Jenny knew, had worked here with her aunt since both women were relatively young; they were as close as sisters. So whenever Manguana spoke of her Aunt Maggie, Jenny listened. The words, though sometimes harsh-sounding, were always laced with love and affection.

"Tore it up? That isn't like her to do that."

"She gets angry too quickly, sometimes. I expect it comes from missing her man. When he died, she acted like he'd only gone to town and he'd be coming back for supper. But at night, we used to hear her cry. Sometimes we still can hear her." She suddenly looked sad as she rolled raisin dough out for bread. "Dr. Lear is a good man, but your auntie doesn't think so." She spoke with a very slight French accent.

"*Dr*. Lear! You don't mean he's actually a medical doctor?"

Manguana nodded. "He doesn't practice anymore." She seemed to want to change the subject. "You should go over to his lodge, maybe make some friends. You'll get lonely here, with only old women and little children and animals. Over there, you could drink a little red wine, dance to some music—"

Jennifer smiled. "No, thank you; I had all the partying and dancing I want, in New York. I've been very happy here, honestly." She put a fresh sheet of paper in the typewriter. For some reason, in spite of meaning what she'd said about feeling happy here, there was a certain feeling of curiosity in her that had been scratched by Manguana's words. "I might stop by the lodge sometime, if it wouldn't offend my aunt." She bent her head to her work. "And Manguana—"

"Yes?"

"You are not old! And neither is my aunt."

A quick smile. "Old enough to have pains when the rains come."

Jenny resumed her work, losing herself in the letters composed in longhand by Maggie, who did not like to type and seemed glad to have Jennifer to do it for her. The current batch of letters contained a heated complaint to officials concerning the finding of a young bushbuck; its foot and leg had been caught in two snare traps. After surgery, the animal limped about the compound, accepting hunks of coarse brown sugar from the children, but, as the letter stated, he would never be able to survive outside the reserve.

Late that afternoon, Maggie left in the jeep with the elder to visit his village and take gifts. He had come laden with gifts for everybody, baskets of exotic herbs for cooking, some beautiful, sturdy pottery, a shawl for Maggie.

The big house was unusually quiet; Jenny took a rain shower (no need for the bucket to dump on one's head), standing a long time in the silky, warm rainwater, soaping all over, finally going back into the house to dress in jeans and a fresh white blouse. She tied her long hair back in a silk scarf, remembering how she had bought it one day on her lunch hour while still in New York, half-planning to wear it sailing with her boss. She hadn't gone on that trip, and the scarf had been one of the few things she'd hurriedly packed to bring.

The usual cluster of children played quietly on the porch, waiting for time to go with Jenny on her daily visit to see the newborn animals in the compound.

"Can you carry a bucket all by yourself, Mieka?" Jenny asked, pantomiming the action.

The little boy nodded, his beautiful dark eyes full of delight. He spoke no English, but he and Jenny had liked each other instantly.

"Okay, then, off we go, children, and kindly button up your raincoats!"

They were all very proud of the new plastic raincoats Maggie had brought them from one of her shopping jaunts to Nairobi, although some of them looked lost inside the long sleeves and ground-length coats. They stood waiting patiently for Jenny while she filled their little buckets with goodies for the reserve's animal babies, sugar and bits of leftover cake and honey bread and three full buckets of sweet, syrupy water with special vitamins stirred in.

"Mustn't eat the sugar, Tania; Mieka dear, please be careful and don't spill!"

So off they all went, walking bravely in the heavy rain, stopping to admire the new baby eland, waiting while Jenny propped a board against a leap-proof fence and made a note to see that it got mended properly. The next step was a large, tin-can-constructed cage where a lioness was protected for the time being from her mate while she nursed her new cubs. Jenny and the children stayed their distance, pushing a bucket quickly through the door, then closing it.

She felt somewhat surprised at her own new courage around the wild animals, but as Maggie had told her—sometimes one found it far easier to deal with animals in their jungle than to deal with humans in theirs!

"Miss Jenny! *Miss Jenny!*"

Jennifer, who had been taking pictures of the new lion cubs, straightened up and peered through the rain as four of the children came running toward her. One of them, the smallest, tripped on his long raincoat and sprawled in the mud. Jenny hurried over to him and helped him up.

"Mozam—are you hurt?" He was crying loudly. "Mozam, what is it?"

She looked helplessly at the other three children who'd gone with him, carrying their buckets, to feed the monkeys. Their eyes were round, and suddenly, two of them began crying, along with little Mozam.

"Did—is one of the baby monkeys sick?"

The rain seemed to come down harder, drenching Jenny and the children. The older ones, the ones who spoke English as well as French and their own language, were not with her; they'd gone with Maggie and the elder.

"Did one of the animals frighten you, honey?"

Unable to understand her, the little boy stuck both little fists into his eyes and cried harder. Jenny gathered him to her; she had begun to feel not only mystified but helpless as well.

"Did—did one of the baby monkeys—" It was no use; none of them spoke English, except to be able to say Jenny's name. Besides, they were all crying now, even the bigger ones.

"Go back to the house," she told them, pointing. "Leave your buckets here, children, and go back to Missy Maggie's house, understand?" She gave the tallest of them a gentle shove toward the house, wiped off little Mozam's face with the scarf she'd taken from her hair, and, leaving her own full bucket of sweet milk behind with the others, headed for the large monkey shelter.

The animals there gave out a cheerful series of cries when they saw her; most of them began showing off immediately, pushing at each other, pretending to snarl, and rolling around in mock fights. Jenny peered inside the shelter, where it was newly swept and clean, smelling of warm hay. She could see the new mother in there, holding her tiny baby. The baby was very much alive; his beady black eyes blinked as Jenny opened the little door, and he tightened his grip on his mother's neck.

Nothing wrong here. Maybe the children had some sort of private quarrel, something to do with the sugar. She very nearly went back to get them, but as she started to, she heard a strange, hair-raising sound coming from the nearby bush, a kind of hoarse keening sound that sounded almost human.

She stood there, rooted to the ground, fear making her skin crawl. If Maggie had been home, Jenny would have run at once to the big house, but her aunt had left hours before. The choice was very simple—either she go back, try to find Massukuntna to come with her, or else go alone.

It came again, full of agony. *Snares,* Jenny thought suddenly, horror washing over her. She began to run toward the direction where the children had gone before they began crying. Here, the foliage was thick and dense; heavy bushes were bowed low with rain and the tall trees hid the clearing. Jenny pushed her way through; a bush scratched her face and she very nearly cried out.

Then, she had reached the clearing, a wide expanse of trampled weeds and half-eaten grass, surrounded on all sides by a fence. It was raining much harder now; the rain pelted her arms, her face, making it almost impossible to see but a few feet ahead. She walked on, then stopped, her skin chilling, as the terrible, keening sound came once again.

There seemed to be shadows, huge, hulking forms huddled in a group, about a hundred yards away. Still squinting through the rain, she saw that they were not shadows but elephants, females, and one of them was half-crouched on her forelegs. Thinking the beast might have been hurt, or was sick, Jenny walked on, but cautiously; Maggie had warned her strongly about getting too close to wild animals, even to take pictures.

But as Jenny got closer, the huge beasts moved away, all but the one who still crouched, looking almost as if it were doing some kind of well-learned circus trick. The cow saw Jenny and raised its trunk; the ear-piercing sound came once again.

Jenny knew she had moved in too close, but something, some deep desire to help if she could, had driven her on. And now, now that she was this close, she saw: It was the baby elephant, the one she had called Peanuts, dead, lying on its side, the wide little legs already stiffened in death.

She made some sound, a gasp, a half-sob, and moved even closer. The mother cow made no move, but watched her from its tiny eyes. Jenny, her eyes misting with tears, crouched to look more closely at the dead elephant.

It clearly had been shot. The wound was plainly visible between the eyes.

Jenny went no closer. She turned and walked back toward the lodge, remembering only after she'd reached the porch that Maggie had warned her never to turn her back on any of the animals. Apparently, the cow had not wanted to leave her dead baby, or else the poor thing had been so filled with grief that even a human presence posed no threat to her just now.

The children were in the kitchen with Manguana. Mugs of hot tea were on the table; little Mozam had stopped crying, but he looked at Jenny with big, sad eyes as she came in.

"Did they tell you, Manguana?"

"They told me, Missy. Better have tea, you are very wet and cold."

"Who did it? Do you know who possibly could have—"

"People from the lodge did it. My people kill and poach, but not with guns. People from the lodge did it, the rich ones who go there and spend money to hunt."

"But—this is a reserve! And that was a *baby* they killed, only a week or so old! How could they—how dare they—"

Manguana shrugged. She did not seem particularly moved; her face was impassive.

"Better a bullet than a snare, Missy. Death comes to all, and to weep for the dead is foolish. Come and have tea."

Jenny took a deep breath. "No," she said, and her voice trembled so that the children stared at her, as if waiting for her to begin crying. "No—I'm not going to—to just sit back and let them get away with this!" She had taken off her raincoat, now, she reached for it and put it on again. "If my aunt gets back before I do, please tell her I've gone to the lodge; tell her I've gone to tell Damien Lear exactly what I think of him!"

Without waiting to hear Manguana's called-out warning, Jenny turned and ran through the house, through the long, chilly hallway, down the steep porch steps, to the parked Land Rover at the side of the house. Maggie had given her a duplicate set of keys so she could drive into the nearby village anytime she wanted with the children; now, her trembling hand turned the key in the switch and in seconds, she was roaring down the gutted, narrow road leading from the house to the wider but unpaved village road.

Her mind was churning with rage; she drove too fast in the blinding rain, and only the built-in stability of the vehicle kept her on the road as she made a sharp turn. *Calm down,* she told herself, and, taking a deep breath, she slowed down somewhat, reaching to the front panel to turn on the defroster so she could see better. She had no clear idea as to where the lodge was; Maggie had pointed vaguely to the south once, her manner scornful when she spoke of it—or of Damien Lear—and it was in that direction that Jennifer drove now, past the brimming rain forest, past the side road that, she remembered, led directly to the tiny village where Maggie bought fresh produce and flour for Manguana's kitchen.

The road had improved considerably; it had been covered with asphalt and widened. Jenny slowed down and peered through the rain-swept windshield; a sign, neatly painted, announced that Safarilandia Lodge was five miles ahead. She began driving again; signs along the way welcomed the tourist, announced a large sauna bath, three indoor swimming pools, rooms with air-conditioning and a direct communications system to the States and all of Europe. Her rage increased when she read the last sign before the lodge came into view: *Wild animals may be viewed through glass from the convenience of our bar and lounge.*

She pressed down harder on the gas pedal and rounded a final curve. Suddenly, she was in full view of the lodge; it sat in a large grove of trees, surrounded by what appeared to be thousands of blooming orchids. There was a wide, wraparound porch with tastefully placed lounging chairs; the green-and-white-striped awnings of some sort of metal material kept the rain off those people who lounged out there. White-coated servants carried trays back and forth, and a young black girl wearing a long flowered dress pushed a food cart from one lounging guest to another. The entire effect was like something out of a dream, a veritable modern palace in the heart of the jungle, hewn wood and polished glass and plush furnishings in the middle of one of the most primitive parts of the world.

Jenny wasted no time. She parked the Land Rover directly in front of the porch, ignoring the polite sign forbidding parking there, and raced up the porch steps. The girl in the flowered dress paused in serving some sort of iced drink to a balding man smoking a large cigar; she reached out to stop Jenny, but Jenny merely pushed her hand aside and hurried through the ornately carved front door into the vast, carpeted room beyond.

This was a sort of lobby, discreetly decorated. A series of couches were placed around various huge, ceiling-high stone fireplaces, and from one of these, a dark-haired man wearing a neat tropical suit advanced toward Jenny. He was perhaps fifty, smiling, but clearly determined not to let her go any further.

"May we help you, Madame?"

"I came—I want to see Damien Lear."

"I'm afraid he isn't in. He's gone to Nairobi at the moment. Perhaps Madame would care to leave some message?"

She took a small breath. "I'll wait for him, thank you."

"I'm afraid Dr. Lear won't be back for at least several days, Madame."

Jenny looked into his eyes. They were oyster-colored, and something flickered in them; he was lying, she felt sure.

"Tell Dr. Lear," she said quietly, "that if he doesn't see me at once, I shall make such a scene that all of his guests will get in their fancy cars and drive straight to the airport!"

"Madame, I'm afraid I must ask you to leave at once."

"I mean it," she said evenly. "I'm here to see Damien Lear and I know he's here somewhere!"

The man reached out and closed one hand over the upper flesh of her arm, not hurting her, but holding onto her very firmly. His face was close to hers, she could see the small veins in his face.

"I'll escort you out the rear door, Madame—if you'll just—come right along with me—"

"I will not! Let go of me—*let go of me!*"

People sitting in the room, some reading, some drinking, smartly dressed and tanned, all of them, stared. Jenny, her left arm in the man's harsh grasp, suddenly drew back her right arm and raised it, preparing to smash her small right hand into the man's nose.

In that second, a door opened on the far side of the room. A tall man wearing white pants and an open white shirt stood there; the man who had hold of her suddenly released his grasp. The tall man in the unbuttoned shirt walked swiftly across the room; a smile had come on his handsome, tanned face. When he reached them, he put out his hand and took Jenny's; she looked up at him, into his clear blue eyes, startled.

"So," he said loudly, for everyone to hear, "you've come at last! I'm honored. Won't you come inside for a drink?"

And, his arm around her slender waist, he led her across that wide room, through the open door and into a large, obviously private office.

THREE

FOR A FEW seconds, they stood facing each other, Jennifer and the tall, deeply tanned man with the dark hair and the strikingly blue eyes. She was furious, breathing rather hard from her ill-concealed anger and the quick rush this man had given her from the outer room into his office.

For his part, he looked somewhat annoyed, but his hands had left her and his eyes began to look more amused than angry.

"Do you mind telling me what this is all about, Miss?"

Jennifer tried to keep calm, but even her voice was trembling:

"Someone from your hotel—or whatever it is—killed a baby elephant last night, or very early today. Maybe you already know about that—maybe shooting week-old animals is your idea of fair game, good sport, having a fun time! How much money do you get paid to allow people to trespass, how much does it cost those people out there to rent a gun from you, climb a restraining fence and take aim at a poor little—"

"Now wait a damned minute!" He was scowling; his eyes looked bewildered but there was a rising spark of rage in them. "Just calm down a minute and try to make sense! Nobody from my—hotel—as you call it, rents guns, in the first place, and I know better than to set foot on that bleeding-heart game reserve, because if I did, your sweet little aunt would blow my head off as soon as she saw who it was! Furthermore—"

"How dare you talk that way about—" Jenny stared up at him. "How did you know she's my aunt? How—how did you know who I am?"

The ghost of a grin touched his mouth. He went over to a small, portable bar, his back to her, and began mixing drinks. He was a big man, powerfully built, wide-shouldered and slim-hipped, with a broad chest with curly hair on it. With the open shirt, sleeves rolled up, feet bare, he looked more like a man ready to do some kind of bush work in the sweltering sun than the owner of what was reported to be thousands of acres in rich fertile bottom land surrounding his lodge.

"The bush is like a small provincial town," he said, his voice matter-of-fact. "News travels fast." He turned around, a glass in his hand. "It isn't every day a beautiful girl moves into our midst. Of course I heard about you. Besides, you're driving your aunt's souped-up Rover; I saw you when you drove up. Here, have a drink and calm down. I'm really sorry about—"

"Sorry! *Sorry!* Is that all you have to say, that you're sorry one of your spoiled guests—"

"Now hold on a minute," he said, his eyes narrowing a bit. "We don't know it was anybody from here, in the first place. And in the second place, I don't think anybody would be so stupid as to poach with a damned gun, I really don't. The people who come here spend one whole day listening to me harp about fair-game rules in this country, and I can't believe any one of them would be stupid enough to shoot a baby elephant, especially on sacred ground. Bourbon, Miss—"

"Logan," Jenny said evenly, "and I don't like the way you say 'sacred ground,' Dr. Lear. My aunt told me what you think of the work being done on the reserve. I guess you said it yourself, a moment ago, when you called us bleeding hearts." She took a small breath. "Are you saying you know nothing at all about what happened?"

"Absolutely. But I'll have it looked into, I assure you. Would you rather have scotch, Miss Logan?"

"Bleeding hearts don't drink this early in the day, Doctor."

He shrugged, smiling at her over the glass. His eyes, it seemed to Jenny, had warmed; it was as if he were actually enjoying himself. *Cruel,* she thought suddenly, *he has no compassion at all—none!*

"Why don't you go for a swim in one of the pools, and by that time, it'll be late enough for you to join me for dinner and a cocktail. That's the least I can do to welcome a newcomer to this mysterious, dark continent."

"No, thank you. I have your word you'll look into that stupid, pointless slaughter?"

"Absolutely." He put down his glass; he was suddenly not teasing, not treating her as if she were a charming child, a "do-gooder" who had made a silly, pointless scene. "But I think you need to learn a few facts about slaughter—as you call it. It isn't easy, when you first come here, to adjust to certain things. Some people never do, and they don't stay around here very long. The ones that do—some of them—get killed in the bush; they step into a snare or they get their head blown off by some idiot tourist, because they're wandering around where they shouldn't be, or else they drink themselves to death out of a sense of impending boredom or doom."

Jenny smiled coldly. "It looks as if you're well on your way, Doctor."

"Who told you about me, your aunt? I'll bet she painted a nice picture." He picked up the second, half-filled glass and sat in one of the large leather chairs by the wide expanse of window. Outside, lush flowers bloomed in the front garden; five or six men were busily pruning and cutting and mowing. A big fountain sprayed water over the backs of sculpted sea lions and leaping, delicate waterbucks. It was a paradise here, or seemed to be.

"Aunt Maggie doesn't gossip, if that's what you're inferring."

"I know that. Listen—in spite of what she may have said about me, about my ideas, I have the greatest respect for your aunt. As a matter of fact, your Uncle Jack and I used to get together every month or so. I'll bet she didn't tell you that, did she? That in a strange sort of way, he and I were friends."

"Dr. Lear, my aunt and uncle dedicated their lives to caring for animals, keeping them from the very thing some monster did last night to that baby elephant. I simply can't believe that my Uncle Jack would—"

"Lower himself to break bread with me?" He grinned. "As a matter of fact, we used to get a little drunk together and warble old Irish songs."

"Uncle Jack wouldn't—"

"Listen, little girl," he said, his eyes darkening with feeling. "You need a few lessons in survival, and I'm not talking about having enough intelligence to stay out of the bush at night; I'm talking about understanding something about the way people feel around here."

"I don't understand—"

"I know you don't; that's just the point. Here, a poacher isn't always looked upon as if he's some kind of murderous monster; a lot of the time, people just aren't that interested. Some of them are, of course, and I understand they're getting to be more and more that way, but I happen to think it's a damned shame. Most of us aren't involved in any way with the idea of conservation and don't want to be. If somebody tried to blow up your precious parks and game reserves, not many people would give a damn. You're holding your game reserves in trust for a nation that would prefer things the other way, the old way." He put down his glass. "And frankly, I couldn't agree with them more!"

"You mean, I suppose, survival of the fittest."

"Exactly, Miss Logan. The Darwinian theory, if you want to be intellectual about it. There's no aesthetic value here in relation to animals, and neither you nor your aunt or anybody else can change that. Let's face it—in our country, leisure is an important consideration. Here, food and shelter are primary considerations, and the people, a lot of them, honestly believe they have a natural right to hunt and kill for food and clothing, and for enough money to take care of their needs. If you and your auntie don't happen to like that—it's just too damned bad!"

Jenny felt her face growing hot. "I don't like it and I won't accept the idea that, like it or not, nothing can be done to change things!"

He came closer to her. "Do you have any idea what would happen if nobody ever killed an animal here? Do you realize that there would ultimately be no grass, no trees, nothing left of this land except starving animals who would eat their own kind to survive? You have to crop excess, Miss Logan, or else even the strongest and the healthiest will perish."

"That baby elephant wasn't strong enough yet to protect itself! It wasn't—it wasn't fair and you can't convince me that it was!" She had not meant to do this, to begin to cry; she hated herself for the tears that had formed inside her, deep inside her, coming hotly into her throat and finally streaming out of her eyes and down her face. "How can you stand there and try to convince me that it was right to kill that elephant?"

"Damn it to hell, girl, I'm not saying that! I'm saying that you can't stick wild animals inside a fence and pretend you're doing them a big favor because there are other facts you have to consider, facts you simply can't change, believe me."

"I'm going to try," Jenny said, wishing she could wipe her eyes, her face, blow her nose, and leave with some semblance of dignity. "I'll be waiting to hear from you, Dr. Lear. I assume I have your word as a gentleman that you'll find out who killed our little elephant."

"You do indeed, Miss Logan."

"Good day, then."

She started out, but at the door, his voice stopped her.

"I'll get someone to drive you home."

"No, thank you. I drove myself here and I managed just fine."

"Whatever you like. Ah—Miss Logan?"

"Yes, Doctor?"

He seemed to be looking at her with a new gentleness. "Here," he said, walking toward her. "Blow your nose."

And he handed her a lace-edged handkerchief. He had taken it from a drawer someplace; it obviously belonged to a woman. There was the expensive scent of musk about it.

She drove back slowly, feeling somewhat confused, not sure if anything had been really settled at all. It probably had not, and by the time she drove through the wide gate leading to the reserve, she had come to the conclusion that Damien Lear had very likely been absolutely honest with her; he really didn't have the same feelings about protecting animals that she and Maggie did, and he saw nothing wrong in his viewpoint whatsoever. She must, she reasoned, have sounded like a stupid, naive fool, standing there saying that she meant to change things, when she had only been here such a short time.

Perhaps, she told herself, she ought to apologize to Damien Lear for having been so emotional.

The children went about like small, tearful ghosts, not wanting supper or games or anything else, it seemed. Manguana had bread in the oven and the house was quiet and freshly cleaned. Jenny took her typing to the porch, settling herself there with a glass of lemonade and began her day's work, typing requests for straw, feed, watering bins, and first-aid supplies.

But her mind wandered. She kept seeing Damien Lear, his eyes. She had never seen anyone with eyes that blue; they were clear and candid, changing color from the color of a brilliant sky to a much darker, deeper color. She certainly had not expected him to be so—so—

Attractive.

Suddenly, she stopped typing and sat up a bit straighter in the hard chair. Yes; it was true—she had been attracted to him and part of her confusion and ready tears had simply been a reaction to that! What was she anyway, some foolish, love-starved female who wept with desire at the sight of a man's bare chest, at the look of his face when he smiled? If that were true, then she had better get the next plane back to New York! At least she would have a choice of men there, if that was what she needed so badly!

The sound of a jeep or maybe a truck roaring down the road brought her out of her thoughts. For a wild second, she thought it might well be Damien Lear, come to—what? Get thrown off the place by her aunt? Aunt Maggie just might do that.

But it was Maggie driving the jeep; the back was loaded with boxes of supplies and surprises for the children. Jennifer hurried out to greet her and help her unload.

"Stuff to make ice cream in that box," Maggie said. "And in that one, some absolutely luscious dress material. Oh, and patterns to make stuffed animals for the kids; I thought you might like that, Jenny. Your mother used to write me about how clever you are at sewing. I'm no good at it at all—all thumbs and—" She looked again at Jenny. "What's wrong?"

"Someone shot Peanuts, Aunt Maggie. The children found him this morning."

"Oh, God. Poachers, I expect. I'm sorry, honey, sorrier for the poor beast's mother. She'll make dreadful noises all night and for days to come, I expect. We must get the carcass out of there; we don't want vultures swooping around. Come on; let's have a drink before lunch."

"Aunt Maggie, I'm afraid I've done something you might not like."

"Oh? Now you mustn't let this spoil your time here, Jennifer. I expect someone did it trying to hit one of the big bulls and missed, the bloody fool. They hunt for the ivory, you know."

"Aunt Maggie, I got so—so *upset* when I saw what had happened—"

"Of course you did," Maggie said stoutly, going into the house, "and I don't blame you one bit. I remember when Jack and I first came here, there was a darling little monkey that used to sit on our windowsill. I felt sure he was some sort of good-luck omen, and when I found he'd been killed by poachers, I nearly cried myself sick. Jack kept telling me I'd have to get used to things like that happening, but I never have, quite."

"I thought," Jenny said, her voice low, "I'm afraid I felt certain it was someone from Dr. Lear's place. One of the guests."

Maggie turned at the doorway to look at Jenny. "What do you mean?"

"I was—so certain and so angry and—and upset, that I went over there to tell him. To accuse him, I should say."

Maggie was silent until the two of them had begun unloading boxes, putting things on shelves.

"So," Maggie said finally, "you met him. Well, I suppose it had to happen. What did you think of him?"

Jenny hesitated. "I believe he's sincere. I don't agree with him, but I believe he thinks he's perfectly justified in the way he thinks. And it has nothing at all to do with money or greed—"

"I see." Maggie's back was to Jenny as she put away flour and powdered milk for baking. "Did he by any chance call us bleeding hearts?"

"Aunt Maggie—"

"He usually does. Well, to be perfectly honest, I'd hoped I could keep you two from meeting."

"But—why? He's a very intelligent man, and I'd think you'd be pleased to have a doctor fairly close at hand."

"Damien doesn't practice any longer, Jenny. He hasn't for some three and a half years. Besides, I've never liked him because I don't happen to agree with anything he believes in. The very idea of that place he owns, that expensive, moronic palace where people pay a lot of money to sit around, get drunk and go out and kill animals! Oh, I know what he told you, most likely, that hunting with a gun is more fair, more decent than killing with arrows or traps, but all the same—"

"He didn't tell me that, Aunt Maggie. He only wanted to explain some things to me, but I'm afraid I got rather emotional and left."

"I see. Well, it's just as well. My advice is to conquer any feelings you might be having for the man and concentrate instead on your life and your important work here, my dear."

Jenny felt her face flush. "I don't have any—any particular feelings for him. And I'm very happy here."

There was a brief, rather uncomfortable silence. Then Jenny's aunt came over and gently touched her hand.

"I'm sorry, dear. I guess I'm getting used to being alone, or at least I'm finding I can bear it, and I forget that young people ought not to live their lives without someone to share it with. I just don't want you to get involved with the wrong man, that's all." Her blue eyes were steady and kind. "I expect you've done that already, haven't you? Isn't that why you came here so suddenly?"

Jenny had expected this question; it had only been a question of when her aunt would get around to asking it.

"Yes," she admitted, "I was—involved with someone. But not to any degree that—what I mean is—I—we—didn't—"

"But you thought about it. Am I right?"

"Yes; I thought about it. A lot."

"Well, what on earth was wrong with him? Why didn't you marry him?"

"He didn't ask me."

"Oh."

Jenny began putting boxes of crackers away. She hoped the conversation had ended; she very nearly changed the subject to ask about whether or not it was time for the children's daily treat of crackers and some of Manguana's honey butter, but Maggie was clever; she'd know there was more to the story.

"Jennifer?"

"Yes, Aunt Maggie?"

Maggie put the last of the candy treats in the cupboard and closed the door. "A girl who looks the way you do—it just doesn't make sense for a man not to want you."

"I told you—he wanted me. He just didn't want to marry me." She took a small breath. "I didn't want to marry him either."

"I see. Then, that means he couldn't marry you, doesn't it?"

"Yes," Jenny said, her voice low. "He—he was married, Aunt Maggie." Sudden tears flooded her eyes. But this time, they were not the same; there was no pain connected with them, only a deep sense of remorse. "I didn't mean to feel about him the way I did; I guess I was horribly lonely without Mother. This was my first job, and in the beginning, he was just very kind to me, that was all. I—I had this room at first, just a room, in one of those dreadfully dreary little hotels where odd people sit around in the lobby and watch television together at night, and I used to do that, only—only they were old and there I was, just turned twenty, and I didn't have any friends my own age—" She sat down at the table, folding her hands, which had started trembling. "Brendon began taking me places, showing me a different view of New York. I knew it wasn't right—I didn't let myself admit it was wrong, but I certainly knew it couldn't be right, even though he told me his wife didn't mind, that she often went to lunch or dinner with a man friend." She closed her eyes, hating the memories. "He was lying, of course. One day—one day I was shopping on Fifth Avenue; I couldn't afford the outfit, but I'd been given a nice raise, probably as a part of his whole plan about me. Anyway, I was looking at this dress, standing in front of one of those three way mirrors, and I—I glanced up and there he was, Brendon, sitting calmly in a chair with a lady sitting next to him. They were watching their daughter try on coats. She—the daughter—was about my age, very pretty, and his wife kept smiling and leaning close to him to ask him if he liked it. And Brendon just sat there ignoring me, his face kind of pale, but other than that, he didn't let on." She shook her head. "I quit the same day. I just didn't go back to work, and that's when I decided to come here."

"It's over now," her aunt said kindly. "Best to forget it all, Jennifer. Look—let's do something special this evening, shall we? I know you get bloody bored doing nothing but sitting around with an old lady like me—"

"You aren't old! Not at all!"

"Well, it's selfish of me to expect you to be satisfied feeding animals, typing reports, and dozing on the front porch. Tell you what. Put on your best dress and we'll go to dinner!"

"All the way to Nairobi?" Jenny's eyes had widened.

"If you like. We'd have to stay the night, though, and I'm afraid that wouldn't be a good idea, since we've got two bushbabies about to give us more bushbabies. Let's give it some thought, though."

Jenny didn't want to miss helping out when the bushbabies were born; she found them charming creatures, with their huge black eyes and curling tails, they looked rather like honey bears crossed with raccoons. At any rate, to go so far away might mean she'd miss out on helping. She had spent one entire day getting the bedding ready for them, washing down the shelter, while monkeys and other bushbabies and even the shy zebras who usually grazed nearby wandered over to watch her with interest.

The heavy rain kept up all day; children napped on mats on the porch and Massukuntna and Manguana dozed in rocking chairs nearby. At teatime, Maggie fixed a sturdy, fragrant pot of scented tea and carried it in to Jennifer, who was busily typing up a series of complaining letters, composed by her aunt, about yet more snares found at the east edge of the reserve.

"I've come up with a marvelous idea," Maggie said, seating herself comfortably across from her niece. "Why don't we go to Damien Lear's lodge for dinner?"

Jenny stared at her. Her heart had begun a slow, heavy beating.

"But I thought—you said you don't like him!"

"True, dear; I don't, not at all. But you're going to be hearing a lot of different stories about him during the time you're here, and of course, you'll be curious about him, I'm sure. I think it's best we go and let you have a good look at his place, see how fancy it is, how expensive, and then, when all's said and done, remind yourself, Jenny, remind yourself over and over, that the whole place is paid for in the blood of innocent animals!"

"I don't think we should go," Jenny said quietly. "Not after what you've told me about that place."

"My husband thought Damien was sincere in the way he feels about hunting, that he had a kind of—spiritual feeling about it, the way Hemingway used to feel about bullfighting. Maybe he does feel that way, but we're still on opposite sides of the fence with him, Jennifer, and don't you ever forget that."

"I'll try not to, Aunt Maggie." She felt uneasy, as if a part of her were going one way and a part of her the other. The truth was, she was very much attracted to Damien, and this fact surprised her, so soon after her bad time back in New York. But there was something else, she felt certain, some other reason why Maggie hated Damien so. But when she asked, Maggie merely shook her head.

"Because he wasted his life, I suppose. I don't think it's my place to talk much more about it, Jenny, but I do want you to have dinner with me at his place tonight. Jack and I used to go there once in a while; he said it wouldn't be neighborly if we didn't. Besides, he liked Damien, in spite of everything."

"And what *is* 'everything'?"

"You'll hear the gossip, soon enough. I'm trying to think of what to wear," Maggie said, as if it were all definitely decided; they were going. "I haven't worn a dress since Jack's funeral. He always said being married to me was like being married to Huck Finn."

"I've already seen the place, don't forget, Aunt Maggie. There's really no point—"

Maggie smiled. "This time, you won't be going in like some woods animal who is hopping mad. You'll go as a guest, as a well-dressed, lovely young lady. And just keep remembering that if they didn't have those people around there who loved to shoot animals, the place couldn't stay open a month!"

It was clear that her aunt was choosing up sides; Jenny would be expected not to like Damien Lear at all, which was going to be a bit hard to do.

She finally stopped her typing. She felt she was beginning to understand both her aunt's side of the problem and at least get a glimpse of how people like Damien felt. Poaching was a terrible thing; they both agreed to that. It was only that Maggie wanted to protect ("over-protect," some called it) the wildlife and men like

Damien believed in hunting as a natural means of keeping the species limited enough so that there was no starvation.

But as long as women went on buying fur coats and leather handbags and jewelry made of teeth and tusks and other parts of animals, Jenny knew there would be poaching.

She finally turned her mind to other things; what to wear, to begin with.

She took a rain shower in the stall, where Maggie had left a fresh bar of hard-milled soap scented with the fragrance of wildflowers for her. The water soothed her, made her feel relaxed, and when she went to her room to dress, there was a small glass of sherry on a tray waiting for her.

She had chosen an apple-green dress, a silk print with tiny butterflies on it in darker shades of green and gold. One of Maggie's pretty shawls, a rich cream color, hung on the door. Jenny dressed, then sat down to brush her long auburn hair. In spite of the cooling shower, her face still had that excited, flushed look. She determinedly reached for a box of Maggie's face powder to cover her burning cheeks, then decided against it.

She touched perfume—expensive, seductive—at her throat and wrists. She had bought the fragrance to wear to the theater in New York with Brendon; when she had suddenly decided it was all a hideous mistake, the perfume had remained unopened until now. It was lovely—heady and touched with musk, not unlike the scent of the jungle itself on some warm nights.

"Aunt Maggie!" Jenny exclaimed at the foot of the stairs. "You look just beautiful!"

Maggie was waiting for her; she had turned to smile at Jenny as her niece came down the stairs. Indeed, Maggie did look pretty in the soft lamplight from the hallway; her red hair was pulled back from her face and tied with a pretty silken scarf and she'd touched her cheeks with a bit of rouge.

"I've almost forgotten what it feels like to wear a dress," Maggie said. "Mmmm—you smell delicious, dear. And of course, green is your color." She suddenly looked worried. "You're beautiful, Jennifer. Please take care not to let Damien Lear overwhelm you. Not that he isn't used to having plenty of women, all he wants, I hear. That place of his is a regular mecca for the rich and idle. Come on, we don't want to be on the road in total darkness."

On the trip there, however, it was nearly dark, not because the hour was late, but because the rain and storm clouds threw great shadows across the plains over which they drove. In back of them, the rain forest had looked black and somehow threatening. Sitting beside Maggie in the Land Rover, Jennifer realized how vastly uncomfortable she felt about this trip. Maggie clearly despised Damien Lear, and he would no doubt be surprised, if not shocked, to see her walk into his lodge!

"Are you sure you don't want to go into the village, Aunt Maggie?"

"Can't hear you. This darned contraption needs a tune-up."

"I said—are you—" Jennifer stopped talking; a lioness had suddenly appeared at the side of the road and was watching them lazily. Jenny sat back, giving herself up to the idea of an evening at the lodge. It had certainly been a change from what she'd become accustomed to since she'd come here; Maggie's big house was comfortable but it was impossible to read very well by the feeble, flickering light of the candles and rush lamps, so Jennifer was usually in bed quite early. The long nights were filled with eerie callings and raspings from creatures outside, and until the heavy rains came, she would often settle herself on the porch, where the air was cooler than in the upstairs bedrooms, and where she could enjoy the scented air, heavy with the fragrance of gardenias.

It was a world—a life—apart from the real world, a world where the children and the animals needed caring for, and where she could give of herself without having time to think much about what the future might hold for her in a place like this. But now, suddenly, her aunt was forcing her to look again at the "real" world, a world filled with grown-ups, not innocent animals and children but instead, sophisticated men and women who, much like Brendon Miles, were interested mostly in worldly things—money and sex and power.

She wasn't at all sure she could handle it. Not yet. Not after what had nearly happened to her in New York.

A canopy had been put up in front of the lodge, running the full length of the porch, so that guests could sit out there and enjoy the magnificent view without getting wet. The whole building was second- and third-story level, so that there was a fine view of the lake. In weather such as this it appeared to be gray and foggy, but nonetheless, the view seen through sparse, pale green grass was magnificent.

A young man wearing a white coat hurried out to park the Land Rover, and Maggie, giving Jennifer a quick wink, tipped him and walked calmly, and with a grace Jenny hadn't noticed before, up the wide porch steps and through the great, polished ebony doors into the foyer.

At once, they seemed to be surrounded by employees—did they have a reservation, would they like drinks served on the porch, perhaps they would like to be seated in front of the fireplace since the rain had chilled—

Maggie chose the fireplace; there was a small table between them and a fire burned just brightly enough not to overwhelm them. From her vantage point, Jennifer could see the bar; it was packed tight with well but casually dressed men, and women who looked tanned and, in most cases, very wealthy. Mostly, the women wore low-cut, summery dresses; they sat on the leather bar stools with their tanned legs exposed to the thigh; a few of them wore dresses so sheer one could see their breasts.

Jennifer sipped her brandy, trying to concentrate on what her aunt was saying—something about poaching, and expensive guns that could be bought by the guests right here at the lodge. *So this is his world,* Jenny thought, watching a beautiful woman with very bleached blond hair walk unsteadily toward the closed door of Damien's office. As Jenny watched, the woman tapped at the door, holding a champagne glass in one hand and her shoes in the other. The door opened; Jenny got a glimpse of Damien as he spoke briefly to the woman then started to abruptly close the door. The woman was pouting; she finished her drink and moved toward him, dropping one shoe as she did. She wore a black cocktail dress that showed off her body, showed too much of it; her breasts seemed about to pop out of the tight bodice at the top.

Damien bent over politely to retrieve the fallen shoe; as he did, he glanced quickly around the room. Jenny saw him start in surprise as he saw her aunt sitting there, then he quickly looked at Jennifer.

She sat very still, returning his steady gaze. Even from where she was, the brilliant blueness of his eyes almost dazzled her; she felt captivated in that glance, held as if she were bewitched. Then, the magic moment was over; he handed the shoe back to the blond woman, said something to her in what appeared to be a good-natured way, and quickly shut the door in her face.

"Are you all right, Jenny dear?" It was Maggie, who was busily studying the ornate menu. "You look a bit pale."

"I'm fine," Jenny lied, and she picked up her menu and tried to read it.

It was written mostly in French; many of the guests were wealthy landowners from the Congo, according to Maggie. A thin soup and tiny tidbits of puffy bread had been brought without their asking, but Jenny felt as if she couldn't eat anything; her heart had begun that slow, heavy pounding again, as if she were waiting for something wonderful to begin.

"Don't look now," Maggie said quietly, "but I think we're about to get the V.I.P. treatment."

A tall man wearing a white suit was heading for their table. He carried with him a bucket full of ice with a bottle in it. He made a somewhat formal bow and smiled at them.

"Compliments of Dr. Lear, ladies. He would also like to know if you would care to have dinner in one of the more private rooms. I'm sure you will find the view even more lovely."

"Well," Maggie told him, "since the view from here shows us only the rear-ends of people sitting at the bar, I expect that might be an improvement." She picked up her purse. "Ready, Jennifer dear?"

"Aunt Maggie, I'm quite comfortable here."

"Nonsense. If Dr. Lear wants us to have dinner in one of his special rooms, I don't see why we shouldn't take him up on it. Lead on, my good man."

And so they followed the man in the white suit, who carried their bottle of champagne, up a polished flight of beige-carpeted stairs, into a breezy hallway with oil paintings of scenes of African wildlife on the walls, through a softly lit and beautifully furnished anteroom, into a somewhat small but very lovely dining room. There, in front of a glass wall, a table had been set for two. Beside each plate there was an orchid, delicate and creamy-white, huge, exquisitely beautiful.

"Are you sure these are for us?" Maggie, even Maggie, seemed somewhat overwhelmed.

"Dr. Lear suggests the venison for dinner, Madame. He asked me to hasten to add that the meat was not trapped or shot by poachers but sent in from Salaam."

"That will be fine," Maggie said. When the man had bowed again and left, she turned to Jennifer. "He's up to something, Jenny!"

"Aunt Maggie, let's just enjoy his generosity and leave as soon as we can." Jennifer stood by the glass wall, looking out. The rain came down like a thin silver veil, but there was still a good view of the lake beyond. From her vantage point, she caught sight of some large vessel moored at the dock; lights blinked on and off from it. "Do some of these people come here by boat, do you think?"

"That's Damien's yacht out there," Maggie said. "He uses it for gambling, I understand. It isn't something I'd be interested in, even if I could afford it. Are you beginning to understand what I'm trying to tell you, Jennifer?"

Jenny could see people getting on that boat; there was a kind of gangplank on it, with an awning over that, and at the top, someone in a white coat was greeting them. She couldn't hear sounds because of the heavy, insulated glass, but whoever they were, whatever they were doing on the boat, they seemed to be having a marvelous time. As she watched, the lights from the boat shone through like beacons.

Jennifer realized she was very curious about Damien, about why he had chosen to come here to Africa to live. It was, at best, an odd choice, for a man, a doctor, to shut himself off from the world and spend his time doing whatever it was he now occupied himself doing. Certainly, he was living in the very lap of luxury, with his yacht out there, and all the beautifully dressed, mostly good-looking people who were staying at his inn.

And yet, she had sensed something about him, some kind of muted loneliness that had spoken to her heart.

They were brought chilled champagne, waited on as if they were grand royalty; the room was subtly luxurious and the view beyond— the sea and the blinking, colored lights of the pier and the moored ship—beautiful. It was most certainly a night to remember, although Maggie seemed to have her mind elsewhere.

"I wonder if the people at the reserve remembered to feed the macaws and let the goat in the kitchen for his dish of milk before bedtime." Maggie frowned. "He's grown to expect that bowl of milk; I don't want to upset him."

"They'll be fine, I'm sure, Aunt Maggie. We aren't going to be away all that long."

The meal was so delicious and perfect that Maggie and Jennifer both sent compliments to the chef. The meat was juicy and succulent; the yams frosted with a sweet creamy topping, and the salad crisp and fresh, with a brilliant sauce prepared right at their table. Music filtered in from speakers in the ceiling and the room was just cool enough to be pleasant. Outside, gentle rain pattered at the glass wall; Jennifer kept her eyes on the ship's lights beyond.

They were finishing their meal with aromatic coffee when the knock, soft and polite, came at the closed door.

"Please," Jenny said quickly, "let's leave as soon as we can!" With her aunt feeling as she did about Damien, there was no telling what might be said.

"I'm far too old to be told to mind my manners," Maggie told her. She stood up. "Yes; come in."

It was, of course, Damien; Damien looking tall and wide-shouldered and exceedingly handsome in a lightweight suit and shirt and tie. He stood for a moment in the doorway, his blue eyes carefully avoiding contact with Jennifer's.

"I trust you ladies enjoyed your meal? I hope the champagne was cold enough—we sometimes tend to forget that back in the States everything must be served very cold. Here, one finds a certain pleasure in tasting—warmth. Or perhaps it's only that we become accustomed to it."

"It was," Maggie said, her voice cool, "perfect, Mr. Lear. Now, if you'll kindly arrange to have our check sent in—"

"Please," he said quietly, still from the doorway, "allow me this small concession, Mrs. Harmon. May I—"

"Of course," Jennifer said quickly, glancing at her aunt. "Come in. Thank you for—the flowers and this private room and truly the most exquisite meal—"

"My pleasure." He seemed in that moment to fill the room. He walked over to the glass wall, pulled back the heavy draperies with one hand, and pointed to the ship through the fog. "There's a birthday party going on down there; perhaps you ladies would like to try your hand at the gambling tables." He smiled. "I'll furnish you with chips, of course."

"We don't gamble, Mr. Lear," Maggie said coldly. "Oh—I forgot, it's *Doctor,* isn't it? Tell me, when a man is a physician, is it the same as it is with priests? They say an ordained priest is a priest forever—it isn't the same with doctors, is it, or is it?"

Damien Lear was angry; his blue eyes had frosted noticeably, but his voice remained cordial.

"I'm still a doctor, Mrs. Harmon. Feel free to call me in an emergency, in case you can't get Dr. Du Mond in Nairobi."

"We've managed to keep in very good health at the reserve," Maggie said crisply. "So far, nobody has been shot or maimed by any of your stupid poachers."

"They aren't my poachers, Mrs. Harmon. And by the way, I found out who killed the baby elephant."

"I hope you kicked them off your property and sent them packing, Doctor."

"They weren't guests here, unfortunately, so there was little I could do. Some tourists, staying at a hotel in Nairobi. They drove onto the reserve—*your* reserve—and took a lot of pictures, I understand, scaring the herd half to death with their noise. When they started to run—the elephants, that is—the little one was behind and when the idiot with the new gun fired, he missed the big fellow he'd meant to hit. It was all very illegal, of course. They've gone now, back home, leaving their mess behind them."

"How can you be sure of all this, Dr. Lear?" Maggie's voice was sharp.

He shrugged. "One of the men who works for me heard about it. Frankly, as long as you people allow strangers to wander in and out of your place with their idiotic cameras, driving noisy, sometimes dangerous vehicles, you can expect things like this to happen. I keep idiots like that off my land."

"And you charge a very high price to the ones you do let on it, don't you?"

Suddenly, he was furious. "I believe in hunting; you know that. But fairly, not with spears, poison spears that cause an animal great agony." He turned to Jennifer. "I'd like to make my thesis clearer, if I may. Why don't you ladies honor me by staying the night here, and when you're rested, let me take you on a brief tour of the bush tomorrow?"

"There's no need of that," Maggie said quickly. "Come on, Jennifer; it's time we were going. Thank you, Dr. Lear, for a most interesting evening."

"Aunt Maggie—couldn't we—"

"It's out of the question." Her aunt looked at her, then seemed to consider something. "Come by in the morning, Doctor; Jenny probably would do well to see more of the bush. But don't try to convince her that you're right."

His eyes had darkened with pleasure. "Would you like to go, Miss Logan?"

She smiled at him. In that moment, she felt wonderful; a warmth flooded through her and she felt like hugging Maggie for being so gracious about it.

"I'd love to!"

"See you then."

Maggie was putting her shawl around her shoulders when Jennifer asked the question. They were in the Land Rover; Damien stood on the porch, having escorted them from the private dining room, through the hallways and the big main room and foyer, to the parking lot.

"Why are you suddenly going along with what he wants, Aunt Maggie?"

Maggie put the vehicle in gear and expertly backed out, turned around, and pressed hard on the gas so they shot forward.

"I'm not. I only want you to see his viewpoint so you'll come around to knowing how right I am." She glanced at Jennifer. "But in the meantime, kindly take care not to fall in love with him!"

FOUR

OUTSIDE, the morning sounds of the bush had begun. The rain still beat against the long windows, but Jenny had gotten used to that, just as Maggie had said she would. Rain, falling every hour and minute of the day, finally became a fact of life, so that no longer was it a topic of conversation, but rather something that was simply there, like the lovely, morning scent of gardenias that came to her every morning.

I will be with him today, Jenny thought, opening her eyes, *maybe for the whole day!* She felt a warmth go over her; there was a soft ringing sound coming from somewhere in the house, probably one of Manguana's little bells; she had them all over the house. The bedroom was still darkish, and would be until Jenny pulled open the curtains, and even then the brightest it would be all day would be a kind of dim, silver swath of light across the polished floor.

But it was a lovely, lovely day, and she felt good, young and

strong and in some mysterious way, whole again.
she had been ill, or hurt badly, and for a long whi
very bad, but then it had begun to lessen and she h
would one day be free of it.

Now, that had happened. She could feel peace again, and
it had not happened yet, she knew she would even be able to fe
if given the chance.

Suddenly, she sat up straight, her eyes wide now. *Is it because of him, because of Damien? And if it is—why? I hardly know him and if Aunt Maggie is right, he's a totally terrible man! Besides, why doesn't he practice medicine any longer? She looked toward the gray window. Probably even medicine didn't bring in enough money for him!*

She got out of bed, quickly brushed her teeth and splashed her face gently from the night's water in the tin basin, then, giving her hair a very quick run-through, she only glanced at her reflection in the mirror before she ran downstairs for breakfast; she looked very much up for the day and her cheeks were much pinker than usual.

But she felt bothered, somehow, as if she needed to know why it was that the world suddenly seemed—different. Oh, it had been good enough the day before, with Aunt Maggie there someplace, wise and good, the memory of Jennifer's mother forever binding them together, because they had both loved her. She, Maggie, seemed more of an older sister than a great-aunt, more like a saddened little girl than a woman who had lived with a man for nearly forty years and who carried the burden of his death with great charm and courage. Days with Maggie around were good days, right sort of days, but today, today was the first time Jenny had felt this way in what—years? Could it really be years since she had been happy, first losing her mother and then moving away and being lonely and then hurt and lonely once again, because of having met Brendon—could it have been so long since she had been serene and looked forward to life? Well, at last she did again—the coffee put in front of her by Manguana (who must have gotten up really early!) had never tasted quite so wonderful, nor had the rain seemed to have quite the same glimmer about it. The scent of flowers coming in the half-opened back door had never seemed this heady; it was as if everything had been brightened, sharpened, since she woke up and she had realized that something or someone had sparked life in her again. And if it hapρened to be the fact that Damien Lear was perhaps the most sensual, attractive man she had ever seen, then so be it.

Manguana was in the kitchen with some of the children; she gave Jennifer a long look that somehow held disapproval in it.

"Good morning," Jenny said cheerfully. "Everyone is well, I hope."

Manguana got right to it. "Your aunt thinks that your head may be turned around like that of the owl, because of Dr. Lear."

"My aunt has a very vivid imagination." So Maggie had been concerned enough to talk about it, and of course, Manguana was very wise. She had probably guessed the truth, that Maggie was hoping she, Jenny, would hate Damien, that she would never stoop to going anywhere with him, never. And that the only possible obstacle to this conclusion happened to be the fact that Jennifer was lonely and worst of all—lately recovering from a near-affair with a most unsuitable suitor.

"Manguana?"

"Yes?" She was spoon-feeding a small boy who sat in her lap.

"If you—if you hadn't met your husband, if you didn't have Massukuntna and you were alone—"

"Not have Massukuntna?" She put down the spoon. "Life would be very sad without him. He is a man who gives great joy to a woman."

"But if you didn't have him," Jennifer persisted gently, "if you had never met him, never heard of him—do you think you could be happy here?"

There was a long, thoughtful pause. "I would," the older woman said gravely, "have been someone else, you see. I am who I am because what we have found together has made me this way. Otherwise, I would have been very foolish. I would be living in a city, with fine furniture and with the wrong man looking at me over breakfast and supper and tea." She smiled a little. "And I might even think myself very fortunate. But from the first, Massukuntna was different."

"Different? How?"

The child squirmed and finally got down. "My village has a custom—when a girl marries, she is given presents by her man. I was—not one of the pretty girls. I was shy and—"

"I can't believe you weren't one of the pretty ones!"

"Not like the others, not like my sisters. So after a while, I got older, and my father worried for fear nobody would ever ask me. He even thought of taking me away, so that my uncles could find me someone suitable. And then, one day came a tall man from Wankie, near the park. His name was Massukuntna and he worked in the park and was, they said, very good with animals.

"On the day he came to marry me he brought with him a donkey. And behind it, another. And behind that one, another—and another and another—all the way, halfway through the village! That was the price he paid for me, you see—he gave my father all of those, such a great price, far more than any other girl I'd ever known had gotten for her father. It was as if he believed me to be a—a very great prize."

They were silent. "Yes," Jenny said softly, "he made you feel priceless and beautiful." Was that, perhaps, Damien's great attraction for her? Last night, he had treated her and Maggie to the most elegant meal she'd ever experienced. He had invited her to see him again today. He had made her feel very, very special.

Going out on the porch with her hot bread and sweetened coffee, it was hard to imagine old Massukuntna, who sat quietly mending his fishing rod, as the sweet and ardent lover he surely must have been. But they loved each other, that was very evident, so, Jenny suspected, Manguana probably didn't really miss the life she could have had, a different sort of life in the city, after all. Jenny could not, at this point, imagine one without the other; although they seemed seldom to be together during the course of the day, they were together each night, every night, and Jennifer had noticed some mornings how happy Manguana seemed, like a young girl in love.

Jennifer took her coffee out to the porch; it was clean-smelling, washed over and over by the rain. There were always many birds out there; they came from the bush during the rainy season, to roost on and around the sheltering porch, and of course, Maggie saw that they got fat from all the seed she was constantly putting out.

The birds screeched when Jenny came out; she had disturbed the sleep of some of the lazier ones. The morning was calm, gray with rain, and very lovely. She had a sudden urge to paint the morning; she could see the touches of sweet lavender drifting around the edges of the dawn, the way it had been this morning. Yes; she would order some paints and canvas from Nairobi, or perhaps go and get the things herself, and she would paint, the way she used to do before she got involved with Brendon.

"That you down there, Jennifer?" It was Maggie; Jenny had heard the sharp sound of her aunt's opening the window above. "What in God's name are you doing up at this hour?" There was another sound, drawers opening; she was getting dressed. "Nobody, but nobody, gets up this early except Manguana. Are you sick?"

"I'm fine—I'm having coffee." Jenny had to raise her voice against the sound of the rain. "Come on down!"

Moments later, her aunt pushed open the door and plopped into a chair across from Jenny. "He's upset you this soon in the game, has he?"

"I'm far from upset, Aunt Maggie. In fact, I feel wonderful this morning!"

"That's even worse." Maggie put down her coffee cup. "I hope it's clear to you why I'm giving my approval about this little tour you're to take with Damien this morning. You do understand, don't you, Jennifer?"

Jenny felt her face begin to color. She wanted her aunt's approval, and yet, some of the lightheaded, giddy feelings she'd been experiencing ever since she woke up made it impossible for her to be totally serious.

"Of course. You want me to think of him as a sinister person who detests all animals—"

"This is no time for frivolity, Jennifer. I want you to listen very carefully to what he tells you—and then, you can decide for yourself about our work here. You see, Dr. Lear thinks we're no better than some sort of local zoo, where we pamper animals to the point of their being unable to survive in the bush. So you understand how important it is for you to weigh the facts and come to some decision on your own." Her face looked weary this morning, as if she had slept badly. "I wouldn't want you to give a moment of your life to this work if you didn't believe in it, my dear."

Jennifer got up, went over quickly to her aunt, and gave her a quick, warm hug.

"Forgive me—I guess I wasn't thinking very straight this morning. Look—I *know* how important this work is to you, and I know you'd like me to be in accord with your thinking. It was wrong of me to say you want me to dislike Damien Lear for whatever reason. I know you're above that sort of thing."

"For a while, I'm sorry to say I wasn't," Maggie said, her voice soft in the early morning stillness. "You see, Jack always wanted this life, but in the beginning, I didn't, not at all. When we lost your mother, it was more like losing a daughter than a niece; we were nearly shattered. Jack thought it would be a splendid idea for us to come out here and work, so we did. I hated it at once."

Jenny smiled. "I can't imagine your ever hating it, Aunt Maggie."

"I did, though. Then, one morning, when we'd been here about five years, I got up and sat at that dressing table upstairs and I looked at my face and I realized that some kind of change had come over me since we'd come here. I had stopped feeling bitter about life; I felt free and as if I belonged here, and I'd never felt that way about any place we'd lived before. Not only that, but I began to feel very lucky, very privileged, to be able to live the kind of life Jack and I lived here. We worked long hours and we were worn out a good deal of the time but we had both gotten a new kind of peace inside." She pressed Jenny's hand. "That's what I want for you, dear. I want you to start meeting people; I'll take you into town so you can start going to some of the parties and lectures."

But Jenny wasn't interested in meeting a lot of new people, making a social life for herself, not just now. For now, just being a part of the reserve seemed to be enough to give her good feelings about herself and about life.

She still wasn't sure just what part, if any, Damien Lear was playing in her life. But she was glad she would be seeing him later on today; that much she knew.

For her bush tour date with Damien, she put on sturdy jeans and a blue shirt-blouse and tied her long hair with a scarf. Her face remained flushed and glowing, even though at the last minute she splashed it with cool rain water from the fresh pitcher Manguana brought to her bedroom.

When Damien drove up in his pickup truck, Jenny was sitting on the wide porch, feeling much better about things. She would listen to what Damien told her on this little sightseeing tour and then later, she would decide for herself what seemed right and best for the animals.

For a second or two, Damien's physical presence blotted out Jennifer's promise to herself about clear-headedness; she could only think that he looked very big and masculine and strong, as he stood waiting for her somewhat uneasily on the porch steps.

He smiled up at her. "I hope your aunt won't think I've kidnapped you if we go into Nairobi for lunch. Maybe you'd better tell her we'll be coming back later than—"

"I'm not a child," Jennifer said somewhat stiffly. "Aunt Maggie won't worry."

"Good. Then we needn't hurry." He turned to look at her, his blue eyes amused. "And you don't have to tell me you aren't a child. I can see you aren't; any man could."

She said nothing, having felt a sudden rush of pleasure at his words. His truck seemed to be filled with papers, invoices of sorts, memos, hunting magazines sent from the States and everywhere. Jenny couldn't help but notice, however, that there was the lingering aroma of expensive-smelling perfume. Either Damien had very recently transported a female guest someplace, or else he had recently had a woman in his truck for other reasons.

"It gets a little bumpy," he told her, his voice loud over the powerful roar of the truck's motor. "Just hang on and don't panic when we come to the river, okay?"

"A river! Won't—won't we sink?" She was clutching the seat with both hands as they went up and down ravines, into ruts and over bumpy flatland.

"Not in the shallow part. I want to take you over to where the snares are."

"I saw them," Jenny said, closing her eyes as they approached the narrow river. "My aunt—"

"I know; she wrote the commissioner in Nairobi and after due red tape, he'll send somebody to come around and sweep them all up and haul them off. But they'll be back within a matter of days, maybe hours."

"But who puts them back up?"

He began to expertly slow the truck down as they approached the river.

"Traders, mostly, a lot of them Americans. Killing animals and selling hides and tusks and teeth is big business here. Maybe you've already realized that."

Jennifer nodded. Even though it was raining, tourists milled around the park, sitting in campers and various motor vehicles, waiting to snap pictures of the first thing that showed itself. One family appeared to be busily (and wetly) removing the sun roof from their van in order to get better shots of animals.

"Against the law to do that," Damien said grimly. "It's a terrible intrusion, all that popping and flashbulb snapping, heads sticking out of the top of a noisy vehicle. It scares hell out of the animals and disturbs the general habitat."

Jenny kept her eyes straight ahead. "And what about poaching—killing with a gun? Surely you agree *that* disturbs the general habitat in a much more deadly way!"

He glanced at her. "Okay, we'll talk about it, as soon as we cross the river."

She did hold on, knuckles white as he inched the truck across the swirling, muddy water. Damien looked very calm; he seemed to know just how high the water would get.

The truck didn't falter; they smoothly climbed the bank on the opposite side and went on down the narrow, twisting road. Now the trees were denser, even greener.

Damien looked at her, his eyes very blue and serious. "There used to be real hunters here, men who hunted with a kind of—mystic fairness, the way the Indians at home once did. An animal was revered and every bit of its carcass was used for something valuable, and I'm not talking about money. The hunters used to use the hide, the organs, even the eyeballs. But now, there aren't any hunters of that kind left. Massukuntna used to hunt that way, but I understand he doesn't hunt anymore, not since he went to work for your aunt."

Jennifer realized he had touched on something she did not and perhaps could not understand—man's relationship to the animal he hunted. To her, it was inconceivable that it could ever be a fair match. But nonetheless, she knew now that Damien's feelings about animals—and killing them—weren't as harsh and mercenary as her Aunt Maggie seemed to believe they were.

They began to talk, finally, about the animals. Jenny mentioned how dear it was to her to see the little children at the reserve with their beloved pets. And yet, whenever an animal died, it didn't shock them; they cried, but they accepted death.

"It's different now," Damien told her, driving more slowly now. His voice was deeply quiet as he spoke about hunters and poaching. "Everybody—tourists, foreigners, local people—they don't care about the animals. They hunt with snares, and even when they have a gun, nobody is really safe. Sometimes, they use poison arrows, although it's against the law, of course. I'm talking about the kind that killed your uncle."

They drove in silence for a little while. Suddenly, Damien stopped the truck and got out. His face looked pale under the deep tan.

"Damien—what—" She realized she had called him by his first name.

"Something caught back there," he told her grimly. "I think it's a deer. Stay here."

But she didn't; she got out and walked quickly over to where he stood, looking down at the poor thing, a young, beige-colored doe, hopelessly caught in the cruel wire snare. Her leg was twisted and bleeding; blood was everywhere. Her eyes looked glazed and agonized.

Jennifer made some sound, covering her mouth with one hand.

"Oh my God—"

"Get back in the truck," he said harshly. "I can't help her; she's nearly gone. But I can stop the suffering. Go on; get back in the truck, damn it!"

She obeyed, shutting her eyes even tighter at the loud blast from his shotgun. Seconds later, he was in the truck beside her, and they drove on.

"They wait days to come and collect their bounty," he said grimly. "It's bad enough when it's an animal, but last summer, a man died in one of the snares. Nobody came to check and see if they'd caught anything, and when they did—"

"Please," Jenny said, her face in her hands. "Please—"

"You'd better get used to things like that," he told her quietly. "Otherwise, you'll hate it. A lot of people hate it, but a lot of people stay because, in some strange way, they love it here. With all its faults, all its problems, this is still one of the most beautiful places in the world." He glanced at her. "Killing is a way of life here, Miss Logan."

"I can't accept that," Jennifer said, her eyes on the road ahead. "It's just too—"

"Cruel?" Suddenly, he pulled the truck to one side of the road and looked at her. "Life is cruel, or haven't you found that out yet? Survival is what counts."

Jennifer turned to look at him; her eyes were misted with tears, but in that second, it didn't matter. In the rain the trees outside looked ghostly, twisted; the animals had apparently all taken shelter, leaving the bush empty of any living thing—except for the two of them, sitting side by side in that damp-smelling, warmish truck cab.

"If you believe that," she said softly, "if you really believe that life is that precious—why aren't you practicing medicine any longer?"

Until this moment, she had certainly not meant to ask that question. For one thing, it was none of her business, none at all, and if her aunt had wanted to gossip, she would have talked more about it. Now, with a sinking heart, Jenny realized she had touched upon some vital pain within this man; she had encroached upon a very personal part of himself, so deep and painful that his blue eyes darkened like a stormy sky; there was a certain tightening of his jaw and his strong hands seemed to move slightly on the steering wheel.

"I lost a patient," he said quietly. "Ready to go on, now?"

"Yes—I—I'm terribly sorry I asked."

"A lot of people wonder as soon as they find out," he told her, starting the truck once more. "Most of them figure I just fell in love with money and since I can make a lot more of it accommodating the beautiful rich, I switched jobs, you might say."

Jenny took a small breath. "I don't believe that," she said quietly.

He glanced at her in surprise. "Thank you."

They rode now in comfortable silence, up and down the soaked hills, until at last, they came to a clearing. Again Damien stopped the truck and pointed. "There used to be at least three hundred animals killed every day in those damned snares," he told her. "It isn't nearly that bad now, in spite of what we saw back there. Now, they use poison arrows with seeds of the *Strophanthus* plant."

"Is that—what killed my uncle?"

"No, that was *Acokanthera,* made from the wood bark. It's more potent than the other. Jack knew all about the stuff; we used to talk about it sometimes, about how many people got killed by arrows meant for animals."

"I had forgotten you were actually friends with my aunt and uncle."

He smiled. "Not with Maggie, no. But she always knew I'd like to be, and maybe we would have been, in time. But when Jack died, it changed her a lot. I'm still a great admirer of hers." He got out of the truck. "Come on," he told her, reaching for her. "I want to show you something."

"But it's pouring!"

"It isn't far. I want to show you the rain forest. It's something you'll never forget."

It was true; she would never forget it. Suddenly, with her hand in his, she was led into a giant, emerald room, a room made by the heavy overhead branches, the green, green trees. Inside there was no rain, only the smell of the good brown earth and of the rain itself, washed clean and heavy with the scent of jungle flowers. It was a world in itself, one of those unexpectedly heart-stopping, beautiful moments in time.

Later, Jennifer was to ask herself if it was because of the beauty of the place, the exquisite serenity of the rain forest, or if it was merely because Damien shared it with her that made it so precious, so special to her.

"I've never seen anything like it," she said, standing in the middle of that greenness. "You were right."

He stood watching her; they were perhaps ten feet away from each other but there had sprung between them a kind of swift, electric closeness. She was very much aware of his steady gaze and surprisingly, she was bold enough to meet his eyes without trembling.

"You," he said quietly, "are like nothing I've ever seen. You can't imagine how—how magnificent you look in this moment."

Jenny looked quickly away. She had never thought of herself as beautiful, except for the inherited red hair; that was the pride of all the women in her family. Aunt Maggie had once said that there had only been two brunette girls born into the family in the last century, and, she had added darkly, nothing any good ever came of either of them.

But she was not, and could not be, magnificent to look at, not by a long shot, her with her share of freckles, even on her arms, and her mouth a bit too wide, just like her mother's, only on her mother it had somehow seemed sensual and lovely.

"I must bring the children here some day for a picnic."

"You," he said, coming toward her, "are a picnic—a feast—"

And he was nearly, very nearly, kissing her. There was, coming from the moist air around then, a sweet, heavy scent, mingled juniberries and mint and gardenia, and she felt suddenly dizzy with the sweetness of it, that and his arms around her.

But she suddenly, as if a picture had been flashed on a screen, saw Brendon that day in his office when he had told her how much he lusted for her, how he had wanted her from the first day she worked for him. . . .

"I think we'd better go," she said now, turning, half-twisting away from him. He suddenly looked bereft, then; he was changed, and a curtain had come down over his eyes. "Let me know when you want to bring the children, Miss Logan. I'll send one of my guides along to look after everyone."

She felt uncomfortable for the rest of the afternoon with him. He drove her into Nairobi and they had lunch on the top floor of a white, very modern American hotel. The appetizers they ordered were deplorable and she didn't really want the expensive wine he ordered.

"Listen," he said finally, reaching over, putting his tanned hand over hers. "I'm sorry about what—I mean, I had no right to talk the way I did—say those things. I know I embarrassed you and I'm sorry." His blue eyes looked into hers; he was smiling gently at her. "Okay?"

Suddenly, she looked at her plate. "What makes you think I was embarrassed? Maybe I—liked it." She looked steadily at him. "A lot."

A slow flush was rising on his face. "Then why—I mean, if you wanted me to kiss you, why the devil didn't it happen?" He touched her cheek gently with one finger. "I know I wanted it to happen, but on the other hand," he said lightly, "I don't want your aunt coming around my place with a large pistol, shouting that I've been fooling around with her favorite niece. Let's try for a steak here; I understand they're terrible but I want to see you eat a nice hearty meal."

"I really don't like to eat much meat," she said, feeling that she was suddenly being treated rather like a child that he found charming. "I'll just have the vegetables, please."

"That calls for a drink," Damien said teasingly. "I should have known all bleeding hearts are vegetarians!"

It was dark when she got back to her aunt's; Damien had bid her goodnight quickly and she'd gotten out of his truck, hurrying through the dark rain.

"There you are," her aunt said from the dark living room. There was a burned-down candle in a dish beside her. "Well, I'd given you up. I must admit I had fantasies about your spending the night with him in Nairobi."

"Fantasies, Aunt Maggie?"

"I assure you, I didn't get past the part where he asked you to dance. I understand from some of the people here that in the beginning, Dr. Lear dances with a girl. Holds her close and puts his mouth close enough to her ear so that she can feel him breathing. It's evidently very successful because he's had scores of women, my dear, or have you already figured that out for yourself?"

"I'm going to bed, if you don't mind," Jennifer said, realizing she was unwilling to talk about Damien. "I'm sorry I missed dinner—we had a late lunch. Aunt Maggie—there's something I need to talk to you about, but it can wait until tomorrow. Goodnight." She bent and gently kissed her aunt's forehead. "Sleep well."

"Jennifer!" Maggie had followed her into the hallway. "Now you turn right around and look at me, young lady!"

Jenny turned. "Aunt Maggie, I really don't care to—"

"Didn't he tell you his big-shot ideas about the bushland? Didn't he talk about survival of the fittest, which means he thinks we're all a bunch of dodder-headed busybodies who capture animals and take care of them, whether they want to be cared for or not?" Maggie was clearly angry; her voice was heavier than usual, thickened with wrath. "That's what your Dr. Lear thinks about us, Jenny. Don't you see?" she demanded, and Jenny realized her aunt's voice was wavering. "If Damien Lear is right—if my husband and I worked this hard, this long, just to be some kind of zookeepers—then Jack's whole life was a failure—and mine is too!"

"Damien and I didn't talk much about that," Jenny said. "Please— don't put me in this position, Aunt Maggie. Besides, I don't think it's all that important that everyone agree with everyone else. Life is more interesting when people don't, sometimes."

"It isn't—just that," Maggie said suddenly. She walked up to Jenny and put her arm around her niece's waist as they walked toward the stairs. "It has to do with my husband, you see. Anything that might have saved him makes me start a whole, wild train of thinking. And it's far too late tonight for me to get started on my what-ifs. What if I had made him promise me never to try to come home if he couldn't get here before dark? There'd been a run of poaching about then, natives using the spears dipped in poison—he knew it wouldn't be safe, but he wanted to get back to me." She smiled a little. "He didn't want to break our record."

Maggie was switching on rush lamps, turning them up a bit, so that suddenly, her face was outlined in the soft light. She looked a bit, Jenny thought, like a lonely child, standing there without him, without her husband. They had been together so completely, for as long as Jenny could remember, that it still seemed odd, seeing one of them alone.

"Record? Aunt Maggie—you're stepping on your gown."

"What? Oh," Maggie said. "Yes. This was one of Jack's favorites. Our record had nothing to do with sex, not really, although sometimes we used to make love with a kind of glee, because we'd been able to keep our promise to each other." She took a little, sharp breath. "We made a promise when we first got married that we'd never sleep apart if we could help it. He was trying to keep his promise."

They were very close in that moment. The sense of loss, of grief, was so profound to Jenny that long after she'd crawled into bed and closed her eyes, something was nagging away at her, bothering her. She finally sat up in bed; the thought was coiled inside her mind. She felt she had to find it, grasp it and look at it, because if she didn't, she'd have missed something very important.

She needed to feel as blessed as the women who had fallen deeply in love with one man and stayed that way, through it all, for all of their lives. It was a sort of special blessing she thought, some magic given to some women, to love only once and then forever. Not all women could know it; she had known many women who had been in love various times. Her own mother had had lots of lovers, quite a potpourri, but she hadn't, as far as Jenny could tell, actually been in love with any of them. A lot of people apparently never fell in love at all, not even once.

Am I afraid that will happen to me? Am I even more afraid that if it does, it won't be so bad after all?

So it might, she told herself with her face pressed on the pillow to shut out the look of the slanted rain outside. *It might only be that I've decided it's time to fall in love, after a very bad experience with Brendon, and I might just be looking for someone to—*

The thought trailed off in sleep. She dreamed, of course. She was in a great, vast sea, very green, a deep and beautiful green, and she was being sweetly and soundly kissed by Dr. Damien Lear.

FIVE

THINGS at the reserve were cracking, as Maggie would say, as soon as it was dawn, the following day. By the time Jennifer came downstairs, Maggie had gone with Massukuntna to help with the birth of lion cubs and the kitchen was cluttered and steamy; it was canning time and Manguana silently and with great concentration boiled dark, sweet berries to make jam. Several children, giggling, hid under the big preparing table, waiting for the first taste.

It didn't seem to be the day to discuss her plan with Maggie, even though it kept rolling around in her mind. She longed to talk to someone about it and since Maggie might be gone all day and Manguana was going to be in the kitchen all day, there was no one.

Except for Damien, of course. All morning, typing, pressing the official stamp onto the neat letters, Jenny waited for some message from him. She even thought Damien himself might suddenly drive up in front of the house, big and wide-shouldered, telling her to get in his truck, telling her that he wanted to talk to her about something, or that he wanted to show her another secret place in the rain forest, the way he'd done yesterday.

But there was no word, none at all. She could not get what had happened—or nearly happened—off her mind, however; she felt foolish for having made a mild fuss about a near-kiss, but still, if she and Damien had kissed, would it have meant anything at all, or would it only have been some unexpectedly dear pleasure, to be taken and then never repeated?

At noon, over a steaming bowl Manguana brought to her (soup, clear, deliciously flavored with herbs and root vegetables grown in the kitchen garden), Jennifer began to wonder if perhaps the tour with Damien had not been a mistake. She was perhaps too attracted to him, and at this point, she wasn't really sure if she belonged here or not. Africa had been a shot-in-the-dark, a place to run to, but now that she no longer thought of Brendon, except with a sense of shame and regret, it seemed to her that her life needed more meaning. She felt she had wasted enough of the precious time of her life, being a part of Brendon's foolish world.

She wanted no more of that.

Jennifer had just finished lunch when Manguana suddenly came in from the kitchen.

"Dr. Lear is here; I told him to wait in your aunt's study."

"Dr. Lear is—here? Thank you, Manguana." Suddenly, she felt a deep sense of joy at the prospect of seeing him once again.

There was no time to primp, to go off to her bedroom and comb her hair or perhaps put on a trace of lipstick. Besides, she had promised herself that she would be very sober and mature about Damien, since her emotions had run away to some selfish never-never land as far as her ex-boss was concerned. Actually, she knew very little about Dr. Damien Lear, since Aunt Maggie had told her practically nothing and didn't seem at all inclined to.

"Well," Jennifer said cheerfully, facing him in that book-filled room, "to what do we owe this honor, Dr. Lear?"

She nearly always forgot how tall he was, how he seemed to fill a room with his physical presence. Today, he wore high hunting boots, black, with the cuffs of his white pants tucked in. The blue denim shirt was casual, with sleeves rolled up over strong, muscled arms.

"Things would be much simpler if your aunt would have a phone installed," he told her, smiling. "That way, I could have called to invite you to lunch."

"I just had lunch, thanks."

"Dinner then, in Nairobi. And this time, I promise you the food will be great. I'm afraid," he said quietly, "yesterday almost turned into a disaster. I acted a little like an overly eager teenager who hadn't seen a girl for ten years."

"I'm sure," Jenny said, beginning to smile, "that nothing could be further from the truth."

"Does that nice display of dimples mean you'll have dinner with me?"

"My Aunt Maggie isn't here and I—there's a lot of work piled up." He waited silently, and suddenly, she burst out: "I have something— a sort of idea—and maybe, instead of talking to my aunt, I ought to be talking to you about it!"

"Sure, I love to listen to people with big plans. Ready to go?"

"Dr. Lear—this is serious! It's about getting the children together—"

"And having a picnic in the rain forest? Great, but not today. Today I want to introduce you to some very nice people, friends of mine. In case," he said, leading her gently but firmly out of the room, toward his waiting truck parked in front, "you're wondering why I haven't chosen my lodge as our place to have dinner, it's because there are so many stupid, boring people wandering around there."

"Listen," she said suddenly. "I—I'm not dressed—if we're going to dinner, I'd like to change. And I'll have to tell Manguana, so she can tell my aunt."

"I guess that means you want me to come back later." His gaze was warm. "Frankly, a girl like you doesn't wander into the jungle every other day. There must be at least fifteen guys at my lodge, guests from various places all over the world, who would love to squire you around." He shrugged his wide shoulders. "Don't forget, mine is the first bid."

And so she had plenty of time in which to shower, standing in the little stall under the warm rain, using the lovely, fragrant soap Maggie always kept on hand, then sudsing her long hair so that it would be fragrant too.

Shortly before she went back downstairs, she heard Maggie come in. First, there was the roar of her aunt's ancient Rover, then the excited voices of the children in the kitchen; apparently, there were presents and surprises for them, as usual.

"Jennifer? I've got you a raincoat; come down and see!"

"I'll be right down, Aunt Maggie." Why did she feel guilty, reluctant to go downstairs?

Her aunt was in the savory-smelling kitchen, with six or seven children tugging at her.

"This doll is for you, Tania, and if you pull off this one's arms, I won't bring you new clothes for her when I go next time. And we've got—let's see—building blocks and—oh," Maggie said, "there you are, Jennifer. Why, you look just beautiful, dear; what a pretty dress. Rather fancy to wear to type up reports, isn't it?"

The dress was sunny yellow, silk and clinging, draping softly over her hips and breasts. She had bought it to wear with Brendon Miles, but thank God, she never did. It was expensive and looked it.

"If it's all right with you, I thought I'd go out."

"Out? In that? In this rain?"

"Aunt Maggie, could I speak with you a moment?" Jenny's face felt warm; she actually dreaded what she must say. *Dreaded?* Why? And why should she feel so terribly disloyal?

"Of course, dear. Go in the study and I'll show you the raincoat I brought you." Maggie smiled, but her eyes were wary. "I want to finish giving the children their surprises."

When her aunt came into the study where Jennifer waited, Jenny had made up her mind to come straight out with it.

"I'm having dinner with Damien," she said quietly. "I'm sorry if that displeases you."

"I see." Maggie laid a square box on the table and began unwrapping it. "This might seem rather big, but out here, the idea is to cover oneself completely from the rain, you see. They're imported from London, very sturdy—"

"Aunt Maggie, are you angry with me?"

The blue eyes met hers steadily. "I did feel anger, but only for a moment. You see, all my anger is bound up in Jack's memory. Now that Jack is gone—it's terribly important to me to know that the work here is vital. Dr. Lear doesn't think it is. I explained that to you before, Jennifer."

"Aunt Maggie, I don't see that a difference of opinion—"

"Have you ever loved a man, Jennifer? Really loved a man, the kind of love that goes beyond the grave?"

"No. I don't—know anything about love, not really. I've only played at it."

"Then," Maggie said quietly, "you don't have any idea what I'm talking about."

Jenny took a small breath. "I don't want to hurt you. I couldn't do that. If you really don't want me to go—"

"You must make your own mind up about Damien Lear, Jenny. Let's not talk about it anymore, shall we? Here—come and try on your new raincoat."

Jenny lifted it from the box. "It's lovely—thank you." Suddenly, she was hugging Maggie. "I promise you, I'll ask questions today. I'll try to understand what his real feelings are about your work here. I'm sure he respects you and I'm sure he was very sorry about Uncle Jack's death. But if he's the way you say he is—cruel to animals, uncaring—"

"I didn't say that, Jenny. I said his ideas about reserves mean that animals must fend for themselves, and sometimes that means an early death."

"Aunt Maggie—that baby elephant died an early death, and it happened right here on the reserve!"

"Of course. We can't keep the poachers away entirely, but at least we don't have animals starving to death! Out there, the people take the land and plow it and plant it for food, driving the animals out. Or else they graze cattle until the land is overgrazed and destroyed. Or they make a living by putting up snares, so they can sell hides. The farmers say they can't very well have lions roaming around on their farmlands and they can't grow a patch of corn and allow elephants to wander through it, helping themselves, so what they do is build fences—or else they kill whatever sets foot on their land."

"And Damien agrees with all of that?"

"No. He thinks he has another answer, but as I said—it's up to you to decide about him. Well, dear, I'm famished and I smell Manguana's soup simmering. The coat fits you very well. See you later." She turned at the door. "Thank you, Jennifer, for not asking all those questions about him that I'm sure you're dying to ask."

Damien came promptly at five, standing at the foot of the stairs in the hallway, his eyes admiring Jenny as she came down the stairs.

"I asked myself why I was putting on a shirt and tie," he told her, "when my friends in Nairobi will probably be wearing the usual blue jeans and bare feet. Now I'm glad I did." He took both her hands in his. "That's a fantastically beautiful dress. Or maybe it's just you in it that makes it look so great."

"Did you say we're going to have dinner with some friends of yours?"

He was helping her on with the new coat. "You'll like them. Well, either you'll like them or you'll think they're a little crazy. He's a doctor; she's a nurse. They run a clinic just south of the city. Crazy place—they've got nearly as many animals running around as your aunt has."

The truck was cool; he had left the windows down and he had parked so that the rain and wetness wouldn't blow in. Settled in the seat beside him, Jennifer watched as animals on the reserve scurried to safety as the truck roared by. Several lazy-looking lions perched in trees, watching them as they drove by.

"Fat cats," Damien said suddenly, breaking the silence between them. "Did you ever stop to think that they couldn't survive without people? They were here a long time before we were, you know. Now they just lie around on tree branches and look stupid."

So that was the way it was going to be! He was going to jump right into an argument and get it going. *Well, fine,* Jennifer thought, *let him! I'm not going back to Aunt Maggie's until I make my mind up about this man—one way or the other!*

"I think," she said quietly, "they look beautiful."

"Well, take a good look," he told her, "because before very long, you won't be seeing them anymore. Even people like your aunt know that they're on their way out. Right now, the signs are all there, but frankly, a lot of bleeding hearts don't want to talk about it. In another fifteen years, Kenya will have about twenty-five million people. They have to be fed, so the animals get pushed off grazing land, out of the bush, even out of game reserves, so food can be grown. It's a losing game." He turned the truck swiftly to the left. Now they were approaching the smooth road leading to the city.

"Dr. Lear—"

"Damien." He glanced at her. "After all, I nearly kissed you yesterday in the rain forest. That makes us buddies, or something, after such a close encounter."

"You said yesterday that as long as people buy fur coats and handbags made out of hide, the poaching would go on. In other words, there's a solution to the problem of poaching."

"Grow up, little girl." His voice was grim. "I could count the number of women I've known on one hand who wouldn't accept a fur coat. Make that one finger." He shook his dark head. "And that lady was my mother. All the others would wear that bushy-tailed impala over there just as soon as somebody could get him shot or hung up in a mesh trap, or maybe caught between the eyes with a poison spear. Skin him, put in a cloth lining and a label and she'll pay a lot of money for him."

It was true; all one had to do was walk down a street in New York at noontime in the winter, past the fancy stores or the chic disco places, and there would be scores of women wrapped up in mink, sable, and other animal furs.

"You think it's hopeless then." She looked at him; his profile, she couldn't help but notice, was lovely, like a piece of sculpture—the strong jaw, the indent that became a smile crease, the good, straight nose, the thick, sooty lashes. "I don't," she told him. "And that's what I wanted to talk to you about. Please, Damien, before you put me down as another bleeding heart."

He looked quickly down at her; his eyes were warm and smiling. "Say that again, please."

"I said before you write me off as what you love to call a bleeding heart—"

"No; not that. My name. It sounds different when you say it."

"Please don't tease me. I'm very serious. I just sort of got this idea yesterday and it's stuck with me. I'm going to talk about it to my aunt, but first—"

"I am serious," he told her, turning his attention to the road once more. "I like it when you say my name."

"Damien—" Jenny folded her hands in her lap; they had begun to tremble slightly. "Haven't you ever considered approaching the problem of poaching from the other side? What I mean is, to educate the children not to—"

"Look!" He didn't seem to be paying much attention to what she had said or was about to say; in fact, he seemed to be treating her rather as if she were a sweet, charming and desirable female, but nobody to be taken all that seriously.

A pack of impalas had reacted to the sound of the truck with their usual quick, soaring jumps. These were beautiful, sleek and black-faced, bounding over the flatland as if they were on strings. To the north of them, Mount Kenya showed itself like a hulking shadow through the rain.

"They're lovely," Jenny said appreciatively. "Damien, will you please listen to me?"

"Of course. You have a beautiful mouth; I like to watch it move over a word. But right now, I'd better concentrate on not running over any of our furry friends."

So Jennifer put the words away, for then, promising herself that at the first opportunity she would talk to him about her idea. At first, the thought of embarking on a plan to help solve the poaching problem seemed a little wild since she was so new here. But it kept bothering her, and there were the children, the children who would grow up to be poachers like their fathers and grandfathers; there would be no end to the grisly, hideous slaying of innocent animals. Unless . . .

The city was in sight at last, low-lying, rather grim-looking in the rain, but very busy. Almost until they entered the city, they had seen wild animals for a small band of elegant zebras had run alongside them for nearly a mile, manes flowing backward in the wind.

Now, Damien turned to look at Jenny. "I'm sorry if I sounded rude back there. But I didn't want you to miss seeing any of the animals. Like I said, if you decide to come back thirty years from now, most of them will probably be gone."

He had parked the car in front of a small café, a crowded, noisy place with an awning stretching out to the front. Tables were set up near the street; nobody had bothered to take them inside when the rains began. Now, he led her inside; holding onto her hand, he went in first, shouldering his way through the noisy crowd. Many of them were office workers from the downtown section, petty officials who had come in to have tea before going home from work. It was a dreary place, with rough wooden tables and limp-looking curtains hanging from the windows.

"Don't be discouraged," Damien told her. "This is the best place in town to get an American beer, black market, of course. Save your appetite for food, though—my friend's wife is a gourmet cook."

"An honor, Dr. Lear," the waiter said, bowing slightly. "You have been too long away from us."

"Busy trying to educate tourists on the fine art of handling a hunting rifle, Saiwan. This is an American friend of mine, Miss Jennifer Logan. This is Saiwan Kairobe, the proud owner of this establishment."

The man grinned and bowed again. "Two cold beers," Damien said, "frosted glasses."

"Damien, I really don't want anything to drink. Just tea."

"Tea for the lady, please." He leaned closer to her. "If the tea makes you dizzy forget it. Sometimes they spice it with weird jungle herbs."

"Will you kindly listen to what I have to say now?"

"Of course. You're going to save the animals from poaching with a brand-new idea."

Her face flamed. "I know it sounds foolish, as if I'm some—some—"

"Intruder?"

"Yes, that. And worse, an idiot. My aunt, for instance, would probably think, without telling me, of course, that I was a silly, very vain girl to get the idea that I could come here straight from New

York, never having been any closer to wild animals than a trip to the zoo, and start spouting ideas about teaching people."

He looked at her, some kind of emerging interest coming into his eyes.

"Teaching people? Are you talking about educating the kids?"

"Exactly." She leaned closer to him, so he could hear her above the general noise of the place. "I heard some of the children talking this morning about animals they'd seen last week, and all the time they talked, Manguana had to tell them they were calling some animal by the wrong name!" It was true; even her aunt had gently reminded one little boy that it could not possibly have been a cow running in the kitchen garden, since all the wedding cows were always tied up at the house of Manguana and her husband Massu-kuntna. It must, her aunt had told them, have been a wildebeest. "Damien," she said earnestly, "those children have lived here all their lives—and they can't tell a zebra from a cow or a cow from a wildebeest!"

"I often wonder about that when the meat comes in to stock my larders at the lodge. I'm not sure some of my hunters can tell one from the other. It makes the meals interesting, though—the guests never know whether or not they're eating monkey."

She stared hard at him, then finally she sat back in her seat. Her manner was cool and reserved.

"You aren't listening, are you? You can't possibly imagine that there just might be some value in what I'm talking about!"

"Sorry." He was still grinning, still teasing. "Look, nobody gives a damn what they shoot, just so it's edible. It comes down to that. Anything else is pure—"

"Fantasy? Is that what you're thinking?"

"Look," he told her, "if you're going to get mad at me, okay, but—"

"You actually think that it's all well and good for the children not to really care about the animals! Because you don't care, you can't understand why other people do, why children can grow up and change things—"

"I do care, dammit! But I happen to believe the answer lies in a totally different direction from fencing wild animals in, that's all!" His eyes were growing dark. "Tell me, Miss Logan, have you always had some cause to get excited about? I'll bet you carried placards and went to marches back home, right?"

Anger, slow, chilling, began to go through her. "You really do think my aunt and I and everybody else at the reserve are nothing but a bunch of crazies, don't you, Doctor?"

Suddenly, they were furious with one another.

"Frankly," he said, "yes, I do. But that doesn't mean I don't like your aunt and that I didn't respect and admire your uncle a great deal. It simply means that I happen to believe their energies have been gravely misdirected."

She looked quickly down at her cup. The waiter had come over with a large, copper kettle filled with tea; it smelled deliciously fragrant, scenting the moist, warm air around them with the aroma of spices and rose petals.

"Do you have any children staying at your lodge, Doctor?"

"No. I always try to avoid having them around the place."

"I see." She heard her own voice, quietly, relentlessly going on with it. "Are you against children, then?"

"Of course I'm not against children. What the hell is that supposed to mean?"

"It means that you won't show any interest whatsoever in what I have to say, even though you have the power to make my plan possible!"

"If you're asking me to help build a school, the answer is a flat-out no, Miss Logan. I happen to feel that children are not safe here and shouldn't be encouraged to stay. If at all possible, they should be taken out, transported, taken to some place where they aren't likely to die because they stumbled into a poacher's trap, or perhaps get their eyes put out from a poison arrow meant for a gazelle!"

She was silent again, feeling the quick, heated anger flow out of her, feeling a certain relief that it was gone, almost as if she had actually hated having to hate him. It would be so easy to feel something else for this man, something wonderful and exciting.

"Your face is red, Miss Logan. Did I say something to offend you?"

"No," she said softly. "I'm just glad that—I understand where you are. I don't fully, but at least I've got a start." She smiled at him, a beginning smile that began to clear the air about them at once. "You don't think it's safe for children to grow up here?"

"My dear girl, I don't think it's safe for children to grow up anywhere on the face of this earth!" He raised his glass to her. "Here's to a peace treaty until at least dinner tonight? Good." His eyes met hers and suddenly, things were right once more. The argument, the anger, had come about quite unexpectedly; one minute he had been teasing her, and the next moment, she had touched on something vital in him and he'd become coldly furious. Not because he didn't care, she suspected, but because he did care, very much indeed.

She finished her tea, then went into the powder room to freshen up before going on to Damien's friends' place. There was nobody there; the rooms smelled clean and powdery. Jennifer bathed her warm face, then stared at her reflection for a few seconds. Had she ever, in the past, when she was living and working in New York, felt this way about a man? The answer to that was yes; she had thought she was in love with Brendon, all of which pointed to the fact that she was unstable, likely to fall in love far too easily, still upset over her mother's death, still searching for a life of her own, something of importance.

So if this man attracted her, she must remember he attracted many women, dated many women from all over the world, rich, spoiled, beautiful women who came from places like Monte Carlo and Paris and Berlin.

"I think we'd better be going," Damien told her when she got back to the table. "Heller gets very annoyed when people are late to dinner. You'll like her—she's an animal nut too."

Dr. Paul and Heller Du Mond lived in a rather large, airy upstairs flat over a bakery. There was a white-washed balcony with a half-dozen hanging plants, suspended from a wooden rafter roof. The city surged about the building, but once Damien and Jennifer stepped inside the downstairs door leading up a flight of rather dim-looking stairs, the world and sounds were shut off. Jenny stood beside Damien in the small, darkish entryway, her shoulder touching his arm.

He had been peering at mailboxes. "Here it is," he said, turning to look down at her. Suddenly, he very slowly put both arms around her and gently drew her, quite willingly, closer to himself, in the warm circle of his arms.

Neither said a word. Jenny closed her eyes and rested her face against him, against his chest; she could hear his heart beginning to beat very hard.

His hand gently stroked her hair. "Once I found a little wildebeest, caught in a trap just east of the rain forest," he said quietly. "Scared to death—wouldn't let you get near her for a while. But she and I got to be friends because whenever we'd see each other around the lodge, I'd hold her for a while." He smiled down into Jennifer's warm face. "Look at me, Jenny. Do you know what finally happened?"

"No."

"That little devil got so she thought she owned the whole place! She'd bite people if they didn't throw her enough peanuts from the bar. Come right up and snarl at them. Scared a lot of 'em off the premises."

Very gently, she withdrew herself from his arms. "Is that how you feel about women in general?"

"I guess you could say that. Ready to go up?"

The apartment door was not solid wood but instead, a sort of swinging door made of a light material that led directly into a large, breezy room, a patients' waiting room. Beyond that, Jenny could see a room with a table and medical equipment, and to the right of that, a bathroom with a gleaming white tub. There were hanging plants everywhere, charming wallpaper, and the aroma of a fragrant, simmering stew.

"There you are," a woman's voice said, and Jenny turned to look at her hostess. The woman was perhaps thirty, black and good-looking in a wholesome kind of way. Heller Du Mond wore a large-flowered smock and her hair was tied back in a ribbon, yet one felt instinctively that she was a nurse. "I was afraid Damien had spirited you off to see something he particularly likes. One day he took a pregnant patient he was supposedly bringing to see my husband for a joy ride and she delivered her baby as Damien was pointing out the sights of Lake Naivasha."

"She wanted to get up and walk on home with her baby," Damien said with a slight smile. "Very strong-minded women around here." He glanced at Jenny. "If you should marry here and have children, be prepared to be back at work within twenty-four hours. Otherwise, we'll all think you're a slacker."

A man about Damien's age, probably in his early thirties, had emerged from one of the inner rooms. He was stocky, powerfully built, with a smooth black face and freshly clipped beard. He seemed delighted to see Damien; they shook hands and clapped each other on the shoulder like raucous schoolboys. This was Dr. Paul Du Mond and because he and his wife ran a "twenty-five hour a day" clinic, Jenny soon found herself alone once again with Damien, on a sort of long, comfortable back porch with a view of snow-capped mountains beyond.

"Well, what do you think of their clinic?" Damien sat across from her, holding a glass of wine that Heller had served to them. Night city sounds floated to them; a car horn blared, then abruptly stopped. From inside one of the rooms of the clinic, a baby began crying steadily.

"I guess I imagined a sterile, scary hospital. This place is charming."

"It isn't what we—what they had planned to have, of course." He looked beyond her, out at the lights of the city. "To tell you the truth, after your Uncle Jack died, I found myself wondering if he'd been able to get to a hospital, if there'd been one nearer the reserve— but that wouldn't have helped. That poison works very fast, usually. The fact is, he shouldn't have been here at all, wasting his time. If he'd stayed in the States, caring for ladies' poodles, he'd still be alive." He leaned forward, putting his glass on the low table. "Don't look at me that way, because there's no point in our getting into another power-struggle argument about things we don't agree on."

No, he was quite right; there wasn't. "Your doctor friend," Jenny asked coolly, "Dr. Du Mond—have you been friends for a long time?"

"Since medical school at the Sorbonne. We got drunk together in Paris the night we learned we'd both passed, and ran into some good-looking American nurses who were touring the Left Bank. Paul asked Heller out and she hasn't seen Kansas City since." He picked up the decanter. "More wine?"

"No, thank you. What would he have done with his life, do you think, if he hadn't come here to practice? Surely there must have been many choices."

"Paul? Mmm—let me think. Well, his father is a plastic surgeon in Paris, makes a stultifying amount of money doing film stars' faces. Paul could have gone into practice with him, I imagine. Of course, he never wanted to."

"And why didn't he?" She leaned forward a little, enjoying getting through the shell Damien had around himself much of the time, in spite of the charm and polished manners.

He was silent for a few seconds. "I suppose," he said finally, "because he wanted to do something important."

"And you, Damien? Did you feel that way too, when you first came here?"

His eyes didn't waver. "I came here to get away from the woman I was married to at the time. Getting lost in the jungle may seem a rather unique way of making the best of a bad situation, but in my case, it was the one place I felt Pamela wouldn't follow and try to drag me back to Cape Hampton. That's a very rich, very snotty little town just north of New York, where her father owns the bank and a lot of the shopping centers. I had a practice going there; my kids went to private schools and Pam and I had a lot of credit cards. The great American dream." A kind of bitter quality had crept into his voice. "I got letters from Paul, telling me about life here. He talked about the bush and the rain forest and the way things looked on a quiet morning, very early. I didn't come, at first, because I didn't—I didn't want to leave my kids. When I did go, I gave Pam an option—either she let me have custody or I'd get it on my own terms. What happened was that she showed up with the children. I hadn't counted on that."

He had said her name—Pamela. His past suddenly changed things; it was as if such a strong involvement with someone else put a kind of shadow between them.

"And your wife—didn't care for Africa?"

"She hated it, loathed it, every minute and second. Her father kept sending her poison-pen letters about how I'd ruined her otherwise dandy life, and from her point of view, I suppose I did. It takes a very special kind of woman to live here, day in, day out. The life style can be ruthless." He stood up abruptly, as if the conversation were ended. "Come on—I'll show you Heller's greenhouse. She says she raises orchids instead of kids."

She followed him down some open steps in the back, a narrow stairway that led into a private walled garden. Here, a pit had been dug in the ground for the roasting of meat; plants had been placed carefully along the stone wall, and there was a small, carved birdbath near the gate. The entire effect was one of tranquility and order, as if Heller spent a lot of time working out here.

The greenhouse was at the far end of the yard, a small, green-glassed room with the most amazing flowers growing there—huge orchids, some a pale lavender blending into a deep purple; some cream-colored blending into a pink or peach shade—all of them huge, exquisitely lovely.

"I've never seen anything like them," Jennifer said, bending over a huge flowering white orchid plant. "They're so beautiful they seem unreal!"

"A lot of life is like that." Damien's voice was surprisingly serious. "Too beautiful to be real. Did you know that those plants bloom just once a year, and when the flower is finished, the plant itself is very ugly? Look at that stalk—would you ever think anything as beautiful as an orchid could come from that?"

"I suppose everything is beautiful at some time or another in its life," she said gently. He looked so—*unhappy*. That was the only word for it; she looked at him as he stood there by the doorway, like some kind of stranger in this moistly warm world of blooming, beautiful flowers. "You don't care for flowers, Damien?"

"Not as much as I used to. Ready to go?" He didn't wait for her, but instead, turned and stood outside. She took one last look at those beautiful, potted plants and then closed the greenhouse door behind her.

"Why did you show that to me? That place—it upsets you, doesn't it, Damien?"

He walked protectively close to her in the slanting rain. "I always stop in when I'm here. Those flowers are Heller's pride and joy."

Their host was waiting for them in the large room where now there were no waiting patients. Paul Du Mond was smiling, still wearing his white med jacket, but he held a cup of coffee in one hand and poured brimming cups for Damien and Jennifer. They had a glimpse of Heller, busy out in the kitchen.

"So you've come from the States, Miss Logan. I imagine you're still in a state of shock; am I right?"

"Shock, Dr. Du Mond?"

He smiled. He was a handsome man, with a certain weariness around his eyes. There was something in his manner toward Damien, a certain tone he used, that she couldn't decipher. For now, she settled into one of the large, very soft chairs and sipped the coffee.

"Of course—it happens to everyone who comes over here. First, you find the animals delightfully amusing, then you find the heat or the flies or the rain not very amusing, and then, when you've been here for a while, the crucial time comes." He seemed to be teasing, yet there was that note of seriousness in his voice. "The time when one must decide to go or to stay. I hope you, Miss Logan, will decide to stay on. It's very refreshing to see my friend Damien with someone like you."

"Thank you." What, Jennifer wondered, was their secret; what was the mystery that seemed to exist between these two men? One could easily sense the camaraderie between them, but there was something else—unspoken. Whatever it was, Heller, Jenny sensed, knew about it too. She, like her husband, was perhaps a shade too teasing, and during dinner, both Heller and Dr. Paul kept talking about the shortage of doctors, the expected rash of yearly illnesses that the heavy damp rains caused, the babies that would be born in the bush unattended.

The meal, served in a dining room overlooking the street, was simple but delicious. Heller had utilized ingredients she had bought at the local street market—rice, chicken and the staple, couscous with big, plump raisins all through it. The talk drifted from the weather to the need for a regular clinic and hospital closer than the one here in the city.

"You're just trying to get patients out of your living room," Damien said, his voice joking, but still with that odd restraint to it. "My compliments on the wine, Paul."

"A gift from one of my patients. Makes it himself. By the way, this is the chap with the toes missing; I told you about him last time you were here. I'd like to discuss the prognosis with you for a while after dinner."

Something had leaped into Damien's blue eyes. "The man who got caught in the snare—yes; I remember your telling me."

After dinner was finished, the two men remained at the table; Heller had cleared it, bringing more coffee and a decanter of brandy.

"I really don't need help with the dishes," she told Jenny. "Someone comes in every day, and if there's nothing to do, she stands on the balcony and flirts with men down in the street. We'd best leave her something to keep her busy." She smiled at Jennifer, this slight, calm little woman who seemed perfectly contented living here in the midst of a teeming, sometimes violent city so far from home. "Why don't we go and have a look at my babies? My flowers, that is. I grow—"

"Orchids," Jennifer said. "I know; Damien showed me. I was very impressed."

Heller, who had been reaching for a heavy raincoat from a peg in the kitchen, seemed to pause. "Damien took you out there? That's strange." She shoved her thin arms into the coat. "He hasn't been out there for years."

"I thought he was a regular visitor. He seemed to know a lot about them."

They were outside now, hurrying through the rain and early darkness. Heller held open the greenhouse door and once again, Jennifer stepped inside to a quiet, moist world where every inch of space held a blooming or near-blooming orchid plant.

This time, she stayed much longer, walking up and down the earth-floor aisles with Heller, while Heller explained about the plants, pointing out the ones with buds, the ones whose flowers were fading.

"I suppose it might seem strange to you, the way I treat my plants as if they're people," Heller said, poking a small drainage tube inside a clay pot. "In a way, it's what I like to think of as my controlled world. In here, if I nourish my flowers and feed them certain things and keep them well watered, chances are about ninety-five to one they'll bloom for me. But with people, it's different." She turned to look at Jenny. "I'm a nurse, but I've never been able to get used to seeing people die. And a lot of people die here, when there's really no need. We need a clinic closer to the bush country, and we need one badly. My husband is a brilliant doctor, but even he can't save someone who needs help in a hurry and has to come all the way into the city to get it."

Jennifer paused over the head of a lilac-colored, nodding orchid. "Does this have something to do with Damien, Heller?"

Heller's eyes deepened. "How much do you know about him?"

"Why—very little, actually."

"Your aunt hasn't told you anything about him at all?" There seemed to be a certain urgency in Heller's tone.

"No," Jenny said slowly. "Aunt Maggie hates gossip. Heller—what is it about him that everyone seems to know but me?"

Heller had bent her head over a flower; when she straightened up, she looked vastly uncomfortable, as if some unwanted task had been thrust upon her.

"Well," she said quietly, "you're bound to find out sooner or later."

"If you feel I ought to know that Damien has been married," Jenny said somewhat uncomfortably, "yes; I know that."

"Is that all he told you about his marriage?"

"Heller, I really don't think it's any of my business. Please—"

"Okay then." Heller put a watering can high on a shelf and dusted off her hands on a handy rag. "Come on, I've got some very good sweets you can take back to the kids at your aunt's place."

"You don't think I'm being rude?"

"Of course not. It's very nice of you not to want to pry. However, if the two of you are going to go on, shall we say, I hope Damien has a nice, long talk with you."

Suddenly, Jenny felt as if she wanted to run, to get out of there, away from that enclosed, warm little place with its boxed-in beauty, away from this very nice, sensible lady who seemed to want very much to talk about Damien's past. Somehow, his past frightened Jenny. To know about it would be like opening a door on something she had no right to see.

"Dr. Lear and I haven't got a romance going," Jenny said, her voice low. "It—it's nothing like that. I especially wanted to see him again because I've got a rather wild idea concerning the children and I wanted to bounce it off someone. Not only that—he can help me make it possible."

"You're wasting your time," Heller said drily. "Look, the truth is, he doesn't think anybody should stay here. He thinks people should pack up and get as far away from here as possible. He wants to leave it to the hoot owls and jackals."

"And yet, he stays." Jenny looked through the rain, to the Du Monds' brightly lit apartment. She could make out the forms of the two men, sitting at the table, talking. A kind of fierce yearning flooded over her, so electric that it startled her. *Why,* she thought, *I'm falling in love with him, reacting like a stupid schoolgirl at the very sight of him! Am I so starved for love, so desperate for affection that I'd let myself tumble again, this soon after my last near-fatal mistake?*

Surely not. Very quickly, she buttoned her raincoat, ducked her head and hurried across the dark expanse of grass leading to the apartment's open back stairway.

"There you are," Damien said from the dining room, getting up. "Did Heller give away any of her secrets?"

"No," Jennifer said quickly, perhaps too quickly. "She—she's very close about her lovely orchids. She wouldn't tell me a thing."

But everyone in that room knew what she was really saying: *Don't worry, Dr. Lear; if you want me to know your secret, you're going to have to tell me yourself, because neither my aunt nor your good friend Heller seems to want it to wait much longer!*

And if he didn't—it really didn't matter, did it? Since he wouldn't help her with her plan to bring the children around to a totally new way of thinking about the bush, she probably wouldn't be seeing him again anyway.

Or so she thought.

SIX

BY THE TIME they left Nairobi, the rain had slackened somewhat, so that it was only a light spattering against the windows of Damien's truck.

"You liked them, didn't you?" His voice was warm in the close darkness.

"Of course. They're lovely, dedicated people."

"Kindly stop sounding like a travel folder. What did you really think of them?" He made a sharp turn off the road; they bounced along in silence for a while. Jenny didn't remember having come this way on their trip in.

"I think there's—something lacking. Something wrong. Not wrong enough to keep them from loving each other, but wrong, all the same."

Now it was his turn to be silent for a moment. Finally, he pulled into a clearing, light-streaked, silent, somehow lonely.

"You're a very astute girl. Yes," he said, "something is missing. But you know what they say about best-laid plans of mice and men."

"She wanted to tell me something," Jenny said softly. "But she didn't. She said—she also said that you wouldn't help me help the children."

He let his breath out. "I won't be party to some goody-two-shoes fool plan to make the kids love all the nice lions, because it won't work."

"It might. All I'm asking," Jenny said quickly, "is that you furnish transportation. I don't mean just for picnics in the rain forest. I mean taking them into towns where they have hides and animal ivory for sale. They need to be told that there aren't going to be any more animals if poaching doesn't stop. They need to be taught the—the history of wildlife and then maybe they'll respect it."

He looked at her in the half-darkness of the truck cab. "What about your precious reserves? Are you going to teach them that's the only way to save Africa?" Suddenly, he reached over her and opened the door. "Get out," he said. "I want to show you something."

He came around the truck and took her hand, walking with her on the firm, wet ground; the wet grass clung to her ankles.

"Now," Damien said, pointing, "this is elephant country, or used to be. People, well-meaning people like your aunt and uncle, have confined thousands of them to unnatural boundaries, sanctified ghettos, a lot of them, and what nobody seems to want to admit is that the animal population increases beyond the limits of food supply. Believe it or not," he said, his voice low, "this used to be a food base, a forest. Then, it became grassland. Next, it'll be desert, where nothing grows and nothing feeds."

"You never have anything good to say about my aunt and uncle's work, do you?" But seeing that vast expanse of seeming wasteland, her heart had begun beating in something close to shame. "I can't believe their work isn't helping animals," she said finally.

"Helping them exterminate themselves, that's what it's doing. You've heard, I suppose, of that place where elephants go to die?"

"Of course. But I don't see—"

"A lot of us," Damien told her, "happen to believe that place is none other than one of your precious game preserves. Come on; I'll drive you home."

It had not been a totally satisfying evening, although she found that, once in bed, she could not stop thinking about the events of the evening—the Du Monds, their rather cramped quarters, their seeming longing for something they didn't have, something they felt was essential. . . .

Suddenly, Jennifer sat up in bed, eyes wide. The rain outside made its steady, hissing sound and from somewhere in the house, a clock chimed.

It's Damien, she thought clearly. *That's what the problem is—he's what the problem is! They want him to go back into practice, along with them!*

She did not know if it was because of that, or because she feared her own feelings concerning him that made her decide not to like him, not to like him at all, to be totally on her aunt's side and never set foot anywhere near his lodge again.

Finally, she slept, hoping she would not again dream of herself in that emerald garden, the rain forest, in his arms.

She did not. In fact, she did not dream at all, and when Manguana came in with morning tea, Jenny felt tired still.

"You have company downstairs, Missy. Your aunt says to hurry up."

"Company? Do—is it Dr. Lear?" She was suddenly wide awake; all her resolutions about him seemed to have vanished and here she was, eager to see him again!

"Only his truck. And three jeeps. And drivers. And a letter from the doctor. If you want hot bread, it is being baked in the kitchen."

"Did you say—his truck?" Quickly, Jenny went to the window, shoved it up and stuck her head out into the rainy day. There outside, in the driveway, was the big truck she had ridden in the evening before with Damien, plus, as Manguana had said, three jeeps. The drivers were nowhere to be seen; they were very likely having honey and bread in the kitchen.

"You want me to bring his note up to you?"

"No, thank you," Jenny said, turning from the window. "I'll be right down."

Downstairs, she found Maggie on the porch, feeding the roosting birds. One of them, a macaw named Father Pierre, clung to her wrist as she moved about the porch.

"Good morning, Jenny. We're going to need a soft-drink bottle with a nipple on it for that new baby zebra. Be sure to pick some up when you go into Nairobi today." She looked hard at Jenny. "I assume you *are* going in."

"Aunt Maggie, I can explain everything."

"No need, my dear. Obviously, you charmed Damien Lear to the point where he is laying his treasures at your feet. I've never seen anybody drive that truck but him. I guess one could say that settles the question."

"Aunt Maggie, I only asked him to provide transportation so that I could take some of the children into the city. I—I've had an idea swirling around in my head that has to do with poaching. . . . Suddenly, she felt almost ashamed. "I know it must seem as if I'm forward and arrogant, coming here and wanting to change things. But please, even if it doesn't work, the children will enjoy the ride, I'm sure."

"Nothing good can come of any dealings of any kind with Damien Lear," Maggie said darkly, turning back to the birds. "Be sure the nipple fits tight on the bottle and while you're there, you might as well load some sugar cane in the back of that truck and bring it back too."

"Aren't you afraid we'll all be contaminated, Aunt Maggie?"

"Jenny!"

Jenny let her breath out. "I'm sorry—I didn't mean to be rude. I'd better start gathering up the children so we can get started."

But she hadn't reckoned with any of the problems that she would have to deal with, just to take four carloads of children into Nairobi.

While she was fixing lunches to take along, she read the brief note from Damien, which had been carried by one of the drivers:

> *Stop in the café where we went last night. A hot meal will be waiting for you and the kids. The drivers have been instructed not to make any stops on the way due to poachers. It won't work, Jenny, but give it a good try. At least the kids will get to have a nice outing.*

How dare he say her plan wouldn't work!

But she found, finally, that she would only need one jeep and the truck; there simply weren't enough children allowed to go. Most of the parents who worked for Maggie were off someplace doing chores or tending to the animals, and the well-behaved youngsters would never leave unless given permission. So in the beginning, there was only one little girl and finally, her younger sister, then four from the village, grandchildren of Massukuntna and Manguana, piled into the jeep. So off they went, Jenny, the two drivers, neither of whom spoke any English at all, and the half-dozen children.

All along the way, the vicious wire nooses were in plain sight; the poachers had made no attempt at all to conceal them. They gaped between bushes and across trails; none contained living animals, Jenny was relieved to see, but one held a carcass, an impala, largely devoured by scavengers. She felt her stomach lurch at the sight.

"Chimungu," the children beside her began chanting, pointing to one of the huge black birds circling overhead. "Boss bird," one of them said, his voice matter-of-fact. "First he comes and then the vultures. First, he eats the eyeball."

"Tongo, kindly don't talk about it, okay?"

The boy grinned. "Okay."

"Oh-kay," said one of the little girls. And then they were all chanting the word, making it into a little song.

Strange, the sight of that poor dead animal hadn't bothered them one bit. They drove on, while above them, in the clouded, gray sky, the vultures wheeled and waited.

The gift of transportation from Damien had come so suddenly and unexpectedly that Jennifer wasn't quite sure where to begin on her personal campaign to help stop the poaching. To talk to the children was going to be difficult; some of them understood and spoke no English at all, except for their favorite word: *okay.*

In Nairobi, over hot tea and a very sturdy meal of baked fish and peanut dressing, she remembered the painting she had wanted to do. *That's it,* she told herself, wiping the chin of a little girl who had spilled her tea, *I'll buy paints and plenty of poster paper and teach the children through drawings!*

It seemed like a splendid idea. She ended up buying not only poster paper and paints but canvas as well, finely grained, shipped from London. Then, holding the two smallest children by the hand, she set off for the nearest store with teeth, tusks, and skins for sale in the window.

The children stopped when Jennifer did; some of them pressed their little faces admiringly against the pane of window, peering inside at the gleaming animal teeth strung on a necklace of cowhide. For a brief, fleeting second, Jenny felt a kind of despair wash over her. They were so small and innocent; they saw absolutely nothing cruel or wrong about the horrible traps, the painful wounds of animals caught in those traps, the selling of the animals' parts for money. They had seen, after all, their fathers and uncles and probably their older brothers, to say nothing of their grandfathers—set traps and calmly extract wounded or dead animals from them, to be skinned, declawed and detoothed, and ultimately sold. Why should they feel any differently?

Then, looking down into the liquid dark eyes of one of the little girls, Jennifer suddenly hugged her, hugged them all in a sweeping gesture, then she sat on the curb in front of the store, where rainwater in huge droplets fell from the covering awning and made small pools, and she began to draw.

The children were fascinated. First, she painted a sign on a large piece of posterboard that said in English: *Protectors Of Tomorrow.* Since the children seemed delighted with the bright red coloring, the pretty letters they couldn't read, and the nice way Jenny went about doing it, with a kind of flourish, they all wanted to try their hand at it. At that point, they went back to the café, and with more tea in front of them, they were each given a piece of posterboard and crayons.

"Elephant," Jenny told one little girl. She fashioned a trunk for herself with one arm and the children laughed delightedly, in unison. "Draw an elephant for me, Katula. Understand?"

They did; they all did, surprisingly swiftly. Twice, the words had to be translated for them by Damien's friend, the café's owner, but then, they all got down to work, heads bent over their drawings.

The final results were simply astounding.

Jenny looked at them once, twice, three times and then again, the last time with tears in her eyes. Three of them had drawn animals caught in traps. One of them, when asked to draw a bird, any bird, had chosen the *chimungu,* the "boss bird" they had seen on the trip down. The bird looked satiny black and beautiful; its tilting wings shone much like their own skin.

Clearly, they saw no evil at all in the killing of wild animals. The same quiet acceptance of life that allowed the children to assist in the birth of babies told them that animal killing and skin selling was a fact of life, much the same as the work of a boss bird was.

They ended the trip with a visit to the shop with the long awning in front. There, they quietly stood staring into showcases filled with small stuffed animals, elephant teeth, jewelry made from ivory, and handbags and suitcases covered with the stunningly beautiful skin of the cheetah.

They sang songs on the way back, sharing the boxed lunches Manguana had prepared for them. The rain had slackened somewhat;

they passed within a hundred yards or so of the road leading to Damien's lodge, and quite suddenly, on impulse, she turned to the driver and tapped him on the shoulder.

"Will you take us to Dr. Lear's house, please?"

He looked a bit startled. She had forgotten he spoke no English.

"Dr. Lear's," Jenny said again, pointing toward the lodge. "That way!"

The driver stopped the truck and in turn, the jeep behind them stopped. Both drivers got out and, standing in the rain, had a conversation Jenny could not understand, except that twice they said Damien's name.

Then, they climbed inside again and started the vehicles. The children squealed in delight and awe when they saw the porch of the lodge, with its elegant furniture, exquisite screens and flowers, and people wearing western clothes sitting there viewing the world.

"Come on," Jenny said briskly, once they'd stopped in front of the sprawling lodge. "That's right, bring your drawings. Don't step on them now—come on, out of the truck, kids."

And so they went, the six little ones, from the tallest, most dignified black boy to the tiniest, shiest little girl, who clung securely to Jenny's hand, across the wide lobby, past the staring, amused patrons who sat at the long bar or else lounged in soft easy chairs, straight to the forbiddingly closed door of Damien Lear's office.

Jennifer knocked firmly but quietly, twice. Then, she found herself looking up into the startled blue eyes of Damien, who seemed to be looking at the children as if they were some rare breed.

"I'm afraid there's been a mistake," he said finally, his voice just on the edge of coolness. "The loan of the jeeps and truck didn't mean my guests can be—disturbed."

His words stung like a slap; they were totally unexpected and, it seemed to her, uncalled for. The boy who spoke very good English looked at Jenny uneasily.

"I—I thought you'd—the children did some drawings, of—of animals and I thought you might like to have them," she told him in a quiet little voice. "It's a sort of—payment for your kindness in lending us the jeep and truck."

Something, some fleeting look that held deep longing, came into his eyes, it seemed to her, as she held out the children's drawings.

"Thank you. I'll send them along to Heller; I daresay she'll do something clever in the way of decorating the waiting room there with them. I trust you had a very stimulating day?"

"Very. And thank you," Jennifer said evenly, "for the meal at the café. I'm sure the children would thank you too but some of them don't speak English."

"My pleasure, Miss Logan. And now, if you and your little friends will excuse me—"

"Damien—"

Cold eyes regarded her as if they were strangers. "Yes?"

"What—what is it? I thought you'd be pleased to see us—that is, I thought, when you sent the truck and jeeps, you'd become interested in what I'm trying to do."

"I sent the jeeps and truck to take a crowd of very nice kids to the city for lunch," he told her unflinchingly. "Whatever else happened is none of my concern. However, I do have a house rule here: no children allowed as guests or as visitors. I told you before, this isn't a place for children."

"I apologize if we contaminated your million-dollar establishment, Doctor."

There was a second or two of silence between them. For the life of her, she could not understand his seemingly sudden swings in mood; one moment he seemed generous to a fault, wanting to help her by giving jeeps and a free meal to the children, and the next, he was practically throwing them off the premises!

"We'll go back in the truck if you don't mind," Jenny said finally, nearly asking for the drawings back, then thinking better of it. "We can all crowd in there easier than the jeep. Unless, of course, you're afraid the children might get it sticky. I understand the truck is one thing you're truly fond of."

A small smile touched his lips. "Obviously, Miss Logan, you haven't heard about some of my lady guests."

She could not recall, later, having walked back through the lobby, past the grinning, overdressed, overfed guests, back to the waiting truck with the children. On the trip back to the reserve, she carefully looked out the window, holding a sleeping little girl in her arms.

It was only when the children sat quietly and tiredly in the kitchen, at the long table with Massukuntna at the head of it, telling him stories about their happy day, that Jennifer finally allowed herself to assess what had happened. Manguana was too busy in the kitchen, apparently, to have lit the rush lamps, and her Aunt Maggie was nowhere to be seen. In the twilight, the big, sprawling house seemed somehow to become a part of land, like a bird's nest or a refuge made by the animals. It smelled vaguely of flowers and jungle lime; the only sounds were the soft murmur of the children's voices and the ticking of Maggie's big old clock, a nine-day wind, coming from the adjoining room.

On the porch, Jenny leaned against one of the posts and thought of him.

It was almost as if she dared herself to, promising some inner self that this time, there would be no possibility of inflicted pain, since she was immune to all of that now. She liked to think she had passed far beyond the capacity for that kind of hurt; after Brendon, she'd made her mind up never to put herself in such a vulnerable position again.

But Damien's words had stung, hurt her; his coldness had somehow chilled her heart, so that she wanted not to strike back at him in any way but instead to withdraw, to leave, to—hide. *Hide.* An ugly word, and yet, she reminded herself, wasn't that just what she'd done by coming here? The truth was, she'd run as fast as she could from anything that might remind her of what had nearly happened with Brendon.

"Hello," Maggie said suddenly, coming in from the side door. She wore a long raincoat with a hood. Her glasses were fogged and had slipped down her nose a bit. "I saw the truck ambling by a moment ago, so I suspected you were back. All intact, I hope?"

"Everybody is fine," Jenny told her. "I think they're all in the kitchen."

Maggie was taking off her coat, watching Jennifer. "Well," she said, her tone hearty, "do you want to talk about it?"

"I don't know what you mean."

"None of that, Jenny. What did he do this time to upset you?"

"Nothing. I mean, nothing that I shouldn't have known would happen."

Maggie smoothed back her auburn hair; there was bird seed in it from the evening's feeding. "To tell you the truth, I was amazed that he sent the jeeps and truck around. Since it has to do with children, I rather imagined he'd flatly refuse to help you in any way."

"Aunt Maggie, why does he seem to—to dislike children so?"

Quite suddenly, Maggie's attitude had changed. She always seemed to be very open and candid with Jennifer; now, however, she seemed markedly vague.

"I wouldn't say he dislikes them, Jennifer. There's nothing he's done to indicate that. He simply doesn't like to see them growing up around here."

"What does he advocate? That nobody have babies?"

"He'd probably like that, I'm sure. Then, according to Damien, we could all pack up and go home or someplace and let the animals take over what is rightfully theirs. Would you like a nightcap, Jenny?"

"No, thank you. Aunt Maggie, you aren't going to tell me, are you?"

Maggie had started toward the fragrant aroma coming from the kitchen. At the doorway, she turned once again to look at Jennifer.

"Tell you what, dear?"

"Why Damien is so uncomfortable around children. It—it seems very strange," Jenny said, "for a doctor—"

Suddenly, she stopped talking. She and her aunt looked at each other across the room.

"Aunt Maggie—" Her voice trembled in the stillness. "Damien's patient, the one he—lost. Was it—was it a child?"

Maggie's eyes didn't change or waver. "I told you, Jennifer, I detest gossip, and it seems to me that your question comes easily under that heading. If Damien Lear wants to let you in on his life's business, I'm sure he will."

"And in the meantime, I'm free to think whatever I want. Aunt Maggie, don't you think it would be kinder of you to tell me the truth?"

"Kinder? Perhaps," Maggie said softly. "But certainly not wiser. Damien himself would tell you that here in the jungle, we don't always do the kindest thing—but we try to do the wisest."

Her work had piled up on the small desk near the porch; Jennifer, having taken a brief bath in the darkness of the shower stall, while a wild bird hooted at her nakedness, had wrapped herself in a snug robe and, in the flickering light from the rush lamps, was busily typing up letters for Maggie.

Her aunt had said goodnight hours before; the children had been taken to their homes by parents, except for the ones who lived in the house with Maggie, along with their young mother, and now, it was a silent, fragrant world that Jenny felt herself a part of as she sat at her work.

But her fingers missed the proper keys and she made so many mistakes that finally, leaning back in the chair, she gave it up. No use to keep on trying to think about budget figures to be sent to the central committee; Damien had spoiled her thinking for the night, anyway. Perhaps tomorrow, when the children were around the house and Maggie was up and about and the birds were yelling for breakfast and the new day had begun in earnest, she would feel differently.

Now, all she felt was a sort of burning hurt, pain not physical and yet it was surely pain. Why had he been so downright rude and nasty, when she'd been filled with all sorts of warm feelings, when she had wanted him to applaud the children's paintings and perhaps even admit that she may have made some small beginning in the changing of their thinking about animals?

Because he doesn't care, idiot, that's why! Because he doesn't care about what happens to people here, or animals here. All he really cares about is running that super-swank lodge of his, his ivory tower, where he's a sort of god, and he can sit there in his fancy, air-conditioned office and announce to everybody that he loathes the jungle, hates the country and only stays because rich fools pay him a lot of money to go off and shoot animals!

She got up from the small desk and walked onto the porch. In some odd way, she wished she could hear music coming from the lodge; she could be angry then. But Damien had complied politely with her aunt's order that he stop bothering them with sounds in the night, and now, there was only an oppressive silence around Maggie's house.

Why should she care so much?

Sometime in the night, she thought she heard the sound of a motor, but she turned over, shut her eyes, and ignored it. Tomorrow was going to be an important day. It was time to explain to her aunt what she hoped to do. With Maggie's support, there was no telling what might happen!

She woke up to the lovely aroma of Manguana's coffee. Stretching, Jenny turned her head to the window, seeing the endless rain; she got out of bed and, for some reason, looked out the window.

That was when she saw the truck, Damien's truck, plus the jeeps—four of them. All five drivers were eating breakfasts they'd apparently brought from the lodge. Her heart began beating harder—he had sent the vehicles for her to use again, for the children to use again! She certainly hadn't expected this.

Maggie, glasses slipped to her nose, peered over them at Jennifer, who was busy eating her grapefruit and making notes in a small notebook.

"Are you by any chance writing Dr. Lear a poison pen letter, dear?"

Jenny looked up, her face coloring a bit. "Of course not. I'm not writing to him at all—there's no reason to."

"What about his truck out there? Pass the brown sugar, dear, please."

"What about it?" Jenny put down her pencil, taking a small breath. "Aunt Maggie, if he wants to loan us the transportation, I'm going to take it. Otherwise, I'd have to worry about how to get all the kids into Nairobi again today."

Maggie gave her a long, level look. "Jennifer," she said finally, gently putting down her spoon, "I think it's about time we talk. Now don't start looking nervous, dear; I'm only going to ask you to kindly explain why you feel the sudden need to round up as many children as you can find and take them to the city again today." Her gaze was steady. "And more than that, why you allow Damien Lear to infringe upon our work and our life here by having property owned by him parked in front of my house!"

"Aunt Maggie," Jenny said carefully, quietly, "I—I know how you feel about Damien. And more and more, I'm finding myself agreeing with you. He *is* rude; he *is* ruthless; he really doesn't seem to care much about the people here or the animals. A little, perhaps, but not much. He certainly isn't dedicated to anything, except maybe the making of a lot of money."

"Go on, Jennifer. What else about the man do you find so repulsive that you feel you must still keep in touch with him?"

There was a silence. "It isn't that," Jenny said finally. "Honestly, it isn't. It's that I've got a plan that concerns the children and it's going to work, Aunt Maggie; I can feel it working."

"*Feel* it working?"

Jenny nodded. "Yesterday, the way the children behaved, the way they loved being together and with me. The paintings they did—they were just so—thoughtful and—and detailed—"

"Paintings?"

"I bought them some supplies in Nairobi, pencils and paints and posterboard. I had no idea they would do such beautiful work! You see, they probably know more about animals than they realize. It's just that someone needs to—to put them in tune with—with feeling differently about them, that's all."

"That," Maggie said drily, going back to her breakfast, "will never happen, my dear. What we have in these children is the sum total of generations of people who depend upon killing animals, by poaching if necessary, so that they can survive. And you expect the children to suddenly want to make house pets of them all!"

Jennifer looked at her aunt. This was painful for her, for them both, but the moment had come to try to explain what she hoped to do. If Maggie didn't approve, then, Jenny had decided, she would simply have to decide whether or not she dared go ahead with a project without her aunt's help or even her consent.

"First of all," she said evenly, "I need to take some kind of crash course on wildlife. I plan to go to the library and send away and do anything that's needed, so that I'll know things like—how long is a giraffe's tongue and how much water can an elephant hold in his trunk. Then, as the group of children begins to grow, I can teach them things they might not know, or if they do already know, they can teach me." She leaned forward, closer to her aunt. "The really important thing is that we'll be communicating to each other about the animals, learning new things about them, so that they won't just be meat and skins and teeth and tusks to be sold in shops for money!"

"In other words, you hope to wipe out everything they've learned about animals, turn them completely about and start anew." Maggie shook her head. "How do you know their parents will put up with that? What makes you think these people are going to allow their kids to spend much of their time sitting around measuring a giraffe's tongue?"

"Aunt Maggie, if only you'd not feel that it's a sort of mission impossible! For one thing, all children feel love for other living things; we need only tap that source and let it spill over and then, they'll begin to care about the wildlife near them! I want to take them to shops and let them get angry because handbags are being sold there, made out of cheetah skin; I want them to be furious when they see animals' teeth strung as beads—"

"I see. And while you're changing the face of this part of the world, what is Damien doing? What, Jennifer? Helping you out with jeeps and a nice truck, maybe sending along food for the children's lunch—what?" Her voice was quite cold. "Let me tell you something, my dear. No matter how hard you try to get that man interested in your project, it won't work. Damien Lear is beyond caring. He's dead inside, Jenny, just as surely as if that fever had taken him too!" Suddenly, her face went pale. "I've said too much. If you're going into Nairobi with the children, tell Manguana to pack lunches—if Damien Lear hasn't already sent along food."

"Aunt Maggie—" Jenny's voice was low; her heart had begun that slow, heavy beating again, the way it did when some new truth about Damien suddenly became clear. "What did you mean when you said the fever—"

"I told you; I've said too much. Excuse me now, Jennifer, I've got correspondence to take care of. It seems my new helper has been spending a lot of her time driving around in a borrowed truck!"

"I'll do it tonight, I promise!" But the words she wanted to say, the questions she wanted to ask, she held back. Even when she made the arrangements to once again take the children into the city, her mind seemed to be spinning, reeling with questions. Maggie had said something about a fever—how had she put it? That fever, something about a fever that might have taken him too. What fever? And who was taken, while Damien was left behind? Dead inside, her aunt had said. Was he? Could it possibly be that a man who smiled and spoke and almost kissed a woman could be so full of agony inside his heart, his spirit, that he could be referred to as "dead"?

This time, there were enough children to fill the truck and the waiting jeeps too. They began their procession shortly before ten, heading once again for Nairobi, where, the driver had said through his ten-year-old interpreter, lunch would be served for all the children; Dr. Lear would take care of the bill.

On the drive there, past the gleaming wet rain forest, past the heavy bush country that strung itself around the winding lake, Jennifer's mind refused to leave Damien. She saw, in her mind's eye, his blue eyes, warming only briefly when he looked at her, deepening with some feeling the time they nearly kissed, clouding when she tried to talk about his past, and finally, cold as winter, frosty, steel-blue, the time she gave him the children's little drawings.

They spent hours in the library that day, while Jenny pored over books on African wildlife, trying to remember each species, trying to put down facts in her mind that she could repeat to the children.

She got a lot of help from the librarian, a pretty girl who had, she told Jenny, studied library science in London but had decided to come back home to work. The children were behaving very well that day; they sat like small angels, heads bowed over books about animals. More and more, Jenny was beginning to understand that there were many, many other people besides herself who felt as she did in this country, people who wanted permanent protection for some of the endangered animals. There were certain types of monkeys that were once plentiful but that were now nearly extinct; at one time, the soft-spoken librarian explained, monkey-fur coats were considered very fashionable. Not only that, many of the cute, tiny little monkeys had been snatched away from their mothers' breasts and hauled off in crates to other countries, badly cared for on the way over and very often dead when they finally got there.

It was, of course, heart-breaking, but new, strict laws had done away with a lot of that.

"Oh," the girl said suddenly, looking up from one of the books she'd just handed Jenny, "I nearly forgot—there's a message here for you, from Dr. Damien Lear."

Jenny's heart lightened. "Dr. Lear left a message?"

"Yes. He said to tell you to stop by the same café for picnic-box lunches to take to the rain forest today."

"Thank you," Jenny said, hoping disappointment didn't show in her voice.

They picked up the box lunches, however, then she herded the children back into the truck and jeeps and along with their drivers, they headed for the vast rain forest. Once there, Jenny felt a strange sense of peace coming over her; it was almost as if she could leave her anger with Damien, her feelings of alternate dislike and deep attraction behind her and here, in this mysterious place, allow herself to remember only the feelings she'd had when they had been so close, when he had made her feel the way every woman yearns to feel, the way Manguana's man had been able to make her feel all these years—*beloved*.

Still, she had to admit that what she proposed to do might well seem impossible. There were moments when it seemed that way to her, too. She really knew so little about what she wanted to teach.

Could she ever cram her head full of enough facts to tell the children?

A feeling of defeat had begun to creep over her, although she tried to push it down. There were capped cups filled with comforting tea; she sat on the forest floor and ate and drank with the children, the sense of doubt spoiling what should have been a very nice picnic.

She told them about giraffes and even took a yardstick out of her bookbag to show them how long fourteen inches was, the average length of a giraffe's tongue. She talked about how they got their food and was delighted when one little girl asked if they ever got a sore throat.

"Okay now, let's go on to elephants. Bama, how many gallons of water can an elephant hold in its trunk?"

"Two!"

"Right!" She smiled at them, feeling much better. "Tomorrow, I'm going to tell you about spoors and how to recognize them. And I wanted to compliment all of you on your drawings—"

A sudden, piercing scream broke the quiet. It came again and then again—a child's voice!

At once, the other children sprang up, eyes wide with fear. One of the drivers, who had been dozing in the truck, leaped out and came running toward Jennifer, who stood frozen in horror. *An animal,* she thought, *an animal is killing one of the children—*

The drivers were all pointing, running to the east, toward the narrow road. Jenny ran after them, not really knowing what she could do, but ready to do anything to help. There was a wide clearing on the far side of the trees, and there, although she couldn't see the child, she saw the drivers huddled around a small circle. Her heart began pounding in slow dread.

Then, getting closer, she saw that it was not an animal that had done harm to the child, but one of the wire mesh traps. Somehow, the little boy had wandered from the group and had gotten himself caught in one of the poachers' traps. He was very small; his little face was stained with tears, and when he saw Jenny, he held out his arms to her.

His leg was caught in the wire; bright blood spurted from the side of it. Behind Jenny, the other children stood in terrified little clusters.

"Too much blood, Missy," one of the drivers said in broken English. "Got to go to see Dr. Du Mond."

Jenny's mind was racing. They were miles out of Nairobi now; the drive was slow and arduous at best. It would take them perhaps thirty minutes or more to reach Paul and Heller's apartment, and by that time the child might well have lost more blood than he could stand losing. One of the drivers had carried the crying child to the truck; suddenly, Jenny turned to face the circle of drivers.

"We've no time to go back to the city. Drive to Dr. Lear's lodge as quickly as possible. The rest of you take the other children back to my aunt's."

It was, to say the least, a wild trip. The driver seemed intent on either getting them there in record time or killing them all on the way. Jenny, who held the bleeding child on her lap, crooning and whispering encouragement to him, thought at least twice they would surely go off the road and turn over. She held the little boy close to her, closed her eyes and silently prayed they would make it to the lodge without a wreck, that Damien would be there—*please God, let him be there*—and that the warm, sticky blood which had soaked through the makeshift bandage onto her skirt wouldn't mean that the child's life was draining away.

Finally, the truck spun from the narrow road onto a wider, paved one, leaving the dense jungle behind. This was another clearing; the lodge was in plain sight now. The driver skidded to a jolting stop right in front of the red-carpeted steps leading up to the porch; guests sitting there got up from lounge chairs to come and stare.

The driver helped Jenny out; she carried the bleeding child in her arms, and the driver sprinted ahead of her to hold open the door. Inside, the cold, air-conditioned air, scented with the aroma of expensive perfume and rich food, came at her. Two women sitting at the bar stared, faces going pale, as Jenny ran toward the closed door of Damien's office.

Then, the door opened and he stood there, Damien, shirt sleeves rolled up over strong arms, eyes narrowing as he saw the child in her arms.

He came forward in three giant steps and gently took the boy from her.

SEVEN

"WHAT the devil happened?"

Damien was bending over the child; he had spoken to the boy softly, kindly, placing him on the huge, polished desk, one strong hand on the child's chest.

"Snare got him, Doctor," the driver said, from somewhere behind Jenny.

"You know better than that," Damien told the boy, "but you'll be fine, so stop crying. Just let me have a good look, okay?" He leaned closer. "I can do a patch-up job here, but he'll have to go to the hospital."

The child began howling.

"Okay," Damien said, "okay, maybe I can do it here. It's surface, mostly, nothing vital touched. Do you know there is poison sometimes on the snares?"

The tearful little boy nodded miserably.

"And that you are very, very lucky to only have a nasty gash on your leg?"

The big eyes blinked.

"Good. Then I'll patch you up and we'll put you in a spare room for the night." His eyes met Jenny's. "Perhaps Miss Logan would like to keep you company."

It worked. The child grinned and nodded and suddenly Damien was giving quiet orders to everybody—the desk must be sterile; everybody must wash up, and where the devil was his bag; he hadn't used it for years and it was locked up someplace—

"Eight stitches," he said finally, and he smiled at the boy. "You did very well indeed. I think a nice supper and a present or two are in order." He lifted the child into his arms. "Tell you what—while you rest, I'll send word to your mother and you can be thinking about what you'd like for a present."

"Ice cream," Biano said promptly.

"Sure; we've got plenty of that. And we'll come up with something else."

Jenny, feeling slightly faint, leaned against the door.

"You okay, Miss Logan?"

She straightened up. "I'm fine, Doctor. I was just getting my second wind."

The room was actually a suite, probably the most expensive in the lodge. It consisted of a huge bedroom, with a low, king-sized bed covered with a lovely spread that looked like zebra skin but wasn't, Jenny saw with relief. There was an adjoining room, a living room with sleek, modern furniture, and a sweeping view of the jungle beyond.

The presents for Biano began coming about ten minutes later, mostly from guests. There was a jungle hat sent from Damien, too big, of course, but Biano wore it anyway, sitting up happily in the huge bed, eating the peach ice cream Jenny fed him from a silver spoon. Outside, it was beginning to get dark; a message had been sent to the boy's parents and to Maggie.

It looked as if Jenny would be spending the night there.

She wasn't sure just when it was it happened; she only knew that she woke up, there on the cot in the room with the sleeping child, and at once, she knew something had happened, something had changed. She sat up in the near-darkness, wearing only her slip, and stared out the wide window.

There was a moon, and moonlight lay like a blue-silver pool on the polished floor. Strange, the moon was so clear, so lovely and bright, so much brighter than usual—

Then, she realized what it was. It had stopped raining!

It was odd, that new silence, a world without the heavy, constant beating of rain against glass, against wood and pavement, slanting, slashing, never-ending. But it had ended; the night was clear and cloudless and, when Jenny unlocked and opened one of the windows, the air was rain-washed and fragrant, sweet with the scent of jungle moss and flowers, heady and somehow pure, as if a new beginning had been made.

When the knock came at the door, she wasn't surprised; it was as if she had only half-slept, lying close to the sleeping child for a while, to comfort him with the warmth of her body, then going to the cot to try to sleep through the night. But she had not slept well; she had dreamed of riding in Damien's truck, a mad, wild ride through tangled, soaked brush, an agonizingly slow trip to get help for the bleeding boy, and finally, Damien, Damien in her dream, lifting the child, bending over him with great kindness and tenderness, much the way it had actually happened.

The knock came again, quietly, but not secretly. She slipped into her clothes and opened the door.

"Did I wake you?" He wore pajamas and a robe; he was smiling at her.

"No. That is—I was in bed but the rain woke me up. I mean the lack of it."

"Didn't anybody tell you that it doesn't always rain in Africa?"

"No," she said, and she saw that he was teasing her. "I should have known the sun always shines, sooner or later."

"Very true, Miss Logan. Now, if you don't mind, I'd like to take a quick look at my unexpected patient."

Without waking the boy, Damien gently lifted the sterile bandage and addressed himself to the wound. Then, having quietly covered the child once again, he walked across the large room to the door. Jenny had stood behind him, glad he had come, that he had been concerned enough to come to the child at this time of night.

"Damien?" She looked at him as he started to leave. "I—I was wondering if—are you sleepy?"

"No," he told her. "As a matter of fact, I was just thinking of going for a drive. Care to join me?"

"But—will the boy—"

"He'll sleep until dawn with that sedative. The best way to celebrate the close of the rainy season is to go out and view the world at once, you know—before the nights begin to get very hot and steamy and you find yourself wishing it would rain again."

The truck was parked where the driver had left it, in front of the lodge. Jenny dressed and then waited on the porch while Damien went to change. When he reappeared, he wore the usual faded slacks and a white shirt, sleeves rolled up. He started the truck, backed it out, and then they were speeding down the twisting, narrow road that led to the thick underbrush. Here, the trees were still bowed from months of heavy rain, but the moonlight was crystal clear, lighting the brush and forest like a huge spotlight. To their left lay Lake Victoria, calm and black, except where the moonlight spilled across its rippling surface.

Damien stopped the truck in a clearing near the lake.

"I want you to meet a friend of mine," he said. He got out of the truck, came around and opened the door on Jenny's side.

"A friend? Here?"

"He's a night prowler. Doesn't sleep when the rest of the herd does. Come on; don't be afraid. See that stretch of woods over there? He's eaten most of it himself, the old devil. He's particularly fond of acacias."

He took her hand, leading her off the road into the bush. Now Jenny could hear sounds, the night sounds of the jungle. From high above, shining eyes watched her; she looked up and cried out in fright.

"It's only a lioness," Damien told her calmly. "She won't jump you—not unless you try to hurt her cubs. Come on, old Max is probably around here somewhere, having a late snack."

She stayed very close to the comforting presence of Damien as he led her deeper into the bush, using a powerful flashlight to guide them. Then, very suddenly, he stopped walking, turning off the light.

"Hear that? That's got to be old Max."

"You must know him very well," Jenny said nervously, "to call him by his first name."

"The natives call him 'One-tusk', but I didn't think that was a very dignified name for such a great animal. Apparently, he was speared as a youngster and the poachers got one tusk but something happened—he probably got up on his feet and scared hell out of them, so they didn't get the other. Look," Damien said, switching on his light again. "There he is!"

There he was indeed—a huge, magnificent elephant, calmly and daintily nibbling on some twigs and leaves from a giant tree. He blinked in the bright light, threw his trunk in the air in some sort of protest, then calmly went on eating.

Damien and Jenny drew closer; he held her hand and suddenly, she wasn't afraid any longer, not at all. She stood silently next to Damien, who had now let go her hand and had walked up to the beast, putting out one hand to quietly, kindly stroke the trunk.

"I'm surprised he remembers me," Damien said quietly. "I used to come here a lot, looking for him. Whenever I had something vital to decide, I'd look up old Max and talk to him. Maybe it was myself I was talking to, but he seemed to symbolize something to me. Max," he said, "go back to the herd and go to bed. If you hang around here all the time, they'll get the other tusk and the rest of you with it." He walked back to Jenny. "Come on—he'll probably be here all night—he isn't really hungry. I think he has trouble sleeping. But he'll be around for a long time; he's one of the smart ones."

When they were back in the truck, driving smoothly across the flatland, Jenny turned to look at Damien. His profile was clearly outlined in the moonlight.

"Thank you for bringing me," she said softly.

"My pleasure. We get around 2500 elephants here in the wet season. For a long time, they stayed away, probably because of the ivory hunters. Now, they're back, and of course, poachers are killing a lot of them."

"Damien?"

He glanced at her. "You aren't still frightened, are you?"

"Not a bit," Jenny said. "I want—I want to be able to feel the way you do in the jungle—at home, not afraid, at ease."

"Stay here long enough and you'll get that feeling," he told her. "Maybe you've got it now and you don't even know it."

"If I do," she said quietly, "it's because of you. Look, I don't want us to be unkind to each other. I don't want us to be enemies."

"We never were."

"No," she said, "we never were."

The truck slowed down and stopped. Damien cut the lights and turned to her without saying a word. Jenny, as if spellbound, felt herself move closer to him on the seat, until their shoulders and arms touched.

"Will you tell me, Damien?"

"Tell you what?"

"Tell me about—about yourself. Please—I want to understand." She touched his hand, close by hers. "When I brought the child to you today, I brought him because I knew you would help him, even though you don't seem interested in practicing medicine any longer."

He had started the truck once again. A certain coolness had come over him; the warm moment, the close feeling she'd experienced only seconds before was gone.

"That's right," he said, switching on the headlights. "I'm not interested."

"That's pretty difficult to understand."

"Then don't try. I'd better get you back; it's late."

They drove in silence until they reached the lodge. Then, in the parking lot, Jenny suddenly touched his hand once again.

"I'm sorry if I seemed to pry. I had no right."

He looked at her. Then she felt his hand on her face, warm and gentle, tracing the outline of her cheekbones, her temples; one finger lightly touched her mouth.

"People come to a place like this for a reason," he said. "It doesn't always turn out the way they thought it would."

"You think I've been foolish, don't you, Damien? Taking the children to Nairobi—if I hadn't done that, the child wouldn't have been hurt."

"He could have been hurt, or killed, some other way, Jenny. It just happened that he was with your group at the time. Look," he said quietly, "there's no harm in your taking the kids around to look at animals and there's no sense in your feeling guilty for any reason. In fact, I find that charming, your interest in children."

"I don't want you to find me charming!"

"Oh? And what do you want from me?"

"Nothing," she said loudly, reaching for the door handle, "nothing at all!"

She was outside, hurrying across the moonlit parking lot, up the porch steps, into the now-darkened lobby of the lodge. Two guests sat on the porch, drinks in hand; the women stared curiously as Jennifer fled into the lodge and down the long hall to the suite.

At the door, she fumbled for her key, suddenly realizing she had forgotten to bring it.

"It isn't locked," Damien said from behind her. He had followed her. "We never lock doors around here." He held the door open. "I'd like one more look at the boy before I turn in."

"Of course."

Jenny went into the softly scented room; the child was still comfortably asleep. While Damien bent over him, she sat on the nearby cot, taking off her sandals. Then, she waited silently, her heart beating in a mixture of emotions, as Damien quietly, gently covered the child once again.

"He'll be able to go home in the morning," he told her. "I'd suggest you take him by Dr. Du Mond's in a few days, just to be certain no infection has set in."

"I'll see to it," Jenny said.

He was looking at her. "Goodnight, then."

She started to speak, to say goodnight, to say something, but the words didn't come out. Instead, she had stood up by the cot; her feet were bare and under them the floor felt smooth and cool and clean. Moonlight filled the room; the window she had opened earlier was still open, the scent of flowers, gardenias, came to them. From somewhere in the bush, a night bird called and another answered.

"Jenny." Damien came over to her, standing close, arms at his sides. "I want you to know that the jeeps will be there, at your aunt's, in the morning, for you to use."

"That won't be necessary," she said quickly. Her face was hot; she had the unexplainable urge to run out of there, to run from him and the wild feelings churning inside her. "Since you obviously think I'm simple-minded to want to change things—"

"I don't think that. I think you're very sweet and—"

"And a child. So much a child that I arm myself with crayons and poster paper and think I can change an entire continent! Well for your information, Dr. Lear, I can't and I know it, but maybe, just maybe, the children can!"

"Where did you get the idea that I think of you as a child?"

"You—you just said—"

"I said nothing of the sort. As a matter of fact," he said, his voice low, husky, "I find you extremely appealing as a woman. You're very lovely, very—"

Their eyes met. Jenny's heart was thundering, a wild drumming in her ears; she moved like a sleepwalker into his arms and then, as he pulled her roughly to him, his mouth crushing down on hers, she yielded, gave herself to the moment, to this slot of time when the world was only silver moonlight and the heavy, musk-scent of jungle flowers and his arms and his body pressing against hers with a fierce urgency and his mouth, moist and deep and full. . . .

Suddenly he left her, turned from her. He shook his head as if to clear it.

"Forgive me. I'll check on the boy before he leaves in the morning." He looked at her then, his eyes masked. "Goodnight."

She didn't answer. She was trembling, so much so that, when she heard him close the door softly behind him, she went to the window and sat on the floor by it, to let her burning face cool in the rain-washed night air.

What was wrong with her? How had it happened, this quick entrance into a world of symbols—the moonlight, the scents, the feelings she thought she had locked somewhere inside herself, perhaps forever, or at least until she could get her thinking straightened out completely. How had it happened, this sudden intrusion into her privacy by a man she hardly knew and wasn't even sure she liked?

And yet, back then, moments ago, her young body had arched toward his and her arms had wrapped themselves around him as his did her and she had, while he was kissing her, heard herself moan, as if she were already in a kind of dark ecstasy. . . .

All night she tossed and turned on the little narrow cot. At dawn, the child woke up, spoke in a language she didn't understand, but she knew he wanted his breakfast and his mother, in that order.

She was in the bathroom taking a shower when Damien came back to check the child, who was not only up and feeling fine but didn't want to leave without all his new presents. Through the closed door of the bathroom, Jenny could hear Damien's voice talking to the boy, teasing him, then silence.

He was gone when she came out. She had dressed and now she quickly combed her hair, sitting at the large dressing table in the room, carefully avoiding meeting her own feverish eyes in the glass.

One kiss, one brief moment of passion and need—and it was over. He had wanted her as much as she had wanted him, perhaps even more, but Damien had abruptly stepped back from her, avoiding her this morning, not even bothering to tell her goodbye.

So be it. She promised herself to avoid him at all costs. But the really troublesome thought was this: What if he was right, right about her plan, after all? What if she could never, ever change a single thing, what if she was only a silly, idealistic female who had to have, as Damien had said, a "cause"?

Now that the rain had stopped, there seemed to be a new surge of energy at Maggie's place. A truckload of equipment arrived, and there was new fencing to be put up. That kept most of the men busy for a while, and because Jenny found she had trouble sleeping, she began to get up very early, long before dawn, going to the little desk near the porch to do the typing for her aunt. By seven, when Manguana served breakfast to the children, Jenny's chores were done for the day, except for helping to feed the animals.

Each day Damien's truck and several jeeps arrived with their drivers. He may have thought her plan was foolish, but at least he kept his promise to furnish transportation to and from the city. For a week or so, she gathered up her little brood with their packed lunches and doggedly went in the truck to the city, where most of the day was spent in the library. Jennifer studied there, reading about ivory trading, trying to assimilate everything from why great swaths had been cut through forests along the Seronera River by elephants, to why big safari firms, places like Damien's lodge, were flourishing, making people very rich. Somewhere between poaching and hunting, there had to be another way, a better way for the animals.

Could she really change the children's thinking, so that as adults with families to care for, they would turn to some other way of making a living?

She returned to the reserve feeling very discouraged.

Maggie was on the porch, enjoying the view in a nicely mellow mood, possibly from the brandy she'd had with her after-dinner coffee.

"Jack and I used to take walks on nights like these," she said. "We'd never go far, never into the bush, just on the cleared meadow. On one of those very quiet, very beautiful nights, I decided I loved it here." She turned her head to look at quiet Jenny. "It came as a complete surprise; I thought I'd been dissatisfied and aching to go back home. It was a little like suddenly realizing you're in love with somebody you don't want to love."

"Aunt Maggie?"

"Yes, dear?" Her aunt put down her cup. "You aren't crying, are you?"

"I never cry, Aunt Maggie."

But she was; she was crying, and she was horribly ashamed of that fact. For nearly three days now, she had found herself waiting, waiting for something—she didn't know what—to happen. It was as if she were suspended in time, as if all her plans and her life here had come to some sort of standstill.

"Of course you are," Maggie said quietly. "You are crying, my dear, and that's a very good sign, you know."

Jennifer took a deep breath. For a moment, she didn't trust herself to speak; tears rolled silently down her face; her nose needed blowing and her throat felt full. It was true that she didn't cry, at least not very often and only for something that was deeply wounding her. She had cried at her mother's funeral, and years before that at her father's, but these present tears were embarrassing and baffling. She did not really know why she wept.

"Go ahead, dear," Maggie said gently. "It's good for a woman to let go once in a while, if only to make herself feel more of a woman."

"Aunt Maggie—that's silly!" Jenny wiped her eyes with a tissue her aunt handed her. "There," she said, "I'm finished with it. And I don't feel anymore womanly than I did before I began."

"Well it ought to be good for something, Jenny." Maggie gazed out at the darkening jungle sky. "I think you'd better ask yourself what it is in your life that is making you unhappy."

"It's—I'm not sure." Jenny blew her nose, leaning back in her chair. She somehow felt better. Maybe it really was the good, cleansing cry, or perhaps it was that crying afforded her the opportunity to talk about things she'd been unable to bring up before. "I'll be sending that truck and those jeeps back to Damien in the morning," she said quietly. "It—it hasn't worked. I don't know why I thought it would, Aunt Maggie. I can't change anything here. I can't even take good care of the children."

"You mean the accident with the wire trap?"

"Yes," Jenny said. "That little boy might have died! He might have been hurt much worse; Damien said he was very, very lucky."

"I see." Maggie was silent for a moment. "So you're giving up?"

"Yes; I'm afraid I am."

"There's more to it, Jennifer. What is it? Did something happen between you and Damien Lear?"

Jenny was very glad the light from the rush lamp was so dim; her face suddenly flamed.

"From the start, he hasn't put any stock in my great plans to re-educate the children about poaching, if that's what you mean."

"Well," Maggie said, "that isn't what I meant, but if you'd rather not talk about it—"

"There's nothing to talk about." The sudden memory of that deep and unexpectedly passionate kiss came to Jenny like a blow. She suddenly felt achingly lonely, almost bereft, as if she had lost something lovely.

Her aunt was watching her closely in the near-darkness.

"You mustn't blame him, you know." Maggie reached out, gently patting Jennifer's hand. "Jenny, I told you before, it's not my place to speak of this; it isn't my place to tell you what happened to Damien Lear to make him feel the way he does about things."

"It doesn't matter," Jenny said, getting up from her chair. "I'll send his jeeps back in the morning and there won't be any more children caught in animal traps because of some silly idea of mine. Goodnight, Auntie."

"Jennifer, wait!" Maggie followed Jenny through the living room into the hallway. Here, the fiber rugs were cool under their feet and the smells of the jungle, musk mixed with flowers, was very pungent. Jenny felt dizzy, heady, ready to cry once again. "I don't ever want you to say it doesn't matter."

"Well it doesn't," Jenny told her. "Damien was right about my silly little outings—they were a futile waste of time and if it hadn't been for my—my do-goody ideas, that little boy wouldn't have gotten hurt!"

"Nonsense. The children around here play in the bush all the time. It's a part of their everyday lives. It wasn't because of you, my dear. You didn't put the traps there; the poachers did. You were trying to do away with them, just as I am. Now stop feeling sorry for yourself."

"Maggie, please, I'm very tired and I'm going to bed."

Her aunt's voice, quiet and yet firm, followed her up the stairs:

"Did Damien make love to you by any chance?"

Jenny froze on the stairs. She turned around, hoping her voice wouldn't tremble the way her insides seemed to be doing.

"I don't know how you can think—"

"I'm sorry," Maggie said gently. "It's none of my business, is it? But something happened; *he's* made you unhappy and you don't want to admit it!" She walked closer to the stairs, barely outlined in the shadows. "Jenny, he can't help it, you know. My husband used to tell me that Damien doesn't respond like other people because he can't, not anymore. Not after what happened to him."

Jenny's voice was very quiet. "What was it?"

"All right," Maggie said finally. "It was his child, his son. Damien brought his family here because he and Paul Du Mond planned to open up a clinic, a big free clinic. But Damien's wife hated it—she spent most of her time in London. She had an apartment there, they said, and the parties and men—never mind. It isn't for me to judge, and it wasn't that kind of thing that changed him."

Very quietly, Jenny came back down the stairs, facing Maggie.

"What did change him?"

Maggie looked at her. "His son died, of fever. That isn't the medical term, of course, but a very high fever goes along with the illness. He'd been in Ghana with his mother and probably contracted it there. Anyway, Damien did everything he could, and so did Paul Du Mond, but the child died."

"I wish I had known," Jenny said, stunned. "I wish I'd known. . . ."

"His wife left Africa right after that and filed for divorce in London. I suppose Damien felt even more guilty after that; it was as if she were blaming him, you see, for having brought his family here. I understand he went into the bush and stayed with friends there, living in one of their huts, not practicing medicine and mostly drinking heavily. Anyway, when he came out, he built the lodge and began to get very rich indeed."

"Thank you," Jenny said unevenly, "for telling me."

"I still don't think he had any excuse at all for dropping out of life, however," Maggie said firmly. "Jack felt the same way, although he was a lot nicer about it than I am."

Jenny felt haunted all that night by her aunt's words. It was a long, lonely night, and she spent a great deal of it sitting by the window, looking out at the forest beyond, listening to the night sounds.

What Maggie had said was true, very true. Damien Lear had simply dropped out of life. He didn't care about anything.

Which meant, of course, that he could never really love a woman or be faithful to her.

EIGHT

BIANO, the child who had been hurt, was waiting on the porch for Jennifer early the next morning. He limped slightly, but not much. In fact, he seemed very excited about what had happened to him and all the attention he'd been getting.

"We're going to be seeing Dr. Du Mond this morning," Jenny told him, lifting him into her aunt's Land Rover. "Not the doctor who lives at the lodge."

She'd just rounded the curve, driving slowly, when the vehicles from Damien's passed her on the road. By the time she'd made a U-turn and headed back for Maggie's, the children who usually composed her little study group had all piled into the jeeps, ready, it seemed, for yet another day at the library, visiting curio shops or sitting quietly in the rain forest while she talked to them.

"Driver, will you please take those jeeps back to Dr. Lear's? Come on, children, we won't be going today."

Eyes misted, in some cases; there was a feeling of disappointment.

"You promised to talk about little moles today." The little boy's voice held a faint note of resentment.

"And you promised to tell us about the great marshal eagle!"

"I'm sorry," Jenny told them. "We just can't go until—until some other time." She felt their rising sadness. "Please, I'll bring you all a surprise, I promise!" She turned to the surprised drivers. "Thank Dr. Lear for me, please. Tell him I won't be needing them anymore." She would tell the children later that, although she would gladly take them on little visits to town, there would no longer be a class to teach.

She had started down the road, Biano next to her in the Rover, when she realized several children were running after her. She stopped and waited.

"We can't go with you? Everybody say we'll be very good." He glared at Biano's bandaged leg. "Not go near the snares."

"I don't think it's a very good idea anymore," Jenny said gently.

"I think you can have a better time helping my aunt. Or playing in the kitchen and talking to Manguana. She knows a whole lot more than I do."

"We like to draw the pictures."

Jenny smiled at him. "I know that, honey, but you don't need me for that. Now you tell everybody not to chase after me when I start the car. I don't want anybody else getting hurt. Manguana is making honey cookies today, did you know that?"

But her heart felt very heavy as she drove off, leaving the little, sad-eyed band of children standing in the middle of the road. Damien's vehicles had already headed back toward the lodge; she had told the drivers not to come anymore with them.

So it was over, her great plan to change her part of the world.

She switched on the car radio. On one channel there was a newscast, and another station carried American western music; the rest was static. She tried to clear thoughts of Damien from her mind and get on to the next problem.

Which was, of course, whether or not to stay here in Africa. She was over her ex-boss now; she hadn't thought of him in ages, it seemed, except with a kind of vague disgust. Her aunt, whom she had supposed would be horribly lonely, actually wasn't; Maggie would be busy and involved until she died.

What was there here, then, to hold her?

The Du Monds' apartment was filled with waiting patients. Heller, wearing a white nurse's uniform, came out carrying a baby in her arms and smiled when she saw Jenny.

"I've been meaning to get over to your aunt's to thank you for the drawings you sent us," she said. "You'll see them inside, in Paul's office." Her eyes narrowed. "Are you okay? Don't tell me you're coming down with something, Jenny."

"I'm fine," Jenny told her, although she didn't really feel fine at all. Not sick, just strangely sad. The last time she had been here, she'd been with Damien. "I'm afraid Biano here got tangled up in a wire snare."

"I see he did." Heller bent over the child. "Hold still, darlin'." She straightened up. "It's clean as a whistle, but Paul will want to look at him anyway, I'm sure. Who took care of him?"

"Damien."

"It was an emergency measure, I imagine, right?"

"Yes. I took Biano to the lodge."

There was something, some look, in Heller's eyes. "And instead of having you come back there, he told you to bring him here to us?"

Jenny nodded. "Heller, I was wondering if I might speak to you later on."

"Sure. I'll try to get a minute between the next flu case and the lady with the broken toe. Just wait for me, okay?"

Jennifer waited patiently for nearly an hour. When everybody had been seen, when the last tearful child (he'd just been given a shot) was carried out by his mother, holding a honey bar in one small hand, both Paul and Heller came out to Jenny in the waiting room.

"We honestly meant to come by and say thanks for the kids' drawings," Paul told her, pulling on his pipe. "They're in my office; come and see."

They were indeed; they were tacked up all over. There was a bright crayon drawing of a slightly cross-eyed cheetah next to his medical degree from Paris.

"Dr. Du Mond—" Jennifer moved about the room, a glass of fruit juice in her hand. Heller had brought a tray with cookies for Biano.

"Call me Paul—I thought we'd all become friends."

"Paul—I've decided not to try to—to teach the children. I'm not even sure I want to stay here any longer." She put down her cup; her voice had taken on a husky quality. "Damien and I aren't—really friends, you know. I'm sure he's a very dear friend of yours, but I'm afraid I can't agree with his reasons for having given up."

Heller and Paul were watching her closely. Finally, Paul asked the question:

"Has someone told you about what happened to Damien?"

"Yes," Jenny said quietly. "My Aunt Maggie did. I think she wanted me to know so that I could draw more reasonable conclusions about him."

"I see." Paul went over to the window. "It's a city you hate sometimes," he said quietly. "Sometimes, I feel guilty as hell for having brought Heller here, staying here, making her live out her life with me in this bug-infested, disease-ridden—"

"All of which means," Heller interrupted cheerfully, "he's in love with the place. Where else can you look out your window and see flowers like we have here? Where else can you find the kind of mutualism the animals teach us? In the jungle, whatever happens—life, death—it's always for the best, always for the benefit of the creatures living there. I'm not talking about man's killing them, of course. I'm talking about the way God has allowed one creature to live because of another creature's existence. The next time you take the kids out for a walk, tell them about the swallows who feed above the buffalo, eating the insects the buffalo attracts."

"I told you," Jenny said, "I've decided not to—"

Someone had come into the outer room, the waiting room. Heller got up quickly, putting down her cup and opened the door to the office. Then, a wide smile came to her pretty face.

"Damien! What on earth are you doing in town?" She opened her arms and as Jenny watched, heart beginning to pound in something close to pleasure, Damien came into the room, hugged Heller and then, as his blue eyes caught sight of Jenny, an unmistakable look of gladness came into them.

"I'm here to borrow a few things," he said. "Forceps, for one thing, although I doubt if they'll be needed."

"Forceps!" Paul had turned from the window. "What's going on?"

"A friend of mine is making me keep a promise I made to him once," Damien said. "How are you, Jennifer? Well, I hope. And how's the patient today?" He leaned over the child on the floor. "Dr. Du Mond taking good care of you? I see you've got more honey bars than you can handle."

"Damien," Heller asked persistently, "would you mind telling us who is having a baby and why you're—"

"I promised the young chief I'd deliver his first-born, that's all. I stayed in his village for a while, a few years ago. This morning I got a message, so I'm on my way." He looked at Jennifer once again. "I was surprised to see all my drivers back at the lodge with the truck and jeeps."

"Yes," Jennifer said quietly. "I—I won't be needing them any longer. I planned to send a personal note to you, but I might as well thank you right now."

"You've given up on the kids then?"

Her face colored. Why did he always spoil the good moments by saying something or doing something to hurt her?

"Yes," she said coolly. "I've given up."

Heller quickly covered the bad moment by offering Damien tea, which he refused, saying he was in a hurry.

"I've probably got hours," he told them, "but anyway, these women are usually healthy and not at all afraid, so it probably won't take long. She's in first-stage labor now, according to the message."

"Good luck, old man," Paul told him. "Glad to see you're keeping your hand in. First the boy, now—"

"I'm still an innkeeper," Damien said. "I'm just keeping a promise, that's all. And yesterday, I frankly didn't have the courage to say no to Miss Logan. She's a very tough-minded girl." He smiled. "Why don't you come with me, Jenny?"

For a second, Jenny felt stunned with surprise. She'd felt sure he didn't want to see her again, that the kiss and embrace had only come from some physical need in him.

"I'm not sure I'd be any help," she said finally.

"Don't need help. The women there usually stand around and wail —it's part of the ceremony. There's bound to be a big feast afterward, though, with dancing and singing. It's a time to remember." His eyes deepened. "I doubt if you'll find anything like it back in the States, in the discos."

"But I have to take Biano back."

"No, you don't," Heller said firmly. "I'll drive him back to your aunt's. I've been meaning to call on her anyway; one gets lonely for female talk sometimes. And God knows I wouldn't want to chat with those jet-set morons who stay at Damien's lodge! Go on, Jenny; you wouldn't want to miss this."

So Jenny found herself in Damien's truck once again, sitting next to him as he drove slowly through the crowded, teeming city, past the modern, whitewashed buildings to the European-influenced suburbs, and finally, past the squalid shacks that lined the road leading to the bush. Here, there were herds of cowlike wildebeests, tended by men in the traditional dress—sandals and a colorful, wraparound robe. Damien honked as they drove past, and without fail, these native shepherds waved cheerfully.

"It's going to get dusty pretty soon," he told Jenny. "Better roll up the window."

In the closed-up cab of the truck, cooled by air-conditioning, she suddenly felt herself to be in a tight and intimate world with him. They were deeper into the jungle now; the road had narrowed and was pitted with holes.

"I'm sorry for what I said back there," he told her suddenly. "About your having given up, I mean. That wasn't a very civil way to put it."

"It was what you wanted me to do, wasn't it, Damien?"

He was silent for a moment. The greenness of the bush reflected itself against the glass windows; a horned eland stared at them silently as they passed by.

"I wanted you to understand that old ways die hard here, very hard. But I'm sorry for the kids—I know they'll miss being with you every day." He glanced at her. "I know I would."

Once again, she felt that sudden surge of something close to joy go through her. How odd that this man could do that to her; with a word, a glance, a smile, he could suddenly color her world.

"It was very kind of you to ask me to come with you," she said quietly. "I just hope I won't be in the way."

"You've got a special feeling for children, haven't you, Jennifer? Don't deny it; when you discover something you do very well, you shouldn't turn your back on it, you know. People who paint beautifully shouldn't decide to bake cookies for a living."

"I beg your pardon?"

"Now take Manguana," he said. "A very wise lady, very wise. She knows what she does best and she does it. Haven't you ever wondered where all those honey cakes come from that the Du Monds pass out to their patients? Manguana makes them. She has a lot to give to the kids." He began to slow the truck down as the road got steep and even more narrow. "Now you," he said, "you should be working with kids too. And painting, of course."

"How did you know I like to paint?"

"Your picture of the female monkey with her newborn was with the package of drawings that were sent to Heller and Paul. I hope you don't mind—I kept yours."

She had forgotten that she had sketched the monkey that day in the rain forest, while the children were coloring and drawing and having such a lovely time. So he had kept that!

"You'll find some beautiful views in the village," he told her. "Did Maggie ever take you here?"

"No."

"Have you ever heard the drums at night?"

Some sense of excitement touched her. "No, but I'd like to."

"This country," he said quietly, almost as if he were speaking to himself, "it grips you, holds you like a fist, and when you try to get away—you very often find you really don't want to."

"And you, Damien—do you want to?" She realized she wanted to touch him.

"Sometimes," he said softly.

They rode on into the nearby village in silence. Jenny's mind went back to her brief, sad conversation with Maggie; this man had suffered deeply and yet, he never spoke of it. How angry he must be, she thought, to have turned his back on medicine! How wounded, how deeply wounded his spirit must be, to call himself an innkeeper, to have decided he was no longer interested in saving human life, except to keep a promise or as a kind of polite accommodation, the way he had done for little Biano.

She found herself grasping for ways to talk about it, about his dead son, his little girl who was in school someplace—London, Maggie had said. Some easy, polite way to say she was sorry, sorry his life had become ashes.

But he never allowed anyone to reach past his hurt; he was always, as far as she could tell, easygoing, flippant and caustic, treating life as if it were all some enormous joke, comic in its cruelty. And in some strange way she hadn't quite thought out yet, didn't fully understand, her knowing this about him, even understanding, in a way, that thick shawl of hardness he had drawn about himself, as a kind of armor from further agony made her feel a different kind of love, different than the passionate rising of her feelings the time he had kissed her at his lodge. But it was love all the same and its addition to the other only bound her closer to him, increasing her feelings for him.

This knowledge stunned her, made her sit beside him in a kind of muted resentment. She had not meant to fall in love. She had come here because something, some ugly thing in the guise of love had tricked her, nearly caused her to become a man's mistress. She had run from that, thank God, to a place where there were good women, Maggie and Manguana, living in a peaceful house in a land where New York's life style seemed very remote indeed. And shortly thereafter, she had been freed from her unhappy experience with Brendon so much so that it seemed, finally, as if a different person had once thought she loved him. . . .

And now this.

They went up another bumpy, rocky hill and then he stopped the truck and Jenny leaned forward to see. The windshield was somewhat scratched and quite dusty, so she opened the truck door and got out, standing on the top of the hill. The view was spectacular; a warm, moist breeze blew up from the clean river beyond. It was sweet and fragrant, touching her hair and face.

"There it is," Damien said. The village lay in a thick clump of trees, nearly invisible from this vantage point. "We'd better leave the truck here," he told her. "Give me your hand. I keep telling Kuana that he ought to be ashamed of himself for not putting in a road, but he never does, the old fox. He doesn't want strangers bothering them. By the way, it's his daughter-in-law who's having the baby."

He helped her over a series of rocks; she was afraid, at first, because there was a steep drop, but then she very suddenly didn't feel afraid at all. It was beautiful to be here in this lush paradise with him, close to him, about to witness a miracle with him. She stumbled once; he caught her in his arms and then he was looking down at her with some honest, surging need rising in his eyes. He bent his head, drew her body close to his, and then he kissed her mouth.

It was another moment of wild feelings, with the world gone for an instant; it was like being transported into some dark and secret and lovely place with him. It was like being a part of him entirely, totally belonging to him for an instant in time.

"I hope that little one isn't going to decide to be born in a hurry," he said then, smiling. "The young chief is one of my best buddies— he'd be very angry with me if I missed the big event."

She realized that he had once again assumed his light manner; as they pressed on, she began to realize that once again, Damien had put on his cloak of teasing toughness. *Isn't he ever going to say something to me that is real, that happened, that hurts him?*

Apparently not. They had reached a plateau in some way; she certainly wasn't going to mention his dead son, his divorce, any of it. If he only wanted them to be kissing friends, with a cheery, surface kind of relationship, then that was what she would accept.

The village lay in a kind of pocket, surrounded by heavy green trees and the most beautiful flowers Jennifer had ever seen. There were orchid trees everywhere, heavy with the gorgeous blossoms, violet hues and cream white and a very pure and beautiful pink. The people there lived in what were obviously permanent huts; there were hearty food gardens growing around them, and everything was very neat and clean-looking. Damien and Jenny had been met at the edge of the forest by the chief himself, a tall, very polite man who spoke no English.

She felt high on her present state of mind—being here with him, feeling a new closeness in her feelings for him. Once she had been able to accept the fact that, like it or not, she was in love with him, she had begun to enjoy it, *revel* in it.

She was happy, and strangely at peace, as she stood, during the birth of the child, in the back of the hut. Some very old women were given the place of honor around the grass mat on the floor where the young woman who was about to give birth squatted.

Damien leaned over the girl, talking softly to her. The watching women, including Jennifer, held hands; a young girl with strong, beautiful white teeth held Jenny's right hand while the mother-to-be's grandmother held the left. They made, in unison, a kind of singing, a soft and mellow sound like keening. It sounded like some kind of prayer, a lovely, soothing chant rather like the mourning sound of doves.

Jenny couldn't see much of what was going on, not until, when the chanting suddenly stopped, she gently pushed her way forward until she could see clearly. Damien had his hands on the girl's face. Her eyes were closed; she made no sound at all except, finally, a soft, low moan.

Then, holding Damien's hands, in a sitting-up position, she delivered her son.

The place was filled immediately with pure joy and goodness. One of the girls hugged Jenny, then another did, and she hugged back, crying and hugging everybody. She went closer to the baby; he was fat and beautiful.

It was night now; Jenny sat next to Damien on the hill facing the village. They had walked from the hut where the child had been born and even up here, they could hear the singing and joyful sounds coming from the village. There was a huge bonfire and the tantalizing aroma of well-spiced meat being cooked.

Jenny sat on a smooth rock. The light from torches cast a soft, orange-colored glow over the men and women who sang and danced in celebration.

"They liked you," he told her. "They're a very strong, independent people, you know. They were under British rule for a while, with all opposing parties done away with, that sort of thing. But not any longer. Frankly, I don't think they need anybody, not even a doctor."

"Something could have gone wrong," Jenny said practically.

"If it had," he told her, "they could probably have done as good a job as I could. Just because a man lives out here and doesn't read medical books, it doesn't mean he may not have his own methods of dealing with illness. Frankly, most qualified doctors are amazed at the cures that come from other means than cutting people open. We carve people up too much. Here, they depend on natural herbs and keep themselves and everything else very clean."

"Damien," she said carefully, choosing her words, "what you're really saying is that these people can get along just fine without a bona fide doctor. Somebody like you to look after them on a regular basis."

She realized, with a sinking feeling, that she had somehow spoiled the moment with her words as surely as if she had stood in front of a plate glass window and hurled a brick through it. Even in the moonlight, she could see the frost come into his blue eyes.

"If they need a bona fide doctor, as you call it, they can find one. There are a lot of them in Nairobi, including Paul Du Mond."

"So you don't think it matters that you no longer practice? You don't think that's a terrible loss, a terrible waste of—"

"Kindly don't tell me I'm wasting my life. If I want to listen to that kind of garbage, I can go into any bar in Africa, sit down and tell them my life story and they'll tell me my life is wasted." He stood up impatiently. "Do me a favor and spare me the violins, will you?"

"I don't mean to pry," she said uneasily. "I know that—that when people are dreadfully unhappy, they sometimes don't think too clearly about what their priorities should be."

"Have you by any chance been talking to somebody? The Du Monds?"

Her hands suddenly felt moist. She did not want him angry with her; the coldness in his eyes wounded her. She hated that, that new sense of being so vulnerable, but for now she didn't try to fight it.

"I wanted to know about you," she said, her voice low. "I wasn't— I didn't mean to be nosy, it was only that I was interested in you. I found myself wanting to know about you." She felt horribly humiliated having to explain. "I thought you might have told me, but when you didn't I suppose I just decided at some point to find out for myself. I'm sorry if that offends you in any way. I'm not trying to get into your private world, Doctor." She was not begging; some sense of pride or perhaps dignity had come to her, so that she found herself refusing to let his sudden withdrawal affect her.

"I have my reasons," he said, not looking at her. Then, he turned his head; she felt his steady, smoldering gaze on her. "Do you know what they are, Jenny?" His voice was quiet. "Did someone explain all of that to you, somebody who would like to make it all sound very twisted and not very gentlemanly, like somebody who decides to jump ship for some crazy reason? Sorry," he said, "I don't feel that way."

"I know about your son, Damien."

The only thing that changed was his eyes. He shot her a quick, blazing look, brimming with sudden, spurting emotion, a look so filled with need that it was almost like a scream, a cry for help.

Then it was gone.

"Good. I'm the guy that people love to sit in taverns in Nairobi and get drunk reminiscing about. The local doctor who quit doctoring and decided to get rich instead, running a hotel nobody around here can afford to come to. I've accepted that," he said, and once again, that thread of amusement had crept in. "I'm very used to being the local antihero."

"How about becoming the local hero, instead?" Jenny said.

"How about minding your own damned business?" he said, his voice good-natured but his eyes cold.

And suddenly, as she started to say something, something tinged with abruptness and anger, he grabbed her, pulled her roughly to him and closed his open mouth over hers. She struggled, tried to get away from him, but she seemed to grow suddenly tired, tired of not telling him she cared about him, that in spite of everything—including not wanting to—she did love him.

"You're very dear," he told her, his face in her long hair. He stood holding her; he had kissed her three times, deeply, and now they both were shaken, unwilling to let go of the sweet closeness. "I know," he said quietly, "I'm not doing what I ought to do, most of the time. I'm very aware of that. But I've made a conscious choice and I'm standing by it. If you and the rest of the world choose not to like that, it can't be helped."

She closed her eyes. "Please say it, Damien. Please, please say you were very, very hurt when your son died and you couldn't go on with your life. That happens to people," she said gently. "It happens to people and then they get over things somehow and they go on with their lives."

"I'm doing that." He took his arms from her but before he did, there was a certain tightening of his fingers against her flesh, the beginning of anger, most likely. There were always signs, flashes that said quickly: *Don't interfere in my life!*

"No," Jenny said clearly, "no; you aren't. You came out here with Paul and Heller to help people and because you lost one of your own, you're going to give up, quit, hide out in that fancy lodge of yours. I'll bet you get drunk at least once a week so you can feel sorry for yourself!"

He turned and strode down the hill, leaving her behind. His wide shoulders were hunched in anger.

NINE

THE CELEBRATION went on all night. Jennifer, having walked alone down the hill and back to the village, had sat among the women, the younger ones, and when they passed her a warm coconut shell filled with delicious, steaming food, she ate it, using her fingers, the way everybody else did. A few times she found herself looking for Damien, watching the hut of the chief, for it was surely there that Damien would be spending the night, while she herself had been assigned to sleep with some of the children.

But he was nowhere to be seen, and she finally concluded, with a sense of growing anger, that he had indeed gone to bed to sulk. *Let him then,* she told herself, with a surging new sense of conviction, *let him sulk! I'm right; I'm absolutely right. He should be practicing medicine, not hiding himself in the bush, pretending to be an innkeeper, tricking himself into believing he can turn his back on life. . . .*

She sat cross-legged in front of the flickering fire, watching the people dance and talk, their voices soft over the Swahili vowels. *If I stay,* Jenny thought, dreamy now, dreamy and warmed as she sat with other girls by the fire, *if I stay, I'm going to learn to speak their language. That way, we can learn from each other—if I stay, I'm going to . . .*

And quite suddenly, she sat up straighter, putting down the now-empty coconut bowl, and she looked around the orange, flickering firelight at the faces, the black-satin faces, sleepy children and beautiful young girls and proud mothers and the old ones, gentled and loved by the whole tribe.

In that moment, Jennifer realized that she loved them, loved their children, and she could not, would not leave here. Not even Damien, who did not believe in anything she did, could force her to leave!

And so now she could sleep without worrying, without thinking about whether or not she would allow herself to be hurt by him. Only people in love could be wounded by the wrong word, the careless glance, the gesture that meant love was received but not given back. Or maybe not even available to give back. That might be it, after all; Damien might, at this point, be totally incapable of loving her or anybody else.

The child lying on the mat next to Jenny's crooned softly in her sleep and turned over, snuggling close to Jenny. Jenny's arms went around the little girl, and, feeling strangely strong and safe, Jenny slept in the sweet-earth smelling hut, with ten of the tribe's children.

There were shy goodbyes in the morning; Jenny gave away her mirror and her lipstick and a bottle of pink nail polish she found in the bottom of her purse. As a special gift to the new mother, she impulsively took off her watch and handed it to the chief. She pressed it into his hands, pointing to the hut where the new mother and baby were. The chief nodded and smiled at her.

"You handled yourself very well," Damien told her as his truck bounced them along, back to Maggie's. "Look—I'm sorry about last night. I was a bastard to bring you here and then ignore you part of the night." His words sounded heavy, as if it had been a struggle for him to apologize.

Jennifer said nothing. They rode along for a while and she was conscious of his taking sneak glances at her now and again.

"I said I'm sorry," he told her. "I'm usually a gentleman—ask Maggie if I'm not." His hand touched hers almost gingerly. "Jenny?"

"I'm still here."

"Will you forgive me? And let me take you to dinner tonight?"

She closed her eyes. It was a beautiful morning; green and still, with a silver-blue sky and no clouds. It was hard to realize that not far from here an animal might be lying bleeding and in agony, trapped by a snare of mesh wire and cruel snap clamps that might have caught his leg.

"I think it best we don't," she said quietly.

"I told you, I know I shouldn't have lost my temper the way I did. I—I'm very grateful to you for a lot of reasons and I want to go on seeing you. More importantly," he said, not looking at her, "I want you to want to go on seeing me."

"Why?"

"Why?" He shrugged. "Okay. If you really want to know, it's because I happen to like you very much. You—let's just say you're different."

"Different from whom?"

"There," Damien said, smiling now, "you see? Most women would be content to know they'd just had a very nice compliment laid on them. The lady has been told she is not only different from most women, but she is decidedly admired. Most females would just lie back and bask in that. You, however, don't. You keep pestering me. And," he said, "I hate that but I like it."

She turned her head quickly to look at him. Suddenly, it was all right, what he had done, the walking away from her; the dark, brooding anger and pain that had caused him to treat her that way had caught hold of him, that was all.

"Damien, I've decided to stay. And I've decided not to give up with the children." He turned to look at her, his blue eyes suddenly brimming with feeling, and at once, her heart lightened. "I'm not just going to take the little ones with me; I'm going after some of the older kids too, the ones in school. I can talk to their teachers and maybe get them to work along with me. For instance, did you know that the poachers' ringleaders ship skins from Kenya by way of forged export documents? Young people should know that. . . ."

She didn't realize it until they pulled up in front of Maggie's, but she had talked non-stop about her plans for her work with the children.

"Jenny," Damien said, looking totally charmed and amused at her eagerness, "please change your mind about dinner."

"I don't see—"

"I'll give you the chance to tell me what I'm doing wrong all the time. I seem to make you very angry, did you realize that?"

She smiled. "Yes," she said softly, "you do make me angry."

"Good. Making up can be—"

"Damien," Jenny said firmly, getting out of the truck, "I have what I believe to be very serious business ahead of me. I'm going to spend most of my time trying to fight the killers who put up those snares." She took a deep breath. "Now a lot of those kids I'm talking about are going to begin to care—and I think that's important."

"I think it must be your face," he said slowly, eyes narrowing. "Yes; it's got to be your face. Or maybe it's something else—I don't know. All I know is that you can make me very very angry and I keep wanting to see you. Dinner, I promise you, will be private, delicious, and I'll behave myself. You, on the other hand, can tell me more about your project."

"Will you at least try to take me more seriously, Damien? I mean —my work."

"Only," he said lightly, "if you'll promise to take me less seriously. I'll be by about eight."

She found Maggie out in back in the round summerhouse, standing on a low ladder, stringing up strands of colored paper streamers.

"Hello," Maggie said, some of the paper held up between her teeth. "I was hoping you'd get back in time for the party. Hand me those flowers, dear."

"It looks lovely," Jenny said, handing her aunt the paper flowers. "What's the occasion?"

"I'm afraid I've forgotten. Jack used to keep a record of all the holidays here, so we'd know when to celebrate, but I never knew—I still don't. All I know is that Manguana asked me to give a party so I'm giving a party." She jumped down. "I know it's none of my business, dear, but did you by any chance spend the night with Damien Lear?"

"Yes—but I can—I mean, it wasn't—"

"I see. In other words, you fancy yourself to be in love with him."

"Aunt Maggie, I don't want to talk about it, I really don't."

"Very well then," Maggie said, beginning to gather up boxes of paper flowers. "But when you get hurt, don't say I didn't warn you." She headed for the kitchen. "I think today is in honor of the birthday of one of Massukuntna's ancestors. I hope I ordered enough Coca-Cola."

"Aunt Maggie," Jenny said worriedly, following her through the cool, freshly polished hallway into the living room, where Maggie, on her knees, began taking more decorations out of a big cardboard box. "What are you trying to tell me? Are you trying to tell me something to make me hate Damien? Is that it? Because if you are, that's totally unfair!" She had not meant to speak so bluntly, even rudely, and it surprised her a little to realize that she was so ready to defend her relationship with Damien.

"My only interest has been to keep you from getting hurt, Jennifer."

Jenny let her breath out. "I'm sorry. I guess maybe last night's events put a rosy glow on everything. I keep forgetting about the fact that there are a lot of things you say that I run from simply because they're true."

Maggie smiled. "Come and have some coffee. Did you know we had a baby elephant born last night? Looks just like little Peanuts did. . . ."

It was a very nice day, a very happy day, one she would remember for a long, long time, trying to recapture in her mind the way she had felt this day, the day she had made up her mind to stay here and follow her dream. All of it, of course, had a great deal to do with Damien, although Jenny didn't really want to admit that to herself. She knew that she often saw his face; his image would come suddenly and abruptly and rudely into her mind as she was doing something else, thinking some practical thought or reminding herself of some chore she yet had to do, and there he would be, and she would remember his arms and his probing mouth on hers and she would suddenly feel changed, warmed, as if she had walked closer to the fire—

Or perhaps it was only a step to the edge of hell.

She walked with the smaller children to view the newborn elephant, who did indeed resemble Peanuts as she stood on wobbling, fat legs and nursed. Two of the children had witnessed the birth and they told Jenny about it in sweet, broken English, black eyes wide with wonder.

At teatime, Jenny took out a sky-blue dress, nearly the color of

Damien's eyes, and she pressed it in the kitchen, heating the flat iron on Manguana's busy stove. There was semolina with brandy-soaked raisins baking in the oven; the large, clean kitchen was moist and warm and somehow very dear to Jenny as she stood by the open back windows ironing her blue dress. There were children huddled under the table, their favorite hiding place, looking at an animal book from the library, and upstairs, Maggie's voice could be heard talking to more children. *Family,* Jenny thought suddenly, looking at them, at the room, with its sun-bleached wooden table and the blackened pots and pans and in the darkening backyard, the crowned cranes with their beautiful golden halos. That's what they were, these gentle people, they were her family.

And that being so, what was Damien to her?

She took a shower when it was dark, standing under the smooth, flower-scented water for a long time. Then, with her hair wet, she hurried inside the house, her mind on the blue dress, getting her freshly washed hair dry enough so that she'd not look like she just came in out of a monsoon, and whether or not it would be wise to put on some of the perfume she'd brought from New York.

New York. She tried to think of it, only briefly, but she tried very hard and yet, only pictures, not feelings, came to her. She saw herself as if from a distance, a rather pretty young woman sitting in an empty office very late one night, standing at the long glass wall that looked out over the great city. Brendon's offices had been on the twenty-eighth floor of a skyscraper, and one wall of each room had been total glass. It had given one the scary feeling of standing somehow exposed to everything out there, although she had never stopped to consider just what she felt she ought to be hiding from.

There had been many nights when she would sit in the office, trying to find extra work to do, so that when he phoned her she would still be there. Just catching up on some odds and ends, she would say. The fact that she lied should have told her how wrong it all was, what a fearful mistake it was going to be. The truth was, she stayed there because she knew he usually went uptown to his club for a few drinks before heading back across town and then on to the suburbs where he lived. If he saw the light on in the office, he would probably stop downstairs and call up to find out what was going on. Later, she understood that he wanted her to be up there, so he could come up, so he could flatter her, appeal to her lonely, confused heart and get her to imagine herself to be in love with him.

It all seemed now as if it happened to someone else, some other poor, misguided girl. Why hadn't she known that love had nothing to do with the few times she allowed Brendon to kiss her there in the office?

City streets, cement, glass, stop lights, bars, and all the rest of it seemed very remote to her now, sitting in that warm, moist upper room, brushing her long damp hair, with the gardenias and orchids thick outside the screened windows, and the night birds beginning their calls in the nearby jungle.

She pulled her hair back, coiling it into a bun at the nape of her neck. Then, she opened the window, and with a kind of reverence, chose a very creamy and particularly beautiful orchid, gently broke it from the vine, and tucked it into her hair at the back. In the light of the rush lamps, she looked flushed and, if she did say so herself, extremely pretty.

Maggie's grandfather clock downstairs in the front hallway chimed a discreet eight-thirty. Well, it was like him to do that, to be late, perhaps to make certain she would not think he was running to her, or that he needed her.

At nine o'clock, however, she was beginning to ask herself just what her role, if any, should be. She was pretty sure she knew what he wanted her role to be, but that didn't mean she was going to be absolutely pliant, sitting around waiting for him to leave his wealthy friends at his inn or lodge or whatever it was and finally remember her.

He was now more than one hour late. Jenny sat on the porch, watching guests come to Maggie's party, families with children, the young missionary family and some shopkeepers from Nairobi and the nearest neighbor, a very old man who lived with his old daughter in a grass hut just outside the reserve.

"When Jack was courting me," Maggie said suddenly from behind her, "I used to have a rule: more than fifteen minutes but not less than thirty didn't mean a thing. Everybody in that big, crazy family of his drank, so I figured he'd stayed a bit longer at home to have another squiff with his dad. If he was more than thirty minutes late and he hadn't called, I knew something terrible had happened. Of course, he was never more than thirty minutes late, though, so I never had to put the rule to the test."

"Yes," Jenny admitted, "he's very late. I was just trying to decide whether or not to be angry, and I decided not to be. May I come to your party, Aunt Maggie?"

She was in the round summerhouse, with the decorations holding up beautifully, as Maggie said, when the message came. At first, for a wild, happy moment, Jenny thought it was surely Damien, two hours late, but finally here and in one piece. Then, as she walked quickly through the house, having run across the lawn to the back door, she saw the outline of the jeep parked in front of her aunt's house, and the driver getting out. It was one of the young black men who used to drive the children to the city and the library and back.

Maggie's words—*something terrible*—came into her mind and for a moment, Jenny felt only unreasonable fear rising hot in her, unthinkable that he would be hurt or dead—

"A message from Dr. Lear," the man said politely. He handed Jenny an envelope with the lodge's crest on one corner of it. Holding it in her trembling hand, she thanked the driver, shut the door, and then leaned against it, letting the panic ease out of her. *Foolish to have gotten so concerned about him when here I am, being stood up!*

The envelope was not sealed. The stationery was impersonal, the kind she felt certain he stocked every guest room with. The writing was in black ink, bold, blunt-looking script and the message straight to the point:

> *Unavoidable circumstances make it impossible tonight. Sorry. D.L.*

Disappointment, followed by a quick surging of pride, came over her. She put the message in the pocket of her skirt and walked back through the silent house to the back door. Everybody out in the little summerhouse seemed to be having a wonderful time. They were chanting, all of them, and dancing around. The dance looked very African, but the minister and his wife were dancing as if they'd been born to it.

Beyond lay the mountains, giant shadows this time of night, and before them Africa spread herself out like a feast—the lush rain forest, the calm, infinitely blue lake, the flat places where wild animals ran in packs, so utterly free and beautiful, the flowers, so huge and fragrant they surely must have come from another world—

This *was* another world. And with or without Damien's love or support, she was going to stay, just as she'd decided the night before.

She was going to enjoy her life here. She would not run as she had done the last time, in New York. If Damien's treatment of her hurt, she could bear it, because now she was far, far stronger than she had been before.

With a great sense of peace she realized she was strong now, and she would stay.

The party had been over for more than an hour, and Jenny lay on her bed, eyes wide. She had enjoyed herself—danced, ate, and had two glasses of some kind of drink made from fermented rice, far too strong for her taste; she didn't like leaving reality. Her new-found reality was here, and she wanted to face it. She had thought she would sleep at once, when she got to bed, but she didn't.

Suddenly hungry, she sat up in bed, reaching for her flashlight. "I'd love a sandwich," she called to Maggie, who was sitting out on the porch. "Is there anything left?"

"We can heat up Manguana's couscous, if she left some wood for the stove."

And so they ate together, sitting on the porch, a comfortable silence between them. Maggie had made spiced tea, and when the dawn began to show its coming, the black night sky began to be streaked with strands of silver, and then came the first pink blush over the horizon. Maggie stood up to watch it all happen and so did Jenny.

"Aunt Maggie?"

"Yes, dear?"

"I'm staying. I mean—for good. Even though things aren't—even though Damien and I are at odds when I'd rather we weren't—I'm still staying."

"Yes," Maggie said quietly, "I thought you'd get around to that. For a while, I must admit I thought you were just trying to dream up some impossible chore so that you could trick yourself into believing you weren't hanging around because of Damien Lear. But then that changed, Jenny. Now, I'm sure you're very sincere, and of course, that's the first step in a long series of steps that Jack and I took and that I'm still taking."

"Steps?"

Maggie nodded, beginning to gather up the plates and silverware. The sky had turned a bright pink in places; it was filling up with color. "You'll find that sincerity means you're under some kind of spell. That you think this place, with all its faults, is actually a kind of Eden. A savage Eden, but paradise, nonetheless. Well it isn't, my dear, and once you're able to accept the fact that it isn't, then you can remain here with a calm heart and no illusions."

There was no use trying to go back to bed now, Jenny decided. Instead, having said goodnight once again to Maggie, she dressed in jeans and a loosely fitting shirt, took her paints and equipment and set up shop on the front porch. As she worked, she began to feel tension leaving her; it was lovely, catching, or nearly so, the exact blue of the lake, the rose color of the morning sky. As she painted, two giraffes browsed along, turning gold-pink in the reflected light, and Jenny very quickly sketched them into the background.

Manguana came, nodding and taking off her sandals to pad barefoot through the house to the kitchen. Almost at once, delicious smells began to filter through the house, coffee and the sweetish aroma of frying eggs and sometime later, bread baking.

Tired now, Jenny leaned back and looked hard at her work. It had been a long time since she'd wanted to paint as badly as she had a few hours earlier, and from this one fact alone came a kind of strength, a feeling that her day could be a good day, with or without Damien in it.

"Very nice, Jenny dear." Maggie yawned, wearing her robe. "Those bloody jeeps woke me up."

"Jeeps! You mean he—did Damien send them again?"

"I'm afraid so. I'm surprised you didn't hear them. I guess one of the children must have been banging on the piano. At any rate, you'll find them lined up in front, as usual."

"May I use your Rover today, Auntie?"

"Of course. You can pile a heap of kids in that thing."

So she didn't need him, didn't need his jeeps, and she would tell him so herself!

Maggie was right; there was enough room for the usual number of children to go, although they were a bit packed in. But they were a cheerful, merry little bunch, armed with their crayons and their poster paper and their library books. Jenny gave orders to the drivers to head back to the lodge, and she followed them, bumping along over the uneven road until at last, they drove in a single line up to the front of the lodge.

It was nearly ten now; the morning had begun in earnest. White-coated waiters served continental breakfasts to guests; at one end of the awninged porch a group with a guide prepared to leave on safari. Jenny, ignoring the curious stares, walked quickly up the porch steps, calmly into the main room and then, straight across the polished floor to Damien's office.

"Please," a voice, very worried, said from behind. "The doctor is not in, Madame. He is having his breakfast."

"I see. And where is that?"

"On the east porch, the upstairs veranda, Madame. At the moment, he is—"

"Excuse me," Jenny said politely, walking past him. "You needn't announce me."

She hadn't the faintest idea where the east porch's upstairs veranda was, but it certainly had to be upstairs. She had been followed halfway up by the pleading but polite man from behind the front desk, but he apparently had given up and left her to wander about upstairs. These were guest rooms, fronted by a wide hallway with a soft green carpet. The motif was pure African, all done by some clever designer to make the indoors seem like outdoors. Some of the bedroom doors were open, showing sunny rooms, beautifully furnished in subtle and exotic colors. A small hallway to her left showed some kind of porch. She went through and found herself on a wide, shady upstairs veranda, with lush hanging plants everywhere. Now, to find the east porch—

She heard his voice then; slightly loud, and the clatter of silver or a spoon against a cup. Jenny walked forward, coming to a little bend in the structure. Then the porch widened, and at the end, a small table had been set up, covered with a floor-length cloth.

Damien sat facing Jenny; a look of surprise and then something else came to his face. He looked vastly uncomfortable.

The woman's back was to Jenny. She was a silvery blonde and her slender, pretty arms looked white, not tanned, so she must have just recently arrived. She turned partially in her chair and stared rudely at Jenny, who, at that moment, seemed to have trouble finding her voice.

"I—returned your jeeps, Dr. Lear."

"No need to." He had stood up; his face was slowly turning a burning, embarrassed red.

"I won't be needing them."

And of course, he was about to begin tedious introductions; Jenny spared them all that by turning on her heel and walking quickly around the corner of the veranda, and then, when they couldn't see her, running the length of it to the door that would take her down yet another flight of stairs, down the hallway and into the lobby and at last, down the porch steps, into Maggie's waiting Rover and away from there, away from him.

In the cool library, she finally managed to calm down, control her thoughts, and get to the business of researching the mating habits of the sable antelope. Then she took the children to lunch, but not at the usual café. They had spiced meat spread on thick white bread and cold bottles of a canned fruit drink; they were all in very high spirits.

In the park, Jenny told them about elephants along the Seronera River, and invited them to bring their friends to view the new baby elephant at the reserve. She decided to have a baby elephant-naming contest; surely if they loved this new creature they would, at some later point in their lives, find it very difficult to shoot or spear or set a trap for a wild elephant in order to sell his tusks and teeth for money!

It was suppertime when she pulled up in front of Maggie's with her sleepy little band. The children tumbled out; Manguana was waiting on the porch with a pitcher brimming with cold milk and a tray of goat-cheese sandwiches.

"Nothing for me, thank you, Manguana. I'm going straight to bed."

"First drink the goat's milk," Manguana said wisely. "It's rich and sweet—makes you feel nice and sassy."

Jenny smiled. "I'm afraid I'm in no mood to be—" She heard a sound; a door opened from somewhere downstairs. Was that pipe smoke she smelled? "Is someone here, Manguana?"

"In the library, Missy."

The library was a large, airy room where Maggie kept all her late husband's manuscripts and books. Now, the door was partially opened. Jennifer walked toward it as Maggie swept out, looking slightly flushed.

"Good evening, Jennifer," she said somewhat stiffly and headed directly for the stairs.

"Aunt Maggie—what—" Jenny had reached the room and now, she opened the door and looked in.

Damien sat in one of Maggie's chairs, looking as if he might go into a rage any second.

TEN

THERE WAS a brief moment of mutual anger—*How dare he come here and behave as if he's some kind of warlord!* Jennifer started to turn and leave, before they began to argue. Somewhere behind her eyes there were tears; she had a horrible mental picture of herself sitting on the bottom step of the stairs, weeping like a child.

"Just a moment," he said, and in two giant steps or so, he had a tight hold of her arm. "I want to talk to you."

"Of course," Jenny said softly, sweetly, "but not now. I'm very busy—"

"Listen, dammit—I want to explain—"

She pulled her arm from his grasp. Her heart was pounding now and she realized she had somehow gone beyond the tears to a kind of calm, cool, and collected anger. Invisible anger, the best kind, because he would not see it, would not know how he managed always to churn up her feelings.

"When are you going to understand, Dr. Lear, that there is absolutely no reason for you to feel you must make some—some statement to me about your comings and goings? You've no need to defend yourself because as I believe I told you, I'm very busy with my work here. I have a job to do here that I believe in, and in spite of the fact that you think it's a joke, it just might turn out to be something very important!"

She had started for the staircase, not to cry on it but to return to her room and get to work on letters to the nearby schools.

"Jennifer, will you listen to me?" He followed her to the stairs, looking up at her as she began the ascent. "Jenny, I came here to talk to you about my daughter!"

She slowed, stopped, turned around and looked down at him.

"I beg your pardon?"

"Judy, my little girl. I want you to include her in your field trips from now until she leaves. Will you?"

She felt stunned, unable to grasp what he was saying to her.

"Your daughter is here, in Africa?"

His eyes were steady. "She arrived last night, with her mother. You didn't give me a chance to explain to you, and you certainly didn't give me a chance to introduce you to my ex-wife, Judy Anne's mother."

Jenny felt her face color. "I'm sorry. Perhaps if you'd been more revealing in your note, I'd have been more understanding. Good evening, Doctor. I'll see to it that—Judy, is it?—will be picked up in the morning. Kindly have her ready and waiting on the porch; I'll provide her lunch. We usually return—"

"I know what time you usually return. Will you have dinner with me tonight? No more surprises, I promise. Her mother vowed she had to talk to me about Judy and that was why the cozy little meal. Please, try to understand."

"I do," Jenny said quietly, "I do understand. I understand that your family is here from London or someplace and if you think that for a moment, I'd ever interfere with—with a man and his wife—" She looked at him. "I did that once. I wasn't—we didn't—but all the same, I took something from his marriage simply by wanting to be with him, be near him, look at him. That was wrong, Damien, and I'm not ever, ever going to put myself in that position again!"

She was in her room, door closed, when she heard the sound of his truck starting.

And of course, she thought about that woman, his ex-wife, who had sat on the veranda across what appeared to be a very lovely table on that veranda; she had sat across from Damien and when she had finally turned to look at her Jenny had seen a beautiful face, delicately fragile, with a fine straight nose and expertly made-up eyes and a pretty, pouting little mouth. It was the face of a lovely woman who was quite used to getting her way with men.

After all, he had stood Jenny up, hadn't he? And written a very terse, even rude note, simply saying he couldn't help it but he wasn't interested in seeing her. He certainly hadn't been very interested in seeing her when she had quite suddenly appeared on the upstairs porch!

She wondered if by some outside chance, he wanted to keep his ex-wife's attention, perhaps make love to her while she was here— and have handy little Jennifer waiting in the wings, so that when his beautiful Pamela went back to London, he'd have—

That, Jenny told herself firmly, *is quite enough of that line of*

*thinking, thank you! Whatever is happening right now, or did hap-
pen, has nothing at all to do with your life! Kindly remember that
and do not, repeat, do not make a fool of yourself by being jealous!*

She wrote the letters to the schools, got correct addresses from
Maggie, and put them on her nighttable, so as not to forget to take
them to Nairobi tomorrow, when she once again went in with the
children. She envisioned seminars in mud-walled village schools,
around campfires, and in some kind of club buses, touring with the
children, going to different national game parks. The kids could become as knowledgeable and as dedicated as the experts, like Maggie.

There was definitely no time to let herself cry over Damien Lear.

She was up early the next morning but not before Maggie.

"Well," Maggie said, looking up from her morning tea. "I hear his
little girl came along too." She put down her cup. "In case you're
wondering how I found out, I told you before, news travels very fast
here, very fast indeed. Manguana has a cousin who is employed at
the lodge, you see, so almost as soon as they knew that our doctor
friend was to pick up his ex-wife and daughter at the airport, we
knew about it too. I would have told you, dear, but as I recall, you
simply wouldn't give me a chance."

"It's nothing to me," Jenny said, reaching for the juice. "He asked
me to pick up his daughter and take her along with the rest of the
group while she's here." She looked at her aunt. Suddenly, she softened. "I saw his wife yesterday, Aunt Maggie. I didn't mean to spy,
but for some reason, when he stood me up the way he did, I guess I
just wanted to—to spit in his eye or something. That was what I was
really doing when I decided to tell him not to send 'round his jeeps
any longer. And there he was, sitting with—with Pamela and she
was—"

"Beautiful?" Maggie's voice was calm. "Oh yes; she is that, all
right. She was always very social, too; Jack and I would run into
them sometimes at social things on the Ivory Coast. She always
dressed expensively and with great taste, while he, poor man, always
looked as if he'd far rather be doing something with his sleeves rolled
up. They were, to say the least, an unlikely-looking couple." She
leaned closer to Jennifer. "Are you ready to hear more about that
so-called lady, Jenny? Because this one time, I am going to forget
that I detest gossip, and I am going to tell you some things about
Pamela Lear that will make your hair stand on end! She hated

Africa, tried every way she knew to make him give up the idea of starting that clinic, discouraged him at every turn. She made him feel foolish and idealistic and I wouldn't be at all surprised if she didn't cause him to lose his manhood for a while. I daresay that would explain all the women he's been with since—"

"Aunt Maggie," Jenny said, starting to leave the table, "I don't want to hear or know anything about the two of them!"

The two of them.

Try as she would not to think about what that meant, she did think about it; in fact, as she showered and dressed for the long day, she finally allowed herself to give in to that train of thought, to examine it and then put it away forever.

Damien had been married to a beautiful, if unfaithful woman, and now she had come back to him, which wasn't any of Jenny's business, and she vowed not to let Maggie say anything more; she'd heard quite enough. The fact was, at this very moment, that cool-eyed, silver-blond woman who had borne children by Damien might be in his arms, in his bed. And she, Jennifer, must face that fact.

She told the children about Judy before they left Maggie's, the usual, well-scrubbed little group, carrying their lunches in sacks. There was an extra lunch for Damien's daughter, and the children who spoke English were told to be very kind to the new little girl.

Jenny had absolutely no preconceived notions about the child, so that when the Rover pulled up in front of Damien's lodge and for the first time Jenny saw her, she was not ready for the delicately lovely little girl who primly and somehow shyly came alone down the porch steps and introduced herself to Jenny and the others while her father watched from the doorway. She had a lovely, crisp little accent, picked up at school in London, and Jenny immediately began to love her.

All day, she found herself watching Judy without letting the child know. The little girl, although always polite and cordial, seemed not really to join in. In the rain forest, where they went to have lunch, they ended their day by holding hands and singing songs in English; the children who didn't understand all the words nonetheless understood that it was about a great lion who was smarter than the men who hunted him. After a few verses, repeated over and over, little Judy knew the simple words, but there seemed to be no joy in her singing, and once, she looked across the circle of children and Jenny saw in those eyes, the same blue as Damien's, his own reflected agony.

The child is desperately unhappy, Jenny thought clearly, and it was as if a knife had gone into her heart. She did not know if Judy Anne meant so much to her because she was Damien's child or only because she was an unhappy child.

She drove straight to the lodge after that; some of the children had nodded off, the way they always did at the end of the day, but sitting there beside her, Judy was wide awake.

"I hope you're going to be staying with us awhile," Jenny told her. "We do a lot of interesting things, you know. Perhaps you'd like to do a drawing for us and bring it tomorrow, Judy. Do you remember the herd of wildebeests we saw back there? Could you draw them, do you think?"

"I'll try," Judy Anne said. She was five, a slender little thing with pale blond hair and those startlingly blue eyes that Damien had. Beauty had stamped itself on her lovely face; she would be breathtakingly beautiful as a woman. "But I may not be staying very long, you see. Mother told me we might be going back to London soon."

"I see. I'd hoped you would stay longer and make more friends."

"I thought I'd be staying," Judy said, turning her head to gaze at Jennifer. "But it's my father, you see. Are you a friend of my father's?"

"Why," Jenny said, flustered, "I—I guess so. Yes; of course. He's a very nice man."

"He isn't at all nice."

Jenny took a small breath. "I'm sure," she said carefully, "that your father loves you very much, Judy. Look, tomorrow we'll all sit quietly on the library lawn and the other children will talk about stores—shops—that sell animal skins. The next day, we'll go and visit some. You aren't afraid of little snakes, are you? Because the next day, we're going to study them and maybe even touch one."

"I'll have to ask my father if he'll let me stay on a little while," Judy said, primly folding her tiny hands in her lap. "He doesn't want to, you see."

"I'm sure he does, honey."

"Oh no," the child said, and she seemed oddly adult, as if this was a simple fact of life. "He doesn't want me at all. My mother brought me here because she can't take care of me and she wants my father to do it. But he doesn't want to."

Either. The word came to Jenny's mind and stayed there. Ugly, terrible, unthinkable to think two people, parents, would not want this lovely child. . . .

Pamela and Damien stood on the porch of his lodge with a small group of guests. They all held cocktail glasses, and when Jenny pulled up in the Rover, hot, dusty, tired and angry, she got out, held Judy's hand and walked with her up the lodge steps. Pamela watched, gray eyes narrowing as Jenny walked toward her.

"Hello, darling," Pamela said to Judy. "Did you have a fun time?"

"I'm going to draw a lion, Mother. For tomorrow. I can go tomorrow, can't I?"

A cold little smile from Pamela, who was looking directly at Jenny.

"We'll have to ask your baby sitter, darling. Would you mind awfully if my daughter tags along? I'm afraid she's a dreadful crybaby—did she do that today, Miss Logan?"

"Of course not," Jenny told her. "She was lovely. A perfect lady. Please allow her to come tomorrow; we love having her."

Pamela turned to speak to Damien, who had come over to them carrying his drink. Jenny carefully avoided meeting his eyes.

"I was just saying that Judy's father is very lucky to have a young American girl living so close by," Pamela said sweetly. "So—convenient."

"Pamela has a remarkable ability to insult people," Damien said lazily. "I see you haven't lost the knack for it, my pet. Drink, Jennifer?"

"No, thank you. I have to get the other children home."

"Why not give them supper here, then I'll see to it that my drivers go with you. I'll send one of them ahead, to tell your aunt and the kids' parents."

"I don't—"

"Please," Damien said, his voice low, "my daughter has been very lonely. Having the kids here would be good for her."

Before Jennifer had a chance to answer, Pamela cut in. "It's amusing, darling, the way you want her to be happy on one hand and on the other, you can't be bothered with her." She raised her glass. "Here's to the Father of the Year, everybody!"

It was a monstrous moment; Damien turning on his heel and walking quickly inside, slamming the wide front door behind him. Other

guests on the porch looked vastly ill-at-ease, and little Judy stood
there about to cry.

"Of course we'll stay," Jenny said quickly. She gently touched
Judy's soft hair. "Go and tell your father I said thank you very much
indeed." She looked into Pamela's frosty gray eyes. "You're very
blessed, Mrs. Lear, to have such a wonderful child."

"Tell that to her father, will you?" Pamela walked away; someone
came up and poured more champagne in her empty glass.

Yes, Jenny thought suddenly, *I will tell him!*

She walked across the porch, but inside the lobby someone came
up to her and, handing her a glass of wine, began talking about New
York. It was a man, a tanned, handsome, probably rich young man
here, he said, on safari. He spent most of his time working for his father in New York; he'd heard there was a beautiful American girl
from the East living nearby and he was delighted she'd stopped by.

Jenny took a small sip of the wine and told herself to relax, to
wait until the proper time. The evening stretched out ahead of them;
there would be the right time to ask Damien why he was rejecting his
child, when she obviously needed someone to love her.

Tables were set up on the porch; the staff obviously was surprised
that children were allowed at the lodge; they ran around having a
marvelous time, delighting and charming all the guests. There didn't
seem to be one grump in the place, Jenny noticed; they all seemed to
enjoy watching the kids.

Candles were lit at dusk and the children, including little Judy, sat
at little tables fashioned from packing crates in the storage room,
then covered with very elegant cloths. Jenny, declining the handwrit-
ten request brought to her by one of the white-coated staff members
asking her to join Dr. Lear and the others in his private dining room,
sat on the porch instead to watch the children enjoy themselves.
From time to time, one of them would bring her something delicious
they wanted her to eat, taken from their plates. It was one of the
ways they told her they loved her so she ate every piece of bread,
every little bite of potato or vegetable or meat that they brought her.

Finally she was quite full. She sat in one of the chairs, with Judy
sitting next to her. It was a peaceful moment; the children were
happy and well-fed and they'd all had a very good time, including
Judy.

"There you are," Pamela said from the doorway. She walked
across the porch rather unsteadily; she still carried the glass of cham-

pagne in her hand. Her pretty face looked flushed and cross in the moonlight. "Time for bed, Judith, and no whining, please."

"But the other children are still—".

"Mother doesn't give a damn about the other children, darling. Now go upstairs and go to bed." She shot Jenny a quick look. "Damien missed you at dinner, or did you know that? I really think he'd much prefer to sit out here with you, instead of inside with the rest of us."

"That's very flattering," Jenny said uncomfortably, "but I'm sure it isn't so. If you'll excuse me, Mrs. Lear, I think I'd better be getting the children back. Goodnight. Goodnight, Judy."

She left quickly, getting the kids into Maggie's Land Rover. Then she reluctantly walked back up the porch steps, into the lobby and into the bar, looking for Damien.

He sat at the end, surrounded by several women who alternately leaned on him, leaned against him, and leaned low enough to make their breasts quite obvious.

"Disgusting," Pamela said from behind, her voice thick and amused. "Little do they know that Damien is absolutely turned off by such vulgar displays." She smiled coldly at Jennifer. "You're in love with him, aren't you? Oh—don't deny it; I saw it in your eyes. How much, may I ask, do you know about me?"

"All I care to," Jenny said crisply, and she walked right on by, across the room, to stand squarely in front of Damien.

"I'd like to speak to you," she said quietly. "Alone."

ELEVEN

DAMIEN GENTLY shouldered his way from the bar to his office with Jenny following close behind him. Most of the men smiled her way; a few of them tried to convince her to join their party.

He closed the door of his office behind them and headed straight for the small portable bar near the long window.

"Drink, Miss Logan? Or would you consider that a step into debauchery?"

"Damien," she said clearly, "I want to talk to you about your daughter."

He was not looking at her and she had the feeling that when and if he did, his eyes would be masked, their secret hidden somewhere in the blue depths.

"Charming kid, isn't she? As beautiful as her mother."

"What kind of beauty are you talking about? The kind that hurts children?" Jenny stood her ground. "All right, look startled. I mean what I say."

"Well, the little cricket-by-the-fire turns out to be a tiger in disguise! It isn't nice," he said putting ice into his rather stout-looking glass of whisky, "to talk badly about the mother of one's child. So I never do it, my lady."

"I know it's obviously none of my business," Jenny said evenly, "but she—your daughter—told me that you don't want her. She actually thinks you don't want her! And frankly, she looks so—so unhappy, for a little child—"

"She's quite right," Damien said at once. "I don't want her." He tilted the glass to his mouth, avoiding Jenny's stunned look. "At least, I don't want her here, here in the bush. I told you before, little Jenny, this place is not what it appears to be. It is filled with death traps. And it is no place for a child."

"Damien, she seemed happy with us today, at least part of the time. For an instant or so, there would be flashes of gladness in her little face; I honestly think she could get better here."

"My daughter isn't ill, thank you. I'm a physician; I ought to know."

"Are you, Damien? I thought you'd quit that. I thought the closest you ever got to practicing medicine anymore was to watch a woman have a baby as a favor to her husband and father-in-law, or looking after a child with a hurt leg only because you had to—"

"Is that why you wanted to see me, to tell me this?" He put down his glass, then began refilling it.

"Look," she said, "I know we don't agree on very many things. But what I'm doing is good for the kids, Damien, and it was good for your daughter! Why won't you let her be a part of it? You've a beautiful place here to make a home for her, and there are all these children to be her friends, and when she's ready to go to school, there are very good ones in Nairobi, I understand—"

Suddenly, he slammed his glass down with a loud thud. His eyes were blazing with emotion. "I know about the schools, Jennifer! I had a son, remember? I had a boy who died in this cursed garden, of an illness I couldn't stop; nobody could stop it. I'm not taking any chances on losing my daughter too, do you understand that?" He turned to the window; his wide shoulders seemed to fill the space of glass. "Judith Anne is returning with her mother to London. And that's final."

The moments ticked by; the silence was hostile. Jennifer turned to leave, but suddenly, he bolted across the room, caught her with one hand and before she could move, he pulled her to him; one of her hands shot out to push him away but it was too late; he was kissing her. There was anger in that kiss, and as his kiss grew deeper and wilder, Jennifer felt both excited and insulted. She felt herself sinking, giving in; she felt the deep yearning, the attraction to him begin to overtake all reason, but then, in her mind's eye, she saw his child, his little girl, lonely eyes wide in that lovely face. . . .

She raised her hand—she had pulled away from him at last—and soundly, with full thrust ahead, she slapped his face.

They stood facing each other. He had gone quite pale.

"Your daughter needs you," Jenny said quietly. "I don't."

She opened the door and walked out into the hallway. Just beyond, the guests seemed to be having a wonderful, noisy time. Jenny pressed her way through, hurried down the porch steps, and got into the waiting Rover with the children.

It had been a nasty scene, a brutal confrontation, and it left her shaken. At Maggie's, she went quickly to her room, washing her face in the fresh, cool water in the basin. Her mouth felt bruised, violated; she hated him for having kissed her that way against her will, as if to physically overpower her would prove something to them both.

Maggie was outside feeding the animals when Jenny left the next morning. She piled the children in the Rover and headed down the bumpy road toward the lodge. It would be painful to see Damien this morning; she actually hoped she wouldn't because she wasn't at all sure about her feelings. She did not understand how she could feel anything but anger concerning him, and yet, close to him, she always seemed to black out, to forget everything except that closeness.

The jeep rounded the corner, nearly forcing them off the road. Jenny stopped the Rover, opened the door on her side, and leaned out.

"Is that you, Biwauka?"

He grinned. "Yes, Missy. Dr. Lear says you don't need to come by because his daughter isn't there."

"You mean she's gone off to London with her mother?"

He nodded. "Early this morning, to get early plane out. So the doctor sent me along to tell you."

"I see." Jenny experienced a feeling of sadness. "Thank you."

It was a long but fruitful day. Between lunch and tea, she and the children researched Serengeti lions and they talked about how, outside the parks and reserves, the lion might soon be gone forever.

But Jenny's mind kept wandering; she kept seeing that sad but eager little face, Judy looking at a picture book, singing with the others, holding Jenny's hand. I could easily have loved her as my own, she thought at one point, and she wished fervently she had never met Damien Lear.

They got back to Maggie's shortly before dusk. The children scurried all over the place as they always did; Jenny had stopped to glance at the hallway table to see if there was mail for her. Maggie had promised to try to get her on the payroll as extra help; if that didn't work out, Jenny knew she could probably get something for her paintings, enough to pay her room and board here and maybe buy an old bus to transport the kids back and forth in—

She was still standing there when she heard the truck roar up out in front.

She half-turned, then, seeing Damien striding quickly up the front steps, she picked up the letter postmarked New York and fled for the stairs.

"Jennifer!" His voice was like thunder.

She stopped at the bottom of the stairs, hoping, praying she would not have to face him.

"What the devil have you done with my daughter?"

She turned quickly around. "Judy? Why—I haven't done—I didn't pick her up today, if that's what you mean."

"Are you saying you haven't seen her all day, she hasn't been with you?"

She saw his eyes; they held a totally new look, a burning look filled with fear and anguish.

"Your driver brought a message," Jenny said, suddenly wanting to put her arms around him. "He told me you'd said not to stop by because Judy and her mother had left early. Damien, what is it?"

"She's gone," he said heavily. "I've got an emergency call in to Pamela, at Heathrow in London, but God knows when she'll row in to England—she'll probably stop in Paris to go to a fool party or something—" He shook his head, turning away from her to stare out the open front door. "Judy's out there somewhere. As far as we can tell, she ran away sometime last night."

"*Ran away?* Oh Damien—" Jenny went up to him, touching his arm. But she couldn't help but look out there too, to where the lawn ended and the deep underbrush began. Out there, not too far away, hidden from the casual eye, were hundreds of snares, quick-acting, strong enough to pierce flesh and cause a child to bleed to death quickly. Jenny felt sick, faint.

"Pamela didn't take the time to look in on her this morning," he said, his voice bitter. "She was in a hurry to get out of here—she planned to just take off and leave Judy."

"But—the driver said they both—"

"He *thought* Judy went with her mother. It wasn't until I found out they were both gone that I put it together. Pam went to the airport all right, but she didn't take Judy with her!"

"Damien, I'll do anything I can to help; you know that."

He closed his eyes for a second. "Call Paul Du Mond and tell him I need him to help search. Tell him to bring anybody he can find!"

He was gone then; she had a thousand questions to ask, but there was no time. She had begun to shake, to tremble, only slightly at first, and then harder, until finally she realized she was either going to have to grab hold of something or else she would faint. The agony and guilt in his eyes had been like sorrowful windows to his soul; Jenny had a quick glimpse into them and she would never again be able to tell herself he meant nothing to her.

From this moment on, no matter what, she would love him with certainty, and if she could prove that to him, she would, gladly.

It was Maggie who managed, coolly and calmly, to get the entire story from Jenny and then relate it to the others, speaking Swahili. Then, with the help of Manguana, small groups of people were organized to do various things—the men and boys of course, were all out searching the bush, but inside, there was food to be prepared, coffee to make, and of course, all the time they were doing those things, silent prayers to be said.

There had been, Jenny knew, much valuable time lost. From the time Damien and the others began searching the heavily vegetated bush to the time darkness fell was only a matter of hours. Little Judith Anne had been out there somewhere not only the entire day, but perhaps the night as well, or at least a part of it. She had run away sometime in the night, without ever going to bed.

The question was, why hadn't her parents looked in on her, to say goodnight or to kiss her goodnight? Her mother hadn't even bothered to say goodbye to her when she left for London.

But there was no use blaming Damien now, not for anything. From time to time, he would come back to the house in his truck, his eyes holding a muted kind of agony. Was there any word? Did anyone bring the maps he had ordered? He stood in the kitchen, very tall and big, looking down at the maps they brought to him, and, surrounded by whatever men were there, he mapped out territories to be covered. Two of the men ran into snares; they were briefly treated in Maggie's kitchen by Manguana, who remained stoic, silent, and a rock for everyone. Most of the children who lived on the reserve huddled in the kitchen, under the big preparing table or near Manguana's old wood stove. They knew; their frightened eyes said they knew.

Nothing Jenny could have said to them, no posters she could have painted, no words she could have asked to have translated so that they would understand, could possibly have had the impact this was having on them in regard to poaching. There was, they had been told gently by Manguana, a child out there, the little American girl who had come to visit. She was out there somewhere, and they must all pray that she did not become entangled in one of the traps set by their fathers or uncles or older brothers.

From time to time, Jenny would go to the porch. Most of the time, she worked close to Manguana, helping to peel potatoes for the hot meal that was being served to any and all as they filed into the kitchen. Then, either Maggie or Jenny would serve the weary men who came in, handing them iced glasses containing a tea made from the herbs Manguana carried in a small pouch around her fat waist.

It was dark when Heller and Paul Du Mond came in. Heller came straight to Jenny, her face anxious.

"We just got back from Mombas. Paul's giving lectures there twice a week. A friend of Manguana's met our plane and told us about Judy." She shook her head worriedly, openly upset. "Judy Anne was always a spunky kid; never did like her mother very much and who can blame her? Somebody should have checked on her!" She was pacing the floor. Paul had already hopped into one of the jeeps out in front, taking off for the bush with five other men who'd been out there for hours. "I know," she said, gentling a bit, "how Damien feels about his daughter, how he *really* feels." She looked at Jennifer with steady eyes. "I think," she said softly, "it's important for you to understand that about him, Jenny. I also happen to feel that it's important for you to stay with him, no matter what happens."

Jenny's face was moist from the steam in the large room. She went to the back door and at once, a small, warm breeze touched her face.

"I don't understand him, Heller. I don't think I ever will."

"He lost his son and he can't pull himself out of the depths; it's that simple. Paul and I have known that all along—we waited, at first, because to medical people, death is so common that you build a fence around your feelings. We thought Damien would grieve, but he was always very strong, very tough-minded, very dedicated, you see, so we thought in a matter of months or even weeks, he'd be fine again. Maybe if Pamela had been a real wife to him—but she wasn't, not ever, and I suppose that was why his children always meant so much to him."

Jenny turned from the door. "He was cold to Judy. She—she told me he didn't want her." Tears of frustration filled her eyes. "Heller, if Damien had only gone in to kiss Judy goodnight, he'd have seen that her bed was empty and a search party could have been sent out last night, barely twenty-four hours ago." She took a shaking breath. "That," she said, "is what I can't understand!"

She wanted to hate him; she really did. It would be easier. Hate him instead of feeling the way she did about him, despise him instead of seeing the agony in his eyes and wanting to stop it. If she could only convince herself that the agony was deserved; that he had failed his little girl and now he was paying for that failure to love and want the child.

But she could not hate him. She could not.

"Jenny dear," Heller said quietly. "Damien's loss, when Robbie died, was far greater than any of us realized. His future was wrapped up in his kids. He brought them here, and when his son died so soon after they got here, Damien blamed himself. After a while, Paul and I talked about it, when we realized he'd gone into some kind of cocoon. We understood that he would have to either come out of it more dedicated than ever to medicine, to this country and its people, or else he'd go the other way."

"And he went the other way. Totally."

"Yes," Heller said. "He put on a mask and became a kind of—of rich overseer, a man who deals with dollars and cents, nothing to get emotional about. Jenny, the reason he didn't want his daughter to stay here, the reason he didn't go to her room to kiss her and behave like a loving father, has nothing to do with his feeling for her. Or maybe it has everything to do with it. He didn't want to love her so much that he couldn't bear to have her leave him. So he tried not to love her at all." Heller came over to the screened-in door where Jenny stood. She put her hand on Jenny's shoulder. "He did that with you, too, you know."

Jenny closed her eyes, trying hard not to break down. She must not; she must not.

"If Judy dies, Heller, what will happen to him?"

"I don't know," Heller said softly. "But whatever happens, please, please be there with him!"

Jenny nodded. Another truck had pulled up in front, filled with men who had been searching the bush, calling, hacking away at the thick undergrowth with sharp machetes. She went at once to the food table and began filling plates. One of the men came up to her, his kind face haggard with worry.

"Don't think we'll find her. We found many snares, but didn't find the child. Some think maybe something came and found her caught and—"

Jenny's heart seemed to stop. "Some animal found her, you mean? Found her and—"

"Animals don't tell no difference between an elk in a snare and a child in a snare. They got to eat."

"Oh my God." Jenny went out on the porch and leaned against the post. She looked beyond, at the dark lake and somehow, its peaceful tranquility gave her hope. *Please, Lord, don't let that happen to Damien's child. Spare her; give her back to him—You know how much he has already suffered!*

It was nearly midnight when the message came for Damien. Jennifer hadn't seen him for hours. He had come in to drink tea and check to see if there was any news, and he had briefly glanced at Jennifer. In that moment, she saw his eyes—they were veiled, hardened. It was as if she meant nothing at all to him.

Shortly before he folded up the maps and started to go back out to his truck, the boy came in, breathless. He spoke first to Manguana, then to Damien, in a trembling little voice. Manguana bent over him kindly, listening; when she straightened up, she looked hard at Damien, but said nothing.

Damien answered, speaking quietly but firmly; Jenny couldn't understand any of what he said except for the name, *Dr. Du Mond.* He shook his head, pointing to the darkness outside.

"I have to leave," he said finally.

Jenny came a bit closer to him. "Is there news?"

"No. Nothing about my daughter. The boy came to tell us a child is sick in the village." He looked at Jenny; it was as if a fire blazed in his eyes. "If they find my daughter and she is dead, leave her here, please. I'll take her to Nairobi myself."

"Yes," Jenny said, her voice surprisingly steady. "Damien, let me come with you, please—"

But he was gone, out the door into the black, threatening night.

TWELVE

ONLY MAGGIE and the stoic Manguana seemed sane that night, as the carloads and truckloads of men increased, as more heard the news of the white man's lost child and came to help. Only a very few spoke English; between her kitchen duties Manguana patiently translated. The children refused to go to bed; they slept on the floor, huddled close to each other. Some crept under the big kitchen table and some brought their little grass mats and lay down on the porch, eyes wide and frightened.

Jennifer tried not to think of the little girl out there. She tried very hard to think of the child here, brought back safely, hugged, kissed, loved. She tried to picture Damien's eyes when he knew Judith Anne was safe.

But it was hard; the cruel snares with the deadly loop of wire that caught a neck or a leg in it so easily kept sliding into her mind. When an animal became caught in the woven strands of the steel wire, the frenzied struggle to escape only sank the noose deeper into its flesh.

She could not bear such thoughts. Whenever they crowded in on her, Jenny went to Maggie's side, pretending to be busy bringing coffee or hot tea or whatever was being served. Or she stood silently next to Manguana in the kitchen, washing dishes, cups, and pans, gaining strength from doing the mundane things.

Nobody cried, not even the children. Death was nothing new to them; they had all seen animals gravely hurt and suffering, caught in the pliable yet unstretchable and unbreakable snares. Unlike a hunter with a gun or a spear, the deadly snare did not distinguish between young or old—or even between species. They could kill a child as easily as they killed animals.

The search went on; sometime before dawn, Jennifer saw the big searchlights mounted on trucks that had been brought all the way from Nairobi. They flashed like comets in the dark jungle beyond Maggie's house.

"You'd better get off your feet awhile," Heller told Jenny some time before morning. "You don't want to pass out on us, you know."

"I'm fine," Jenny told her.

"You aren't fine. Look, I'm a nurse, remember? Now come and sit down and have a cup of tea. We're just spinning our wheels in here anyway, waiting. We've got enough food ready to feed all of Africa, I'd say. Come on, Jenny, there's a nice, obedient girl."

They sat in the kitchen at Manguana's big table, which groaned with food she'd cooked all night. Outside there was the sound of an occasional vehicle starting up, but other than that, silence. Maggie had gone upstairs to sleep for a few hours.

"What will happen to Damien if they find Judy dead, Heller? Will he be able to survive, do you think?"

Heller had put the tea kettle on. Now she sat across from Jenny at the end of the table, her face calm. There was a certain serenity about Heller that was enchanting; one felt that throughout any kind of crisis, she would remain the same, calm, capable and good-natured. No wonder her husband seemed so much in love with her!

"I don't ever predict what will happen to people under terrible pressure because there's always the human spirit to deal with," Heller said, "and that's an unknown quantity. Sometimes what we think we hate we will eventually come to love—or at least respect." She began buttering some of Manguana's bread for them both. "I came here because Paul and Damien had a dream," she said quietly. "I hated it here. I refused to give my husband a child here. I grew orchids and babied them instead. I refused to get involved in the running feud between your aunt and people like her, and Damien with his ideas about survival of the fittest. Then, I suppose I began to change, from inside out. It's hard to live here and stand back and refuse to get involved."

"Do you mean you're actually happy here?"

"I suppose I am, in a strange way. I know that poaching is deadly and wrong, but I'm not so sure that locking animals up, so to speak, the way Maggie and all of you do, is the right answer. Paul thinks the future of Africa lies in game ranching, Jenny. Animals are controlled by slaughtering them to sell, just as farmers do cattle. Or farmers let people come onto their property to take pictures or to hunt game, for a price. That way, the people eat, the forests don't get chewed away because of animal overpopulation, and the animals survive as a species. It's very likely the only way out of what's been happening here."

"Then, teaching the children about farming, getting them acquainted with this kind of life style—"

"Exactly. If it works, it would do away with poaching forever."

Jenny looked out the window to the breaking dawn. *God, let Damien's child be safe this day! Bring her back to us—her father needs her so!*

She thought there had been a breakthrough when she heard the truck roar up. It was nearly seven; the day was going to be moist and hot. Already some of the men had taken time out to sleep; they lay about the grass in front, catching perhaps thirty minutes of sleep before going back out into the bush to search.

It was Damien's truck; he jumped out and hurried quickly up the porch steps, striding toward the kitchen where Heller and Jenny and Manguana were preparing breakfast for the children.

She saw at once that he looked terrible, like a man in a nightmare. His voice was low and controlled, but his eyes held agony. He needed a shave and he looked exhausted.

"Anything?"

"Nothing yet," Heller said stoutly. "Come and eat, Damien. Now that it's light, it will be much easier to find her."

"Is everybody out now?"

"Most of them," Heller said, pouring coffee for him. "How's the baby?"

"Pneumonia. He'll be all right; I left medicine. Where's Paul?"

"Out on one of the trucks, I think." Heller glanced at Jenny. "I'm going to check and see if he needs a lunch sent out there for everybody. Excuse me."

So Jenny found herself alone with him. She put the dish of coarsely ground sugar in front of his cup and then busied herself with the frying eggs.

"Jennifer?"

She did not turn around. There was a certain depth, a quality to his voice that she had not heard before.

"Yes, Damien?"

"I'm going to go back into medicine. When we find my daughter, one way or the other, I'm going to talk to Paul about it." She turned to look at him; he shook his head like a wounded fighter. "I've been dead ever since I lost my son. If I'd reacted differently, with the attitudes that these people have about death, my daughter wouldn't be out there now. She wouldn't have felt that nobody wanted her." His eyes closed. He was, Jenny saw, weeping, weeping silently, trying not to, unable not to. "I didn't hold her; I didn't tell her I cared for her, that I had missed her every moment of every day, because I was afraid to keep her here, afraid for her to stay here. If only I'd held her in my arms and told her how much I love her—"

His head dropped to his folded arms. The wide shoulders suddenly shuddered, although he made no sound. Jennifer watched him for a few heartbeats, then she went to his side, kneeling next to him, reaching out with her arms to hold him.

She held him as she would a child, with her arms tight around him. His face was buried in her soft hair; he made no sound as he wept, but she felt the wetness from his weeping moisten her hair. Her gentle hands touched his face as she murmured to him, trying to give him hope, telling him it wasn't finished, wasn't over, that a new day had dawned and surely, surely this day they would find Judy—

Suddenly, he moved in her arms and looked at her. His blue eyes were bloodshot from worry and fatigue; there were tears swimming in them.

"I love you," he said, very quietly, not moving. "I want you to know that."

She put her cool cheek against his. And from that moment on, from the essence of herself, from the depths of her spirit, she dedicated herself to making this man happy, to being a comfort and a friend to him, to loving him now and forever, no matter what.

That was the way Maggie found them when she burst into the room, wearing her long white nightgown, her feet bare, a look of excitement in her eyes.

"Something has happened! From upstairs, from my window, I saw two of the jeeps coming down the road, coming fast! Surely they wouldn't drive that way unless—"

Damien jumped up. "Get the food off this table immediately. Spread newspapers on it and get everybody out of the kitchen and keep them out!"

But there was, Jenny saw moments later, no need for any of that.

The jeep pulled up in front, after having stopped to pick up Damien, who had run down the road to meet it, his medical bag in one hand. The women waited on the porch; Jennifer's hand reached for her aunt's and she held on very tightly.

Damien was in the back with his child on his lap; he had his arms around her. Jenny held her breath, hoping against hope, as he got out, carrying little Judy in his arms. There was a hush; not a person made a sound as he proceeded toward the porch.

"Stand by to assist me treat some mild scratches, Heller," Damien said, and then a sudden roar went up from the crowd gathered around and Jennifer saw that the child moved in her father's arms. Judy's face was pressed against his chest.

Fifteen minutes later, Damien came around the back of the house, to where Jennifer stood on the porch.

"I want to thank you," he said quietly. "You saved Judy's life. If she hadn't heard you talking to the kids about the snares, she never would have stayed put, waiting for us to find her, instead of wandering around looking for us."

"We all prayed for her," Jenny said. And then, because she knew that was what he wanted, she went into his arms. They stood very still, close. Finally, he gently raised her face with one hand, so that she was looking into his eyes.

"My daughter and I need you, Jenny."

She smiled, wise as all loved women are wise.

"I know that," she said. And she raised her face for his kiss.

The
Marriage Contract

The
Marriage Contract

by VIRGINIA NIELSEN

To Mac,
my husband, critic and friend.

With the exception of the few historical per-
sonages mentioned in setting the stage for my
story, all my characters and the events in which
they are involved are fictitious.

The Author

ONE

HAD it not been marred by an unfortunate intrusion, the entertainment Monsieur and Madame de l'Ouvrier gave at their plantation, Les Chênes, to honor their guest, young Armand, *le comte de Valérun,* would undoubtedly have been called incomparable by that little band of émigrés who had succeeded in transplanting a small remnant of Versailles to this remote bayou wilderness of Louisiana. Instead, as Madame de l'Ouvrier told herself in angry humiliation, it was destined to become one of the most memorable.

Her friends, alas, were amused, and her enemies delighted. Her usually mild and somewhat vague husband was in a temper, the elder of her two daughters, Claudine, for whose benefit the elaborate affair had been staged, seemed to be in a daze. What *monsieur le comte* thought, no one knew.

Fuming, Madame de l'Ouvrier did not even wonder what her younger daughter thought. Amalie, after all, was not yet of marriageable age. But Amalie, dark eyes sparkling, was wickedly enjoying herself.

Maman had really outdone herself for Count de Valérun's visit. Anchored out in the bayou was a flatboat, transformed into a veritable fairyland by a profusion of flowers and colored paper lanterns whose glowing lights were reflected in the still dark water. Aboard it, musicians played, and a pair of jugglers alternated with dancers in providing diversions. On the grassy slope between the galleried house and the bayou—beneath more colored lanterns—Maman's guests sat or strolled, resplendent in the court dress most of them had managed to bring out of France when they fled the revolution the year Amalie was born.

In the warm, starry night, fragrant with the scent of orange blossoms, the mended rips in a lace cuff or the shiny elbows of velvet worn napless were easily overlooked. Bewigged or powdered, the guests gossiped wittily as they dipped snuff and sipped the wine that liveried slaves passed among them, enjoying the illusion of their magnificence.

Amalie had seen the smaller boat immediately, although the bend around which it appeared was partially concealed by the moss hanging almost to the ground from a large old oak. It carried a single lantern and obviously was heavy laden. In it were a white man and his slave, the biggest black man Amalie had ever seen.

Their surprise at seeing the spectacle of Maman's entertainment was comical. Their oars stilled in midstroke, their mouths fell open and they stared. The exclamation of the young boatman—for he was young and clean shaven, though rudely dressed—carried clearly over the water, attracting the attention of Maman's guests.

Amalie could hear their murmurs: *"—yanqui—coureur de bois—"* Increasing numbers of the Yankee trappers were finding their way through the tortuous bayous of Louisiana since Napoleon had sold them to the United States—to the outrage of Papa and his émigré friends.

The murmurs increased when it became obvious that the *yanqui* was heading his boat into the landing. The hospitality of the planters along this remote bayou was famed, but—after all! Perhaps, Amalie thought, the young trapper realized too late that in order to approach the landing he would have to pass between the flower-decked stage and its audience on the bank.

As he stood up, ready to cast his rope, Maman gasped, *"Mon Dieu!"* He wore a loose shirt which fell open to his waist, revealing a well-muscled, sun-browned torso. What his trousers revealed, as he came nearer, was that he must have waded in muck—probably making a portage from bayou to bayou in the swamp.

He threw his rope and left his slave to make it fast to the half-submerged pole alongside the landing. Someone tittered as he leaped ashore and started toward them.

"Arrête!" Never had her indulgent Papa sounded so angry!

The *yanqui* stopped, and said something incomprehensible.

"Speak French!" Papa commanded. There was outrage even in the cut of his coat, flying out above his white satin legs as he strode stiffly forward. "I do not speak your barbaric tongue!"

The young man flung back his head. He was not apologizing—with his feet spread and his hands on his hips, he looked too defiant!—but saying something in barely understandable French about Papa's hospitality.

Monsieur de l'Ouvrier interrupted, "State your business, m'sieu, or I will loose my dogs."

Amalie heard Clotie cry, faintly, "Papa!" She turned to look at her sister. Soft-hearted Clotie was gazing at the young trapper in wide-eyed distress. But Amalie was beginning to understand that poor Papa was defending his injured pride before his guests.

The situation was deliciously absurd. The Yankee had to ask his slave to translate for him, and that brought more titters. He was requesting food and drink before he continued his journey. Perhaps if Maman had not been so distressed, Papa would have sent the two strangers to the kitchen.

But Maman, all too aware of her guests' malicious amusement, moaned, "Oh, I shall never live this down."

And so Papa gave a reckless order.

From around the house the big dogs came, barking wildly. Women screamed, and their escorts helped them climb up on their chairs. But the dogs unerringly recognized the intruder. The young *yanqui* gave them one incredulous look, then with an exclamation turned and leaped for his boat.

"*Vite,* 'Ti-Bo!" he shouted, and his black slave pushed off just in time to save his young master's pantaloons from the bitch who led the pack.

Amalie laughed aloud.

She looked at Clotie, but Clotie was still gazing after the unfortunate trapper in sympathy and distress. "Didn't you hear, Amalie?" she murmured. "He was trying to say they had been lost in the *prairie tremblante.*" And, indeed, he and his servant did look as if they had been mired in those swamps the Acadian settlers had named the "trembling prairies."

It was unfortunate for him that he arrived in the middle of Maman's entertainment—but so comical! Unexpectedly, Amalie's eyes met those of Papa's handsome guest. The count, standing beside Maman's chair, was looking down at the two girls, and his face, so formidably aristocratic, was alight with amusement, making him all at once much more handsome. It was a moment of shared laughter, unplanned and delightful, that Clotie had missed, and it left Amalie catching her breath.

She was awake and remembering that delicious moment when her *femme de chambre* came into her room the next morning, bringing her *café au lait*. Amalie sat up, hugging herself.

"Julie, do you think the count will offer for Clotie?"

Her chambermaid shrugged. She had come with the de l'Ouvrier family from Saint Domingue as Amalie's nurse when Amalie was a toddler. "That is why he was invited, *n'est-ce pas?*"

"Yes," Amalie said impatiently. "But will he?"

"Who knows, m'selle?"

Amalie sipped the hot milk drink. "I should like to marry a count, but Maman says there are few left since the revolution. I am afraid there will be none left when I am ready to marry."

"Oho!" said Julie.

"Is Maman up?"

"You' maman has a headache."

"I don't wonder. And Clotie?"

"M'selle Clotie will most likely take breakfast in her room."

"I shall get up," Amalie decided.

While Julie went for water, Amalie pulled her nightgown over her head and, pinning up her hair, looked down at her body with dissatisfaction. It was still slim as a boy's, and her small breasts were not yet as full as Clotie's who was, after all, only a year older. Amalie sighed and stepped into the chair-shaped tub, washing herself while Julie poured water over her from a pitcher.

Already the day was warm enough so that the tepid water was pleasantly cooling. Outside the shuttered windows, the cicadas were noisy in the trees. The voices of the servants in the detached kitchen behind the house rose and fell musically, mingling with the songs of mockingbirds and cardinals.

Julie dried her with a soft towel, then leisurely dressed her in one of her simple white gowns. Amalie opened her shutters and walked out on the wide encircling galérie where the de l'Ouvriers spent most of their day. To her intense pleasure, she found the count there, alone at a small table, sipping his morning coffee and gazing out across the grassy scythed slope to the landing where the flatboat, its flowers withered and drooping, was still tied up.

"It is not so pretty this morning, *non,* m'sieu?"

"Ah, *bonjour,* Ma'm'selle Amalie." He stood, tall and slender, and raised her extended hand to his lips quite as if she were his hostess. His nose was long and straight and his eyes below the finely shaped brows regarded her with smiling interest. "Are we the only early risers?"

"Yes, and it is a pity. The morning is the best time in the bayous, m'sieu."

"The morning is the best time anywhere in the world, ma'm'selle."

"Ah, I would not know! I have been no place but to the convent in New Orleans, and that only for one year to learn my catechism. How I would like to travel as you have traveled, m'sieu!"

"Where would you go, ma'm'selle?"

"Everywhere!"

"You are not as retiring as Ma'm'selle Claudine, are you?" said the count looking amused.

"Papa says I am the lively one," Amalie confessed. "But then, I am Papa's favorite."

"Truly? And is Ma'm'selle Claudine your maman's favorite, then?"

She observed that he seemed eager to discuss Claudine. "I think Pierre was Maman's favorite. Pierre died on the ship that took us from France to Saint Domingue, so I don't remember him. Perhaps he was Papa's favorite, also. But since his death Papa has spoiled me outrageously. So Maman says."

"And is it true?" He was openly laughing at her now.

"I do not know—but he can refuse me nothing." What a handsome brother-in-law she would have if Clotie married him!

"Do you know what I think, ma'm'selle? I think you will someday break some hearts."

"Someday, m'sieu?" Daringly, she asked, "When is that?"

"Perhaps when you are as old as your sister."

"Oh, but there is not that much difference between us. Because, you see, in some ways Clotie is such a goose. Papa says—"

At that moment Monsieur de l'Ouvrier appeared at the far end of the galérie.

"Yes?" The count teased her, under his breath. "Papa says—?"

But Amalie was suddenly appalled at herself. Clotie would not thank her for chattering like a magpie! "Good morning, Papa!" she called.

"Good morning, my dear. Good morning, m'sieu. Has my daughter been boring you?"

"On the contrary, m'sieu."

Monsieur de l'Ouvrier's manservant was following him with his coffee, which he placed before him when Papa seated himself opposite his guest. "My servants are stocking the boat now. We can leave when we have finished our *cafés,* m'sieu."

"Are you allowing Papa to take you on a specimen-hunting expedition?" Amalie inquired. "I warn you, m'sieu, that you will come back sunburned and mosquito-bitten, and you still will not have found where the rare hair-plant grows."

"There is no need to frighten the count. I am merely taking him on a tour of the plantation."

"—with a small detour or two to see if you can find a new plant for your collection? Botany is Papa's passion, m'sieu."

"She is right," Monsieur de l'Ouvrier admitted, "and I flatter myself that what I am doing will someday be of great value to France."

"I have no doubt of it," the count said courteously.

Amalie leaned against the galérie rail, listening as Papa expounded on his hobby, and thinking what beautiful manners the count had. While she listened, she watched a procession of slaves carry provisions for a sumptuous picnic lunch toward the boat dock, where they stripped the flatboat of its withered décor and set comfortable chairs under its awning. So Papa planned to keep Monsieur out all day. What a pity!

She stayed on the galérie until the two men descended the stair and sauntered toward the loaded boat, then went inside and along the wide central hall to Clotie's room. She found her sister awake and looking ravishing, sitting up on her bed with her *café au lait* and roll.

"Papa has taken the count out with him," Amalie told her, sighing, "so we shall not see him again until this evening. Clotie, is he not handsome? Are you not transported at the prospect of marrying him?"

"He has not offered for me yet."

"But it is very possible that he will. He cannot speak without mentioning your name," she said, with slight exaggeration. "Clotie, are you not wriggling with excitement?"

"I should like to be a countess, certainly," Clotie said, dreamily chewing on her roll.

"Is that all you can say?"

Clotie had a look of being far away which Amalie found not only baffling under the circumstances, but annoying. "Promise you will not tell, Amalie? I dreamed of the *yanqui coureur de bois* last night.

In my dream I was crying, because the dogs attacked him and he was all bloodied."

"How awful, Clotie!"

"It was dreadful, Amalie," her sister said, her eyes filling with distress. "It was cruel of Papa, don't you think? And he was so handsome, standing there with his head high! So brave—"

"—until he turned and ran! Oh, Clotie, you are such a goose!" Amalie cried, in exasperation.

Madame de l'Ouvrier lay in her shuttered room with a wet cloth over her eyes and tried not to think about what would happen to them if the count did not offer for Clotie.

She could not prevent her thoughts from going step by step over the events that had brought them to these severe straits. At times like this, when some frustration provoked the headache which utterly incapacitated her, it seemed to her that what she had lived through in the fifteen years since the revolution was more than a woman should have to bear.

The terror of that flight to the coast from their pleasant estates north of Paris, with three small children and a single nurse—the only servant to be trusted!—who had deserted her rather than take ship to a land she had never seen. That dreadful sea voyage to the West Indies—but her mind shied from that, even now unable to face the crippling pain when their oldest, their only son, sickened and died and was sewn into a canvas bag and consigned to the sea in a ceremony she could not bear to witness.

Instead, her thoughts made a leap to the disquieting days in Saint Domingue on the plantation of Monsieur de l'Ouvrier's cousin where her husband had first fallen under the enchantment of the novel tropical plants. Exhaustedly now, she wondered at the gaiety of those elaborately planned entertainments with which they filled their hours, continually assuring each other that they thought of their exile as a pleasant holiday in the country. From the distance of time she wondered if there were not a certain feverishness in that early gaiety, a macabre sort of self-congratulation as heads rolled from the guillotine across the water. Or did it seem so to her only because her emotions had been paralyzed by her grief?

And then, those long, indolent, sociable evenings, so pleasant on the surface and secretly so charged with fear of the threatened slave uprising! Until she had insisted, forcibly insisted, that they remove to

Louisiana—where they had learned, after some months, that Monsieur de l'Ouvrier's cousin and his entire family had indeed been murdered by their slaves, just as she had feared.

It was at her insistence, also, that they left the pleasant social life of New Orleans to acquire land on this remote but lovely bayou with its wide, grassy banks of rich soil and, with their dwindling capital, most of it proceeds from the jewels they had smuggled out of France, purchased the slaves who could plant it with indigo. Alas, her husband was not in the least interested in becoming a planter. He had been born a gentleman and he would die a gentleman, without ever soiling his hands except in the service of his beloved botany—nor soiling his mind in the pursuit of profit!

Count Armand was a gentleman, also, but he was shrewd. Young enough to adjust to the loss of his ancestral estates in France and shrewd enough to be practical about the necessities of his situation. Moreover, he was not without funds. His family had invested in the West Indian colonies long before the revolution and some of their investment had been salvaged before the bloody uprising.

Oh, if only it were possible to place the management of Les Chênes in the hands of a shrewd young man who, as their son-in-law, would have their interests at heart! Perhaps, Madame de l'Ouvrier thought, she would be able then to tolerate her husband's preoccupation with the plants of the new world, and his obsession with plots against Napoleon. (She strongly suspected that he had been sending their precious capital to Europe in the hope of furthering the restoration of the monarchy!) As for herself, Madame de l'Ouvrier had long ago dried her tears over the fate of her poor beheaded queen, and given up all hope of ever recovering their French estates.

She moaned, and signaled her *femme de chambre* to replace the wet cloth on her brow. It was absolutely necessary that she be able to preside at her dinner table tonight, for in the morning the young count would leave to pay his other local visits.

Wherever he went, she knew he would be entertained with witticisms at her expense, thanks to that impudent *yanqui* intruder. And in nearly every émigré household he would visit, there was at least one daughter of marriageable age who was her family's only hope of escaping poverty, now that the fields of indigo were blighted with disease.

In her mind Madame de l'Ouvrier ran over the list of eligible girls.

From here the count was to go to Monsieur and Madame Costeau for an indefinite visit. With her hand over her eyes—the light was so painful this morning!—Madame de l'Ouvrier compared their Délie with her Claudine. Délie, almost seventeen, was not as pretty as Claudine, who was very nearly beautiful. The Costeau girl was short and her figure inclined to stockiness, but she was more animated than Claudine, with quite engaging ways.

Claudine was sweet and pliable, excellent qualities which could very well seem dull to a worldly young man who was accustomed to dividing his time between New Orleans and the capitals of Europe. (Madame suspected that Count Armand acted as courier for the royalists with whom her husband plotted.)

On the other hand, the young count had seemed quite enchanted with Claudine. And was not her pliant nature the very quality a man should value most in his wife? She must take an opportunity to call that to Armand's attention. And somehow she must manage some new gowns for Claudine, for they would be receiving invitations to the entertainments her neighbors would plan for the count.

Without opening her eyes, Madame de l'Ouvrier lifted a hand to summon her chambermaid. "Have the cook come to me, Hortense. I must speak to her about the dinner. It must be perfect."

"*Oui,* madame." Hortense, experienced in Madame de l'Ouvrier's sufferings, tiptoed from the room.

Madame de l'Ouvrier sighed. For all her scheming, she knew quite well that it would be the very shrewdness she admired in the count and not necessarily Claudine's beauty which would dictate his choice. But there she was at no disadvantage. The de l'Ouvrier name was as old and honorable in Bourbon France as his own, and could furnish records showing the three legitimate generations required by the best Creole families when making a marriage contract. And the dowry could scarcely be matched by any of her neighbors who also had a son to inherit, for Monsieur de l'Ouvrier was offering Les Chênes itself—with the proviso, of course, that they could continue in residence.

If only her husband had the good sense not to bore his young guest with his interminable discourses on the botany of the new world!

Fortunately, Monsieur brought his guest home before the heat of the day reached its zenith, and the two men spent the somnolent hours before dinner in pleasant relaxation on the galérie. By that time, Madame de l'Ouvrier had recovered from her headache with the merciful aid of a small glass of brandy, the cook was preparing an admirable dinner with no mishap, so far, and her two daughters appeared, looking fresh and sweet in their pale, short dresses.

They remained on the galérie, in easy converse, until the night began to glow with fireflies and buzz with mosquitoes. Then Madame de l'Ouvrier took the arm of the young count and led them into the dining room. As she glanced around her table, its crystal sparkling in the candlelight, she thought that Claudine looked unusually lovely. Her expression was dreamy, her eyes luminous; she looked, in truth, like a girl in love. The young count caught her eye and smiled at her, and a faint blush appeared on her cheeks. Ah, he must be moved by that gentle beauty!

Monsieur de l'Ouvrier, all unaware—or at least insensitive!— insisted on telling her what they had discussed during their tour of the plantation. Not, alas, a marriage contract, but the coronation of Napoleon as emperor of France.

"They are saying that his court is as royal as any Bourbon's ever was. Can you believe it, my dear?"

"Incredible!"

"It is quite true, madame," said Armand. "All Paris—indeed, all Europe—is talking about it, and not all with disapproval. Indeed, fashionable Parisian women are already following the style of dress set by his empress."

The servants began removing the soup course, and another of succulent oysters was brought in.

"The audacity of it!" Monsieur de l'Ouvrier was growing red in the face just thinking about it. "That a little Corsican upstart should proclaim himself *emperor!*"

"With, they say, the right of succession," said Count Armand. "It is said he hopes to put an end to the attempts on his life by producing an heir who will succeed him."

Madame de l'Ouvrier's heavy eyebrows shot up at this hint of what the royalists whom her husband and the count supported had been up to in France.

"Attempts on his life?" Amalie repeated, alert as a bird, but Claudine only gazed dreamily at a lone fly buzzing in the crystal flytrap before her on the damask.

Madame de l'Ouvrier sent a daggerish look down the table which both Amalie and her husband ignored. Count Armand, seeing it, said only, "There have been—plots, all unsuccessful," and added, "The incredible thing is that the Pope traveled to Paris to bless his coronation and to remarry him and his West Indian consort."

"*Mais, non!*" Madame de l'Ouvrier laid down her fork. It was one thing to become resigned to the terrible fate of the royal family under which she had grown up, but quite another if the Pope approved of this usurper of the French throne! This was a thing that disturbed her deepest religious feelings.

"Impertinent upstart!" growled her husband.

"It is true, madame," Armand told her. "It is said the Pope hopes to regain some influence in atheistic France."

"But is Napoleon a Catholic, then? I understood he was an atheist."

The count laughed. "He is said to have been a Moslem while he was in Egypt! Obviously, he wants the Pope's sanction of the hereditary monarchy he hopes to establish."

"He has not a drop of royal blood in his veins," Monsieur de l'Ouvrier fumed.

"His genealogists will find one, I am sure."

"It is intolerable! Intolerable!"

"Why is it intolerable, Papa?" Amalie inquired. "What has Napoleon to do with us?"

"Amalie!" Madame de l'Ouvrier reproved her.

"You would not ask that, ma'm'selle," Armand said, smiling at her over his wineglass, "if you could see your father's estates north of Paris, as I did recently. Unfortunately, I was able to ascertain for him that they were long ago sold by the government to an official for a fraction of their worth. My own family property is still unoccupied, and I have hopes of one day recovering it."

Madame de l'Ouvrier noticed with satisfaction that although he answered Amalie, his eyes had strayed to Claudine when he spoke of his estates. Her older daughter looked remote, as if her thoughts were far away. If it was a deliberate strategy, it was effective; she looked like an English painting.

"From Napoleon?" Amalie asked. "You are on good terms with him, m'sieu?"

Ah, that one! Madame de l'Ouvrier thought, sending another dagger glance. "That is quite enough, Amalie!" She turned to the count and began a familiar complaint. "Her father has spoiled her, m'sieu. In France he could scarcely find his way to the nursery, but in those years in Saint Domingue he had nothing to do but make a plaything of his infant daughter. Would you believe, m'sieu, that I could not even send her to the Ursuline nuns in New Orleans to be educated, because he would not be parted from her? She and Claudine both have had only the one year of catechism, because I insisted that if Claudine be sent, Amalie must go, as well."

"Peace, madame!" said her husband, helping himself to a fat quail from the platter a servant offered him. "What need have my daughters of the nuns to teach them manners when their mother was herself at court?"

"Of course," Armand murmured, diplomatically.

But Madame de l'Ouvrier gave a little laugh and exclaimed, "You see how he dwells in the past, m'sieu! Me, I have forgotten those faraway days. I think of the future, and what will happen when our crop of indigo fails completely. In Saint Domingue, I became interested in the sugar cane, which seemed a most profitable crop, and I have heard that some planters are doing well with it in Louisiana. What do you think of it, m'sieu?"

"My wife has the soul of a bourgeois, m'sieu," her husband apologized, his tone indulgent.

"You may be right," Madame de l'Ouvrier said, her voice rising a note, "for I can no longer pretend that we are on a pleasant holiday in the colonies, and that soon money will arrive from France."

"Ah, we must not lose our gaiety, my dear. Our dear king, Louis XVIII, has given us his promise that when he is restored to his throne, all our lands and feudal rights will be returned to us."

"I no longer think of that. Instead, I find myself thinking that a little bourgeois thrift may be what Les Chênes needs. Is it that I am becoming a Louisianian, m'sieu?" she asked, turning to the count with an apologetic smile. "Or is it merely that I am growing old?"

"Perhaps, madame, you are growing wise. I am very interested in cane myself. It is making a great deal of money for a few planters, I understand, even though the quality of Louisiana sugar leaves much to be desired."

"You see, Charles? Count Armand does not think a planter's concerns beneath him."

"In your scientific studies of plants, Monsieur de l'Ouvrier, has it not occurred to you to experiment with the different varieties of cane in order to find one that does well in Louisiana?"

"Indeed, no," Monsieur de l'Ouvrier said, lifting his wineglass and looking into it with a faintly superior smile. "My interest is in pure science, m'sieu, my ambition only to collect and classify the native plants of the region."

"A pity, isn't it," Madame de l'Ouvrier asked, shrugging, "when our land is so rich?"

The young count looked thoughtful. It was time to leave the gentlemen to their brandies. And, she hoped, to a more fruitful conversation.

"Claudine, Amalie, bid our guest a good night and a good journey, for he leaves us in the early morning." They rose, the count with them, and he touched the hand of each in turn with his lips. Did he linger over Claudine's, or was it only Madame de l'Ouvrier's wish to see that he did?

In her bed, Madame lay awake, listening for her husband's step. The two men sat late over their brandies in amiable conversation, judging from the sounds of deep laughter that now and then reached her ears. Indeed, the discussion seemed more amiable than serious. She could not contain her curiosity, and when she heard her husband moving about in his room, addressing his manservant in a mumble, she slipped out of her bed, drew on a robe and went through the connecting door.

Monsieur de l'Ouvrier sat on a chair in his shirtsleeves with his servant on his knees before him, removing his boots.

"Did he offer, Charles?"

"He has promised to return to us on his way back to New Orleans in late summer."

"But he did not offer?"

"No."

"And you, Charles? Did you propose the marriage?"

"There is plenty of time," her husband said, mildly.

"*Mon Dieu!*" she cried, throwing up her hands in angry despair, and went back to her own bed.

"It is essential," Madame de l'Ouvrier told her husband the following morning, "that Claudine have a new gown. And I have not another court dress left that can be cut down for her."

"Why is it essential, my dear?"

"Because all our friends will be entertaining the count this summer. We will be receiving invitations and Claudine must go, of course."

"But Claudine looks very pretty, whatever she wears," her husband said. "And will not all her friends be wearing cut-over dresses?"

"That is not the point. She is competing not only with her friends but with all the beautiful women the count has known in New Orleans. Yes, and in Europe."

"Um—ah—*oui*." Monsieur de l'Ouvrier took out his snuffbox, but paused in the act of opening it, gazing vaguely out of the window of his wife's room and across the galérie to the woods. "We met that peasant fellow on our expedition yesterday," he remarked. "You know, the one who lives in the hut down the bayou and traps animals for his living?"

"Do not change the subject, Charles."

"I am not changing the subject, my dear. I was about to tell you that he has a houseguest who may be able to help you solve your problem."

"In what way, pray?"

"It seems that Broussard took in that *yanqui* trader I set the dogs on. You remember that, my dear?"

"How could I forget it?"

"I am afraid that I was quite beside myself."

"*Alors?*" she said, impatient.

"*Eh, bien,* it appears that the *yanqui* is not a trapper, but a peddler. I am told he has some silks."

"Silks!" Madame breathed. "Is he a Baratarian, then?" It was a long and uncomfortable journey to New Orleans, and she seldom had an opportunity to shop—which was just as well, considering their limited funds. But occasionally, smuggled goods were brought up through the maze of bayous from Barataria.

"The trapper says not, but I do not believe him," her husband told her.

Madame's eyes glistened. "I must see his silks."

"I believe Broussard will be expecting you. As you know, the flatboat will be away all day delivering the count to the Costeaus. Shall I have it fitted up for you and the girls tomorrow morning?"

"*Oui, merci* . . . Charles? If I choose some silks, how shall I pay for them?"

Monsieur de l'Ouvrier flicked some snuff and waved the box in a vague gesture. "We shall think about that when he presents his bill, *non?*"

But after he had left her room, Madame, being not at all certain that an itinerant peddler would be agreeable to "presenting a bill," rummaged in her jewel box until she found a sapphire ring that had been the gift of a once-ardent admirer.

The next morning while the day was still comparatively cool she set forth with Claudine and Amalie on the canopied flatboat, with a footman to carry her réticule and her parasol, and two slaves to man the oars. The black water of the bayou, before the oars were dipped into it, was smooth as a dark mirror. From the graceful oaks along its bank, the delicate gray strings of moss hung motionless in the still air.

Claudine dreamily watched the huge dragonflies of metallic blue or rust that darted across their path, but Amalie, after a few restless minutes, slid from her chair and stooped to trail her fingers in the water, amused by her distorted image.

A fish jumped, breaking the surface, and what had appeared to be a submerged log began eerily to move. Madame de l'Ouvrier warned sharply, "Amalie!" and Amalie withdrew her hand from the water. One of the oarsmen began to sing in a low, minor key as the alligator swam silently out of their path.

The weathered cypress house was scarcely three miles from Les Chênes. It was built in a style much favored by the early 'Cadian settlers along the bayou, a simple dwelling on a platform which elevated it some four feet above the ground, with a high roof that sloped sharply down to shelter a narrow front galérie. A crude curtain hung limply in the unglazed window.

At one side of the house and slightly behind it were some bizarre objects which, on closer inspection, proved to be the skins of those fat, furry water rats which inhabited the swamps, turned inside out over a piece of planking to be stretched while drying. A cloud of flies hung in the air above them.

It was a strange place to be buying silks, Madame de l'Ouvrier observed as she directed her slaves to tie up at the pole and plank which was the only landing provided.

The trapper, Monsieur Broussard, appeared on the galérie, his thin, swarthy face slashed by a humorous grin. "*Bonjour,* Madame de l'Ouvrier," he called, neither bowing nor approaching them, but waiting on his galérie as their footman helped them ashore and they walked up the path from the bayou.

"Welcome to my poor house," he said then, his shrewd eyes twinkling. "You and the *jeune filles* have come to see the silks?"

He reminded Madame de l'Ouvrier of the fiercely thrifty, fiercely independent peasants of her own province, from which his ancestors might well have migrated to Acadia. *"Oui,* m'sieu," she replied. "M'sieu de l'Ouvrier said that you suggested it."

"Mais, oui, they are beautiful, beautiful!" He indicated the three chairs that had been placed in a semicircle around a small wooden table, then excused himself. When he returned, the *yanqui* was with him and each of them carried several large rolls of silk. The *yanqui*'s huge black servant followed with several more. The young peddler threw his silks down on the table with a hint of defiance and stood before them, his intensely blue eyes challenging.

"My friend, M'sieu Den-eez Ma-kah-nair'," Jacques Broussard said, grinning. "He is *américain,* but he comes here from New Orleans, bringing silks from France."

Amalie was looking at him with wonder. She had never seen such blue eyes, and the silky brown hair pulled back from his face and tied simply with a ribbon was also a rarity in this émigré community. In spite of his simple dress—a loose white shirt above close-fitting pantaloons—he was a striking-looking young man. He was looking at Clotie, and Amalie glanced at her sister. Clotie's cheeks were slightly flushed and her eyes were wide and luminous. She looked extraordinarily beautiful.

Still gazing at Clotie, the *yanqui* uncovered several rolls. Each was wrapped in plain muslin and as the rich colors tumbled out upon the table, Madame de l'Ouvrier and her daughters gasped.

Monsieur Broussard was not only translating the American's answers to Madame de l'Ouvrier's questions, but giving her a running commentary of his own. "He is the second son of a gentleman, madame."

"Indeed?" she said skeptically.

"Truly, madame! He is come from Philadelphia to make his fortune, and through connections in New Orleans was able to purchase these magnificent materials with which to start his trade."

"Which is?" Madame de l'Ouvrier studied the array of colors spilled between them—diaphanous white and ivory, the pale blush of pink and rose, deep reds and bronzes and burnished greens.

"The importing of luxuries from France and England for ladies like yourself."

"Ladies like myself have little to spend on luxuries any more," Madame de l'Ouvrier said, with real regret. "Pray ask him what he wants for a dress length."

The *yanqui* spoke politely, his eyes still on Clotie, and the 'Cadian said, with a chuckle, "He thinks the sea blue would grace your older daughter, madame, and wishes to make you a present of it."

Shocked, Madame de l'Ouvrier said, "His offer is impertinent! My daughter does not accept gifts from strangers."

"It was not so intended. He hopes, madame, that you will recommend his silks to your friends."

"Tell the peddler that I am not in trade." She was genuinely annoyed. The young rascal had made it impossible for her to take his silks and ask him to present a bill. And now she saw the way his eyes softened when he looked at Claudine, and decided to cut this transaction short.

She reached for her réticule and took from it the sapphire ring she had brought with her. "I wish two dress lengths for each of my daughters, M'sieu Broussard," she said, crisply. "Ask the *yanqui* if he will accept this sapphire set in gold."

Apparently Monsieur Broussard did not have to translate her request, for the *yanqui* smiled slightly and nodded.

"I want a white for each—and I think the pale pink for you, Amalie. Clotie, which color do you prefer?"

"The blue, Maman." Clotie indicated it, with a blush, and the young peddler flashed a smile at her.

Annoyed that she had asked her, Madame de l'Ouvrier nevertheless ordered a length of the blue. The peddler took her ring, examined it with amused satisfaction and tucked it carefully into a small pocket at his waist.

The footman carried their purchases to the boat and helped them to their chairs under the canopy. From the little galérie the two men watched as the flatboat was pushed off and rowed up the almost currentless bayou. The sun was high now, and the heat was a heaviness almost visible in the air. A buzzard wheeled lazily above the trees on the opposite bank.

"The old rooster has a pair of pretty pullets, *non?*" Jacques Broussard said, in broken English.

"Aye," said Dennis MacInerney, "and I'd like to get into that henhouse."

"Oho! He'd do more than set his dogs on you, that one!"

But the young man's eyes still followed the flatboat. After a moment he said, softly, "It would serve the bastard right."

TWO

"STAY BESIDE ME, Amalie," Clotie begged, as Monsieur Armand approached them under the lanterns hung from Monsieur and Madame Dupré's lordly magnolia trees.

"Why?" Amalie demanded. "It is not I—"

Clotie silenced her with a pinch. The count was already beside them, looking handsome and worldly in a pale blue coat over close-fitting white pantaloons. He bowed to each of them in turn, but his expressive eyes lingered on Clotie. Amalie slapped at a mosquito.

"Will you not join us, m'sieu?" Clotie cried in sudden animation. "Amalie and I are going to look at the puppies."

The count looked slightly surprised. "Puppies?" he said, with a curious inflection.

"Ma'm'selle Dupré's favorite bitch has a litter, and she has promised me my choice of the males," Clotie raced on, turning toward the brilliantly lit house. "Come. She has given the new family a bed on the galérie just outside her bedchamber."

"Indeed," said the count. Amalie had the notion that he was not at all interested in newborn puppies and, furthermore, that he had hoped to find Clotie alone, but he good-naturedly offered each of them an arm.

Amalie took it reluctantly. She and Clotie had already been shown the puppies by Marthe Dupré, who was besotted with her dogs, and Amalie suspected that Clotie, like herself, had been quite satisfied with one visit. She could not remember Marthe promising a male.

They strolled toward the house. From somewhere inside came the faint strains of a minuet, eerily diluted by the strident and incessant rasping of the cicadas. After her sudden burst of enthusiasm, Clotie had fallen unaccountably silent, and finding her unresponsive, the count turned to Amalie.

"I am forced to take back my remarks to you when first we met, Ma'm'selle Amalie."

"Which remarks were those, m'sieu?"

"It is not someday that you will break hearts, but very possibly to-night."

"And will one of them be yours, m'sieu?"

"You see? I am right about her, am I not, Ma'm'selle Claudine?"

"What?" Clotie murmured, then colored. "My thoughts were else-where."

"He is teasing me, Clotie. And pretending he does not know that everyone is looking at us only because he is walking between us."

"You wrong yourself, ma'm'selle," the count protested, laughing.

As they climbed the stair to the galérie, with the eyes of Madame de l'Ouvrier—and several other mothers among her friends—following them, Amalie wondered at her sister. The Duprés' *soirée* was the third entertainment for the count to which Monsieur and Madame de l'Ouvrier and their daughters had been invited this summer, and each time Amalie had noted that the count was endeavoring to speak with Clotie alone, but Clotie had been adroit in avoiding him.

Amalie observed that the effect of all this on the count was apparently to make him more ardently desire a private interview, and she wondered if Clotie, who was a goose in so many ways, had been clever enough to foresee this.

They were passing a salon with its shutters standing wide. Amalie glanced in and saw their father with a group of men standing around an enormous silver punch bowl. When he looked up, she waved to him and he smiled at her.

With mingled curiosity and amusement, she stood beside the dog bed where the patient bitch lay with her babies crawling over her, while Clotie stooped to coo endearments to the wriggling creatures— who had not even opened their eyes and were interested only in finding the source of food—all the while pretending to be quite un-conscious of the count.

"Look, Amalie! Shall I choose this small spotted one? Or will he be frail? He is so tiny, poor precious! Perhaps this one? Oh, they are all precious!"

Amalie looked to see if the count were bored, but he was watching Clotie—who did look ravishing tonight—with a bemused smile.

"Oh, there you are, my dear count." Monsieur de l'Ouvrier had followed them along the galérie. "I thought I saw you pass. Come with me," he urged warmly, all unaware of the annoyance Amalie knew her mother would feel if she could know what he was doing. "I have been telling *messieurs* the news you brought us from Paris, and they have some questions for you, my friend."

"But certainly," said the count, and making his excuses, he accompanied Monsieur de l'Ouvrier back to the punch bowl.

Amalie watched him go, thinking that he walked as proudly and carelessly as if the earth were his estate, and envying Clotie that look, both tender and amused, that he had bent on her as she fussed over the puppies.

"He will offer for you," she murmured to the retreating backs, her father's slightly stooped, so that his ancient coat flared out at the bottom, the count's straight and slim with his coat fitting like a second skin.

Clotie was looking after them, too, with that faraway expression on her face. "Who?" she said, absently.

"Who!" Amalie exclaimed, startled. "Oh, Clotie, can you really be such a goose?"

But Clotie did not even hear, so lost in thought was she.

"She is in love," Madame de l'Ouvrier told her husband late that night after the flatboat had taken them back to Les Chênes. "He must offer, for her sake as well as our own, for I think she is in love."

"Who?" said Monsieur de l'Ouvrier absently. He had gone straight to the press he had fashioned in which to dry a new plant—one completely unknown to the scientific world, he was certain!—which the day before he had carefully dug out of the swamp with its roots intact.

"Who?" Madame repeated in weary exasperation. She had sent the girls to their beds and was pouring a glass of wine for her husband and herself before retiring. "Why, Amalie, of course."

"Amalie!" Monsieur de l'Ouvrier almost dropped the press with its precious insert. "What are you talking about? *Amalie* in love? With whom, pray?"

Madame de l'Ouvrier laughed unpleasantly. "I was talking about your daughter Claudine," she said, handing him his wine, "but that did not interest you, did it? How is it that you never fail to hear me if I mention Amalie?"

"Now, my dear, let us not—"

"It is scandalous the way you favor that child! Claudine scarcely exists for you."

"That is unfair of you, madame."

"It is true, m'sieu. One would think you had only one daughter, the way you dote on her. I do not know what will become of Amalie. She cannot hope to meet with such indulgence from a husband as she receives from you."

"It is a strange mother," Monsieur de l'Ouvrier observed stiffly, "who is jealous of her own daughter."

"I am not jealous!" Madame de l'Ouvrier grabbed the back of a chair and held on tightly, pressing her lips together until she was in control of herself. She had very nearly thrown her wine in his face! Then she said, "The wonder is that Claudine is not jealous of her sister. Do you know what would happen if their positions were reversed? Your little Amalie would scratch her sister's eyes out, that is what would happen!"

"Good night, my dear," Monsieur de l'Ouvrier said, wearily, and left her, taking his wine and his press with him.

As the time approached for the count's return visit, Claudine began acting very strangely. She seldom heard when anyone spoke to her. Madame de l'Ouvrier worried aloud that she was not eating enough, and Amalie found her a very unsatisfactory companion. She had taken to rising an hour earlier, and instead of waiting for Amalie to join her for their morning ride, often went off on her small mare without Amalie.

"Why did you go so early?" Amalie stormed, when this happened. "Why didn't you wait for me?"

"I couldn't sleep," Clotie would murmur from deep in her dream.

But when Amalie wanted to ride, Clotie would demur, saying it was too hot, and Amalie would cry, frustrated, "But it is always hot!"

When Amalie complained to her mother, Madame de l'Ouvrier shrugged. "She is in love. You must learn to amuse yourself, for soon you will be the only bird in the nest." She turned away, but Amalie saw her make the sign of the cross, and understood that it was very important that the count should offer for Clotie.

The day of the count's return finally arrived. On that morning, Clotie again went for her ride without waking Amalie, and she did not return for so long that Madame de l'Ouvrier became worried. When Clotie appeared, her lovely face was flushed and spotted with mosquito bites, and she was trembling with fatigue.

Madame de l'Ouvrier sent her to bed and reproached Clotie's bodyservant for allowing her mistress to stay so long in the sun. "Whatever were you doing all that time?"

"Riding, madame."

"You should have returned two hours ago."

Trembling, the slave said, *"Oui,* but m'selle order me. I can do nothing."

"I shall speak to her," Madame said. When the slave followed, she turned and said coldly, "I do not need you, Madi."

"Oui, madame," the black girl said, but the troubled eyes followed her mistress.

Madame de l'Ouvrier found her daughter lying on her bed, her swollen face feverish. Exasperated, Madame exclaimed, "What a day for you to choose to stay out and feed the mosquitoes until you get heat sickness! You know the flatboat has been sent for Count Armand. He will want to see you."

"I cannot face him, Maman. As you can see, I am not feeling well."

"You will rest until he comes," Madame said firmly, "and then you will get up and put on your new blue gown and come to the dinner table."

"Like *this?"* her daughter wailed.

"Mon Dieu, do not weep! It will only make your face more swollen."

With an expression of utter despair, Clotie closed her eyes on her tears.

Madame had a fleeting memory of how anguished was the despair of a sixteen-year-old, and was moved. She laid a cool hand on Clotie's heated brow and said, gently, "You are still lovely, my child, mosquito bites and all. Do you not know that? He will offer for you, do not doubt it."

"Oui, Maman," Clotie said, in a dead voice.

Madame bent and kissed her, then drew the mosquito netting around the bed. "Rest, *chérie."*

In spite of the afternoon heat, Amalie could not remain still. Between her excitement at the prospect of seeing the count again, and learning whether he really meant to make an offer for Clotie, and her apprehension about Clotie, who was behaving so strangely, Amalie was overcome by a fit of nervous energy. She moved from her father's room, where he pored over his collection of dried specimens, to her mother's, where Madame de l'Ouvrier wrestled with the question of tomorrow's dishes for her guest.

Although they might be facing poverty, there was no lack of food, for the woods and bayous teemed with game and fish, and the slaves tended an ample kitchen garden. A clever Frenchwoman could set a marvelously rich table in this bayou wilderness, and Madame de l'Ouvrier had trained her cooks well. The count himself had brought wine, which had been carefully husbanded for his return visit.

Amalie left her trying to decide between a *boeuf en daube* and a *courtbouillon* and went down the stair and across the steaming grass to the landing to see if the flatboat were yet in sight.

It was! And she had been seen, she saw with a faint embarrassment. Count Armand stood in the center of the boat in his shirtsleeves, looking cool and capable, and waved to her. She waved back and waited while her father's slaves tied the flatboat up at the landing and the count stepped ashore, carrying his coat. So informally dressed, with his hair unpowdered, he looked virile, much younger, and rather dashing.

"*Bonjour,* Ma'm'selle Amalie! You are kind to meet me. Where is your sister?"

"*Bonjour,* m'sieu. Clotie is resting."

Her answer seemed to please him and when Amalie saw that, she knew that he had come to offer for her sister. She wanted to rush into the house to tell Clotie. Instead, she directed the servants to take Monsieur's cases to the room which had been made ready for him, and accompanied him to the stair to the galérie where, presently, her father and mother appeared to welcome their guest.

"And how is the puppy?" the count asked, as they walked.

"Puppy? Oh!" Amalie recovered herself, annoyed that he had somehow got it into his head that she was the one who had made a fuss over the Dupré bitch's litter. "We have not got him," she answered carelessly. Let Clotie explain, she thought.

"M'sieu! Madame!" The count advanced up the stair to kiss her mother's hand and to clasp her father's.

"You are welcome, my dear Armand," said her father. "I hope you will remain with us for a long visit. I have planned an extremely interesting expedition for us tomorrow—"

"I am here only overnight, my good friend," the count interrupted, "for I have arranged for a merchant boat to stop here for me tomorrow. It is traveling up to the Mississippi where I can catch a boat down to New Orleans."

"Ah, what a pity."

"I, too, regret the short visit, but I have come to discuss a matter of importance with you. I think you know what it is."

"First let us have a brandy, dear Count," said her father, imperturbably. "There is plenty of time to discuss our affairs."

But Amalie saw the unutterable relief that shone for a second in her mother's eyes, and quietly slipped away to hurry down the broad central hall to Clotie's room.

Her sister lay motionless, staring up at the canopy over her bed. Behind the transparent curtain of gauze she seemed remote and, with her swollen face, somehow strange. She lay so still that for a second Amalie entertained the frightening fantasy that she was dead.

"Clotie! Count Armand is here. He said he has come to discuss a matter of importance. You know what that means."

Clotie did not answer.

"You will be a countess!"

"No."

"But, yes," Amalie insisted. "You will be *madame la comtesse de Valérun!* Is that not exciting? Clotie, what is the matter?"

"I shall refuse him."

"But you can't!" Amalie cried, shocked.

"I shall."

"Oh, Clotie, don't be a goose. You know it is between Papa and the count. What can you do?"

"I shall refuse."

"But what will Maman say?"

Maman, at that moment, entered the room, looking purposeful. Madi followed her with a basin. "Wring out those cloths and lay them on her face," Maman told Madi. To Clotie she said briskly, "We must make you presentable, *chérie.*" And to Amalie, "Leave us."

Reluctantly, Amalie left. There was no place for her to go but to her own chamber. At one end of the house, Papa was closeted with the count over brandies. At the other end, Maman remained with Clotie. At times voices were raised from either room, Papa's and the count's in genial comradeship, Maman's in emotional cries.

When dinner was served, Madame de l'Ouvrier appeared alone. "Claudine is feeling much better," she said, "but prefers to have her dinner in her room."

"It is as well," said Monsieur de l'Ouvrier, unperturbed, "since the count and I have a few matters still to discuss, eh, my friend?"

The count nodded, and Madame said, "I will send her to you when you have concluded."

"Bien," responded her husband.

If the count knew anything was amiss, Amalie could not read it in his face. She bent her efforts to amuse him, since her mother was on edge, and she suspected that her father had been spending more time discussing his hobby than his daughter's marriage. If the count were bored, he was too courteous to show it, but he turned to her light chatter with an air of enjoyment.

The meal over, Madame excused herself, taking Amalie with her, to leave the men to resume their discussion. At Clotie's door, she burst out in sudden despair, "I can do nothing with her, Amalie. She swears she will go down there and tell the count she cannot marry him. She will humiliate and impoverish us!"

"But why, Maman?"

"She will not tell me why. I can get nothing out of her. It is so unlike Clotie to be stubborn. And the pain in my head—it is unbearable!"

"Let me talk to her, Maman."

Madame de l'Ouvrier hesitated, massaging her temples. "Perhaps she will tell you things she thinks I cannot understand," she sighed at last. "I shall be in my chamber."

Amalie opened the door to her sister's room and stepped inside. Clotie was sitting up on her bed, with her dinner tray practically untouched before her. Her face was no longer so swollen, except around her eyes from weeping, but she looked wan and miserable.

"How unhappy you look, Clotie!" Amalie exclaimed. "What is the matter? What can I do?"

Clotie turned toward her, a flicker of hope in her dulled eyes. "Help me, Amalie. Help me make Maman understand that I cannot marry him."

"But why, Clotie? Perhaps if you tell Manan why—"

"I cannot! I cannot tell anyone, not even you, Amalie."

"Then how can I help you?"

Her sister came suddenly to blazing life, seizing Amalie's arms in so fierce a grasp that it pained her as much as the change in Clotie surprised her. "Amalie, do you swear not to tell a soul, neither Papa nor Maman—?"

"Oh, Clotie, how can I promise that? Maman will pounce on me as soon as I leave you."

"Then I will tell you nothing!"

"All right," Amalie said, after a moment. "I promise, Clotie."

"You swear it by the Holy Virgin?"

"I—I swear it," Amalie faltered, frightened.

"Then I will tell you. I cannot marry the count because I love another."

"Oh, Clotie, you goose, how can there be another?"

"If you call me a goose once more, I shall tell you nothing! I love another and he loves me. He wants to marry me."

"Then why have you not told Maman so?"

"Because it would make no difference—and she would prevent my seeing him. She thinks only of Les Chênes, and says I shall make beggars of us all." A look Amalie recognized came into Clotie's face —that look of being far removed from the shuttered room, the canopied bed on which she lay, her ignored tray of food before her, with her eyes gazing through the pale wainscoted walls at a vision Amalie was denied. "Amalie, do you remember the *yanqui* trader from whom Maman bought our silks?"

An image came into Amalie's mind—the young man standing with legs wide apart and head thrown back, his shirt open to his waist as he defied Papa's wrath. "Of course I remember him, but what has that to do—" Amalie clapped her hand to her mouth. She had seen something that made everything clear. On Clotie's finger was a sapphire ring that was familiar—Maman had traded it to the young *yanqui* for their silks.

Amalie's eyes flew from it to Clotie's face. She was smiling strangely and slowly nodding her head. Amalie was struck by the change in her eyes. A moment ago they had seemed dull and hopeless; now they shone softly.

"It is my betrothal ring, Amalie. I have been riding to meet him every morning while you slept."

"Then Madi knows—"

"She goes only a little way with me. I make her stay behind."

For once Amalie was speechless. Clotie was meeting a man *alone!*

"He teases me because I cannot say his name," Clotie said dreamily, "but his French is so ludicrous I have to laugh. Did you notice how blue are his eyes? Oh, he is so wonderful, Amalie! He has come here from Philadelphia to make his fortune. And he will. Someday he will have his own plantation."

"Papa will never let you marry a *yanqui* trader," Amalie gasped, finding her voice at last. "Do you not remember how he set the dogs on him?"

"You do not yet understand, Amalie. I belong to Deneez. How can I marry someone else when I have given myself to him?"

"It makes no difference," Amalie argued. "You know Papa—"

"Does it not?" Clotie said, so queerly that Amalie stared at her. "*Mon Dieu*, Clotie! What have you done?"

"You know quite well what I have done. The question is what am I to do now? Deneez has gone with Jacques to New Orleans to sell the furs Jacques has trapped, and to buy more silks. When he returns with money, Deneez and I will be married, whether Papa consents or not."

"Father Bernard will not marry you."

"Deneez says if it is necessary, we shall go to Philadelphia and be married there. So there can be no contract with the count, as Maman insists. Now do you understand?"

"Are you *enceinte?*"

A look of pure terror flashed in Clotie's eyes, and Amalie guessed she had not even considered that possibility.

"Oh, you goose!" Amalie sighed, and sank down on the edge of the bed. What were they to do?

In the dining room Monsieur de l'Ouvrier and his guest had had their final talk sitting across from each other at the cleared table, and were pouring a toast to their complete understanding. Monsieur de l'Ouvrier, who had seldom had such an opportunity to discuss his hobby with a politely patient listener, and was now certain of his wife's good humor, was in a mellow, slightly sentimental mood.

"She is a gentle and lovely girl, m'sieu, with a great capacity for happiness."

"I shall do my best to make her happy, m'sieu."

"Her capacity for suffering is as great, I fear," her father warned.

"Life is uncertain and unpredictable," said the count, with emotion, "but if I can prevent it, she shall never suffer."

Monsieur de l'Ouvrier raised his brandy. "To the mingling of our great and ancient bloodlines! In this marriage I can perhaps forget the sorrow of having no son to carry on my name."

They drank. Monsieur de l'Ouvrier summoned his servant. "Send word to my daughter that her father and Count Armand await her pleasure."

They waited, relaxed and expansive now that all details of their agreement had been worked out. Claudine did not appear.

"This is an historic event," Monsieur de l'Ouvrier explained. "We know women, do we not, my friend? They must be dressed for such an occasion."

"But, of course," said the count, politely.

Still Claudine did not appear. Monsieur de l'Ouvrier was growing nervous. "She is feeling some trepidation, no doubt. She is somewhat shy—"

"—and it charms me, m'sieu."

At last the door opened. It was Amalie who stood there, and her father looked at her, thunderstruck. Her hair had been pulled up to the crown, baring her tender neck, making her look at once older and more vulnerable. His anger rose as he realized that there was stuffing in the bosom of her dress, but the shining look in her eyes arrested his impulse to shout at her. He could not bear to destroy that look.

He glanced at the count, who looked bewildered, with the beginnings of a scowl on his handsome face.

"You sent for me, Papa?" Amalie asked innocently, and without waiting for an answer, bent in a low curtsy.

Across her head he murmured, swiftly, "Leave this to me, m'sieu, I beg you."

Amalie raised her head and extended her hand to the count. "I am deeply honored, m'sieu."

It was the young man's turn to falter before her look. He raised her hand to his lips and said nothing.

Monsieur de l'Ouvrier moved between them. Placing his hands on Amalie's shoulders, he bent and kissed her brow. "You are my little dove," he said, in a voice strangled with emotion. "Now, if you please, go and tell your mother that I wish to speak with her."

"*Oui,* Papa," Amalie said, and left them.

Monsieur de l'Ouvrier plucked a kerchief from his sleeve and mopped his forehead. "*Merci, mon ami,*" he said. "*Mille mercis!*" He rang for his servant and, while they awaited him, said, "I must ask you, m'sieu, if you have said anything to Mademoiselle Amalie that—er—may have contributed to this—er—unfortunate misunderstanding?"

"I am certain that I have not," the count said stiffly. "However, I have found it extremely difficult to separate her sister from her company."

The servant entered, and Monsieur de l'Ouvrier regarded him sternly. "To whom did you deliver my message?"

"I knock on M'selle Claudine' door, but she in bed. M'selle Amalie answer."

"And what did you say to her, you dolt?" cried Monsieur de l'Ouvrier.

"That you wish to see M'selle."

" 'M'selle?' Just that? Get out, fool!"

The servant fled.

Monsieur de l'Ouvrier wiped his face again. "You may leave everything to me, my friend. I assure you the misunderstanding will be corrected."

"But, of course," the count said, tight-lipped, for he was not at all sure he had not been made a fool of.

"You understand it must be handled tactfully. I am unwilling to hurt Mademoiselle Amalie." Her father groaned. "She is still my baby, m'sieu."

The count's eyebrows rose at that. But he said only, "Since the boat will call for me very early in the morning, I leave it in your hands. I will have the necessary papers drawn up in New Orleans and sent to you."

"I am grateful for your patience, *m'sieu le comte.*"

"Then I bid you good night, m'sieu," the count said, and went to his room.

THREE

MADAME DE L'OUVRIER, summoned by her husband, assumed that she was being asked to share in a toast to the future marriage of her daughter. She was disconcerted when she encountered the young count in the wide central hall. He was obviously on his way to his own room and his expression as he gave her a cold, silent bow was forbidding.

She stayed the startled question that had nearly burst from her lips, and returned his bow. Then she hurried on to the dining room to join her husband. She found him striding back and forth beside the table—on which the wineglasses had been left, her disapproving eye noted in passing—with his coat flaring out behind him and his face suffused with his agitation. He turned on her as she entered.

"This is your doing, madame! You are conspiring to take my daughter from me, but you will not succeed!" He glared at her.

"Since I do not know what you are talking about, Charles, I cannot answer you," she said, more calmly than she felt. "Why did the count leave you? He passed me just now in the hall without a word."

"It is the damnable trick you have played on him! Because of it, he may not offer at all!"

"What?" She was jolted. "You have not agreed upon a contract? Have you botched things, then? Can you not forget your dreary botany and your vain plots long enough to get your daughter married?"

"I? *I?*" He was almost speechless with rage. "It is *you* who have done this thing! You have overreached yourself this time, madame. It is Claudine the count wishes to marry. You have defeated your own purpose by sending down Amalie."

"Amalie! Pray collect yourself and tell me what happened."

"Obviously, Amalie has been led to believe the count is offering for her. Madame, *she had stuffing in her bosom!*"

Now she understood, and her heart sank. "But I sent Amalie in to help her sister prepare herself to come to you and the count." She had gone to her room to try to forestall the headache the conflict with Claudine was bringing on. It had been a serious mistake, she saw now, leaving the two of them to conspire together. "So she answered your summons herself! The little minx!"

Even in his rage, her husband bridled, as always, at criticism of his favorite. "It is a misunderstanding, of course. I have promised the count that it will be straightened out. You must talk to her, madame."

"Talk to her yourself," she retorted. "It is no one's fault but your own that she is so spoiled."

His anger collapsed like a balloon. "Adèle, if you had seen her! I cannot bear to tell her the count is offering for her sister."

"She knows that quite well," Madame de l'Ouvrier said bitterly.

"But the look in her eyes! I am sure she does not know. My dear,

I am sorry if I have blamed you unfairly, but you must do this for me. I implore you to be gentle with her—"

"I shall have nothing to do with it. The count leaves in the morning?"

"*Oui,* very early."

"I shall not be up," she said coldly. "Pray convey my respects."

She left the room, with Monsieur de l'Ouvrier looking helplessly after her. He could still see his darling's shining eyes as she curtsied. Could he shatter that artless happiness? "No, no," he groaned.

Madame de l'Ouvrier's anger grew as she walked toward the rear of the house. She passed by Claudine's door, hearing no sound within, and abruptly opened Amalie's. The room was empty. Moving quietly, she walked across the hall and entered her own chamber. Her younger daughter stood in front of her pier glass, admiring herself in Claudine's blue gown. Her delicate shoulders were bare and—yes, her bosom definitely was stuffed.

Amalie saw her in the glass and turned guiltily. Madame de l'Ouvrier moved forward and with a quick movement snatched the handkerchief that simulated one young breast from her bodice. Amalie giggled.

Before she could control herself, Madame had flicked the handkerchief like a stinging whip across her daughter's cheek. Amalie stiffened, but did not cry out. For a moment they stood in a shocked silence. Tears stood in Amalie's eyes.

Then Amalie said, "What would you have me do, Maman? Go down and tell the count that Clotie refuses him?"

Madame de l'Ouvrier sank heavily into her damask chair. "I should not have struck you, Amalie. Forgive me. I am distraught and my head is bursting. I am afraid all is lost."

After a moment Amalie said, "Perhaps not, Maman. He cannot keep his eyes from Clotie."

Madame de l'Ouvrier looked up without hope. "Yes," she said heavily, and her chin sank to her bosom again. "You may be right." In spite of the fact that her headache was worsening by the minute, she saw that she would have to arise early enough to bid the count a pleasant journey, and to assure him that Clotie was devastated at not seeing him, but too much in love to risk letting him see her face ravaged by insect bites.

She sighed. "Who helped you dress?"

"Clotie."

"You did not have Julie or Madi with you?"

"No, Maman."

"That is good. You must get out of that gown without their help. No hint of what has happened here tonight must escape from Les Chênes."

"But can I not trust Julie?"

"Count Armand is a proud man. In a matter so delicate, we can trust no one. Good night, my child."

Amalie curtsied. "Good night, Maman." At the door she turned, with a sigh of her own. "It is a pity the count could not love me."

Madame de l'Ouvrier looked after the slight figure, so strangely matured by that one little aid to nature, with mixed feelings and, for a fleeting second, saw instead of her nettlesome younger daughter, the infant she had turned over to Julie, the dark-eyed girl child she had been too grieved to love. *Yes,* she said, silently. *Yes, it is a pity.* And she was not willing to look into her heart and ask herself why she said it.

The sun moved south and wheeled across the sky with unbearable slowness; the days wheeled as lazily from dawn to dawn. Life seemed scarcely to move. Summer rains were frequent, and the de l'Ouvriers spent interminable hours on their galérie, enclosed by a cascading silvery wall of water that fell as if the sky were an overturned bucket, and dulled their desultory conversation with its drumming on the roof.

When the rain stopped as abruptly as it came, a shining flood of water often stretched from the pillars beneath them to the bayou, and the steaming silence was as oppressive as the drumming of the rain. Monsieur had temporarily abandoned his excursions into the marshes. Because the high water obliterated the banks of the bayous, the morning rides Amalie and Clotie had once enjoyed were now impossible. Sometimes the servants gathered the crayfish that had been carried by flood waters up the grassy slope to the house itself, and from the small scarlet creatures made a tasty bisque. Once a young slave caught a baby alligator in the storage beneath their living quarters.

When cooler air moved down from the north, the family moved indoors to gather around a fire. The wood, stored beneath the house, was never dry and the acrid smoke hung in the heavy air. Madame de l'Ouvrier supervised the simmering of hot, rich stews and bouillabaisses. Occasionally, between rains, a flatboat appeared on the bayou with visitors from one of the other plantations, driven out by their forced inactivity, and it was a welcome diversion, for the de l'Ouvriers were becoming bored with each other.

The difficulty was that they had exhausted all the safe topics of conversation. No word had come from the count, but it was dangerous to comment on that, for it could lead into a discussion of the disastrous events of his last visit. Monsieur de l'Ouvrier had still not got up his courage to tell Amalie she had misunderstood his summons— for Madame de l'Ouvrier had not enlightened him about her conversation with her daughter later that evening. For their own reasons, Amalie and Clotie kept their own counsel.

At first the matter that occupied all their silent thoughts had been discussed behind closed doors, Monsieur and Madame in their suite, Clotie and Amalie in one or the other's chamber.

"Will he offer?" Madame constantly asked her husband. "Do you think he will send the contract as he promised?"

"The count is a man of honor, my dear." But Monsieur de l'Ouvrier was uncomfortable each time she raised the question, for it brought to his mind that blinding vision of Amalie in the door of the dining room—his little Amalie a woman!

"Then why have we not received it?"

"Do not forget the difficulties he faces in sending it. It cannot come up the river as swiftly as he floated down, for it must be carried over land. Also, we must remember that the waters are sometimes so high that many ferries are obliged to wait until they recede. It is very possible that the contract is now on its way to us."

"It is also possible that he did not send it at all," Madame invariably remarked gloomily.

"He is a man of honor," her husband repeated, bringing them full circle, and thus they went around and around until Monsieur cried, "Enough, madame! Let us sleep on it."

In Clotie's room, curled up with her under the gauze *moustiquaire* draped around the bed to keep out the new crop of mosquitoes brought by the rains, Amalie listened as Clotie worried about Dennis's long absence.

"Why is he not back? I know it takes much time for his business, but why has he not sent a message? *Ma foi,* it would not be so difficult! He could send his slave. He knows we can trust Madi."

"*Mais, oui,* he could easily send his slave a hundred and fifty miles into the wilderness," Amalie mocked her, and teased, "he has forgotten you for a fashionable Orléanienne."

"He will not forget. He will come back and carry me off before the count returns."

"If the count returns."

At first Amalie had been greatly intrigued by Clotie's romance. She listened eagerly as Clotie relived her meeting with her lover. "Do you remember the grassy clearing on Bayou Black where you and I and Papa took a picnic lunch? That is where we first met. I rode alone that morning, and when I came to the clearing he and the trapper were on the other side of the bayou. When he saw me, he—he just threw back his head and laughed. Oh, Amalie, he looked so splendid! And then, do you know what he did? He jumped into the bayou without even removing his boots and swam over to my side! *Mon Dieu,* but I was frightened for him!"

Amalie sighed. "And did you meet him there again?"

"*Oui.* He came back alone the next morning in a pirogue. Afterward, we found a place I cannot tell even you, Amalie, a secret place that will be forever our own. He teased me because I cannot say his name," Clotie said, dreamily. "Always he teases me, asking me to say it. 'Deneez,' I say. 'Deneez.' And he laughs and kisses me."

Her voice dropped to a murmur that was scarcely above a whisper. "When he touches me—here—"—she cupped a hand around one breast—"and kisses me, I love him so much there is nothing I would not do for him. Amalie, I think I could die for him."

Amalie listened with a queer smothery feeling. She laid her hand on her chest—almost flat, alas!—and tried to imagine the handsome count, whom her sister had scorned, cupping her own small breast in his slender hand.

But as the weeks wore on, and it was "Deneez this" and "Deneez that" whenever she and Clotie were alone together, Amalie grew so weary of the *yanqui* trader she wanted to scream. Finally, on a day when Clotie mourned, as she had times without number, "Oh, *why* doesn't he come?" Amalie said, "Because he is a peasant and has forgotten you."

"Amalie, you are cruel!" Clotie burst into tears.

After that Amalie began sleeping in her own room again.

Madame de l'Ouvrier also lay alone in her own bed, with her dismal thoughts. It seemed to her that the future was a dark tunnel down which they must all travel to a bitter end where poverty and humiliation awaited them. Her husband would never change his habits. He could not for his life—for the life of any of them!—make a living, even on this steaming fertile land where now the foul-smelling indigo rotted with disease and the slaves worked only at fishing and hunting alligators and partridges and growing their vegetables.

They were doomed, all of them. She saw Claudine's beauty fade to a mousy shade and Amalie's spirit die as they sat and waited in their made-over clothes for poverty to overtake them. *If my son had lived!* her heart cried in despair.

On a day when the sun came out and the waters had receded enough so that the bayous were navigable again, Amalie impulsively suggested a picnic. Monsieur de l'Ouvrier was deep in the classification of his specimens to which he had retreated during the rains, and Madame was suffering from the headache which came more and more frequently these days. Clotie, at first, was indifferent, but when Amalie said frankly, "If we do not escape from this house, we shall be tearing each other's hair out," Clotie's coolness of the past weeks dissolved and she eagerly agreed.

Having grown up on the plantation with no near playmates, both girls were skilled in handling the tiny, flat-bottomed canoe they called a *pirogue*. Each had taken her turn at accompanying their father on his many expeditions, and they shared an enjoyment of the warm, dreamy afternoons spent drifting through the serpentine lagoons and pushing into the marshes where their father sought strange plants among the grasses that grew higher than a man's head.

They were followed in a second pirogue by Julie and the strong boatman who rowed their father on many of his excursions, for the girls were not allowed to go into the watery wilderness alone. The air was still and humid when they left the majestic bayou with its grassy banks and took a smaller waterway which soon widened into a shallow lake. This was a true wilderness, sheltered in gloomy light by the swamp cypresses dangling long fingers of moss and lifting bony knees above the surface of the motionless black water.

The cypresses gradually thinned as Amalie sculled on. In half an hour they were entering a reedy lake in which stilt-legged herons walked daintily or stood with one leg lifted, while over their heads countless gulls wheeled with cries like mocking laughter.

"There is no shade here!" Julie complained from the other pirogue. "Turn back!"

Amalie kept on, and Clotie demanded, *"Ma foi,* Amalie, where are you taking us?"

"To your secret place," Amalie teased.

Clotie blushed and laughed. "In this bog?"

"Where is it, then?"

"I will never tell you, so you may as well find a *chenière* on which we can picnic."

Amalie headed for a mass of green which indicated an island of firm ground in the marsh where the live oaks grew and where they might find a dry, grassy spot for their lunch. As they approached it, Clotie gave a little cry.

"See? Over there by that clump of reeds! It looks like one of Jacques's traps."

"Jacques?"

Clotie colored again. "The 'Cadian who is Deneez's partner."

"The *trapper* is Deneez's partner?" Amalie asked, incredulous.

Clotie avoided her eyes. "Row nearer, please, Amalie," she begged. "If it is one of his traps, it means they have returned, don't you see?"

Amalie pulled the pirogue over to the reeds and they looked down into the black water. It was, indeed, a trap lying four or five inches below the surface and something was caught in it, something dark and shapeless that did not move. When Amalie gingerly reached out to touch it with her oar, they gasped and drew back in revulsion. What remained of the creature whose leg had been caught in the iron jaws had been there a long time.

"What you do, you wicked girls?" cried Julie, from the other boat. "You want to spoil your lunch?"

Amalie backed away from the reeds as quickly as she could and headed once more for the oak island.

"They are not back," Clotie said, in despairing tones. "It is a trap he failed to bring in before they left." She sucked in her breath. "I am frightened, Amalie, and I don't know why. I fear it is an omen of something dreadful."

"Love has made you simple," Amalie said angrily, "and the good Lord knows what a goose you were before you fell in love!"

"Oh, do be quiet!"

The unpleasant incident had, indeed, spoiled their picnic. They ate indifferently, slapping at occasional mosquitoes, although they were carefully swathed against them, and soon packed up their picnic basket and climbed back into the pirogues to return to the plantation. The sun was lowering and its slanting rays made a mirror of the dark water, reflecting the reeds with such authenticity that Amalie found herself hesitating to put her oar into the reflections.

When they entered the cypress grove it was dark and mysterious and so inhumanly still that the splash of a turtle dropping off a half-submerged log was startling. No one spoke. An alligator moved leisurely out of their path, only his nostrils visible.

Their gloomy mood persisted as they walked up from the landing, leaving Julie and the boatman to tie up the pirogues and bring up their things. But when they reached the galérie it was immediately apparent that something had happened in their absence. There was agitation in the very air. Madi's face as she came toward them to take their hats and mosquito veils was alight with it.

"A letter come from *michie le comte*," she whispered.

Clotie paled and headed swiftly for her room.

"Where are Maman and Papa?" Amalie asked Madi.

"In they room, m'selle." Madi's black face split in an irrepressible smile. "Me, I hear'm say *michie le comte* offer for you."

"*Me?*" Amalie cried, stunned.

But Madi was hurrying after her young mistress.

FOUR

THE LAZY HOUSEBOUND days of the hard rains were over. Now everything at Les Chênes was hustle and bustle. The entire house must be scrubbed and polished, or repainted, inside and out. Crystal and silver were burnished to a sparkle, clothing turned out of chests and armoires to be aired and remodeled or repaired. The gardens must be pruned of an excess of creepers and the grass kept scythed as a precaution against snakes. Madame was enveloped in such a frenzy of activity that she had no occasion for headaches and little time for concern for her pale elder daughter, who seemed to have lost her appetite.

Monsieur de l'Ouvrier wandered through the bustle, looking pinched and unhappy. "Surely this matter can be cleared up when the count arrives," he reproached his wife. "It is plain that Clotie is pining, and that Amalie is not ready for marriage."

But Madame de l'Ouvrier, herself blooming, paused between directions to her servants only long enough to say, "It is too late now, m'sieu." She was ordering the flatboat prepared for another excursion to the trapper's hut to see if she could purchase more silks for Amalie's trousseau. "Julie will accompany us, of course," she instructed the boatman, "for it is she who will make ma'm'selle's dresses."

Only Amalie knew the true cause of her sister's lack of appetite: No word had come from her lover. Amalie herself was in a state suspended between celebration and disbelief. At times, the wildest fancies coursed through her mind. The most fantastic involved herself in a trailing gown with diamonds in her hair (and a bosom), her hand on the count's arm, being introduced as "madame la comtesse." More often, she saw herself thrust aside when she went to greet the count and heard him declare passionately to Clotie that he had meant only to punish her for her coldness.

Sometimes, in pure panic, she tried to call the count's features to mind, and found that she could not. Oddly enough, the memory that came in their place was the proud lift of his head and his straight back in the close-fitting coat going away from her with Papa on the galérie where Clotie had taken them to look at Marthe Dupré's puppies. Not by the wildest feat of imagination could she imagine herself sharing a nuptial chamber with that fashionably dressed man!

On a gray, cloudy day, when the air was heavy with moisture, the two girls set out with Madame de l'Ouvrier and their servants to call on the 'Cadian trapper. The cool air had retreated to the north, and the moist heat was more oppressive than if the sun were shining. Clotie was alternately pale and then flushed with excitement. Amalie was mostly conscious of her discomfort and an irritation with the boatmen who, dripping with perspiration, dipped and poled in an exaggerated slow motion that she found maddening.

It was a silent trip, except for the soft plash of the oars and an occasional squawk from a startled bird. Madame was glad for an opportunity to sit quietly and let her mind sort out her plans for the wedding; Clotie was wrapped in her own secret fears; and Amalie looked at the patterns swirled in the black water by the oars and thought that she was being swept into marriage and the mysterious changes it would make in her life much as the flatboat was being propelled through the mysteriously opaque waters beneath them.

The deserted air of the little 'Cadian house was apparent as soon as they came around the last bend. There was no need to send the boatmen up to investigate. Water grass was waist high between the landing and the small front galérie, and the windows were boarded up. A forlorn appearance, Amalie judged it, and glanced at Clotie who had paled alarmingly.

"*Ma foi,* why did not someone tell me he was gone?" Madame de l'Ouvrier exclaimed in annoyance. "My own folly! I should have sent a servant ahead before setting out! Well, it is of no moment. I shall have to dig deeper into my trunks, Julie, for materials for you to sew for Ma'm'selle Amalie. And I have used this respite to plan my menu for the count's first evening with us. It will be a private celebration of the betrothal—the family only. Anyway," she said, frowning, "I cannot summon our friends for the wedding until I learn the exact date of the count's arrival. At least, the banns are posted and Father Bernard invited to officiate."

Speaking her thoughts aloud and directing the boatmen to return them to Les Chênes, she did not notice the pallor of Clotie, who had turned her face aside.

A scant month after his letter arrived, a boat deposited the count at the landing with his boxes and trunks and his bodyservant. They awaited him on the galérie. He came up the stair toward them, unsmiling. Amalie looked at the stern expression on his long, aristocratic face and wondered how she could have forgotten his direct and penetrating gaze. Her heart fluttered with apprehension.

He bowed and lifted her hand to his lips. "Ma'm'selle." With no change of expression, he repeated the coldly correct greeting with Maman, then Clotie.

Amalie felt a twinge of remorse as she saw the painful effort it was for Papa to greet him. Both Papa and Clotie had grown thinner these past weeks. Clotie, in fact, looked unwell—but even more beautiful.

"I trust your journey was pleasant, *m'sieu le comte?*" Of them all, only Madame de l'Ouvrier's face reflected pleasure. Her cheeks were flushed with triumph.

"It was uncomfortable, madame. But I am here, as you see."

"Amalie will show you to your chamber. Then perhaps you will join us in the salon?"

"With pleasure, madame." He bowed.

As Amalie walked ahead of him down the central hall she could hear her own heartbeat. The count followed her without uttering a word, and she could not speak until they had reached the guest chamber. Then she said, in a small voice, "Will this be satisfactory, m'sieu?"

"Assuredly, ma'm'selle. It is a room I have occupied before."

She had expected some sign from him that she really was his choice, but there had been none. When she stood silent, confused, his eyes took on a malicious gleam. "Where is your lively tongue, ma'm'selle?"

"In truth, I am overawed at the prospect of becoming a countess," she admitted.

His eyebrows lifted politely. "But why?"

"And why not, m'sieu? It is a role I had not imagined for myself."

"Indeed?" he mocked her.

She flushed, knowing what she had told him was not true. She had often imagined herself betrothed to him, but the reality was so much less comfortable than the dream!

"I daresay it is a role you will grow into. *Merci,* ma'm'selle, I shall join you directly."

She had been dismissed—like a child. She curtsied, and left him.

The count, having removed his travel-stained clothing and freshened himself with cool water, was allowing his bodyservant to help him into a pale blue coat when Monsieur de l'Ouvrier's servant knocked at his door and, on being admitted, requested that the count wait on his master in his chamber before joining the ladies. The count found his host pacing his room in an agitated fashion.

"Ah, *merci,* m'sieu. I wish to speak to you on a matter too delicate to bring up before my wife and daughters, yet one it is important to me to settle before the—before we proceed—"

When Monsieur de l'Ouvrier's voice stumbled to a halt (he had found himself unable to pronounce "wedding"), the count said, somewhat amused, *"Oui,* m'sieu?"

Monsieur de l'Ouvrier shook a handkerchief out of his sleeve and mopped his brow. "It concerns my daughter—ah, my daughters. Madame and I assumed—that is, we thought you were offering for Ma'm'selle Claudine."

"Indeed, m'sieu?" The faint surprise in the count's polite tone said plainly that he had never entertained such an idea. This was so dismaying a falsehood that Monsieur de l'Ouvrier abandoned all thought of flying in the face of his darling's—not to say his wife's—wishes and, instead, said in a trembling voice, "Amalie is very young, m'sieu. In some ways it is true she is older than her years, but in other ways she may be younger. Madame tells me that is my fault. Be that as it may, you can appreciate that, as her father, I am concerned that she—that you do not—"

The count's amusement deepened. "Have no fear, m'sieu. Her immaturity does not arouse me."

Monsieur de l'Ouvrier flushed darkly. "It is not easy for a father, you understand. I cannot but think of Amalie as my child. Yet I must concede that she is on the verge of young womanhood. I desire her happiness above all else. I trust to your sensibilities, m'sieu, and so I—" He paused, then with difficulty continued, "I relinquish her to you—to your care."

The count bowed.

With formality, Monsieur de l'Ouvrier picked up the signed contract and placed it in his future son-in-law's hand. *"Alors,* shall we join Madame?" he suggested sadly.

Over Madame's excellent stuffed partridges, she tactfully brought up the subject of the wedding date. Amalie listened, sitting quietly between her father and the count and facing Clotie who sat alone on the opposite side of the long table. There was a faint buzzing in Amalie's head; she had little appetite for partridge.

"It should be as soon as possible," the count said.

"I agree, m'sieu." Amalie thought that Maman looked pleased. "Shall we say in a month's time?"

"I very much fear it must be not later than next week, madame."

"Next week!" Madame gasped. *"Mon Dieu,* m'sieu, but that is impossible! It will take longer than that for the invitations to reach some of our guests. We are not living in New Orleans, you know."

"Then I fear we must be married without your guests," the count said imperturbably, "for I must return to New Orleans immediately. I am required to be present at an inquiry into a lamentable affair in which I am, unfortunately, involved."

Papa's eyebrows rose in a way Amalie knew well. "In what way were you involved, m'sieu?"

"It is a long story." The count reached for his wineglass, which he twirled without raising it to his lips. "But it is one I feel obliged to share with you." He fell silent as Madame signaled the two servants standing behind her to begin removing the plates. Not until they had left the dining room did he continue.

"The inquiry will be conducted to determine the facts surrounding an accident which occurred on my voyage down the Mississippi when I left you last. An accident," he added, "for which I was—indirectly, at least—responsible."

"A fatal accident?" Monsieur de l'Ouvrier asked sharply.

"Regrettably, yes."

Amalie felt a tremor pass through her body. She looked across the table at Clotie. Her sister was staring down at her lap, and from the way in which she held her thin, bare arms Amalie guessed her hands were tightly clenched below the linen.

"A peasant I kicked overboard was unfortunately drowned." For an instant all their shocked eyes were on the count's handsome face, but his own gaze did not waver from Papa's as he said, "I had reason, m'sieu, you may be sure."

"Then pray enlighten us," Monsieur de l'Ouvrier said, with grim hauteur. The pinched look had left his face and he sat erect, his eyes challenging the count.

Madame de l'Ouvrier glanced at her wide-eyed daughters. "Perhaps Claudine and Amalie should withdraw?"

"On the contrary, madame," said the count, "I believe your daughters should hear what I have to tell." Still he did not look at Clotie, yet as he began to speak, Amalie's conviction grew that his words were aimed with deadly accuracy at Clotie's heart.

"It happened our first day on the river. Dusk was approaching and we were looking for a likely place to tie up for the preparation of our evening meal on shore, with the object of spending the night, since navigation of the river, as you know, is hazardous after dark. I felt a need for exercise, and left the salon. I was walking around the boat when I came upon a group of peasants squatting on the deck playing cards and drinking rum.

"I stood not far away, enjoying the cool breeze that had sprung up as the sun lowered. One of the peasants was a rather talkative fellow —a 'Cadian by his speech. I was not listening, m'sieu, until I heard your name. Then I was all ears, for, to my surprise, he was telling of an incident I remembered well. Do you recall the night of Madame's remarkable floating entertainment in my honor which was interrupted by a young boor on whom you set your dogs?"

"*Mais, oui!*" exclaimed Monsieur de l'Ouvrier. "But how did he know of that? Who was the man?"

"I believe he was from this bayou."

Amalie's eyes met Clotie's across the candlelit table. Her sister looked quite ill.

"I learned afterward from the inquiries I made that his name was Jacques Broussard," the count continued.

"Ah, *oui,* the trapper. He has a hut a few miles down the bayou from here."

"*Oui?* It was said he was taking a shipment of his furs to New Orleans."

"The trapper," Madame de l'Ouvrier said, on an exhaled breath. "Of course, he knew of the incident. He took the trader in. Later I bought silks for my daughters from him. But pray tell us what happened."

The servants came in with trays of coffee and fruit, and the count did not speak again until Madame had signaled them to leave the room. Then he said, in a quiet voice, "What I overheard I shall not repeat outside of this room, not even to the inquiry. That is a solemn promise, m'sieu, madame. I shall protect your good name."

Amalie looked again at Clotie whose face was white.

"Well, m'sieu?" Madame said in alarm.

"As I said, the fellow was telling how '*le gran' michie*', as he called you, m'sieu, had set his dogs on the peasant's *yanqui* friend and partner who, it turned out, was squatting beside him. Then he said—and I repeat his words as exactly as I can, m'sieu!—he said, 'But he is getting his revenge, *non?* For all the summer he has been meeting *le gran' michie's* pretty daughter in the woods.' Then, m'sieu, he poked *l'américain* in the ribs and cackled!"

The count's voice was still low, but now it was taut with an echo of his rage. "What would you have done, m'sieu? If he had been a gentleman, I could have challenged him. But he was a filthy peasant! And his friends! Rough riverboatmen, adventurers from the *yanqui* territories—not a gentleman in the lot. I will tell you what I did, m'sieu! I walked over and aimed a vicious kick at the man. He was squatting, *n'est-ce pas?* He lost his balance and fell over the side. It was not calculated, you understand? I acted in pure rage.

"Those nearest grabbed but failed to keep him from falling, and his American friend leaped over the side to try to save him. I immediately raised the alarm. But although the boat was turned to shore and tied up while a hunt was launched, neither man was seen again."

A gasp that was like a sob escaped Clotie.

"*Neither* man?" Amalie breathed, appalled.

The count's face hardened. It was the only sign he gave that he heard. "So I must return to New Orleans to explain in the American court what happened."

There was a sharp tinkle of crystal on silver as Claudine's convulsive gesture overturned her wine goblet. For a moment no one moved. Madame de l'Ouvrier was so angry she did not even think to tap her bell, and the red stain crept across the linen unattended. So that was why he had offered for Amalie instead of for Clotie! And now she knew why Claudine had so stubbornly refused to marry him. Refused a count for that peasant! *I should have whipped her,* Madame thought viciously.

Now at last the count was looking at Clotie. Amalie saw his eyes, and shivered.

Clotie was on her feet, pushing back her chair. "I am sorry, Maman—I feel ill," she murmured. Madame rose hastily, but she was too late. Clotie toppled over in a faint.

And then all was pandemonium as Maman at last rang the bell for the servants, and all—with the exception of the count—rushed to bend over Clotie.

Late that night Madame de l'Ouvrier tapped at the connecting door between her boudoir and her husband's chamber, and opened it when she heard his weary voice bid her enter. He sat in his armchair huddled in a damask robe, looking very old.

"Well, madame?"

"She is sleeping now. Amalie is with her. She is *enceinte,* of course."

A grimace of rage passed across his face. "I wish the dogs had torn him to pieces!"

"He is dead, Charles. Do not waste your energies wishing for what is already accomplished. The question is what to do now." She looked as weary as her husband, but not as beaten. "It may not be too late to save her reputation. I have a plan."

He looked up at her in cynical admiration. "You are truly remarkable, Adèle. And what is this plan of yours?"

She lowered herself into the chair opposite him. "It is simplicity itself. The count and countess will take Claudine and me with them to New Orleans. There the two girls will remain in seclusion, and it will be announced that the countess is *enceinte*. I shall arrange everything. Julie is experienced in midwifery and she is trustworthy. When the child is born, Amalie will raise it as her own."

"You are mad," Monsieur de l'Ouvrier said, his tone wearier than before. "In the first place, madame, there will be no wedding."

"I think so. The count has signed the contract in the presence of his lawyers. The banns have been posted. He will not want a scandal any more than we do."

"The count will never agree to take Claudine's by-blow as his own! Suppose she has a son? The bastard of a peasant inherit *m'sieu le comte de Valérun's* title?"

"It will not be the first time a bastard has inherited a title," she said calmly. "Anyway, what is a title in America? I understand the count better than you do, Charles." She leaned forward. "He will not return to France. He will cast his lot with the Americans."

"Never!" exclaimed her husband. "He is a devoted royalist! He has everything to gain from a return of the monarchy."

"Did you not notice his interest in sugar as a new crop in Louisiana? He will become an American planter," she repeated, unmoved.

She had never had the faith in the success of the royalist plotters that sustained her husband. And since the Caudodal coup had failed, and the poor duc d'Enghien had been executed by that monstrous Napoleon, she was convinced that the royalist cause was lost.

"The count needs us as much as we need him," she told her husband. "He needs Les Chênes. And even though Clotie has humiliated him, I think he wants it badly enough to accept it on our terms."

"And you would put a bastard in the position to inherit Les Chênes!" Monsieur de l'Ouvrier exclaimed, looking on his wife with something near dislike. From what ancestor had she got that bourgeois shrewdness that she claimed to find, as well, in the count? Was she right? Did the prospect of owning Les Chênes now weigh more heavily with young Armand than his loyalty to his king? Certainly it must outweigh Armand's pride, or he would not have returned for Clotie's sister.

Fortunately, perhaps, Monsieur de l'Ouvrier's own pride was not great enough to make him insist that his daughters starve, something his wife claimed would happen if he did not allow this advantageous marriage. Greatly depressed, he muttered, "My poor Amalie!"

FIVE

IN SPITE of the short notice given their guests, the wedding of the Count and Countess de Valérun was a beautiful event certain to be long remembered—longer, Madame de l'Ouvrier hoped, than her last disastrous entertainment for the count! (Madame de l'Ouvrier had not complained again about the count's insistence on haste; haste, now, was essential.)

The guests assembled on the broad lawns between the house and the bayou to watch Monsieur de l'Ouvrier give his younger daughter, attended by her beautiful, pale sister, to the young nobleman; and murmured to each other that they had never seen a prettier bride and bridesmaid nor a more handsome groom.

"But the little one has stolen the count from under her sister's nose, n'est-ce pas?"

"Oui, and she is not so pretty, either. But she is the lively one."

After the ceremony, the count and countess, her hand on his arm, climbed the stair to the galérie where the bride paused to toss her bouquet of roses over the railing. (Amalie tossed it straight at Clotie, who did not lift a hand to catch it; Marthe Dupré snatched it just in time to prevent its landing on the grass.) Then the guests filed up the stair and gathered around the long table which had been set out on the galérie and made resplendent with delicacies prepared by Madame de l'Ouvrier's excellent cook.

The revelries continued until long after dark. At about ten o'clock, some gentlemen in their cups decided to escort the bride and groom to the nuptial chamber. This was done with great ceremony and many ribald jokes. Amalie, who had moved through the past week in a daze, found when the door had been closed on their well-wishers that she was trembling. She could not look at the one great bed which had been prepared for them in the garlanded guest room.

Except for that one moment when she had shown him to his chamber on his arrival, she had not been alone with Monsieur Armand, as she must begin to think of him now. He had spent his days hunting or exploring the plantation, and his evenings with her father and his friends. So Amalie stood just inside the nuptial chamber in her white satin and lace, brave but trembling, unable to take another step.

Monsieur Armand was smiling. "Ring for your servant," he said kindly, "and go to bed. It will be very late when I retire."

He opened the shuttered long windows to the galérie and slipped out to go back to the revelries, and Amalie did as he suggested.

For a long time after Julie had left her—how long Amalie could not guess—she lay alone in the strange bed and listened to the mingling of voices and laughter and music as her guests celebrated her wedding. When there was a lull she could hear snatches of an even livelier celebration in progress at the distant slave quarters.

She wakened to find the sun was high on the shuttered windows. All was quiet. She was still alone, uncertain whether the count had come and gone.

"So I do not know whether I am truly married, or not," she confided to Clotie later, when they had a moment together during the confusion of departing guests, many of whom had come so far they had been obliged to stay overnight, and of seeing to the packing of her wedding gifts and the last-minute toiletries they needed for their journey.

Clotie gave her a quick, sharp look, then with a little acid laugh that did not sound at all like the Clotie Amalie knew, said, "*Now* who is the goose?" These days Clotie was stony-faced, pale as wax, and if she spoke at all, spoke bitterly.

Madame de l'Ouvrier's belongings, as well as her daughters', were being packed and made ready for the boat. Somehow that fact had escaped the attention of the count until that evening when, the last guest having departed, the family was dining alone.

"Les Chênes is our own again," Monsieur de l'Ouvrier said, with relief. "Would you not like to postpone your journey, m'sieu, and accompany me once more on a collecting expedition into the swamp?" He looked wistfully, not at the count, but at Amalie.

"I regret that it is not possible, m'sieu."

"You must forget your absorbing interest in botany, Charles, while I am away," Madame chided him, "or you will find the slaves taking every advantage of your negligence."

"I did not know you were planning to be away, madame," the count said mildly.

She looked at him in surprise. "But I am accompanying you to New Orleans, of course."

"I do not think that wise, madame."

Two red spots appeared on her cheeks. "But my daughters will need me. Clotie—"

"—will be in excellent hands, I can assure you." At this, Clotie raised her eyes and cast a venomous glance at him. "You are needed more urgently here, madame, for I am convinced that the smooth running of affairs at Les Chênes is due to your skilled hand on the reins. M'sieu is a scientist, after all," he said, with a diplomatic bow to Monsieur de l'Ouvrier. "He needs you—and I need not tell you—"

"But *Clotie*—"

"You can serve your daughters best by remaining here, madame. Les Chênes is important to them, *n'est-ce pas?*"

Monsieur de l'Ouvrier, his face pale and aloof, did not dispute what the count said.

Maman's cheeks were flaming. "Amalie—Clotie—you may be excused. We have business to discuss with the count before you leave in the morning."

Once again Amalie lay alone in her marriage bed, and this time she felt very lonely, indeed. She would have liked to go and crawl in beside Clotie, but that did not seem quite proper now that she was a married woman.

The talk at the front of the house continued for a long time. Then Amalie heard the sound of Maman's heels going to Clotie's room. She listened to the low murmur of their voices for what seemed an hour. Still the count did not come. After a while a deep silence fell on the house. Once she thought she heard the count's step on the galérie outside her windows, but he did not come to her.

After a time she realized that he was not coming. She stared into the darkness, wide awake, her thoughts shuttling back and forth in rhythm with the monotonous shrilling of the cicadas that now filled the empty night. Apparently marriage was more complicated than she had realized.

It was then that her thoughts began to dwell uneasily on the curious way in which Monsieur Armand seemed to be speaking directly to Clotie even though he was pointedly ignoring her. And the way in which Clotie all the while was directing murderous looks at the count. Amalie could not blame Clotie for hating Monsieur Armand for what had happened, or the count for being furious at finding himself forced to help protect Clotie from her own folly. But with certain prescience, Amalie saw that it was not going to be very comfortable having Clotie in her house.

The next morning was fair, but the leave-taking at the landing was as damp as if a raincloud had blown, trailing its tears, over the plantation. Amalie wept as she threw herself into her father's ever-indulgent arms, and he left sparkles in her dark hair. She wept with her mother as Maman, exhausted from the incredible task she had performed in staging the wedding in so short a time, instructed her that her first duty on arriving in the city—and Clotie's—was to call on the sisters who were their former mentors at the convent.

"See that you faithfully attend mass," she begged them.

Julie and Madi wept loudly at leaving their families—for they were to wait on Amalie and Clotie in their new home—and the other servants who had gathered on the bank for farewells were all wailing with them.

Only Clotie and the count were dry-eyed—and Jean-Baptiste, the count's citified bodyservant, who stood aside looking down his nose at the lachrymose scene.

Monsieur Armand kissed Maman's hand and Papa's cheeks. "I shall bring your daughters back to Les Chênes in one year's time," he promised. "Meanwhile, do not distress yourselves. They will be kept safe from harm, and I can assure you they will be content, for the city offers many distractions. I will send you word of their welfare whenever the opportunity presents itself."

"*Merci,* m'sieu," they told him, wiping their eyes.

The trunks and boxes were loaded, the boatmen had taken up their oars and poles and the travelers their places beneath the canopy. Soon the flatboat was being propelled up the still, currentless bayou toward that point where it had once been joined with the Mississippi River. Until Les Chênes disappeared around the bend, Amalie gazed back at the sad little group at the landing.

"*Alors,*" said the count, then, "with that tearful parting behind us, let us dry our eyes. Are you not anticipating your new life in New Orleans as my countess, madame?"

"If I can believe it, m'sieu," Amalie said. "It still seems to me that we must return to Maman and Papa before nightfall."

"Then let us pretend that we are on a day's outing. We are provided with the amenities of an excellent picnic luncheon, thanks to Madame de l'Ouvrier's thoughtfulness, and we can tie up at the bank whenever we are hungry. Does that strike you as a pleasant prospect, Ma'm'selle Claudine?"

Clotie's eyes were hostile. "Nothing strikes me as a pleasant prospect, m'sieu."

"That is a pity." Amalie winced at the cold indifference his tone conveyed. It said plainly that Clotie had only herself to blame for her unhappiness.

Clotie took his meaning, too, for she turned her head sharply away.

But Amalie could not take her eyes from her husband. He was dressed informally for the journey in pantaloons and a loose peasant-style shirt. His head was bare and the damp air made his hair curl slightly over his forehead. As a result, his long face looked younger, less formidable and, Amalie thought, quite handsome.

And now, after getting no more than *oui* or *non* from Clotie, he began ignoring her and directing his questions—and all the force of his attention—at Amalie. He asked about Les Chênes and about their neighbors. Amalie warmed to his encouraging gaze and was soon chattering artlessly, quite like herself. Clotie sat aloof, now and then casting scornful looks their way.

Soon, with easy laughter, Amalie and Monsieur Armand were exchanging droll stories about their experiences on Monsieur de l'Ouvrier's obsessive excursions into the swamp for his specimens, and the morning passed swiftly. At midday, the boatmen tied up beside a grassy bank shaded by live oaks, and helped them ashore. Their servants laid out the really sumptuous repast Maman had sent with them, and the count's servant produced a bottle of wine and some glasses.

The count, sitting relaxed on the canvas that had been spread for them, with the sun and shadow from the huge old live oak playing on his face, raised his glass to Amalie. "To our long and happy marriage, madame!"

Amalie flushed, but her pleasure was tempered by the queer edge she thought she heard in his voice. Once again she had the uncomfortable impression that he was speaking through her to Clotie.

After lunch the heat climbed. In spite of the canopy's shade, it was very warm on the flatboat. The travelers dozed in their chairs while Julie and Madi stretched themselves out unself-consciously on the deck and slept. The boatmen poled with indolent movements, singing softly. By late afternoon, when the sun was low and the heat waning, they were approaching the settlement on higher ground between the bayou's end and the west bank of the Mississippi.

The count directed the boatmen to tie up at the landing before a plantation house on their right. It was a house smaller and possibly older than Les Chênes, its first story built of brick and the upper story of clapboard, in the early settlers' fashion, with a hip roof and a double galérie across the front. Connected by a covered walkway to the right was a smaller building, probably, Amalie thought, a *garçonnière* such as many of their neighbors built as independent sleeping quarters for the young sons of the family.

Servants ran down to the bank to help them come ashore. Following them at a leisurely pace came a man in dark clothing and a woman in a pale floating gown. They looked vaguely familiar, and Amalie realized belatedly that these were friends of the count's who had attended their wedding. Several children ran ahead of the couple, coming to stare shyly as the travelers stepped from the flatboat to the landing.

"*Bonjour, bonjour!*" the count greeted them.

The smallest of the girls edged closer to Clotie and said, "You are very pretty, countess."

Clotie drew in her breath sharply, and her teeth caught her upper lip. Before Amalie could speak, the count had taken her hand and was saying, "This is *ma petite comtesse, la comtesse* Amalie, and her sister, Ma'm'selle Claudine. May I present—let me see, now—Robert, Denise, Claire, Jeanne and—and—"

With giggles, the children waited for him to remember their names, refusing to enlighten him. It was obviously a game that had been played before.

"I know there are eight LeClercs," Monsieur Armand told Amalie, striking his forehead in mock despair. "Two great boys, and six little ones of assorted sexes—"

"You forgot me!" the smallest cried in triumph.

"And Jeanne-Marie!"

The children's parents came up, laughing, a small, dark man with a beard, and his round little wife.

"Welcome to Sundown, m'sieu and madame—and ma'm'selle." Gallantly, Monsieur LeClerc lifted Clotie's hand to his lips.

Madame LeClerc tucked a plump arm comfortably through Amalie's. "You are hot and hungry, I suspect. Come with me and freshen yourselves for dinner, which will be served presently." She looked over her shoulder to smile at the count, and said, "M'sieu Armand, we can put Madame and Ma'm'selle in one of the girls' rooms and offer you a bed in the *garçonnière,* if that will be satisfactory. There are so many of us," she apologized, with a charming shrug.

"*Merci,* madame, that will be quite satisfactory," the count assured her.

So Amalie was to be once more separated from her husband.

It was a happy, noisy household that they found themselves joining for the night. After an excellent dinner around the long table, Monsieur LeClerc and the count retired to Monsieur LeClerc's study for a private talk. Amalie and Clotie retired to their room with their servants, escorted by Madame LeClerc and the entranced little girls who chattered and exclaimed over their guests' possessions until their mother ordered them to bed.

"*M'sieu le comte* and my husband have been intimate friends since their school days in Paris," Madame LeClerc said, by way of apology. "To our children, he is an indulgent uncle."

Alone at last with their servants, Amalie and Clotie prepared for bed. Julie had cared for both girls as children and was still inclined to treat them as her young charges, but Madi was ten years younger, still little more than a girl herself.

As she brushed Clotie's long hair, Madi remarked, "M'selle Clotie, you looks peaked."

"I feel peaked, Madi."

"You say, I fin' a voodoo woman in New Orleans."

"Shut you' mouth, you Madi," Julie scolded her. "M'selle Clotie don' want no potion."

"Did I say potion? A voodoo womans—"

"I *want* my baby, Madi," Clotie said firmly.

"I only said—"

"You said enough!" Julie snapped, and Madi shrugged.

Amalie listened without commenting. They would need Madi's and Julie's help in the deception on which they were embarking. Julie was wise and knowledgeable and Amalie trusted her completely, but she wondered how much they could depend on Madi.

"It is a strange marriage, is it not, Clotie?" she asked, after Julie and Madi had left them for the slave quarters, and they lay side by side in the high canopied bed. "I have been married three days and have yet to spend a night with my husband."

Clotie did not answer, but Amalie knew she was not asleep.

Moonlight came through the slatted shutters at the window, but the objects in the unfamiliar room—the faint gleam from a brass candlestick on a table, the black recess she knew was a small shrine beside the armoire on the opposite wall—were veiled by the mosquito *baire* drawn around their bed. All Amalie could see of Clotie was the dark blur of her hair on the white pillow beside her.

After a long silence, Clotie spoke. "I want a promise from you, Amalie."

"What is it?" Amalie asked sleepily, for she had been about to drift into dreaming.

"I must never be separated from my child."

"But of course not, Clotie. You are to live with us. It is all settled."

"When I looked at little Robert, I thought, 'Deneez's son will be like him.' I could not bear to be separated from Deneez's son. You must promise that you will always keep me with you, no matter what the count wants. I—I could not bear—"

"Oh, Clotie, you dear goose! Of course you shall stay with us as long as you want. But you are so lovely—you will find a fine husband in New Orleans, I think."

"I shall never marry. I have given myself to Deneez. It is not something one can take back, you know. I shall always belong to him."

Amalie was silent now and thoughtful. That feeling of *belonging*— would she one day feel she truly belonged to Monsieur Armand? All at once she wished passionately for the journey to be over. In New Orleans, surely, her new life would begin.

Monsieur LeClerc, acting on instructions from the count, had arranged for their passage on a flatboat carrying several other passengers down to New Orleans the next day. "It is a sturdy boat, about fifteen feet wide and sixty feet long," he told them. "There is a small bedroom for the ladies, and since there are no other women passengers, the countess and Ma'm'selle will be quite comfortable. You, *m'sieu le comte,* can share the owner's cabin. The other men will sleep in the small lounge or on deck. Since you will be spending only one night on the river, it should not be too bad."

Monsieur Armand agreed that it was satisfactory, and shortly after breakfast they bade their hostess and her children farewell and climbed into Monsieur LeClerc's carriage to be taken to the landing on the river.

Being carried down the Mississippi current on a sixty-foot barge was different from being poled along a stagnant bayou on their cano-pied flatboat. To Amalie's delight, the count stayed by their side, probably because she and Clotie were viewed with much interest and curiosity by the other men on the barge. He was so attentive that by late afternoon, Amalie was quite transported.

When the count had drawn a little apart in conversation with a planter who was telling him he had plowed under his indigo, and was planting the watery land back of his fields with rice, she whispered to Clotie, "Is not M'sieu Armand charming, Clotie?"

"Oh, quite charming," Clotie said bitterly, "but when I look at him I see only the man who murdered my Deneez."

"Clotie!"

Clotie looked darkly down at the swirling yellow current which was carrying them down the river. "It must have been very near here that he committed that foul crime."

Amalie heard a step and looked up to see the count returning to them. She knew by the cold fury in his eyes that he had overheard Clotie.

"I can show you the very spot, if that is your pleasure, ma'm'selle."

Clotie drew in her breath sharply. She and the count looked at each other. "I am going to be sick," Clotie said, in a voice tight with rage, and fled into the little bedroom.

Amalie lifted reproachful eyes to her husband.

"Go to your sister, madame," he said, and turned back to the rice planter.

SIX

As THEY APPROACHED New Orleans on the second day, Amalie began to feel a tingling anticipation. She did not remember so many planta-tion homes on the river. Around each serpentine bend they came upon a new one, or one a-building. In late afternoon they floated into the crescent around which the city was built, and saw above the greensward of the levee the steep roofs of the line of houses facing it.

"There is the convent, Clotie!" Amalie cried. "And I can see the towers of St. Louis!"

Clotie looked indifferently at the cityscape which seemed to be gliding toward them. They passed two barques at anchor—one flying a Spanish flag, the other the less familiar stars and stripes of America —and were rowed in to tie up beside a line of barges and flatboats at the landing.

The count immediately hired a carriage to take them to the house he occupied on the rue Bourbon. It was a street of two- and three-story buildings with shops at the ground level. Amalie saw a cabinet-maker's shop—the cabinetmaker, a man of color, was working in full view of passersby—a wigmaker's, a shoemaker's. The odor of roasting coffee was strong and beneath it were layers of scents, the fragrance of flowers and of other things less pleasant.

Through the narrow street moved a few carriages and many pedestrians, in a fascinating variety of attire. Among them Amalie saw dandies in fashionable Parisian dress, a Spanish woman wearing a mantilla accompanying two dark-eyed children, and men in the rough dress worn by the boatmen of their flatboat. Some of the latter had short knives stuck in their belts. There were many light-colored negroes on the street and most of the women were wearing bright-colored turbans, giving the scene a resemblance to a ragged flower garden. Amalie was constantly pinching Clotie's arm and crying, "Look!"

Down the street ahead of them, a young servant leaned over an ironwork galérie to empty a bucket of slops into the wooden gutter running along the banquette.

Clotie wrinkled her nose. "I have always thought New Orleans a dirty, smelly place," she said, with disdain.

"It is that, ma'm'selle," the count agreed in an amused voice, "but it has its delights."

Monsieur Armand's house was a two-story building with a lacy railing on the galérie hanging over the banquette. Beneath the galérie was the shop of a wine merchant and importer. "My friend," Monsieur Armand told them, "who owns the building. His family resides at his plantation on the river below the city." A shop sign proclaiming it to be *La Rose* and picturing a full-blown flower hung over the banquette.

They passed through the porte cochère into a courtyard paved with brick. From the courtyard, stairs ascended on each side to the living quarters. Small galéries beneath the windows looking down on the court held pots of bright-blooming flowers. Other pots stood around the well.

"It is a pleasant place, m'sieu," Amalie told her husband, and he smiled at her.

Clotie said nothing.

As they dismounted from the carriage, Monsieur Armand's servants ran out from the kitchen at the rear of the court. There were three: a light brown woman wearing a towering blue turban which made her look even taller than she was, a young girl with short-clipped hair and a slender boy.

After returning their greetings, Monsieur Armand told them, "This is your new mistress, *la comtesse* Amalie, and her sister, Ma'm'selle Claudine. Dulcie keeps my house," he explained to Amalie, "and these are her helpers. Dulcie, take care of Madame's servants and show them where they will sleep. Callou," he addressed the grinning boy, "you take the carriage and return to the landing for our trunks. You will find Jean-Baptiste guarding them."

"*Oui, michie.*" The boy jumped up beside the driver of the carriage with alacrity.

The tall housekeeper was dignified, yet warm. "Ah, *la petite comtesse!*" she exclaimed in a deep, rich voice. "It is a happy day when M'sieu Armand takes a bride! And m'selle—*que belle!*"

"*Merci*, Dulcie," Amalie said, liking her. "Julie was once my nurse. She can tell you what we require, she and Madi, who is my sister's bodyservant. Go with Dulcie now," she told them. "We will not need you until the trunks arrive."

The count was already at the foot of the stair on their left. "This way," he said.

The little glow Amalie had felt at hearing herself introduced as "*la comtesse*" was enhanced by her inspection of the house of which she was now mistress and which she thought furnished in excellent taste, but the glow quickly faded when she discovered that she and Clotie were to sleep in adjoining rooms, while the count "for the present" would remain in his bachelor's suite in the other wing of the house.

When the count informed her further that he would be dining out that evening, her disappointment deepened to a feeling of insecurity. So it was with uncharacteristic timidity that, when Monsieur Armand wanted to know if she required anything, she asked if he owned a carriage.

"You wish to go out?" He seemed surprised.

"Tomorrow. Clotie and I must call at the convent."

"But, of course. Callou will drive you. It is not far to walk, if you prefer, but if you do that, you must take Callou with you as an escort."

"*Merci,* m'sieu."

He kissed her hand and Clotie's and left them for his private rooms.

They were served a light meal by Callou and the girl, whose name was Estée. Afterward, Clotie said she felt unwell and went to her room. For a time Amalie amused herself by looking down on the busy street below the salon windows. Up and down the rue Bourbon, other families were taking the air on their galéries, calling to each other across the narrow street. Amalie noted more than a few curious glances directed her way, and felt a stirring of alarm. She and Clotie would have to be very careful, or their secret would be common knowledge in the city. The sense of danger stimulated her, and she felt not at all sleepy.

When she went at last to her chamber, Julie had put away her clothing and laid out her silver brush and comb. The furniture was richly gilt and the posts of the pretty bed reached almost to the high ceiling. Although the chamber was smaller than her plantation room, it seemed to her luxurious. Julie, however, was gloomy. "How do you like m'sieu's servants?" Amalie asked her, after a few moments of silence.

"They fine peoples."

"Will they keep our secret?"

"I believe *oui.*" But her face was long.

"What's the matter? Don't you like your quarters?"

"It be a nice house," Julie conceded, "but it not Les Chênes."

"You're homesick, Julie!"

"*Oui,*" Julie sighed. "But you an' M'selle Clotie goin' need me."

That was very true, thought Amalie, who was not in the least homesick.

Nevertheless, lying alone in her bed after Julie had left her, Amalie found it difficult to sleep. Her window looked down on the court. Through it she could hear the clip-clop of horses and the squeak of wheels as carriages passed the porte cochère. There were other sounds she could not identify. Occasionally, she heard shouts, some in laughter and good humor, some obviously quarrelsome.

It was excitingly different from Les Chênes, where the noises one went to sleep by were peaceful and monotonous—the shrill buzz of the cicadas, the chorus of frogs from the bayous, and the occasional keening of a mosquito trying to find a way through the gauze *baire*. The sounds of the city were strange to her and not at all a summons to dreams. She could hear distant music so far away she could not distinguish a melody, only an incessant beating of drums such as sometimes came from the slave quarters at Les Chênes but that heard here, in this unfamiliar setting, was disturbing in a not unpleasant way.

The sounds brought her a sensation of teeming activity on the streets around her. It was *life* she heard out there. It would be her life now, and she was filled with such a ravening appetite for it that she was sure she would not sleep. But she did not hear the count return to his rooms across the court.

The next afternoon Amalie requested that the carriage be brought, and she and Clotie prepared themselves to call on their friends at the convent. The way was crowded and lively, noisy with hawkers. A negro woman they passed carried a great basket of rolls on her head. Another chanted: "Fresh strawberries for sale."

At the convent they found that the Reverend Mother was entertaining a distinguished guest in the garden. *M'sieu le vice-presidente,*" Sister Marie who had admitted them confided, eyes sparkling, "is visiting our city from Washington! When she is free, the Reverend Mother will want to give you both her blessing. While you wait, I will send some of your friends who are still here."

Amalie and Clotie embraced the two girls with whom they had shared many of the joys and trials of their days of catechism and lessons. Candide and Dorée had been excused from their classes to come to the visiting room. They were both properly impressed by Amalie's marriage to the count, but as soon as Sister Marie left them alone, Candide suggested they go upstairs. "We can look down on the garden from my room," she whispered.

"*Ma foi,* Candide, she will see us!"

"Not if we take care."

It was like old times and for a few moments, as they went quietly up the stair, Amalie thought Clotie was herself again. Candide raised her window slowly. The Reverend Mother sat with the sister who

was her aide at a table on the grass with her back to them. Facing
them were two gentlemen, one in a gleaming white linen suit, the
other a smaller man in dark clothing.

"He is M'sieu Burr, a famous American duelist," Candide whispered.

"Which one?" Amalie was looking at the smaller of the two men
with interest. His expression was lively and she thought him almost
as handsome as the count, in a different way.

"The small man in black. My brother said he killed a man in
Washington."

At that moment the man in black glanced up and saw the girls.
Laughter shone in his eyes, the most expressive dark eyes Amalie
had ever seen. He raised his finger casually to his lips, signaling his
complicity, although he did not miss a beat of what he was telling the
Reverend Mother. "—And so we conclude that war with Spain is certain," Amalie heard him say, "and when it comes, we are prepared to
liberate Mexico."

"We would not be sorry for that, m'sieu," the Reverend Mother
replied, "since Spain is now taxing the church severely." She rose,
and the four girls quickly moved away from the window.

"Be quick!" Candide cautioned them as they hurried back down to
the visiting room. When the little party passed in the hall, the girls
were sitting primly in their chairs. As he went by the door, Monsieur
Burr glanced into the room, saw them, and winked.

The girls stifled their laughter as the Reverend Mother appeared in
the doorway and came forward to greet them and give them her
blessing.

"Isn't it exciting?" Amalie cried, when she and Clotie were in the
carriage returning to the rue Bourbon.

"What?" Clotie said, the weary indifference back in her voice.

"Everything!" Amalie knew she could not explain what she felt,
but she tried. "It is like leaving the quiet bayou to enter the swift,
strong current of the river. It is here that things are happening, Clotie. Nothing ever happens on the bayou."

"Oh, doesn't it?" Clotie said, with that bitter twist her pretty lips
so often had these days.

Nevertheless, she seemed as intrigued as Amalie was when they
entered the house on the rue Bourbon and found they had a caller, a
fashionably dressed young woman of twenty-five or -six, who rose
from a chair to greet them with outstretched hands.

"Welcome to New Orleans! I am a friend of your husband, *madame la comtesse*," she said, in a golden voice. "I am Madame Héloise Amboy." She had an arresting face, of a beauty that was compelling although unconventional. Her dark hair grew low on her forehead, drawing attention to eyes that sparkled with wit. Her chin was somewhat too pointed, and there were two dimples beside her mouth. "The count has asked me to help him introduce you and your sister to society, and I have come to invite you to a ball."

"*Merci*, madame. You are very kind." Amalie rang for coffees before sitting down.

There was curiosity and—was it amusement?—in Madame Amboy's lively eyes as she looked from Amalie to Clotie and back again, observing, "You are a very young countess."

"I am nearly sixteen, madame," Amalie said, deciding that she did not like Madame Amboy.

"And, I was going to add," Madame Amboy said gently, "a very pretty one. As for you, Ma'm'selle Claudine, our young Creole gentlemen will surely lose their hearts to you."

Clotie flushed and said in a controlled voice, "*Merci*, madame."

Monsieur Armand entered the salon, saying, "Ah, you are here, Madame Héloise! You have met my family?"

"*Oui*, and I applaud your good judgment. Madame and Ma'm'selle will have a great success here where we all enjoy pretty new faces. It is arranged that you will attend the ball, then?"

"Assuredly," the count answered for them.

"And what did you discover at the Cabildo about your inquiry, m'sieu?"

"It is postponed again, for lack of evidence. They have not yet found the victims, nor any boatman who was on the deck at the time of the accident."

Clotie stood abruptly. "If you will excuse me, Madame Amboy?"

The count's expression hardened as she left the salon, but he said nothing.

"My sister is still feeling unwell after our trip," Amalie apologized for her. But she was unhappily busy with another thought. Madame Amboy had known that the count was spending today at the Cabildo —and she, Amalie, had not. And Madame Amboy had known unerringly which of them to address as *madame la comtesse*. There was only one conclusion to be drawn. The count had rushed off last evening to dine with Madame Amboy, leaving his bride alone with her sister.

"You paid your respects to the Reverend Mother this afternoon?" he was asking her now.

"*Oui.*" With an effort she concealed her jealous hurt. "The American vice-president, M'sieu Burr, was visiting her."

"The *former* vice-president Burr," Monsieur Armand corrected her.

"We heard talk of a war with Spain," Amalie ventured.

Madame Amboy shrugged. "There has been talk of war with Spain for years. But is M'sieu Burr not charming? He speaks very good French."

"It is the Americans who want war," Monsieur Armand said. "They have the port they needed, but now that they have Louisiana, they want the Floridas, too."

"And Texas," Madame said with a laugh. "But I think our Spanish friends would like to see the Cabildo fly the Spanish flag again, *n'est-ce pas?*"

"They might jump into the fray on the other side," he agreed. "But wouldn't a Spanish governor be better than being overrun by these sharp-trading Yankee boors?"

"Well, I would not welcome war, with my husband in Paris, and no plantation to which I could flee!"

"She can always flee with us to Les Chênes, eh, *ma petite?*"

"But, of course," Amalie said politely.

"You are too kind." Laughing, Madame Amboy rose. "I must go. I will see you at the ball, then. *Au revoir.*"

"*Au revoir,* madame." He had called her "Héloise," Amalie remembered. Oh, most definitely she disliked Madame Amboy!

Clotie did not reappear for dinner, and Amalie dined alone with her husband, who received her apologies for Clotie with a narrow-eyed reserve. They sat at opposite ends of the long table, with candles burning between them and Callou passing the silver dishes. Monsieur Armand's thoughts seemed elsewhere, and she saw with chagrin that the light chatter with which she had amused him on his first visit to Les Chênes did not engage his interest now.

After dinner the count left the house and Amalie retired to her chamber in tears, wondering what was wrong with her that her new husband left her company as soon as he could.

SEVEN

THE DAY of the ball advanced swiftly. Amalie and Clotie were at breakfast when Monsieur Armand strode into the dining room, looking cheerful, and announced, "I have engaged a hairdresser to come this afternoon to design coiffures for both of you for the ball tonight." He took his place at the head of the table and gestured to Callou to pour his *café au lait*.

Clotie, who habitually excused herself when the count entered the dining room, was apparently as intrigued as Amalie was, for she remained in her place.

"She is a free woman of color," the count continued, buttering a roll, "who, I am told, dresses the hair of half the women of society."

"Then I am surprised she was free today," Amalie observed.

"Ah, but I am paying her well," Monsieur Armand said, smiling at her. "I want *ma petite comtesse* and her sister to look their best."

Amalie's heart turned over. She could not help it when he smiled at her like that. She began asking eager questions.

"All New Orleans will be there," he told them, "including our American governor and his Creole bride."

"Oh, Clotie, perhaps we shall see Lisette—and Renée—"

"—and Isabelle," Clotie put in, a slight flush warming her pale cheeks.

"They are older girls who were at the convent with us, and are now married," Amalie told her husband.

"If they are in society, you will see them," the count promised, "unless they are ill or *enceinte*."

Clotie's head jerked up and she coldly excused herself. But later in the day she joined Amalie as, with the help of Julie and Madi, they pulled out their dresses once again, debating which to wear to the ball. Clotie was refusing to wear the blue silk that was so becoming to her.

"I shall never wear it again," she said, sadly, "because it is the color Deneez chose for me." And although Amalie pointed out that she did not have that wide a choice of gowns suitable for a ball, Clotie was adamant.

"No matter," Julie told Amalie darkly, after Clotie had left them. "I don' b'lieve M'selle Clotie goin' to many more balls."

"Why not?" Amalie was engrossed in her own reflection in the mirror, wondering if the hairdresser would be able to make her look older.

"M'selle too thin, but her *waist* thick."

For a moment Amalie did not understand. Then her eyes met Julie's in the mirror which sat on her dressing table, and she exclaimed, "Already?"

But there was not time to think about Clotie's figure now, nor to wonder if the count's remark at breakfast had been an intentional jibe, for the hairdresser had arrived. She was a slim young woman with skin like pale honey and lustrous eyes that slanted up at the outer corners. Her hair was completely covered by the *tignon* of the free woman of color, made of a gold-tone cloth and wrapped around her head in a turban that towered higher than Dulcie's. She was not beautiful, but she carried herself as if she were. In repose, her lips curled in an expression that hinted at disdain, but when she smiled, Amalie felt a blaze of warmth.

"*Madame la comtesse,*" the woman said, with a brief inclination of her head on its slender neck. Her French was nearly perfect. "I am Madame Laval, at your service. Your husband, *m'sieu le comte,* engaged me to prepare your coiffure for the ball."

Somewhat intimidated, Amalie replied, "*Oui,* madame. I believe you were engaged for my sister, also?"

"*Mais, oui, madame la comtesse,* but I will do your hair first." She turned to Julie, who was regarding her with suspicion, and told her coolly what she would need. Julie gave Amalie a look of outrage before she left the room.

"This is your first ball, madame?"

"*Mais, non,*" Amalie said quickly. "We have many balls and entertainments on the bayou."

"But your first ball in New Orleans, *n'est-ce pas?*"

Amalie looked sharply at the hairdresser to see if she would encounter the amusement she thought she had seen in Madame Amboy's eyes. But the octoroon's expression was one of warm interest. "*Oui,*" Amalie admitted.

"Then you have not seen the jeeg, I am certain."

"It is a dance?" Amalie asked doubtfully. "How many in a set? Or is it like the *valse?*"

The hairdresser laughed. "It is very unlike the *valse,* madame. It is a dance *les américains* have brought with them. It goes hippety-hop— like this!" With her arms at her sides and her feet twinkling, Madame Laval jigged around the chamber to an imaginary lively tune so comically that Amalie's composure broke up in giggles.

"Will I see anything like that tonight, I wonder?"

"Of a certainty, madame, for the governor and his lady will be there and the governor, of course, is American."

"I should be forced to refuse even the governor, if he asks me to jig!" Amalie declared.

"That is very wise of you, madame, for many criticize the governor's lady for dancing in the American fashion. Since you are new to New Orleans society, you would be well advised to 'make tapestry' when the jeeg or the reel is played. Our ladies prefer the *valse* or the *courante.*"

"My maman thinks even the *valse* a trifle naughty."

"Your maman is an émigré, *non?* They cling to the old ways, isn't it so?" The hairdresser's smile invited Amalie to share her amusement.

Julie returned to the room then, and Madame Laval turned her attention to Amalie's hair. Amalie now felt enough self-confidence to request a style that would not be too *jeune fille.*

"If Madame will show me the dress she plans to wear," suggested the hairdresser, and the next forty-five minutes were passed in the pleasant activity of creating a style that caused Amalie to regard herself with secret delight. Clotie came in to watch and to admire while she waited her turn.

As she worked, Madame Laval chattered about the ball. "I hope it does not rain, madame. Are you and Ma'm'selle prepared if it does? You will walk, of course. The Salle d'Orleans is scarcely a square and a half away."

"Indeed? We have raincloaks."

"And boots? If it rains, you must pin up your skirts and have your servant carry your shoes and a fresh pair of stockings. You will find the ladies washing their feet and putting on fresh apparel in their retiring rooms if the banquettes are muddy."

"*Merci* for your thoughtful advice, Madame Laval. Julie, you will accompany us. Take fresh stockings both for Ma'm'selle Clotie and for me."

Julie made a noise that sounded like "Hmmf!"

Later, when Madame Laval was closeted with Clotie in her room, Julie expressed herself more fully. "Why she talk like a fine lady an' give me orders?"

"She is a free woman of color, Julie."

"She too free."

"She told me how things are done here," Amalie pointed out. "Things my husband has neglected to tell me." She could not keep the reproach from her voice, and she caught Julie looking sharply at her in her mirror.

When she was dressed, Amalie went into Clotie's room. Her sister was a vision of loveliness, all in white, with fragrant blossoms woven into the braids that crowned her head, and from which soft curls escaped. Below the dark hair her skin looked as waxen white as the blossoms.

"Oh, Clotie, how beautiful!"

Clotie was looking into her mirror with a melancholy expression. "It is disgusting," she said at last, "that I can look like this. It is disgusting that I can even think of going to a ball—and *escorted by Deneez's murderer!*"

Amalie sighed. She was getting very tired of hearing Monsieur Armand called a murderer. But when she saw tears filling Clotie's beautiful eyes, her heart softened. She put her arms around her sister and touched her cheek with her own. "Pretend you are having a good time," she said, "and, who knows, perhaps you will."

Clotie's soft mouth tightened. "I do it only to protect my child's name."

It did not rain. They descended the stair and went in a little procession across the court and through the porte cochère to the street. Callou led the way, carrying a lantern and rainboots for his master—for it was not at all certain the banquette would still be dry when they left the ball. After Callou came Julie, carrying rain apparel for her young mistresses; then Clotie and Amalie, with the count carrying another lantern in the rear.

Monsieur Armand, in his close-fitting white pantaloons and pale blue coat, quite dazzled Amalie, so she was not surprised when the three of them created a little stir entering the ballroom. Then she began distinguishing murmured words: "—Ravishing—enchanting—a true Creole beauty, the countess—" They were talking about Clotie, of course; they thought *she* was the countess! Amalie's heart sank to the tips of her little satin shoes.

But the count drew Amalie's arm through his and guided her to an imposing-looking gentleman standing with a sparkling young Creole woman, leaving Clotie to follow beside them. The count bowed.

"Governor and Madame Claiborne, may I present my wife, Amalie, *la comtesse de Valérun?*" In the total silence that fell around them, the count stood aside and, indicating Clotie, added, "—and her sister, Ma'm'selle de l'Ouvrier?"

Everyone began talking at once as Amalie and Clotie curtsied. Amalie heard a young man near her say, "He said 'ma'm'selle!' Did you hear?" All at once they were surrounded by young men wanting to be presented to Clotie. It was the kind of social success every girl dreams about; but through it all, Clotie kept her distant, slightly melancholy air, obviously unimpressed—which only seemed to inflame her admirers the more.

Amalie watched her sister with vexation. Madame Laval's elaborate hairdress had not helped, after all. Probably all New Orleans was asking itself, "Why the little one? Why not her beautiful sister?"

It was an unworthy thought. How could she be jealous of poor dear Clotie? If only Monsieur Armand had once, just once taken her in his arms, it would be easier to bear.

Nevertheless, Amalie had her own success, with the affectionate phrase *"la petite comtesse"* on everyone's lips. It was a memorable evening—the glittering chandeliers of crystal blazing with hundreds of candles, the orchestra playing delicate airs, the beautiful clothes of the dancers moving in stately rhythms with courtly manners of which even Maman would approve. What Maman would have said when, in answer to the pleas of the Americans, the orchestra played a lively jig, Amalie did not dare contemplate!

The *valse* was beautiful and its music seductive, but when the count asked Amalie to dance it with him, she cried, laughing, "Oh, *non,* m'sieu! I do not know how. You know Maman considered it somewhat vulgar."

"Indeed?" he said, with a quizzical look. "I would not want to offend Madame de l'Ouvrier, but I can assure you that the *valse* is quite the rage in New Orleans—and with the best families."

He excused himself in a few minutes, leaving her to "make tapes-

try" with the "grandes dames" who filled the satin-covered chairs lining the walls.

A little later Amalie, engrossed in watching the whirling couples
sweep around the hall in dizzy rhythm, was astonished to see the
count dancing with his old friend, Madame Amboy, who looked
handsome and sophisticated in a gown that exposed her rather thin,
nervous shoulders and fanned out above her ankles when she
whirled. But oh, how handsome the count was—smiling down at
Madame Amboy with his arm firmly holding her small waist!

This time Amalie knew with certainty that she was jealous, and
that could only mean that she was in love with her husband. Not just
starstruck, as she had been when he first came to Les Chênes. What
had been a ploy to save Clotie from ruining them all had held a hidden trap into which she had fallen. Young as she was, she had committed her heart.

She closed her eyes tightly against the whirling vision of him dancing with Madame Amboy. Nor would she let herself think that he
might be subtly punishing Clotie tonight by showing her the station
in life that would have been hers had she married him. Instead,
Amalie surrendered to this uprush of feeling which seemed to her so
wonderful in itself that she would not regret it even if Monsieur Armand never learned to love her. (But how could he *not* love her
when she felt so much love for him?!)

The following day was fully as exciting as the ball itself for it
seemed that all New Orleans called or left cards at the house on rue
Bourbon. But Clotie did not share Amalie's pleasure in their success.
Indeed, she was so wan and silent that Amalie suspected she was
afflicted with "morning sickness."

"M'sieu François Arouet," Amalie read, holding up a card. "Is
that not the young man who begged for all your dances, Clotie?"

"I don't remember," Clotie said indifferently.

"You could scarcely have failed to see that he was completely ensnared," Amalie teased. "But then you ensnared half the young men
at the ball! M'sieu Arouet was the one with topaz eyes, wasn't he? I
thought him quite handsome."

"I did not notice."

"Oh, Clotie, don't pretend!"

Clotie said with cold anger, "I did not notice. If you must know,
they all looked alike to me because I saw only that none was
Deneez."

Amalie groaned. *"Mon Dieu,* Clotie, if I hear one more time—"

Clotie stood abruptly and left the salon. Amalie bit her lip. Why was she not more patient with Clotie? Suppose it had been Monsieur Armand who had gone overboard to rescue a friend? She could easily imagine him doing it. Would she not have felt, as Clotie did, that her life was over? She felt a quick stab of terror, imagining it.

That evening, the count said he would be dining at home, and Amalie was delighted. She sat with him in the salon before dinner, discussing the ball and the people she had met there, while he had a glass of wine. Clotie did not appear. After waiting for some time, the count sent Callou to inquire if ma'm'selle were not ready.

"M'selle sends apologies," Callou reported back. "She not coming."

"Again?" The count's face hardened. "What is it, pray?" he inquired of Amalie. "Does she become ill only when I am dining at home?"

Amalie rose from her chair. "I will see—"

He stopped her with a gesture. "Did Ma'm'selle Claudine's servant say ma'm'selle was ill?" he asked Callou.

"Non, michie. She say M'selle take a tray in her room."

"Return and tell her that I require ma'm'selle's presence at the dinner table."

"Oui, michie."

The count's face was hard as he poured himself another glass of wine from the decanter placed at his elbow. Amalie, annoyed and apprehensive, thought privately that Clotie might have shown some gratitude for the consideration and attention Monsieur Armand had shown them last evening.

When Callou returned, he looked frightened. The count set his glass down on the marquetry table top with a click.

"Well?"

"She not coming, *michie."*

"She was unwell this morning," Amalie began, but the count silenced her with another sharp gesture.

"Tell me," the count said in icy tones, "exactly what ma'm'selle said."

Callou began to stutter. "S-she s-say she not eat at a-a-a-"

"Well?"

"S-she say a murderer's table, *michie."* He trembled.

Amalie longed to shake her sister.

"Very well," the count said in a controlled voice. "Go back to the kitchen, Callou. Tell Dulcie that from now on, no food is to be taken to Ma'm'selle Claudine's chamber. No trays. Nothing. Do you understand?"

"*Oui, michie.*"

"*Alors.* You may tell Dulcie she can serve, but that I will not be dining at home."

With a jerky bow, Callou fled.

"M'sieu!" Amalie protested. An impossibly large lump had moved up into her throat. She looked at him beseechingly, then recoiled from the black rage in his eyes.

"I will absent myself so that you may dine with your wenching sister!" he said violently. Amalie clapped her hands to her mouth. He turned his back on her and left the salon.

Amalie stumbled down the hall to Clotie's chamber. "Oh, Clotie, you have made him so angry! Can you not be more forgiving? He was going to dine at home, but now he has gone out—again!"

Clotie was sitting pale and motionless at her dressing table. "*Bien!*"

"You think only of yourself!" Amalie wailed, no longer able to bear her distress. "What shall I do, Clotie? He—he offered for me, and yet he does not want me."

"What can you expect when you are still flat as a boy?" It was a cruel jibe and an unexpected one, coming from Clotie, once so gentle and dreamy.

Tears stood in Amalie's eyes. "Then why did he marry me?"

"Because he hates me as I hate him!" Clotie's face suddenly came alive with passion. Words spilled out of her beautiful mouth. "You're out of your depth now, aren't you? You thought you were the practical one. You called me a goose, and maybe I am. But you have always been so petted and indulged that you can't understand it if everyone doesn't adore you as Papa does. Amalie, don't delude yourself! Yours was a marriage of convenience, just as mine was to have been."

"You're jealous!" Amalie cried, in hurt surprise. "You wish now that you had married M'sieu Armand yourself!"

"Who," Clotie asked viciously, "would wish to marry a murderer?"

Amalie stared at her sister. "And who saved you from that hated marriage?"

Their eyes met. Clotie lowered her gaze first. "I'm sorry, Amalie. I—I am so miserable I want to make everyone else as miserable."

Amalie turned without speaking and went into her own chamber, closing the door between them. Even in her inexperience she saw that Monsieur Armand's friendship with Madame Amboy—whose husband was in Paris, *ma foi!*—was not so grave a threat to her happiness as the fury that flared between her husband and her sister. How could her love compete with a hate so passionate?

EIGHT

THE "LITTLE COUNTESS" and her beautiful sister, so mysteriously sad, were invited everywhere in the next few weeks. There were coffees and soirées and dinners almost every day. To Amalie, the very air of the city, still warm and redolent with its heavy odors of roasting coffee and jasmine, of human sweat and rotting fruit, was exciting. She listened eagerly to conversations about the newcomers, those American businessmen who were so hard-driving and ungracious, who mistrusted the graceful Creole way of concluding a deal over a carafe of wine at the Exchange; about the insistence of *"les américains"* that war with Spain was inevitable and that once it started, Aaron Burr would declare himself emperor of Mexico (and if Spain won, *ma foi,* would their former governor de Salcedo return?); about Jean Lafitte, that gentlemanly blacksmith, newly arrived in town and rumored to be a former privateer, whose shop was said to be a blind for his real activities as a smugglers' agent!

Clotie, as always, was lost in a world of her own, scarcely listening to the talk that swirled around them. But to Amalie's inquiring mind, fresh from the quiet bayous of the back country and the rather old-fashioned formality of the émigrés, it was heady stuff, indeed. She observed that the count was quite at home in these discussions, that he was knowledgeable, and that his friends listened to him with respect. Madame Amboy, also, Amalie regarded with an envious wonder, for that lady did not hesitate to set her opinions against those of the men, but she did so with such wit and charm that the men seemed to enjoy sparring with her.

It was obvious that Monsieur Armand admired Madame Amboy greatly, and listening to her, Amalie wondered how she could have imagined that her own artless chatter had entertained him. She was conceiving the most unreasonable distaste for Madame Amboy's widow's peak and sharp dimples!

The two sisters seldom dined at home *à deux* any more, but on one evening when they did so, they decided to take the air along the levee after the dinner hour, as was the custom of many Orleanians. It was pleasant to stroll on the crest of the grassy embankment with Callou following a few paces behind them, and look down on the flatboats tied up at the anchorage at the foot of Tchoupitoulas Street, loaded with bales of cotton and indigo and hides from the interior; or to gaze out at the barques at anchor in the river, with swarthy, exotically garbed sailors engaged in mysterious activities on their decks.

Gulls with black markings on their wings flew overhead, screeching their calls that were curiously like mocking laughter. The sun had lowered and the breeze that came over the river to ruffle the soft hair at their cheeks was slightly cooler.

"Look!" Amalie said, pointing to a small riverboat. "The red sails of the Baratarians! It is from them that Dulcie buys our oysters, did you know that?"

"From Barataria? Is that not where the privateers have their rendezvous?" Clotie asked idly.

"So I have heard." Amalie studied the colorful boat with curiosity. Then a startled note came into her voice as she exclaimed, "Do look, Clotie! Is that not M'sieu Armand I see talking to the Baratarian?"

"Indeed, it is."

They watched the two men, who were deep in conversation, and saw the count hand the Baratarian a folded note which the rough sailor tucked into the colorful sash he wore around his waist.

"I'll wager he is not buying oysters!" Clotie said, with spite.

Barataria was the bay, separated from the Gulf by the low islands, Grande Isle and Grande Terre, from which a maze of bayous extended into the back country, a most fortuitous hiding place for smugglers and adventurers. Amalie had learned from her assiduous listening that it was somewhere on Barataria Bay that the privateers met to divide their spoils, and it was to Barataria that the men of New Orleans went to purchase luxuries at bargain prices.

Amalie grew very thoughtful, remembering that her mother had once claimed that her father's friendship with the young count was rooted in their mutual plotting with other royalists against Napoleon. Would a Baratarian privateer have ways of getting Monsieur Armand's secret message to someone in Europe? Could he be sending *money?* Maman had been angry, Amalie remembered, because she suspected Papa had been sending money with the count to the royalist plotters.

There was much Amalie did not know about her husband!

At the house in Bourbon Street, Amalie seldom saw Monsieur Armand, who continued to occupy his bachelor quarters across the court and to take few meals in his own dining room. Sometimes she remembered their picnic beside the bayou and their journey down the river with acute nostalgia, because a certain intimacy had existed between them then. Now, except when they were in public, the count treated her with as much formality as he showed Clotie.

It was a state of affairs that grew more galling as her enjoyment of the diversions of the city's social life increased. That came to an abrupt end, however, on a day when the count, encountering Clotie in the salon, looked at her narrowly and said in a curt tone that it was high time she went into seclusion.

"That will suit me very well, m'sieu," Clotie said coldly.

The count turned to Amalie. "Take up your pen, madame."

She sat at the graceful rosewood desk while he dictated a note to be sent to their hostess at that evening's soirée, regretting that a family emergency prevented their appearance. When she had completed it, he rang for Callou.

"Take this note around to number fourteen, rue Dumaine, and when you have done that bring the carriage around for our use." When the servant left, the count said, "You will prepare for a journey, ma'm'selle, with a quantity of empty boxes and trunks. You, madame, will accompany us. We will leave ostentatiously, drive out to St. John's landing, and then along the river to an undisclosed destination, where we will apparently deliver ma'm'selle to unnamed friends. They will escort her by stage to that point on the bayou to which your father's flatboat brought us. Your father, we have learned, is very ill.

"We will return in the dead of night with you, ma'm'selle, well concealed. Later, it will become obvious why the countess did not accompany you to Les Chênes."

"I see you have given considerable thought to this ridiculous charade!"

He ignored Clotie. "You, madame, will now begin to curtail your social activities. It will be necessary for you to remember that you are *enceinte*."

Amalie, taken by surprise and chagrined at his highhanded treatment, said tartly, "Since I have had no experience, m'sieu, that will be somewhat difficult."

The cold distaste in his face revealed how much the necessity for such subterfuge humiliated him. "You will have your sister for a model, madame. But do not forget that the ladies have an unfortunate habit of counting on their fingers!" His quick glance at Clotie was cutting; her face flamed.

Amalie took her courage in hand and inquired, "Would it not be wise, m'sieu, for you to exchange rooms with Clotie? Would she not find a safer seclusion across the court?"

The count said coolly, "I have already arrived at that conclusion, madame. Jean-Baptiste will transfer my personal effects and prepare my quarters for Ma'm'selle while we are away."

Clotie wrinkled her nose to express her distaste at the prospect of using rooms that had once been the count's, but all that day Amalie carried a little glow of excitement in her heart. From now on her husband would be on the other side of a connecting door to her own chamber. Would he come to her? If he did not, would she have the courage to open that door herself, as she had done so many times to look in on Clotie?

She was becoming nervous and unsure of herself around him. Sometimes she recalled the first days of their acquaintance, when she had been secure in the dotage of her father, and could not believe now how fresh and impertinent she had been. It was the unfailing antagonism between the count and Clotie that unhinged her. She loved them both, pitying Clotie and understanding—with pain—her husband's injured pride. But with Clotie in seclusion, surely things would be better!

So she worked swiftly, with a singing heart, to prepare for the farcical journey that the count had designed to protect Clotie's reputation.

It proved to be the most miserable day of her life. She soon learned what the count meant by "ostentatiously." Clotie's empty boxes were lashed to the carriage in plain view of the passersby who could look through the porte cochère at the unusual activity. When they were at last mounted in the carriage, with Madi riding beside

Callou who was driving, they had scarcely passed through the porte cochère when the count ordered Callou to stop and sent him back into the house for his pistol, which he had confessed one day would not even fire.

They sat in the carriage there in the street, bowing to neighbors and acquaintances who passed. It gave Monsieur Armand an opportunity to tell his fable about the illness of Monsieur de l'Ouvrier to friends who stopped to inquire, and for several young men to bid Clotie a flattering farewell.

When at last they were on their way, the carriage was miserably hot, so hot that their traveling clothes already stuck to their moist bodies. The swaying of the carriage and the heat combined to make Clotie ill. As she grew more evil-tempered, the count became more icily withdrawn. But all the way out St. John's road, he bowed to those in the carriages meeting or overtaking them, assuring that they were recognized.

"The news of our departure will run across New Orleans like a river flood," Amalie observed.

"You may spread the rumor of my death, as well," Clotie said in wan despair, "because it will no longer be a rumor by the time this day is over."

"Do not despair so easily, ma'm'selle," Monsieur Armand said unfeelingly, "for I am quite certain that your discomfort has only begun."

"And with it, your opportunities to enjoy my discomfort, m'sieu!"

"Oh, do leave off slashing at each other!" Amalie cried, in exasperation. "It is too hot for fencing."

To her surprise the count chuckled. "You are right, madame, and if Ma'm'selle will stop complaining, I will try to hold my tongue."

Clotie turned her head sharply away, staring out at the swamp which seemed to bob around outside the carriage window as they jogged along.

He looked so handsome when he laughed, Amalie thought; it was a pity he did not laugh more often. She came near blurting her thoughts aloud, but just then Clotie gave a piteous moan and begged that the carriage be stopped. The count's face hardened. He gave Callou the order and, jumping down from the carriage, extended his hand first to Clotie and then to Amalie.

"Attend your sister, madame," he said, and turned his back while she retired to the side of the road with poor Clotie. It was fortunate no carriage passed, for there was scarcely time to get her out of sight.

"He deliberately tortures me," Clotie gasped, when she was able to speak. "He has murdered my lover and now he wishes to murder my child."

"*Mon Dieu,* Clotie! We are doing only what has to be done."

They climbed back into the carriage and went on. Monsieur Armand made sure they were seen at St. John's landing, and soon after that instructed Callou to turn back by a circuitous route and pull off the road behind an abandoned early settler's house. Here they stopped, and Callou unharnessed the horses to allow them to graze while he discarded the empty boxes and concealed the trunks in the empty house until he could return for them. Dulcie had prepared a lunch, but no one had an appetite.

Gingerly, the two girls explored the old house, but it was creepy with massive spider webs and all manner of crawly things, and when they startled a snake curled up at the foot of an inside stair, they ran out shrieking.

It was a tedious, uncomfortable wait until dark fell and they could begin their stealthy journey back to New Orleans, with the curtains drawn over the carriage windows and Madi riding inside—for the *femme de chambre* must disappear with her mistress. When in the ghostly hours after midnight they entered the untenanted streets of the city, Monsieur Armand insisted over Clotie's distressed protests that she and Madi crouch on the floor of the carriage and the curtains be drawn back to show the occasional nightwatchman crying all was well in the streets that only the count and countess returned to the house in Bourbon Street.

Late as it was, Amalie was strangely wakeful, for she and Clotie had slept much of the way back. She found Julie waiting up for her, and sent her with Madi to help the drooping Clotie to her new quarters. Alone, she disrobed and put on her nightclothes, then picked up her hairbrush and began stroking her dark hair, loosened to fall upon her shoulders. She could not stop thinking about her husband, so close on the other side of the connecting door. Try as she might, she could not compose herself for sleep.

She longed for some sign of affection from him. All her short life she had basked in the spotlight of her father's adoration, and she missed it sorely. She had been so sure that she could win Monsieur Armand's love, even though he had first been attracted to Clotie, yet now it seemed that he was slipping farther and farther away from her and she was no nearer becoming his wife in truth than when he had left her alone in their nuptial chamber. Did he feel nothing for her? It seemed imperative that she know.

Before she could reason herself out of it, she left her bed and walked straight to the connecting door and opened it. Monsieur Armand turned, surprised. Jean-Baptiste had just dropped his nightshirt over his head and picked up his boots. The servant stood with the boots in his hand, looking as startled as his master.

"Leave us, Jean-Baptiste."

Silently, Jean-Baptiste left the room, taking the count's boots with him.

"Well, madame?"

The sight of him in his nightshirt had rendered her speechless. His neck was bare and youthful without the usual cravat. Amalie had often admired his straight and shapely legs in the close-fitting pantaloons—they were not at all bowed like Papa's—but now she saw to her paralyzing embarrassment that they were covered with fine black hairs! Her gaze shied away from his bare feet, but not before she had noted how long and narrow were his toes, which seemed a remarkable thing to her.

She forced herself to speak. "I came—I wanted to ask—"

"Can it not wait until morning?" The weary irritation his tone revealed angered her.

"No, it cannot, m'sieu. I can bear it no longer."

"What can you bear no longer, madame?"

"I am ignored, treated like a child! I am neither your wife nor your mistress."

"Your pardon. You *are* my wife, madame. In response to your own wish, was it not?"

She recoiled, seeing for the first time that he blamed her as much as Clotie for the deception they had played on him. But she could not face that truth easily. She stammered, "A strange kind of wife who receives no caress, who cannot enter her husband's chamber without being made to feel unwelcome!"

"I could point out that you would be more welcome if it were not three o'clock in the morning, and I were not exhausted after an unutterably boring day. And has it not occurred to you that it would be more than awkward if you were to become *enceinte* just now?"

"*Oh!*"

"How could I explain my wife giving birth twice within three months? You may rest assured that I will not expose myself to that possibility."

"You care nothing for me, do you?" she cried. "Why did you marry me?"

The candleglow did not reveal the expression of his dark eyes, but she was never to forget the utter weariness in his face which she read as rejection, or the tone of his voice as he said, "For your dowry, madame."

The emotion drained out of her, leaving her feeling very cold. She turned and walked stiffly back to her own room. She was not surprised when she heard the count shouting for Jean-Baptiste to fetch him the key to the connecting door.

She did not climb into her bed. Instead she went to stand before her mirror. Unmoved, she noted that at long last it revealed a gentle swelling of her breasts. It no longer seemed important.

NINE

SOME WEEKS after the date of Clotie's supposed departure from New Orleans, a fat packet of letters arrived from Les Chênes, brought by the master of a flatboat carrying cotton downriver to the port. There was a long thin letter addressed to "Armand, Comte de Valérun," which Amalie laid aside, for Monsieur Armand was not in. The fat bundle was for her. When she opened it, there tumbled out a score of letters inscribed to Mademoiselle Claudine de l'Ouvrier at Les Chênes, all in the same hand. With them was a single sheet in her mother's hand.

Amalie hurried to the rear of the house and the passage through several storerooms which had been opened to make Clotie's apartment convenient without entering the courtyard.

"Letters, Clotie!" she exclaimed when she reached the pleasant room where Clotie sat stitching a fine seam on a small garment. "All these for you! They must surely be from M'sieu Arouet!"

Clotie shrugged her indifference as Amalie tossed them in her lap.

"There is a note from Maman addressed to both of us. Shall I read it aloud?"

"Oui."

" 'Dear daughters,' " Amalie read, her voice quivering with a sudden stab of homesickness.

> " 'Your Papa and I are well, but lonely. Things march here as usual. We received your letter telling of your many invitations. Who is the gentleman who writes Clotie so many letters? I am writing the count to ask if he has inquired about the gentleman's intentions, and if it would be a suitable match. If so, perhaps he can arrange it to appear that your replies are sent from Les Chênes. We beg you both to be discreet, since happiness for all of us depends on your discretion. Do not fail to go to confession, but remember that your child's legitimacy must be inscribed on the parish register when it is baptized. May the good Lord, who understands all, forgive us for our deception! We pray for your welfare constantly. Papa sends hugs and kisses.
> Your loving Maman.' "

When Amalie raised her eyes from the letter, she saw that Clotie's were black with anger. Methodically her sister began tearing up the unopened letters and flinging the pieces on the floor.

Amalie, who was much distressed by the letter—was Maman actually asking them to deceive their confessor?—cried, "Oh, Clotie, aren't you even going to see what he says?"

When Clotie ignored her, she said coaxingly, "At the ball last week M'sieu Arouet requested no fewer than three dances with me, and all for the purpose of talking about 'Ma'm'selle Claudine,' which seemed to give him considerable pleasure. I had to tell him a third dance would be unseemly! I am convinced he is dying for love of you."

Clotie merely tightened her lips and continued the deliberate destruction of poor Monsieur Arouet's love letters.

Amalie left her, feeling vexed and confused. She dreaded what Monsieur Armand would say about this latest evidence of Clotie's defiant spirit, and resolved she would say nothing about the letters until he asked about them. As it turned out, she did not have to tell him anything, for the letter he had received from Les Chênes was never mentioned. She was quite certain he did not approach Mon-

sieur Arouet, and there was pain in speculating on his reasons for ignoring Maman's request.

Did he not consider Monsieur Arouet a worthy suitor? Or did he
not wish Clotie to have another suitor?

Fortunately, Amalie was kept so busy, both socially and at home,
that there was little time to brood, either about Clotie or about the
lack of love in her marriage. Monsieur Armand had turned over to
her the keys of the household. Gradually, she was taking the supervi-
sion of his house and servants into her own small but capable hands,
a little surprised at the things she had learned about such matters
from her mother's example, but depending heavily, also, on Julie for
guidance.

As Clotie had pointedly reminded her, hers was a marriage of convenience, which was the most common arrangement, after all. And
did not Clotie offer a sobering example of the unhappiness love
could bring? Amalie told herself stoutly that she did not want to be
such a goose!

But Amalie's social life, too, was soon to end. One morning Julie
wrapped a strip of muslin tightly around Amalie's waist several times
before dressing her, saying, "Time your gown begin chokin' you!"

Amalie's dependence on Julie had encouraged the black woman to
take charge with all her old authority as Amalie's nurse. Julie was already stitching up a more thickly padded belt which would replace
the binding in a few weeks.

"You'll never be able to fasten my gowns over that, Julie."

"Then I dress you in m'selle's gowns. You can't be too far behin'
M'selle Clotie," Julie warned.

She insisted that Amalie begin taking her breakfast in her chamber, and began telling ladies who made morning calls that *madame la
comtesse* was indisposed. The count was Julie's ally. He insisted that
Amalie send regrets in answer to most of the invitations that came
now.

Such inactivity was, of course, extremely boring. Sometimes Amalie found a diversion in the visits of her hairdresser, for the octoroon
did indeed work at the best houses and never failed to amuse her
with a fund of information about what was happening in the city, although at times what she reported filled Amalie with secret fears.

"Two gentlemen met early this morning in the court behind the
church," she said one afternoon, her hands busy with Amalie's ivory
comb. "I cannot tell you their names, but you know them, madame."

"Why can you not tell me their names? Surely the whole city knows of their duel by now?"

"But *non,* madame. You see, they fought over the *griffe* of one of the gentlemen. Naturally, he does not want his wife to know."

Amalie's heart contracted painfully as she wondered, not for the first time, if the count attended those whispered-about octoroon balls —held on different nights in the same Salle d'Orleans to which she and Clotie had gone, *ma foi!* Sometimes she heard the strains of their music from her own chamber! Did the count's continual absences from the house mean he had an octoroon mistress—a *griffe*—in one of those small, neat houses beyond the *quartier?*

"But how can his wife fail to know? One of the gentlemen was injured, surely—I trust not fatally?"

"Fortunately, *non,* madame. And his secret will be kept. It is the gentlemen's code, you understand."

What Amalie understood, her heart sinking like a stone, was that if one of the gentlemen were the count, she would never be told the real reason for the duel—if she heard it had occurred!

"How did you learn about it?"

"The *griffe* is my friend. Naturally, I will keep her secret."

"And if one of the men were the count?" Amalie challenged her. "You would not tell me what the gossips say about him?"

The octoroon's smile was sly. *"Mais, oui,* madam. Would you like to know what the gossips say about m'sieu? They are saying *m'sieu le comte* is being teased because his *jeune fille* is already *enceinte."*

Jeune fille? Amalie could feel the hot color warming her cheeks. She thought she knew how such teasing, under the circumstances, would annoy Monsieur Armand. But she managed a laugh. "Indeed? And who are 'they'?"

The hairdresser shrugged, smiling, and said no more. But Amalie guessed from her satisfied expression that she would be spreading the news that the count's "little girl" was, indeed, expecting a child. Which, she told herself, was not after all a bad thing. But Amalie was warned that it was dangerous to allow such intimate conversation.

"And what do 'they' say about war with Spain?" she asked, in what she hoped was an idle tone.

"It depends on whether one is listening to an American or a Creole," the young octoroon said with a cynical laugh. "General Wilkinson is said to be moving his army to confront the Mexican army at the Sabine River where there have been border disputes. But the most extraordinary rumor is going about now. It is being said in some places that General Wilkinson himself is in the pay of Spain!"

"A Spanish agent?" Amalie cried, bright-eyed. This *was* extraordinary! *"Mon Dieu,* but I do not understand politics!"

"It is more than politics, madame. If it is true, it is treason against the United States government. But only the Creoles appear to credit the rumor. In fact, I do not think one would dare repeat it to an American."

Amalie laughed with her, highly amused. No one really liked the Americans! It was delicious to think of their being so deceived.

After the hairdresser left, Julie, who had been hovering in the background, ostensibly to fetch whatever Madame Laval needed, began scolding Amalie. "Don' b'lieve ever'thin' that one tell you. She let her mouth run."

"She tells me what I would hear if I were allowed to go out."

"Gossip!" Julie said with scorn. "Bes' you sen' her away and let me comb your hair."

"Oui, the same way you combed it when I was a child on the plantation! You're jealous of her, Julie."

"She up to no good."

"Oh, do be quiet!"

The black woman went off, muttering.

Amalie seldom saw Monsieur Armand, who continued to take most of his meals away from home. She had long ago guessed that her husband began dining regularly with his men friends at the Exchange rather than at home because he was too proud to admit he had repented of his bad-tempered order that no food was to be taken to Clotie's room. He must have guessed that Clotie would simply refuse to eat, and his perception of that streak of soft stubbornness in Clotie's nature surprised Amalie. Now, of course, they had no choice but to send Clotie's meals on a tray to her secluded apartment, but the count continued to dine away from home.

He also continued to accept the invitations to dinner parties and soirées that custom forbade Amalie to attend now. Sometimes when she ventured out of her chamber for breakfast she found him in the dining room, but as often as not Jean-Baptiste had carried *café au lait* to his master when he wakened him, and Monsieur Armand was already dressed to go out.

The ever-thickening padded belts that Julie made for her were increasingly hot and uncomfortable to wear, and Amalie argued that a loose gown would effectively hide her pretended pregnancy. But Julie was adamant. Julie insisted, too, that Amalie spend her hours stitching up infant dresses and petticoats which Amalie found not only tedious, but difficult, since her one year of instruction under the nuns had scarcely made a needlewoman of her.

It was boredom that made her leave her room one morning when she heard a woman's step on the stair from the court and order Julie to admit the caller. It was Madame Amboy, tall and svelte in a stunning green embroidered gown and a saucy matching hat.

"I am so glad you are receiving this morning, *madame la comtesse!* I have called several times and been told that you were indisposed."

"There is nothing wrong with me except ennui," Amalie told her truthfully, and ordered coffees to be brought for them.

The older woman's lively eyes were frankly assessing Amalie's figure. Amalie remembered the count's saying, "Do not forget that the ladies have a habit of counting on their fingers," and was abruptly too conscious of the padding around her waist. It could not possibly have slipped—Julie tied it too tightly. Nevertheless, Amalie felt nervous about it. Madame Amboy was too shrewd!

"You must let a few close friends try to amuse you, *madame la comtesse,* since convention dictates that you withdraw from social life."

"So you have heard the rumor."

Madame Amboy smiled noncommittally, and Amalie wondered if her husband had asked his friend to call, or if she had come out of curiosity. "If you will permit it, I should like to number myself among those friends."

"That is kind of you, madame."

"I know you are very happy to be carrying M'sieu Armand's child," Madame Amboy continued gently, "but it must be difficult for you, being so far from your mother. If I can help in any way—"

The reference to her mother reminded Amalie unfortunately of Madame Laval's report about what "they" were saying. "I am no longer a '*jeune fille,*' madame," Amalie said, lifting her chin. "While I miss my mother, I would far rather be with my husband."

"Of course." Madame Amboy sounded puzzled. "I merely wished to tell you that if you feel the need for a woman friend—"

"You are too kind," Amalie said so coldly that the older woman quickly moved the conversation to less personal topics.

After her guest had gone, Amalie rang for Julie. "I am not at home when Madame Amboy calls," she told her.

"Why?" demanded the black woman. "You needs fr'en's."

"She looks too closely at my padding. I am afraid she will guess—"

"*Nobody* guess that padding not real," Julie said, affronted.

But Amalie insisted. Madame Amboy made her uneasy.

Although it was very nearly winter now, the weather continued oppressively warm. Clotie suffered more from the heat than Amalie did. Sometimes after dark Clotie slipped down into the courtyard to walk with Amalie, taking both air and exercise. Her disposition was no better; in fact, it seemed to Amalie that it grew steadily worse as her ungainly weight increased.

Amalie knew well that while she herself was bored, her position was easier to bear than Clotie's. Amalie visited her sister's apartment daily, but that was Clotie's only diversion, while Amalie's days were varied by her occasional encounters with the count and her daily discussions with Dulcie concerning their food and other household matters.

But it was Madame Laval who made her isolation endurable, for it was only through the hairdresser's visits that Amalie felt herself a part of the city that was now her home. She dared not expose herself to the inquisitive eyes of her friends in society, but the hairdresser came from their houses with scraps of news about their doings. And the woman was entertaining.

"*Les américains*"—the Americans—was an epithet on most Creole tongues, but Madame Laval laughed at them, admitting she took their money for dressing their ladies' hair. "Their General Wilkinson found the Mexicans he hoped to fight had withdrawn from the border," she reported to Amalie. "Nevertheless, he is in New Orleans now, telling us we will be attacked, and trying to raise a citizens' army to protect us from Spain."

"The same who is said to be a Spanish agent?" Amalie cried, highly diverted.

"*Mais, oui,* madame. They are saying that he is very angry with our Governor Claiborne because he refuses to declare the city under martial law."

"But what would that mean?"

Madame Laval shrugged. "I do not know, madame, except that

the general would then control the city. And they say that he has accused M'sieu Burr of conscripting an army to attack New Orleans."

"Mon Dieu!" Amalie remembered the laughing eyes of the small, handsome man who had winked at her and Clotie at the convent and sighed, "I do not understand Americans."

"Nor do I," Madame Laval said. "But you need not worry, madame. Tomorrow's inquiry into the incident on the flatboat involving *m'sieu le comte* will again be postponed for lack of evidence."

"Mon Dieu, does everyone but me know he was facing an inquiry a second time? And how do you know it will be postposed again?"

"That I may not reveal, madame, but you may rest assured." She wove an expert braid in silence, then said, "What a pretty ornament for the hair this is! But is it not a little large for a countess so dainty?"

Amalie looked at the colorful arrangement of stained glass affixed to a comb that had attracted her eyes in a Spanish shop on rue Royale, and said carelessly, "Perhaps you are right. It would look better on you, Madame Laval. Would you like it?"

"Merci, madame." The octoroon pocketed it swiftly. "They say it is the American judge that cannot let the matter of your husband's inquiry drop," she said, lowering her voice. "A jury of his gentlemen friends would long ago have acquitted him of any blame in the matter. I overheard a very highly placed Creole gentleman say that only the other day as I waited on his wife."

"You are kind to tell me so," Amalie said gratefully.

Madame Laval picked up another strand of hair and began brushing it to a silky sheen. "And how is your sister?"

Amalie started, very nearly caught off guard. "S-she is well, *merci.* We have had letters."

"And your father is recovering?"

"He is much better."

"I have heard that a certain young gentleman would be happy if Ma'm'selle de l'Ouvrier returned to New Orleans."

Did nothing escape the hairdresser's sharp ears? "Perhaps she can come for another visit next year," Amalie said, as casually as she could, and sighed in relief that she had avoided telling a direct lie she would have to confess.

Strangely, when she tried to repeat Madame Laval's fascinating gossip to Clotie, it seemed only to irritate her sister. Clotie lived in a world of her own thoughts—and that added to Amalie's loneliness. Amalie spent much of her time in the salon where she could hope to encounter the count when he left or entered the house, and exchange a few words with him. Sometimes she looked out on the galérie that hung over the wineshop, letting herself be glimpsed at the long windows by her neighbors on other galéries, who smiled at her, waving and nodding.

On one such occasion she caught sight of Monsieur Arouet, Clotie's admirer, in the street below. She thought he had looked up, but he stepped quickly through the open door of the chandelier's shop, pretending he had not seen her. After that, she looked for him and discovered that he was spending a good part of each day mooning about and staring up at the count's house. Alarmed, she wondered if their secret were already discovered. Surely, he would not be watching the house so assiduously if he did not have reason to believe that Clotie were in it? Frantically, Amalie went back in her memory over all her actions to see where she might have given their secret away, and could find no indiscretion.

At last, when she could bear it no longer, she sent Julie down to ask him into the house, and awaited him in the salon. He came in, stammering an apology, a fair young man with hair that curled over his collar and features that looked somehow unformed when she compared them with the determined, intelligent face of Monsieur Armand. He was, Amalie thought, exactly the kind of dreaming, romantic young man one would have thought Clotie would fall in love with instead of that dashing adventurer who had seduced her.

Amalie signed to Julie to remain in the room with them. "Please forgive my immodesty, M'sieu Arouet," she said, "but I must put my mind at rest. Why do you stand below day after day and stare up at my house?"

"I have been seeking the courage to request an interview with you, madame," said Monsieur Arouet, his face quite pale with emotion.

"And now you have it. Pray be quick, before my reputation is quite undone."

"I am contemplating making a journey to Les Chênes in an effort to see Ma'm'selle de l'Ouvrier," he blurted.

Amalie gasped. "Surely you would not do anything so rash!"

"Is it so rash, madame? I am determined to ask your father for her hand."

Amalie drew a deep breath to still her racing heart. She must at all costs prevent his traveling to Les Chênes under the impression that Clotie was there—but how? "Does my sister know of your intentions?" she asked, to gain time to think.

"I do not know," he said, a desperate look coming into his eyes. "She has not replied to my letters."

"And she will not," Amalie said. "I am sorry to be the one to tell you this, M'sieu Arouet, but you must put all thoughts of my sister from your mind."

"There is another?" he said, in a tragic voice.

Amalie let out her breath in a long sigh. Of course, the truth! The truth was always best. "Yes," she said, gently, "there is another." When he opened his mouth, urgent questions obviously trembling on his lips, she gestured for his silence. "I cannot tell you more at this time. I am truly sorry, for I like you very much. Forget her, m'sieu."

"Never, madame! And—I beg your pardon! But I must hear my rejection from her own lips."

"You force me to tell you that because of my father's illness you would not be welcome at Les Chênes. Please believe me, m'sieu, when I tell you that you can only harm your suit by going to Les Chênes at this time. My sister may one day return to New Orleans. Until she does, you must put her out of your thoughts."

"That is impossible, madame," he said in the most tragic tones. He bowed, kissed her hand and left her.

Amalie sighed. She did not know whether or not she had succeeded in dissuading him. And what a pity it could not be! She thought Monsieur Arouet and Clotie ideally suited to each other.

TEN

"I SAW Madame Amboy's carriage turn in at your house last week," the hairdresser said, as she set out her jars of pomade and lacquer and began taking the pins out of Amalie's hair. "She is a good friend of your husband, is she not, madame?"

"I believe so," Amalie said, stiffening.

"But he is so handsome, so distinguished! What lady would not want him attending her salon?"

In the mirror Amalie met Madame Laval's eyes. They were slyly amused, bright with some secret knowledge. Amalie's stomach contracted. Before she could stop herself, she had said, "I have a pretty fan that I have grown weary of. I had thought of making you a gift of it, madame."

There was a quick gleam in the older woman's strange yellow eyes. She murmured, *"Merci,* madame." And then, in a confidential tone, "Madame Amboy's salon is said to be a hotbed of royalist plotting."

It had been a transaction, Amalie realized, and felt a sickening twist of apprehension. When had her enjoyment of the hairdresser's fund of gossip evolved into this subtle buying of information?

"It is well known that my husband is a royalist sympathizer," Amalie said. "After all, his inheritance was confiscated after the revolution. Why would he not be happy to see the Bourbons back on France's throne?"

"But the royalists have enemies here, madame! There are many republicans in New Orleans, some of them former soldiers who fought under Napoleon. They are still loyal to him. And there are old enemies of the Bourbons here, families who burned their patents of nobility long ago in sympathy with the revolution. Your husband must take care."

Amalie's heart quailed. There was danger in what the count was doing! She rang for Julie and, when her servant came, instructed her to find the fan promised to Madame Laval.

Julie did so, grumbling. After the free woman of color left, she exploded in indignation. "Why you give that womans your nice fan? Don' m'sieu pay her to come?"

"I wanted to make her a gift. She not only combs my hair, she tells me things I could not learn any other way." *Things like where my husband spends his evenings.* Amalie remembered Madame Amboy's offer of friendship with a surge of anger.

"You playin' with fire," Julie warned, "letting her come here when you got secrets in your own house. She evil, that one."

"Nonsense! You're a plantation negro, Julie. We live in a different world now."

"Hmf!" Julie was offended. "It the same evil, in the field or in the town."

"Oh, do hush!" But secretly Amalie was becoming a little afraid of Madame Laval. The brown woman's knowing eyes made Amalie feel young and vulnerable. Sometimes she wished her worldly wise mother had been allowed to accompany them to New Orleans. She knew Monsieur Armand had guessed rightly that her father's management of the plantation in Maman's absence would be, to put it kindly, absent-minded. Yet she suspected that the count had also been punishing Maman for what he thought was her part in the deception played on him.

If he would just take her in his arms, Amalie was sure she could then pour out the whole story of what she had done and why, and ask him to forgive her because she loved him. But the distance between them seemed to grow wider and colder with each passing day's brief, unloving encounters.

When she felt very distressed, Amalie took Julie with her and, early in the morning, veiled and swathed in loose clothing, ventured out to hear mass. On one such morning, as they were returning to Bourbon Street, they saw Clotie's servant hurrying through the porte cochère ahead of them. When they entered the court, Madi had disappeared.

Amalie went at once to Clotie's apartment and found the black girl with her sister. She demanded to know where Madi had been. "You know, Madi, that you are not allowed to leave the house."

Clotie, dressed in a morning robe, was standing with her back to a window. The light silhouetted the pronounced bulge in her figure and left her face in shadow. "I sent her out, Amalie. To get some fresh fruit at the market."

"*Ma foi,* Clotie! You know that Dulcie sends Estée to the market every morning. Could you not wait an hour for your fruit?"

To Amalie's utter amazement, Clotie laughed and patted her bulge. "One could think so, *n'est-ce pas?* But you don't know how it is, Amalie. No, I could not wait. Besides, this confinement is hard on Madi. I am sorry for her."

"I am glad to find you thinking of someone besides yourself," Amalie said, feeling quite snappish, "but you must know that we cannot allow Madi to be seen without revealing that you are in the house."

"How can you say I think of no one but myself," Clotie retorted, "when day and night I think of nothing but my child and his father?"

"Then you had best begin thinking of other things! Your M'sieu Arouet has been standing in the street, looking up at our windows for days. I do not know whether he also stays through the night, but perhaps you should think about that!"

"Oh, him," Clotie said, with a shrug, but a certain tension revealed that her indifference was assumed. The shaft had gone home.

"Come with me, Madi," Amalie said, turning to leave. "I want to speak with you in private."

"She is my servant!" Clotie's tone was sharp.

"And I am mistress of this house."

For a moment Amalie confronted her. Then Clotie gestured her permission, and moved heavily toward her chair and the needlework that lay on a low table beside it.

Silently, Madi followed Amalie through the passage at the rear of the court. In her chamber, Amalie let Clotie's servant stand waiting, while she discarded her veil and loosened the bulky padding beneath her flowing gown.

"I believe that you are devoted to Ma'm'selle Claudine," she said at last, "and that you would not wish to ruin her?"

"*Non,* madame," the girl said, hanging her head. She had once been very lively, Amalie remembered. Now she seemed subdued. The confinement was hard on her, no doubt, but it was hard on them all.

"If you are seen on the street and recognized as her *femme de chambre,* it would not only ruin her reputation, but forever blight the life of her child. The de l'Ouvrier name would be tarnished. It would bring the greatest distress to all of us. Do you want to cause such unhappiness, Madi?"

"*Non, madame.*"

"If you are speaking the truth, you will ignore such whims of Ma'm'selle as the one which sent you to the market this morning. Do you know what you should have done, instead?"

Madi gazed intently at the floor. "*Non,* madame."

"You should have gone to Dulcie. If she could not supply what Ma'm'selle wanted, you should have come to me."

"*Oui,* madame." The girl's hands, clasped in front of her, were trembling. She was frightened, Amalie thought. Good!

"Go back to your mistress," she said, "the way we came. Make sure you keep out of sight of the court."

"*Oui,* madame." She was gone, swiftly and silently.

Amalie sighed, wondering how her mother would have handled the matter.

It was not long after that incident that a particularly brutal murder took place in the dark of midnight on the old levee road. Death was not uncommon on that row of saloons and bawdy houses frequented by disreputable *yanqui* riverboatmen—and some said pirates!—but it was usually a result of drunken brawling. This crime was different.

Monsieur Beaulieu, a gentleman from a prominent Creole family, was found lying in the road. He had been beaten with blunt weapons, and died soon after the priest was brought without revealing any information about his assailants. The violent deed sent ripples of shock through the city that reached into the house on rue Bourbon. Estée brought the first news of it from the market. Julie carried it upstairs with the *café au lait* she brought to Amalie's chamber.

"A M'sieu Beaulieu, did you say?" Amalie exclaimed. "But he is a friend of the count's! I met him at the theater, and again at a ball—why, I danced with him!" She sprang out of bed and held out her arms to be helped into her robe.

"Your padding first," Julie reminded her.

"Oh, bother the padding!" Amalie seized the filmy robe from her and shrugged it over her nightdress as she ran out into the hall to rap on the count's door.

"Enter," she heard in a sleepy voice. But he had not expected her, for when he saw her he sat up in his bed, his shoulders quite bare, his hair rumpled and his eyes startled. Amalie thought that he must have come in very late.

He pulled back the mosquito gauze that enclosed his bed, and exclaimed, "You, madame?"

"Pardon." She felt a strange fluttering embarrassment. "But Estée has brought the most shocking news from the market. She heard there that your friend, M'sieu Beaulieu, was bludgeoned to death last night on the levee road."

"*Mon Dieu!*"

Jean-Baptiste coughed discreetly in the doorway.

"Don't stand there, Jean-Baptiste! Bring my coffee." The count looked critically at Amalie. "Where is your padding, madame?"

"I will dress presently. I wanted to tell you—"

"You should not leave your chamber unattired," he told her sternly as he took the steaming glass from his servant.

"The padding is uncomfortable, m'sieu, and very warm. Surely, when there is no one but you to see—" She hoped he was noticing the subtle changes taking place in her figure, the soft bulges that made her feel truly a woman, but he sat nursing his coffee, not looking directly at her. His face, sleepy and unshaven as she had never before seen him, looked younger and more vulnerable. She was drawn nearer to his bed.

"Suppose the house caught on fire?" he demanded. "You would be exposed as a silly fraud."

That stung. Besides, he was still talking to her as to a *jeune fille* instead of a countess! "If the house catches fire," she retorted, "Clotie will be exposed, and it will not matter about me. You seem callous about your friend's death, m'sieu. Does it not disturb you?"

"Mon Dieu, can you not see I am disturbed?"

"I cannot help wondering if such a thing could happen to you!"

"But I should not think of going upon that road at midnight unless I were armed and accompanied by a friend, preferably a good swordsman. *Non,* you need have no fear that I will be set upon by murdering thieves. Now, will you leave me so that my servant may dress me? I must call immediately on Madame Beaulieu and offer her my services."

Amalie cried, "You offer them to everyone but me, m'sieu."

"Au revoir, madame!" he said angrily, and she withdrew.

All morning the street buzzed with talk about the dreadful end of Monsieur Beaulieu. Even though Amalie could not hear the talk, she sensed it. Shopkeepers and their customers stood in clusters on the banquette, gossiping. There was much running back and forth from house to house. Her own servants stood in the court gossiping with the tradesmen who came in with their goods.

Amalie took the news to Clotie after the count had left the house, but her sister seemed unmoved.

"You feel nothing for poor Madame Beaulieu, who has lost her husband," Amalie accused her. "No grief moves you but your own."

"Why should anyone be spared what I have suffered?" Clotie demanded. "Why should anyone live, if Deneez cannot?"

Amalie looked sharply at her. Although her sister looked somewhat feverish, Amalie detected a hollow ring to Clotie's sorrow, as if it were now without substance. Had Clotie recovered from her love-sickness, then, and clung to its husks simply because she was bound to it by carrying the trader's child?

Amalie sighed. "I wish I had never heard of Deneez."

At that, Clotie called her an unfeeling brute and burst into tears.

Later that day, the octoroon came to dress Amalie's hair. "It must give you great comfort, madame," she said, when Julie had left them alone, "to know where your husband was last night."

Amalie looked at her in startled anger. "Are you suggesting that *m'sieu le comte* knows anything about that foul deed on the levee road?"

"*Mais, non,* madame! I am sure you have nothing to worry about. But a patron of mine remarked this morning, when discussing that dreadful affair, that it would be unfortunate if *m'sieu le comte* should become involved in a second inquiry before the first is resolved."

"And why did your patron think he should become involved?" Amalie cried, outraged.

Holding Amalie's hair in a firm grasp and brushing it with energy, the octoroon said, "M'sieu Beaulieu was noted for his admiration of Napoleon, madame, and some are speculating that he was murdered because he stumbled upon a royalist plot against Napoleon and would have informed." She gave Amalie's reflection a sidelong glance that added, unmistakably, "*And since any close friends of Madame Amboy's are thought to be royalists—*"

Aloud, she said, "It is known that Napoleon has secret agents in Louisiana."

In spite of herself Amalie felt a chilling apprehension. "Fortunately," she lied bravely, "I happen to know exactly where my husband spent the hour when poor M'sieu Beaulieu was set upon." She blushed a little as she hoped the hairdresser was picturing the count in her chamber at midnight and, inevitably, remembered how he had looked when she burst into his room this morning.

"That is good news, indeed," said Madame Laval, with an enigmatic smile.

The smile told Amalie that Madame Laval had, in some subtle way, been paid for her information. Amalie swallowed the taste of fear, because this time she was not sure what she had paid.

"And why does anyone speak of the count's inquiry?" she asked scornfully. "It is forgotten."

"But, no, madame. Only the other day I heard some friends of the count's discussing it. They were wondering what the peasant said that so offended him. They remarked that he refuses to tell. That is perhaps not wise, madame, for they were guessing the most scandalous things."

The apprehension spread coldly through Amalie's body. It had occurred to her that the hairdresser could be fishing for information. She was certain of it when Madame Laval went on, "They say he told the American judge that he would not reveal what was said, even in the inquiry! His friends say he must be protecting a woman's honor. A Creole understands that, but the American judge says his authority was insulted. That is why they say a second inquiry could result in the Americans sending M'sieu to jail."

To jail! Amalie swallowed hard. "But what a story they have fashioned for their entertainment! I do not know what enraged him, but then I would not expect him to repeat common profanity in my presence."

Blessed Mary! Had she told the count she was not practiced in lying? It seemed that one must learn! For if the octoroon suspected Clotie was still in the house, and why— Now what had put that thought into her mind? Madi's ill-considered excursion to the market, of course. Perhaps it had not been her first? The hairdresser knew Madi was Clotie's servant, for she had dressed Clotie's hair more than once. If Madi had been recognized—

At last Amalie appreciated Julie's warning about letting a gossip in the house that held a secret. But *mon Dieu,* the boredom had been unendurable! And now she dared not dismiss Madame Laval for fear that the woman would whisper her suspicions into the ears of other ladies whose hair she dressed.

Each time the hairdresser came, it seemed, she mentioned Madame Amboy. "Madame Amboy is wearing her hair in a new style that is quite the fashion," she would say and, looking critically at Amalie, add, "but I do not think it would become you, madame."

Or she would mention that Madame Amboy had received a new gown which her husband had bought for her and managed to send from Paris. "It is said that she and her royalist friends are constantly in touch with Paris by way of Barataria and the West Indies." And she would look significantly at Amalie as if this bit of information must have a special meaning for her.

Today she remarked that the absence of Madame Amboy's husband did not seem to distress that lady or curtail her social activities, and Amalie's patience snapped.

"You have something to tell me about Madame Amboy," she said coldly. "What is it?"

The hairdresser's glance, meeting hers in the mirror, was speculative. "I do not know whether it is something you wish to hear, madame."

Amalie bit her lip, her thoughts angry and helpless. She had guessed where the hairdresser's hints were leading, but her need to know was desperate. With an effort, she shrugged. "Then do not tell me."

For a few moments Madame Laval brushed and braided in silence. Then she asked casually, "And how is your sister Ma'm'selle de l'Ouvrier wearing her hair now?"

Amalie raised startled eyes to the reflection of the hairdresser's slight smile. Was there speculation in them? Perhaps even a threat?

"She does not say," she answered at last. "At the plantation we are quite informal in our dress." She paused, reflecting. "I shall not wear my pink ball gown again, for I fear my waist will never again be so narrow." *Blessed Mary, forgive me!* "It could be made to fit you, perhaps."

The smile in the mirror grew more confident. *"Merci,* madame. It is exquisite silk, is it not?" The octoroon laid down her tongs and went to the wardrobe. Taking the dress out of its muslin wrapper, she held it up to her waist and thrust out a foot to spread the skirt, as if marking its size. She could not hide her satisfaction. Draping it across a chair, she picked up her tongs again. "It is a generous gift. How can I show Madame my gratitude?"

"You can tell me what the gossips are saying about my husband and Madame Amboy," Amalie said evenly, although she knew quite well that she was giving the octoroon more to gossip about.

"Naturally I do not believe it." Madame Laval's voice was as smooth as the pink silk gown lying across the chair, and her hands were loving as she picked up another strand of Amalie's hair. "It is their enemies, of course, who say that they were lovers even before M'sieu Amboy left for Paris."

"Of course," Amalie said, in despair.

ELEVEN

AMALIE STOOD behind the shutters opening on her galérie and crossed herself as Monsieur Beaulieu was carried to his stone resting place in the churchyard. A cold winter sun shone down on the procession, led by the priests in their rich vestments and followed by Monsieur Beaulieu's friends and a long, straggling train of curious strangers who had heard of the brutal murder. Monsieur Armand was one of the mourners.

In spite of the somber pace of the procession, there was a subdued air of excitement in the street below her. Sellers of cakes and ginger beer moved along the edges of the parade, chanting their wares. Children skipped along after them, their cheeks reddened by the cold north wind. Amalie longed to be down on the street, pushing through the curious onlookers, sharing in the excited dread the crime had aroused in the city's inhabitants.

Even on this cool day she felt hot and awkward in the bindings that Julie had recently doubled, overlaid by petticoats and gown. Adding to her discontent was the knowledge that immediately after his friend was laid to rest, the count would be leaving New Orleans. He had informed her only last evening.

"Where do you go?" she had asked him, and she recalled his answer with a thrill of fear. She should have known he was going to Barataria, she was thinking, for last week a roughly dressed man wearing a red sash had brought a message for the count. Jean-Baptiste had taken it, and Amalie's curiosity about its contents was never satisfied.

As she watched the progress of the slow-moving cortège, Amalie's thoughts moved back over her conversation with her husband last evening. The count had come in early and found her in the salon, stitching a small garment for Clotie's baby.

"A pretty domestic picture, madame."

Amalie looked closely at him but could detect no irony in his expression. It was so unusual a remark from him that her pulse quickened. "It is an unexpected pleasure to have you home in the evening, M'sieu Armand."

He stood at the mantel, relaxed, his eyes regarding her with bright interest but with an expression somewhat questioning. *"Ma petite,"* he said at last. "I must leave you alone for a few weeks."

"A few *weeks!*" she exclaimed, dismayed.

"I have observed the way you are managing the household, and I am sure you will do very well while I am away. I am taking Jean-Baptiste, of course, but you will have the other servants with you." He added, "I have asked Madame Amboy to call on you to make sure you are well and, if you are in need, to see that your needs are met."

Amalie did not think it necessary to tell him—since apparently Madame Amboy had not—that she was not at home to his friend. "But where do you go?"

"To Barataria."

He will be carrying money was her first frightened thought. *Royalist money!* "But, m'sieu, is not that the hiding place of pirates?"

"They prefer to be called privateers," he said, smiling. "I will leave immediately after the funeral services for M'sieu Beaulieu, which I must attend."

"And what of your inquiry, m'sieu?"

"Inquiry?" he said blankly.

"The inquiry into the deaths of two men on the flatboat which has twice been postponed."

"Oho!" He looked amused. "Your source of information is not reliable, madame. There will be no inquiry."

"It has been dropped?"

"It cannot be held, because no bodies have been recovered."

"But—"

"The captain reported the deaths a regrettable accident. Other witnesses have scattered. The longer the inquiry is delayed, the less the chance that they can be found." He moved impatiently away from the mantel. "If we were still under Spanish rule, the case would have been disposed of in twenty minutes! My Creole peers understand that I could do nothing else. I could not challenge a man who was not my equal, *mon Dieu!* But the Americans saw an opportunity to embarrass one of us."

"I am told there is speculation among your friends about what you overheard on the flatboat deck, m'sieu."

He stopped in his movement around the salon. "Someone has been teasing you for information, no doubt, as they constantly tease me. Do not worry yourself, *ma petite*. The gossips know only that my fiancée's family was slandered, and they will hear no more from my lips."

"And the men who killed M'sieu Beaulieu, will they face an inquiry in the American courts?"

The count's face hardened. "They will hang for it, if they are found!"

A cold draft seemed to have entered the pleasant salon. Amalie shivered. "Even if they are gentlemen? Or," she fabricated on the instant, "were hired by gentlemen?"

"Do not accept the garbage the servants bring back from the market," the count said, with scorn. "A gentleman fights his own battles with his own sword! M'sieu Beaulieu was set upon by murdering thieves!"

"Then are you not afraid to go to Barataria with money?" she blurted.

He shrugged. "One cannot trade without money. Do not let such worries trouble your little head." Moving around the room as he talked, he had come close to her chair. Now he idly picked up the sewing in her lap. She had not time to be pleased at this rare display of his interest before his face altered, and she knew he had just realized what she was making.

"*Bonsoir,* madame," he said shortly, and left her.

She had not seen him this morning, and she would not see him again until he returned from Barataria. And when Clotie's child was born, she was thinking, the child she must pretend was her own and must teach to call the count "Papa"—what then? The road into her future looked impossibly difficult.

The last of the straggling mourners had rounded the corner nearest the church. Amalie turned away from her galérie and made her way through the house and along the passage to Clotie's quarters. It was seldom that Amalie needed comforting, but today she felt painfully alone.

Her sister, however, did not seem pleased to see her. "I am about to take a nap, Amalie," were her first unwelcoming words.

"Oh, Clotie, you have all day to nap! Sit and talk with me. I have something to tell you."

"What is it now?"

Amalie wondered why, when she came into Clotie's rooms, her sister always moved from her chair to the window. Did Clotie wish to call attention to her ballooning figure—as if that were what Amalie came to see—by standing in the light? Facing it, Amalie could not read Clotie's expression.

"The count is going away and will be gone for several weeks. We shall be all alone, Clotie."

Her sister shrugged. "Are we not alone all day and most of the night, anyway?"

"Clotie, do you remember the day we walked along the levee and saw the count talking with that fearful-looking Baratarian?"

"*Oui.*"

"M'sieu Armand is going to Barataria."

"Well?"

She was in one of her nervous, snappish moods, Amalie saw. "Oh, Clotie, I am so frightened for him! He must have been arranging a rendezvous that day. He may be carrying a large sum of money to be sent to the royalists. Madame Laval says that he has enemies, republican followers of Napoleon. And if the Baratarian pirates learn he has money, he could be murdered for it, like poor M'sieu Beaulieu!"

"*Bien!*" Clotie snapped.

"Oh, Clotie," Amalie cried, tears starting to her eyes, "you are no help to me at all!"

She turned to go, but Clotie spoke in a shamed voice. "You are right, Amalie, I am no help to you. And you have been so much help to me. Please do not ever think that I am lacking in gratitude."

Amalie turned back and they embraced, Amalie laughing through her tears as she collided with Clotie's stomach. "It will all be different when this waiting is over. You will be happy again, Clotie."

"*Oui,*" Clotie said, tear-choked.

"Now take your nap. I will come back later."

It was strange how empty and silent the house seemed with the count away. True, as Clotie had not failed to point out, it was actually no different, for the count was usually out all day doing business or visiting with his friends at the Exchange. Yet the house *felt* empty.

It felt stranger still when night fell, knowing that the chamber on the other side of the locked door was empty and, when Amalie wakened, knowing she would not hear Jean-Baptiste's heavy tread pass her door as he carried the count's morning *café au lait*.

The light coming through her shutters was still pale when Amalie wakened one morning and realized that it was early enough that she could go unnoticed on the streets. She rang for Julie and told her she wanted her to help her dress and accompany her to the church to pray for Monsieur Armand's safe return.

Julie approved of the sortie, but she insisted that Amalie's false abdomen must be beyond any questioning doubt in case they encountered an acquaintance among the New Orleans ladies and, as a consequence, bound and strapped her until Amalie wailed, "But I can't move!"

"*Bien.* Then you walk like your sister."

They started out, Amalie feeling awkward and suffocatingly warm. "Poor Clotie. It is not easy for her, is it, Julie?"

"She soon forget all this when her baby come," the black woman said.

Julie knew about birthings; she would be equal to their need, Maman had assured them. As a young girl in Saint Domingue, Julie had assisted a midwife, and she had brought many plantation babies into the world. "We are fortunate to have Julie," Madame de l'Ouvrier had said. Indeed, it seemed quite natural to be depending on Julie. Was that not what Amalie had been doing as long as she could remember?

At the church, she said a prayer for Monsieur Armand, then added prayers for Clotie and for all of them. If it please God, all must go well! *And let him love me.*

Back in the house on rue Bourbon she went at once to her chamber. "If it were summer," she told Julie, "I should be fainting. Loosen these bindings quickly, so that I may breathe! Then bring my breakfast to me here."

Julie lifted Amalie's skirts, the better to undo the knotted ties. As she reached the last knot, they heard Estée admitting someone at the door from the courtyard stair.

"*Ma foi,* it is Madame Laval! Go quickly, Julie, and ask her to wait while I have my breakfast, and then come tie me up again."

"*Oui,* madame."

But the octoroon's step was in the hall. Julie froze with Amalie's skirt lifted, her hands at Amalie's waist holding the binding in place. Amalie swung around to face the doorway and Julie moved awkwardly with her, as the hairdresser appeared.

"*Bonjour,* madame."

"*Bonjour,* Madame Laval." Amalie was a little short of breath because her heart seemed to be going too fast. "I was not expecting you so early. Pray excuse me while I complete my toilette."

The octoroon's tawny eyes moved quickly around the room, and came back to Julie, bright with suspicion. "I came quickly because I have an important message for you, madame."

In her agitation Amalie scarcely heard her. "Estée!" she called to the girl who had let the hairdresser in. "Please take Madame Laval to the little morning room and bring her coffee while she waits."

"But, madame, I must speak with you—" The octoroon's eyes were avidly speculative on Amalie's lifted skirt.

"I will see you directly."Amalie dismissed her with an imperious gesture which was a striking imitation of her mother.

Madame Laval's eyes narrowed to a slit, but she said, *"Merci,* madame," and with another quick glance around, left the room.

Julie tightened the knots on Amalie's binding with an angry jerk, and went to close the door. "How long you goin' let that brown womans come nosin' roun'? She *evil,* I tell you!"

"I am afraid of her, Julie," Amalie confessed.

"Jus' tell her not to come back!"

But if she refused Madame Laval entrance to the house, the woman's suspicions would surely be confirmed. "It is too late," Amalie said, feeling ill. Only now she realized that her too-generous gifts had themselves fed Madame Laval's suspicions. "You were right, all along, Julie. But now it is too late."

Muttering, Julie went off to bring Amalie's breakfast.

When she brought the hairdresser back, Julie followed the octoroon into the chamber and busied herself straightening the bed and putting away Amalie's nightclothes instead of carrying out the breakfast tray.

Madame Laval opened her satchel and set out her tongs and jars. She undid Amalie's braids with long, quick fingers, murmuring, "You may wish to send your woman away, madame, for I was told my message is for your ears alone."

"You may speak in front of my servant."

"I do not think it wise—"

"I will be the judge of that!" Amalie retorted.

Madame Laval picked up a brush and began brushing, holding Amalie's hair so tightly in her left hand that the pulling brought involuntary tears.

"More gently, please!"

"I am sorry, madame." The hairdresser relaxed her hold only a little. "I have a message for you from a very important gentleman who wishes to see you."

"Who is this 'very important gentleman'?"

"He is a Spanish gentleman, madame, a M'sieu Peralta."

"I do not know a M'sieu Peralta."

"True, madame. But the message he has for you is of the utmost importance to your husband's situation."

"My husband?" Amalie faltered. "What has happened to him? Is he in danger?"

"I do not know, madame. I have not been entrusted with the message, only that it is urgent that you receive it."

"Then why does not this M'sieu Peralta come to me?"

"He has his reasons, madame. He has suggested that you meet him at Madame Chouinard's soirée this evening."

"But I no longer go out in society. And I have not met Madame Chouinard," Amalie protested.

"She expects you. She lives in a house on rue Chartres, which is quite near you. Do not hire a carriage, but go on foot. It is extremely important, madame."

"I cannot go out unaccompanied! The man is mad!"

"Take your servant, and ask her to wait for you."

"And how will I recognize M'sieu Peralta among Madame Chouinard's guests?"

"You are *la petite comtesse,* madame. He will know you, and he will find an opportunity to speak privately with you."

Amalie's throat and mouth felt very dry. She did not trust Madame Laval, but at the same time her fear for the count's safety was growing. She thought of the money he must be carrying, and of the desperate men who were rumored to be hiding out in the maze of bayous giving access to Barataria Bay. "And if I do not go?"

"You will regret it," the hairdresser said, with a sudden jerk of her hair that made Amalie cry out in pain. "I am sorry, madame," the octoroon said silkily.

All the time they had been talking, Julie had been angrily pounding pillows and dropping shoes, now and then muttering under her breath. Amalie saw the venom in the look the hairdresser gave her servant and said, "Julie, do try to be more quiet."

But as soon as the octoroon had left, she turned and cried, "Oh, Julie, what am I to do?"

"You ask me now," Julie said angrily. "Why you don' listen to me before?"

Amalie did not answer. She felt a great uneasiness as if some mysterious danger were poised above her, above Clotie, and especially above Monsieur Armand, waiting to pounce. How had it come about? She could see that she had been quite naive, allowing herself to be manipulated. And now, were they not all in the dark woman's power?

Looking back over the small steps that had led her to this unhappy pass, Amalie wondered with a flash of terror if that had not been Madame Laval's goal from the beginning.

TWELVE

ALL DAY Amalie hesitated over her decision to accept the unknown Madame Chouinard's invitation. Her distrust of Madame Laval filled her with forebodings, but, strong as they were, her concern for the count's safety was stronger. She feared that he was involved in a plot against Napoleon—*mon Dieu!* it could even be another attempt to assassinate the man who had made himself an emperor!—and she imagined all manner of dire things that could have happened.

Had the count been captured by Napoleon's secret agents? Was he being held for ransom by pirates? This Monsieur Peralta could be carrying a message from the count himself!

"Then let him come here!" Julie snapped, for Amalie was pouring out her fears to her former nurse, knowing there would be little profit in trying to discuss her predicament with Clotie. "What your fr'en's goin' say if you atten' a soirée now? *They* don' atten' soirées when they *enceinte.*"

"But I do not dare ignore the invitation. If I do, something terrible may happen. You must go with me, Julie."

"You think I let you go alone to a strange house," Julie retorted, "when I nurse' you from your secon' year?"

All day Amalie wavered, going restlessly from her chamber, where she debated what to wear, to the salon where she could look down on the street of shops below the houses and wonder whether the murky clouds that made everything below them look dingy were going to bring rain. Dusk fell over the city, and she still had not resolved the continual debate in her mind between her fears for Monsieur Armand and her distrust of Madame Laval.

As the street darkened and candles were lit in the shops which had not closed their doors, Amalie became aware of a loitering figure she had seen several times before in her compulsive trips to the window. He was an enormous black man in a ragged shirt and frayed trousers, with a nearly bald—or shaven—head. He stood in the recess of a doorway which was across the street and two doors to the left of the chandelier immediately opposite La Rose, the wine shop below her rooms. From the shadowy doorway he was looking directly at the galérie at which she stood concealed by the window draperies.

Amalie called Julie. "Do you see that big black man? He has been there all afternoon."

"He got nothin' to do, that's all."

"Then why does he do it just there, where he can watch this house? Do you know who he is?"

"Never see him before."

"I have a strange feeling about him," Amalie said, dropping the curtain which she had pulled aside to better examine the dark figure. "Who sent him, I wonder?"

"You nervous as a cat," Julie said. "Come, let me dress you. Bes' we fin' out what that Spanish gen'man got to say. You can't learn nothin' walkin' your floor."

Julie was right. She would regret it if she did not go, the dark woman had warned, and whether the threat was to the count's life or to Clotie's guarded secret, Amalie had no choice.

Amalie's gowns had been made to the measurements of Clotie, taken by Madi and carried by Julie to the dressmaker, who was told she must make them without a fitting because of *la petite comtesse's* shyness. They were all loose and flowing, in pale colors. Amalie chose a soft blue, and after dark, with black cloak and veil covering her dress and her hair, she quietly slipped out of the house with Julie, who carried a small lantern to light their way.

There was no moon. The night smelled heavily of the river, of roasting coffee and of the rotting orange peel in the gutter. They looked carefully in the darkened doorways they passed for the giant black man with the bald head, but he was no longer in the street.

"Jus' like I said, a riverboatmans with nothin' to do," Julie commented.

It was a short walk to the rue Chartres where there were fewer shops. The number they sought was painted beside a rounded arch in a blank wall. Julie shone her lantern through the arch, dimly lighting a small paved court. High windows, half-barred with curved iron railings, looked down on it. Only two of them glowed with light. At the left of the court, a dark stairwell ran up between two solid walls. It was a rather somber court, with only a few flowerboxes to lighten its weight of stone and plaster.

Amalie's steps slowed to a stop. Then she saw the movement of a figure behind the glowing curtain of one window, and was oddly reassured by this sign of normal habitation. "Come," she said to Julie.

Julie proceeded her up the stair, lighting her way, and Amalie waited as Julie lifted the brass knocker they found at the top of the passage.

The door was opened almost immediately by a liveried black servant who said politely, "Enter, madame."

Amalie stepped forward, and Julie followed her. The servant led them down a hallway and opened a door, ushering them into an empty salon. The room was pleasantly furnished, Amalie thought, with a brocaded sofa and gilt-and-velvet chairs arranged in a comfortable grouping. On a low table, beside a carafe of wine and two glasses, stood an exquisite framed miniature of a young matron. Amalie wondered if it were a portrait of her hostess.

It was thoughtful of Madame Chouinard to have them ushered into an empty room for Amalie's interview with Monsieur Peralta so that she would not have to face the curious eyes of the other guests. But the house was strangely silent!

Amalie walked about the room, fingering the bric-a-brac—an ornate brass clock with a glass dome caught her approving eye—and examining the portraits on the walls. Julie stood, silent, just inside the door. Then Amalie paused and they both listened to a firm tread approaching in the hall. The door opened and a man entered.

He was old enough to have thinning hair, but young enough to have rosy lips showing through his luxuriant beard. His eyes were large and luminous with an almost caressing softness, and he was a little too plump.

"M'sieu Peralta?" Amalie asked, a slight note of surprise in her voice.

He bowed. "Your servant, *madame la comtesse.*" He came toward her, took her hand and raised it to his lips.

"You have a message from my husband, m'sieu?"

His already large eyes widened slightly. Then he smiled. *"Oui,* madame, a message from your husband."

She withdrew her hand, which he had continued to hold, and he went to the carafe and poured wine into the two glasses. Watching him, Amalie thought with dread, *He is preparing me for unpleasant news.*

Extending one glass to Amalie, he glanced toward the door where Julie stood, a solid, unyielding figure. "It was foresighted of you to bring your servant, madame. She can wait for you in the entry."

"But I cannot speak with you in private, unattended!" Amalie protested.

"How unfortunate. It is impossible for me to address you, madame, in the presence of your servant." He spoke in a curiously light, amused tone, almost as if he were teasing her. He raised his wineglass. "To—to *m'sieu le comte!*" The rosy lips parted over white teeth.

His toast frightened Amalie. She signaled Julie to await her outside. Glowering, Julie left the salon.

When they were alone, Monsieur Peralta gestured toward Amalie with his glass, and she drank with him. Then she set her glass down, and begged, "Now, m'sieu, what have you to tell me?"

Again she thought he looked pleasantly surprised. "My servant has left us a cold repast, madame. Would you not like it before we—er—talk?"

"I did not come here for food, m'sieu—" she began, baffled.

"Ah, madame!"

"—but for your message, which Madame Laval said was most urgent."

"It is, indeed, madame, and now that you have come it grows more urgent!"

"Then, please do not torment me, m'sieu," Amalie said, becoming impatient with his simpering manner. "What is it that you have to tell me?"

He drained his glass and set it down. "That you are a delicious confection, *madame la comtesse!*"

Amalie said, startled, "I beg your pardon!"

His eyes glistened. "I have looked forward to this moment ever since I first laid my eyes on you. It was at the Salle d'Orleans as you curtsied to the governor and his lady. I begged to be presented, as you remember—"

"No, m'sieu, I am sorry—"

"So dainty you were, so delectable! Everyone was saying '*Que belle, la petite comtesse!*' As for me, madame, every word I overheard you speak struck at my heart."

Amalie, greatly shocked at this outburst, was backing away from him as he moved toward her. "M'sieu, you forget yourself! I did not accept Madame Chouinard's invitation to hear these wild sentiments."

"Madame, can you not see that I tremble with desire? You must take pity on me!"

"Pray restrain yourself," she begged, "or her other guests will hear you."

"Ah, but you are charming! You must know there are no other guests. The invitation was mine, *ma chérie.*" His too-red lips were moist. "Madame Chouinard is with her husband on his plantation downriver. My sister does not spend much time in the city, and I use this house as my own. Have no fear, *chérie,*" he said, as she blanched. "I sent my servant away after he let you in. We are alone."

"*Mon Dieu!*" Amalie cried. "I was right to distrust Madame Laval. She has tricked me, m'sieu. She told me you had a message of the utmost importance for me."

"But I do, madame. The message is that I can no longer contain my passion for you. And since you have said you did not come here for food, I see that you share my impatience. Do let us drop the coquetry, shall we? Now that you have come at last, I can support no delay. *Ma chérie*—my charming little flower—"

"Did that wicked woman lead you to believe that I would make an assignation with you?"

His eyes narrowed. "It is delightful of you to pretend such virtue, but I assure you it is not necessary to tease me further—"

"Pretend!" Amalie had retreated from him until she had backed against a table. He came insolently close to her, his face alight with pleasure. He was *enjoying* this!

"I am sorry to disappoint you, m'sieu," Amalie said, with such icy anger that it finally pierced his flirtatious manner.

"Madame, I will not be disappointed now!" he said, reaching for her.

Amalie realized, incredulous, that whether or not he believed her to be flirting with him, he meant to take her by force. "But, m'sieu," she faltered, for the first time becoming afraid for herself, "I—can you not see that I—?"

His hands were on her waist, squeezing it. "Aha! Padding!" he exclaimed, in such triumph that Amalie knew Madame Laval must have confided her suspicions. "Is this how you keep your husband from your bed, madame?" With a darting movement he snatched at her clothing and ripped away both gown and petticoat, exposing Julie's artful padding.

Amalie drew a shocked, speechless breath, for a second incapable of action. It had not occurred to her that a man of society could behave in such ungentlemanly fashion.

He laughed. "You are a clever one! Ah, darling—"

She screamed then, a scream that was cut off abruptly as his hands came up to her throat. His beard brushed her averted face as his bloodred lips sought her mouth. She was fighting for breath now, but his hands did not loosen on her throat until he had covered her mouth with his own. His kiss was the cruel kiss of a strong man bent on having his way with her. Amalie reached behind her, frantically groping for some heavy object with which she could strike him.

The clock! She almost had it in her grasp when the table crashed over. She heard the clock strike the floor with a tinkle of broken glass and a soft *bong!* of its bell.

She did not hear the door open, but she became aware of Julie's presence in the room through soft sounds of movement that the man attacking her was too inflamed to note. Now, as she struggled in his arms, she maneuvered to keep his back to Julie. She knew when Julie picked up the heavy clock and she heard the sickening thud when Julie struck the back of his head with it.

He slumped against Amalie and she sank, weeping wildly, to the floor, half under the heavy weight of his body.

"M'selle Amalie, M'selle Amalie," Julie was crying softly, over and over, as she helped Amalie extricate herself and rise to her feet.

Amalie looked down at the unconscious man who now lay on his back. A tiny trickle of blood ran out from under his head on the French carpet. "Is he dead?" she whispered, in horror.

Julie dropped to her knees and bent over him, leaving Amalie swaying on her feet. *"Non,* madame. He lives. Come, quick, before he wake." Getting up, she looked at Amalie's ruined clothing and disarranged hair with dismay, and snatched up Amalie's cloak, which she had laid across a chair. "Can you hol' up your skirts?"

Amalie nodded. Her breath was still coming in gasps. Julie closed the door on the prone Monsieur Peralta and, with her arm around Amalie, now draped in her cloak and veil, hurried her down the hall to the entry. She picked up her lantern there and held it above the stair. They ran down to the cheerless court into a soft spatter of raindrops, and through it to Chartres Street.

There Amalie stopped in the shadowed porte cochère. "How can I go through the streets like this?" she cried, trembling, clutching at the torn bosom of her dress with a gesture that let her cloak fall open, exposing still more of her *déshabille.*

With an exclamation Julie wrapped her in her cloak again. It was still early, and there were a number of New Orleans citizens abroad. With a little cry of distress, Amalie recognized a strolling couple whose soirée she and Clotie had attended with the count. She ducked back into the courtyard, out of sight of the street.

The raindrops were falling more quickly now, a gentle tattoo on the broad leaves of a tubbed banana beside them. Abruptly, it became a tropical downpour, nearly drenching them before Julie pushed Amalie back into the protection of the porte cochère's arch. They dared not remain in its shelter too long. The man upstairs might awaken, or a servant might come—how did they know Monsieur Peralta had told the truth when he said they were alone in the house?

But the rain had driven others to seek shelter, and now the street was deserted except for a man running with his coat pulled up over his head. The drumming downpour of several minutes became a soft rain again, and they moved out of the porte cochère and ran along the banquette. They had not gone far when a carriage drawn by a smartly equipped pair of grays turned into the street and came swiftly toward them. Amalie shrank against the blank wall, trying to hide her face.

The carriage stopped directly in front of them. A woman's hand drew aside its curtain, and a woman's voice said, *"Ma foi!* Get in, quickly!"

Amalie cowered against the wall, frozen, but Julie put her strong black arm around her and pulled her forward. They climbed into the carriage and the woman, who sat alone in it, gave an order to her driver, who started up smartly.

"*Merci,* madame." Amalie turned to face her benefactor and gasped, "*You?*"

"I am taking you to my house, *madame la comtesse,*" Madame Amboy said quietly, "where you can compose yourself."

THIRTEEN

"YOU SAY that he sent his servant away?" Madame Amboy asked.

"*Oui.*" Amalie sat, white-faced and shivering with a chill, before a small fire in Madame Amboy's elegant boudoir, wrapped in one of her rescuer's velvet robes. Nearby, Julie sat stitching up the rents in Amalie's damp garments as best she could, while they answered Madame Amboy's deft questions and gratefully sipped her wine.

"He said we were alone in the house. Madame, if he should die—!"

"Do not assume that he will," Madame Amboy said, smiling. "M'sieu Peralta has a very hard head." She rang for a servant. The young black man who had driven her carriage entered. "You know M'sieu Peralta's manservant, *n'est-ce pas?*"

"*Oui,* madame. They call him Henri."

"He has been given a night out. You must find him as quickly as possible and tell him that his master has met with an accident and needs his assistance. It is urgent that he return home without delay. Has the cannon been fired for curfew?"

"*Oui,* madame."

"Then you will have to be very careful. Do you think you can find him without encountering the gendarmes? They must not learn of his mishap."

"*Oui,* madame. He will be with his woman."

"*Bien.*" She explained to Amalie, "When the cannon is fired in the Place d'Armes, the streets must be cleared, as you know. But my Anatole is clever. He will get help for your unfortunate suitor."

When the servant had gone, Amalie put her hands to her face and cried, "I am ruined! Everyone will know that I went to his house—"

"*Non,* madame, I do not think it likely. It was fortunate that I was returning along rue Chartres at that moment, and fortunate, too, that the rain kept many people off the street."

"But the count—my husband—when he learns how I was duped, he will think more than ever that I am but a foolish child!"

"You must not tell him what happened tonight," Madame Amboy warned, "for if you do, he will be obliged to challenge M'sieu Peralta."

"I do not see how it can be helped," Amalie said miserably. "The count has many friends. Someone will tell him, and if I do not tell him the truth of it, what may he not believe?"

"I am sure that M'sieu Peralta will fabricate a story to explain the lump on his head. Do you imagine he will want to admit that you and Julie bested him? He will be too humiliated. You will see! But how did he persuade you to come?" Madame Amboy's quick eyes could not have missed the padding beneath Amalie's torn clothing, but, discreetly, she had not mentioned it.

"I was told he had a message of utmost importance to my husband's situation, and since my husband is away—I have been concerned about him, madame, ever since he left on a dangerous mission. For reasons of secrecy, M'sieu Peralta requested that I meet him at his sister's soirée, but I was tricked. There was no soirée."

"Did M'sieu Armand tell you his was a dangerous mission?" Madame Amboy asked thoughtfully.

"He tells me nothing!" Indignation sharpened Amalie's voice. "He thinks me still a *jeune fille.*"

Madame Amboy leaned forward to pick up the poker and stir her fire. "May I ask how old you are, *madame la comtesse?*"

"I am sixteen!" Amalie looked at her rescuer defiantly. "Madame, I know the count is engaged in activities that could bring him into danger. I have been warned that he has enemies. And he told me he was going to Barataria!"

"But many men go to the privateers' province, and for many reasons. They go there to buy slaves and other luxuries that no longer may be legally imported—"

"And for other more secret reasons, *n'est-ce pas?*" Amalie challenged her.

Madame Amboy shrugged. She looked very thoughtful.

It was a tacit admission, was it not? Madame Amboy could hardly say more, could she, when she herself was in the thick of the plotting? A hotbed of royalists, Madame Laval had said of her salon. Probably Madame Amboy knew more about the count's journey than he had seen fit to tell his wife! Amalie asked, in a small voice, "Is it true that you are the count's mistress?"

"Ma foi!" Madame Amboy said, startled. "Who has been telling you such gossip?"

"Madame Laval, the hairdresser."

"Indeed! You must not believe everything that mischief maker tells you!" She looked even more thoughtfully at Amalie. "Was it, perchance, Madame Laval who sent you to M'sieu Peralta's house?"

"Oui."

Madame Amboy reached across the hearth and took Amalie's cold hands in hers. Her brilliant eyes had grown very soft. "M'sieu Armand and I are old friends," she said gently, "and I was happy for him when he married. I have wanted to be a friend to you, also. I can at least thank the octoroon for giving me that opportunity. But you must have nothing more to do with her. She has been playing a little game with you, hoping to be able to make both you and M'sieu Peralta pay her for keeping a scandalous secret. Do you see?"

Amalie saw only too well. Madame Amboy's view of her situation only confirmed the apprehensions about her hairdresser which she had been trying to suppress. She looked at her new friend in despair, knowing herself to be hopelessly in Madame Laval's power. For she was almost certain the octoroon suspected what Monsieur Armand and Maman had joined forces to keep secret—Clotie's folly!

"I been knowin' that one evil," Julie said darkly from her corner. "She have the evil eye."

"Julie," Madame Amboy said, "will you go down to my kitchen and ask my cook to make us some coffee to warm your mistress? I believe she can find some fresh-baked sweet cakes, also."

Julie put down her sewing and rose.

"Carry that candle—the one in the brass holder there—and take the stair at the end of the hall." After she had left them, Madame Amboy said, "Julie was your nurse, *n'est-ce pas?*"

"How did you know?"

"Have you never thought of how galling it must be to be a slave? There are only two ways black women can achieve any power in our society. The first is as our nurses. We never quite lose our dependence on them, do we?"

Amalie acknowledged the truth of this with a rueful smile. "Julie is always telling me what to do. And most of the time it would have profited me to listen."

Madame Amboy nodded in amused understanding. "The second way is the way Madame Laval has taken. She has purchased her freedom—who knows how? Possibly with the threat of telling a secret, *non?* Now she trades in secrets and plays on our fears in order to gain an ascendancy over us. She is notorious in New Orleans. It must have given her much satisfaction to be able to frighten you, a countess, into going to meet M'sieu Peralta after she had led him to believe you were enamoured of him. If his ill-considered assault on you had succeeded, Madame Laval would hold a whip over you both."

"I have been a fool!"Amalie exclaimed. "I allowed her to come with her diverting gossip because I was bored. And now I greatly fear her. If I refuse her entrance to my house, she will—I fear she will spread gossip about me."

"Come now, are we not her equal in wits?" Madame Amboy said gaily. "We must outwit her."

"But how?"

"We will find a way. After all, her nasty little scheme has failed."

Amalie told herself, depressed, that Madame Amboy could not know how completely the octoroon had it in her power to ruin the de l'Ouvriers, and with them the count's expected heir, for neither her parents nor Monsieur Armand had the means to buy the octoroon's silence.

But Julie returned just then with steaming cups of coffee and a plate of small cakes, and after Amalie had eaten three she found she was less gloomy about her situation. She was beginning to feel more relaxed, not only from the warmth of the fire and Madame Amboy's excellent wine, and now the hot drink, but from the heartening glow of the older woman's confidence.

"Julie, is my gown wearable yet? I am growing intolerably sleepy."

"*Non,* madame, I have not finished."

"And since I have sent my coachman out to find M'sieu Peralta's servant," Madame Amboy said, "I cannot summon my carriage for you. I am afraid you will have to spend the night here, *madame la comtesse,* for he will not brave General Wilkinson's martial law to drive you home after curfew."

"Are we under martial law, then?" Amalie exclaimed. "I thought the curfew was only for slaves and the soldiers from the barracks."

"You are too isolated, *chère.* We must do something about that. Yes, General Wilkinson, who still talks of war with Spain, has taken matters into his own hands, since the governor would not act. The American general is a tyrant! His curfew is onerous and quite ridiculous, but it is dangerous not to observe it. Will your absence from home be noted?"

Amalie considered. She had not told Clotie she was going out, but Clotie would not leave her apartments unless there were a fire. The servants doubtless were all fast asleep by now. "I think I will not be missed until early morning, madame, unless there should be trouble."

"What trouble could there be?"

"None that I anticipate."

"Then I shall wake you and take you home at daybreak," Madame Amboy promised.

Amalie did not see what else she could do. Taking a candle, Madame Amboy led her to a small bedchamber and provided her with one of her own nightgowns that on Amalie fell to the floor and trailed on it by at least two inches. As she settled herself sleepily behind the mosquito curtains, Amalie reflected that Madame Amboy probably was able to look the count squarely in the eye, which must be something of an advantage.

To her surprise, she did not relive Monsieur Peralta's assault upon her in nightmares, but slept soundly until Julie came in with her morning *café au lait* in one hand and a candle in the other. There was a soft pelting of raindrops on the roof and the galérie outside the window. As Amalie sat up in bed and drank her coffee, the rain rose to a fierce rattle, but while she dressed it subsided again to a dull drumroll.

It was still raining from a black sky and the wet streets were deserted when, a little later, Madame Amboy drove her and Julie through them to the count's house.

"M'sieu Peralta is in bed with a slight concussion he got from falling down in a fit," Madame Amboy told Amalie with a mischievous smile deepening her dimples. "At least that is the story he gave his doctor, according to Anatole, who stayed to help his man get him to his bed."

"And what of the clock?" Amalie asked anxiously.

"Is that what struck him?" Madame Amboy laughed at her own wit.

"I smash' it on his head," Julie explained.

"He probably hit his head on it when he fell. But we shall let him fabricate his own story, *n'est-ce pas?*"

As the carriage entered through the porte cochère, Amalie's servants ran out into the rain toward them. Estée, in the lead, was laughing and weeping, crying, "Madame, oh, madame!" Then, as she came up to the carriage door and looked inside, her expression changed to one of dismay. "M'selle is not with you?" she blurted.

Behind her Dulcie, her honey-colored face contorted with worry, said sternly, "Hush, Estée!" and Estée clapped her hands to her mouth.

M'selle? She could not mean Clotie! "What is it?" Amalie cried, thoroughly alarmed, "What has happened?"

Callou, his skinny body hunched in a taut question mark of fright, answered her. "She gone."

"Gone?" Amalie repeated sharply. "Gone where?"

They were silent, their faces stamped with guilt and fear.

Callou put out his hands to help her as Amalie, oblivious now of Madame Amboy beside her, jumped from the carriage and started running across the court. When she burst into Clotie's rooms, a few minutes later, she stopped and recoiled. They looked as if a hurricane had swept in from the Gulf to blow through them. Bedding was stripped from her bed, some of it missing. Clotie's wardrobe stood open and clothes were thrown over the bed and trailing on the floor. Her jewel box was missing from its usual place on her dressing table.

"Mon Dieu!" Amalie whispered. "Was she abducted?"

Beside her, Julie demanded, "Where that worthless Madi?"

"She gone, too." Estée had run after them. Dulcie and Callou came into the room behind Estée, and Dulcie began explaining, with excited interjections from both of her helpers.

"We hear nothin'!"

"Nothin' but the rain, all night."

"It silent as the grave, whatever took 'em—"

"Oh, madame, we think you an' Julie gone, too!"

After a little, Amalie began to make a connected story of it. Callou, the first one up, had gone by Julie's open door on his way to the kitchen to make the fire, and noticed that her bed had not been slept in. When he reported this to Dulcie she thought it best to carry the tale to her mistress. But in Amalie's chamber she found that madame's bed had not been used, either. Alarmed, they did not panic until Madi failed to come for M'selle Claudine's *café au lait*.

"So we come an' fin' this!" Dulcie finished, with a tragic sweep of her arms.

"Did I hear you say Ma'm'selle Claudine is missing?" It was Madame Amboy, standing in the doorway behind them.

Amalie turned reluctantly to face her. "Madame, it seems you are fated to learn all my secrets."

"They are safe with me, *ma chère*."

"*Merci*, madame. Yes, these are my sister's rooms. She has been living here, although we gave it out that she had returned to Les Chênes."

"I think I understand. You are planning to take her child as your own, *n'est-ce pas?*"

Amalie felt an admiration for the older woman, and a gratitude that she had gone straight to the heart of her problem without asking for the details that gossip fed on. "I did not think you could have missed seeing my padding," she confessed. "M'sieu Peralta saw through my subterfuge—or was told by Madame Laval. I am sure she suspects the truth."

"And now Ma'm'selle Claudine has left the snug nest you made for her?"

"Or been carried away! Madame, she would not leave here of her own wish. She is five months pregnant! Where would she go?"

"To the nuns?"

"*Mais, non!* She would not wish her child registered as illegitimate, and that would have to be done if the nuns should bring it into the world."

Madame Amboy surveyed the wind-tossed room with the thoughtful expression Amalie was beginning to find familiar. "Let us look around a bit and see if Ma'm'selle Claudine has not left you a message."

"I am not thinking!" Amalie took a deep breath and tried to control the panic that was causing such confusion in her mind. "Dulcie, you return to the kitchen and prepare a heartening breakfast for everyone. Take Estée and Callou with you. Julie, you stay and help us. We will go through Ma'm'selle Clotie's belongings and see what was taken besides her jewel box."

It was soon obvious that the disarray in the rooms had been caused by haste rather than a struggle. "Very little of her own clothing is missing," Amalie announced, after a quick inventory. "A warm cloak and several gowns." She could almost hear Clotie's voice saying scornfully, *I want nothing bought with the money of a murderer.* "But all the small garments she stitched are gone."

"That shows forethought, does it not, even in haste?"

"But why was the bed stripped?"

"Is more than a blanket missing? She could have wrapped her layette in the blanket to protect it from the rain."

"No, nothing—yes, a pillow! *Mon Dieu,* she is not sleeping outside somewhere?"

"More likely in a carriage."

"Then her abductor is not inconsiderate of her comfort." Monsieur Arouet's desperate face, on the occasion when he had come seeking encouragement to follow Clotie to Les Chênes, flashed in Amalie's memory.

"I do not think she was abducted," said Madame Amboy. "I think she has run away."

Tears gathered in Amalie's eyes. "She hates M'sieu Armand, madame, but she would not run away from *me*. Without penning a note? Why, she made me promise to keep her with me always!" She looked pleadingly at Madame Amboy, who returned her look questioningly.

"I know I have been impatient with her, but a person in love can be so *tiresome!*"

"You have never been in love?" There was a hint of amusement in the older woman's gentle reproach.

"I love my husband very much, but I intend never to be tiresome about it!" Amalie's voice held a tremor. "Do you think perhaps Clotie has resented it that Papa indulged me? Maman thinks me dreadfully spoiled, and perhaps I am, but Clotie was always the beautiful one. I loved her, madame. I thought her a goose, but I loved her! Let us look further. She must have left a note for me."

"Perhaps," Madame Amboy suggested, "she sent it by her servant to your rooms."

"*Oui.*" Amalie's spirits lifted.

It was still raining on the courtyard paving stones, drenching the tubbed plants whose leaves quivered under the pelting drops. Amalie led Madame Amboy through the kitchen passage to her wing. It was fortunate that she did, for they had scarcely gained Amalie's chamber when the sound of the knocker echoed imperiously down the hall, and they heard Estée coming to answer it.

Listening, Amalie paled when she heard the visitor's voice. "It is *la* Laval!"

Madame Amboy drew a sharp breath. "She is coming for her pound of flesh."

Now the octoroon's quick steps sounded in the hall. She was ignoring Estée's protests and coming unannounced directly to Amalie's chamber.

Amalie was looking, dismayed, at her reflection in the mirror. Her dress, still damp and badly wrinkled, plainly showed the rough handling it had received, in spite of Julie's hasty stitching. "I cannot let her see me like this!"

"Quick! Into your bed!" Madame Amboy ordered. "Let me confront her."

FOURTEEN

THE TURBAN which the Creoles called a *tignon* was no longer mandatory for free women of color, who had been required to wear it when Louisiana was under Spanish rule, but Madame Laval still affected it, and on her it became an exotic headdress. Today, her *tignon* was of a light vermilion silk that made her cheeks shine like burnished copper, and added a golden sparkle to her eyes. She advanced toward Amalie's open door with a brazen confidence but found her way barred by Madame Amboy, tall and elegant and quite formidable in bearing.

"*Madame la comtesse* does not require your services this morning."

The octoroon's eyes, bright and inquisitive as a bird's, darted around Madame Amboy to take in the entire room before coming to rest on Amalie, who was in bed with the coverlet pulled up to her chin.

"Madame?" the hairdresser inquired, a faint amused insolence in her tone.

"As you see, I am indisposed." Amalie did not have to pretend to be ill. Under the coverlet she trembled. She was quite pale. Julie stood beside the bed holding a glass of water, her face dark as a thundercloud.

"I am sorry, madame," the hairdresser said in her silkiest voice. "I will return tomorrow." She turned away with an ever so slight flip of her hip in the direction of Madame Amboy.

"Hmf!" said Julie.

They listened until they heard the soft clack of the hairdresser's step on the outside stair. They heard her pause to lift her cape to cover her headdress, then run splashing through the rain-drenched court.

"*Tiens!*" Madame Amboy said then. "We must give that one her just deserts, *non?*"

"But she suspects that Clotie never left here," Amalie said in despair. "I am certain she told M'sieu Peralta I was wearing padding, and she must have guessed why. She can ruin us all, madame."

Madame Amboy considered this in her deliberate way. "Perhaps, by running away, Ma'm'selle Claudine has given us an opportunity to silence the woman."

"I cannot think how, madame. But then, I am so distraught by what Clotie has done that I cannot think. Where can she have gone?"

"She must have gone to someone she trusts, someone who could help her."

Amalie climbed out of her bed and let Julie unbutton and discard her ruined gown, and slip a simple, white morning dress over her head. "But she had no friends she would trust with such a terrible secret."

"Are you sure? No one? She could not travel far without help, I think. But why did she go?"

Amalie sat down and let Julie begin brushing and braiding her hair. "She was not happy here, madame, but she had no other choice —or so I thought."

Estée arrived with hot coffee and fresh rolls and butter on a tray which she placed on a small table between the two women. Madame

Amboy's clever face was animated, her eyes bright with interest. "I think you do know someone who might help her, *n'est-ce pas?*" she said, when the girl had gone. "You may speak plainly, *madame la comtesse.*"

"Do you know a M'sieu Arouet?"

"François Arouet? A young man who writes poetry?"

"*Oui.* He stood for hours outside this house, staring up at my windows. I had him brought inside and questioned him. He had been writing love letters and sending them to Les Chênes, and was distraught because Clotie did not answer them. He had some notion about seeking permission to follow Clotie there and offer for her hand. You can imagine how that disturbed me, madame! I am not sure I dissuaded him."

"Then perhaps he—"

"But Clotie scorned his notes! She would not—" Amalie stopped, remembering her strange impression lately that Clotie's grief for her "Deneez" had become mere habit. Was she mistaken in thinking Clotie would not consider Monsieur Arouet's suit?

Madame Amboy was watching her shrewdly. "Suppose he did suspect Ma'm'selle was still in your house? How could he have communicated with her?"

"Her servant!" Amalie exclaimed. She had remembered the day she caught Madi outside the house, and Clotie saying, so defiantly, *She is my servant!* Had Clotie been trying to prevent her from questioning Madi? And Madi—Amalie had a vivid memory of the slave staring at the floor, twisting her trembling hands. What secret had Madi known? If she had only wrung it out of the girl!

Clotie had been different that day—perhaps *since* that day!—standing with her back to the light, mechanically repeating her wails of grief for her lover. How deceptive she had become, Amalie thought angrily.

"But if he did discover her presence here," she argued aloud, "and managed through her servant to communicate with her, he must have been shocked to discover her condition. Would he still want to offer for her?"

"He is a romantic," Madame said enigmatically.

"But surely his parents would object."

"M'sieu Arouet is independent because he controls his inheritance. Could they be returning to Les Chênes to face your father?"

"I think it unlikely," Amalie said, remembering Papa's rage and Maman's distress at Clotie's predicament.

"Any inquiries we make must be very discreet," said Madame Amboy, "but it will be a simple matter for me to discover whether or not M'sieu Arouet also left his home last night. In the meantime, let us turn our thoughts to that mischievous hairdresser. I think we must clear away all traces of your sister's occupancy of those rooms before *la* Laval returns tomorrow morning, hoping to find you alone."

"*Ma foi!*" Amalie began, alarmed at the prospect of facing Madame Laval alone.

"There is no time to waste, my dear. Once everything that belonged to your sister is put away, we will discuss my idea. Can you trust your servants?"

"I must," Amalie said simply. "The count trusted them."

With all helping except Dulcie, who had kitchen work, they tore into the task with energy. The gowns Clotie left behind were put into Amalie's armoire or packed away in boxes with every feminine trinket they found. Callou transferred some of the count's possessions to restore a certain masculine look to the rooms Monsieur Armand had once used as bachelor quarters.

When all was ready for Madame Amboy's inspection, that young woman stood in the middle of the room and clapped her forehead. "Perfume!"

"Madame?" Amalie said, startled.

"The octoroon is no fool. She will *smell* your sister's presence! Callou, go and bring us some of M'sieu Armand's snuff. We will scatter it, rub some into the carpet. These rooms must reek of it!"

"Bring the small brass spittoon that sits in your master's chamber," Amalie called after him as Callou ran off, grinning, and she was too absorbed to note that Madame Amboy was using the count's name with easy familiarity. When all was ready, Amalie and Julie sat down with her to plot the octoroon's comeuppance.

The following morning, when Julie admitted Madame Laval, the hairdresser found Amalie still in her bed. Beneath the coverlet Amalie's hands were tightly clenched. She closed her eyes briefly and silently implored the Blessed Virgin, then lifted her chin. She did not wait for a greeting but plunged into her attack in a cold and imperious voice.

"I shall not require your services any longer, Madame Laval."

The hairdresser's eyes narrowed to slits. Amalie noticed with the detachment of desperation the jungle of dark lashes through which the eyes glittered like gold. "Madame is being hasty. It is no doubt her—indisposition." Her tone implied that she knew a demeaning secret about Amalie's feigned illness.

"Indeed?" Amalie asked icily. "Did you expect me to overlook the lie you told me about Madame Chouinard's invitation? Fortunately, I sent my servant"—she nodded toward Julie, who stood, scowling, beside Amalie's dressing table—"to tell Madame Chouinard I was indisposed."

She saw the faintest flicker of doubt in Madame Laval's face, but it was quickly gone. "You did not go, madame?" Her eyes widened, became brilliant with alarm. "Then you did not receive the message concerning your husband? But he could be in grave danger!"

In spite of her resolution, Amalie's heart skipped a beat with fear. "This messenger, if he is not a product of your imagination, knows where to find me, does he not? Certainly, I shall not go looking for him when, if I am to keep my child to full term, I find I must remain in bed."

At these words a change came over Madame Laval. She tossed her head in a curious gesture of satisfaction and took a step forward. "Your child?" she said, with the most insolent insinuation. "You have no child to lose! You may be able to fool your friends, *madame la comtesse,* but you cannot deceive your hairdresser."

"What nonsense are you speaking now?" Amalie said angrily, but beneath the coverlet her palms were wet. "I am no longer amused by your stories, for I find no substance in them—only an unworthy desire to excite or alarm. I must ask you to leave my house, Madame Laval."

The woman's yellowish eyes flashed a warning of what she was about to do. Like a cat she sprang forward with her hand outstretched to snatch the covers from Amalie's bed and expose her. But Julie had been watching for this. She moved incredibly fast and stood, large and implacable, barring the slender octoroon's way.

"You cannot turn me out so easily, madame." Madame Laval's whisper was more menacing than her voice. "I know your secrets! Your sister is hidden in this house, and I know why."

Amalie regarded her for a long, silent moment during which she could see Madame Laval's sense of power swelling. Her implied threat was now an open challenge. A cold dread of the woman threatened to paralyze Amalie. How close she had been to delivering herself up to this woman's wicked will!

"And what do you propose to do with this knowledge you think you have?" Amalie asked at last.

Madame Laval's eyes glittered with triumph. "I should not like to embarrass Madame," she said smoothly, "or to repeat information which the count's enemies could use to discredit him."

"Wouldn't you?" Amalie hoped she was concealing her involuntary spasm of fear at this reminder of the count's enemies.

"*Mais, non,* madame. I am sure we can make some arrangement."

Amalie stared at the woman, who had begun by serving and diverting her and now stood before her, swollen with power and threatening her. It seemed to Amalie that for the first time in her life she was looking into the very heart of evil. Her revulsion changed to indignation at the woman's bland assumption that she, Amalie, was her helpless victim. Anger made her young voice crack like a whip. "Julie!"

"*Oui,* madame?"

"Show Madame Laval through the house. Be certain that she inspects every storage room and closet," she said, in cold contempt. "When she has satisfied herself that Mademoiselle Claudine is not, and has not been, concealed in my house, show her the door. From today, she is to be refused entrance."

"*Oui,* madame." With an echo of Amalie's contempt, Julie jerked her head at the octoroon, whose mouth had curved in a little smile of disbelief.

Julie was capable of projecting menace, too, Amalie saw in sudden delight. With a new confidence ringing in her voice, Amalie said, "One thing more, Madame Laval. I am sure Madame Chouinard would be horrified to learn of her innocent part in your deception. I believe she would join me in lodging a complaint with the gendarmerie if we hear any more of this matter."

She had not planned to go so far, but she could have hugged herself when the hairdresser stared at her for a stunned moment.

Then Madame Laval said, contemptuously, "And implicate her brother?" But she followed Julie to the door. There she turned, her full lips curling. Speaking very deliberately, she said, "If your husband does not return, madame, I suggest you inquire of the American general who is at present busy snatching spies off our streets and putting them aboard American ships bound for Baltimore in chains."

Amalie caught her breath. Was it true?

With an angry exclamation, Julie shut the door between them, and Amalie sank back on her pillows. The woman was lying, trying to frighten her with her vague warnings and implied threats. But, oh, if only she could know whether Monsieur Armand was truly safe, and where Clotie was at this moment!

At that moment Monsieur Armand was sitting down to a bountiful breakfast of partridges at a plantation not far away. His host, a Monsieur Doradou, was a successful sugar planter, with an adoring Creole wife, six lively children and over ten thousand acres of land, if one included the forests of swamp cypress and the acres of marsh bordering the lake at the rear of his canefields. It was Monsieur Doradou's canefields that the Count de Valérun had come to observe.

At the moment Monsieur Doradou—a generously proportioned man with a handsome black beard only half concealing the twinkling geniality of his expression—was more interested in discussing his children, who hung their heads in pleased embarrassment as their father teasingly enumerated their faults and their accomplishments.

"Etienne, that one, he will be a planter. But not so good as little Marie-Thérèse, there, if she were a man. Eh, *chérie?*"

Marie-Thérèse, obviously her father's favorite, said, "I shall marry a planter, Papa."

"And Bo-Bo there, he will build houses, I think. He does not like the canefields, but has his head always in a book. He goes to Paris next year. They are our finest crop, eh, m'sieu?" he said, looking around at the blushing young faces as he added, "And you, m'sieu, they say you have already planted the first seed?"

"And the little countess so young!" Madame Doradou murmured from the foot of the table where she sat observing her husband fondly. "Is she well, m'sieu?"

Armand stared fixedly at his plate, struggling with the wave of rage and humiliation that unexpectedly threatened his customary aplomb. His firstborn, his *heir,* sired by an American—and he must endure this sly teasing about his child bride so soon *enceinte!*

When he could speak coolly he said, "She is well, *merci,* madame," and turned back to his host. "You are havesting the cane now, m'sieu?"

"We commenced cutting last week. Another breast of partridge, m'sieu? We hunt them in my forests, you know. *Non?* Then try one of these oranges. They are from my own trees."

"*Merci,* m'sieu. It is a beautiful fruit. Tell me, how do you judge the cane ready to cut?"

"Ah, it becomes a sixth sense, m'sieu. Here we cannot allow it to ripen fully. The heavy rains, you understand. And the steaming heat. If the stalks are left in the ground too long, they turn sour. When you have finished your breakfast, we shall take a look." He gave an order over his shoulder. Horses would be saddled and waiting for him and Monsieur.

Making their excuses to Madame Doradou, they left the breakfast table and went out on the long galérie where Monseiur Doradou took out his snuffbox.

"Will you join me, m'sieu? It is my own tobacco. The leaves are cured and ground by a slave I brought with me from Saint Domingue."

Laughing and shaking his head, the count accepted a pinch. "*Mon Dieu,* but it is a little kingdom you have here!"

"But yes! Come, here are our mounts."

They sauntered down the stair from the galérie toward the grass where two dark slaves waited with horses from Monsieur Doradou's stables.

"I did not want to alarm my wife and children, m'sieu, and so I must tell you now that you will find the situation in New Orleans has worsened during your absence. The general of the American army has succeeded in imposing martial law and there is a strict curfew in effect. Last week, two Americans were seized and accused of conspiring against the United States. They were not given any kind of hearing, m'sieu, but put in chains aboard a ship leaving immediately for Baltimore, with no opportunity, so I was told, to bid their families adieu. It is said the general expects an attack against New Orleans momentarily."

"An attack by whom?" the count said violently. "How can Spain or anyone else attack us now with Napoleon rampaging through Europe?"

Monsieur Daradou shook his head. "Myself, I think the general is mad. But watch yourself, m'sieu."

"Me? I have done nothing to offend the Americans."

"Our dislike of their ways offends them, my friend. Sometimes I think our very presence in Louisiana offends them."

"But they are the immigrants! We have been here a hundred years!"

"*Mais, oui.* Half of New Orleans would welcome Spanish rule again, *non?*"

"The other half would welcome the French, even Napoleon!"

"That from a royalist? No one wants what we have, eh? Except the Americans." Monsieur Doradou laughed heartily.

As they rode away from the gleaming pillared house, going inland from the river, a sweet mist rose in the air to meet them. "It is the boiling molasses," Monsieur Doradou explained. "My doctor tells me the vapors are healthful. In truth, Madame's sister claims to have been cured of an affliction by breathing them last season."

They were riding along a grassy track through rounded dark-green trees dripping with orange globes. Beyond them was an expanse of grayish green, tinged with lavender, so thick it hid the earth. Against the green wall they could see small figures moving, dwarfed by the massed stalks of cane. As they rode nearer, Armand could see that the dark men, the women and some of the older children were wielding wicked-looking knives with a swift skill that amazed him. A flash of the blade in the sun down one side of the stalk and then another, and it was bare of leaves. Another slash severed the stalk close to the ground; a second one lopped off the unripened joints at the top. The stalk was cast into one pile, the top discarded in another, and the next stalk slashed bare.

"Sections of the jointed stalks will be put back into the ground. Each joint will produce a new stalk in next year's crop."

"*Ma foi,* it is self-perpetuating!"

"*Oui,* m'sieu."

The piles of stalks grew high and were loaded on carts by the children. Riding slowly, with Monsieur Doradou patiently answering Armand's eager questions, they followed the carts to the sugar mill.

Here, under a rough shelter, more workers were unloading the carts and feeding the stalks of cane into a grinder, the chief feature of which was a pair of stone wheels slowly being rotated in opposite directions by a gear operated by a mule harnessed at the end of a pole boom which forced the animal to walk in a wide circle.

The sweet juice ran out of the crushed stalks and was carried down a trough into a large kettle set over a fire kept going by workers who were cutting wood in the forest and hauling it to the mill. The bubbling juice dripped from one kettle   another, each a little smaller than the one before.

"The molasses finally separates, as you see," Monsieur Doradou explained, "and gradually becomes crystalline." With unembarrassed pride, he displayed a small heap of brown crystals and invited Armand to taste.

The thick, sweet mists swirled around them. In the glare from the fires, the muscular limbs of the black workers glistened with sweat.

"The harvest season is a happy time, although it is a time of hard work," Monsieur Doradou said, beaming. "There are extra rations for the slaves and many sweet treats for all. We make sugar water. We string nuts and dip them in the thickening molasses. Delicious! We have a great celebration when the cane is all cut and ground. Our friends come, and the slaves sing and dance and feast. It is a time of rejoicing for all of us. And of course, m'sieu, it is all enormously profitable! So much so that I am installing more grinding equipment."

Armand's eyes were brilliant with his excitement. The musical cries of the workers and the sweet-smelling smoke—the smell of money!—inflamed his senses. Mentally, he was transferring the lively color of the whole scene intact to Les Chênes. Like his fellow émigrés from France, Armand was proud of his superior birth, taking for granted that he should have all the advantages that wealth and a title traditionally brought. But unlike some of his émigré friends, Armand was also quick-witted and adaptable, and he could view his changed position since the Revolution quite realistically.

Monsieur Doradou, he saw, was an American prince, a former colonist who lived in luxury—*mon Dieu,* what luxury!—his petite empire built by his own efforts. It was an inspiration.

Armand returned with his host to the comfortable house for an aperitif before lunch and the customary rest during the heat of the afternoon with his head full of glowing schemes for Les Chênes. His humiliation at the way it had come into his possession was—for the moment, at least—forgotten.

The following morning, after another breakfast of fruits and game and sweet black coffee, all plantation grown, Armand bade his host and hostess *au revoir* and mounted his horse for the ride to New Orleans, with his servant following on his own mount. An hour and a half later they trotted down rue Bourbon to the sign of La Rose, the wine merchant's shop which occupied the ground floor of the count's house. As they reined up at the porte cochère, they met a carriage coming through the arch.

Madame Beauclerc, whom Armand knew slightly, halted her driver and bowed. *"Bonjour, m'sieu le comte!* I have been calling on *madame la comtesse.* Such a sweet girl! Please accept my deepest sympathy in your misfortune."

"Misfortune, madame?"

"Ah, perhaps you do not regard it so?" Her laugh was peculiarly edged, he thought. "It is misfortune, indeed, to a woman, m'sieu, even one as young as madame. But your marriage is still new, is it not?" With another bow, she signaled her driver, and her carriage rolled past the bewildered Armand, who jumped down and tossed his reins to Jean-Baptiste.

In the court were two more carriages awaiting their owners. Running up the stairs, Armand encountered several ladies of his acquaintance leaving his house, and was greeted with little compassionate cries.

"Ah, m'sieu, *bonjour!* She is so brave, your little countess! It is so sad." And they passed on down the stair to the court.

Deeply alarmed now, Armand strode down the hall to Amalie's chamber and stopped in the open doorway. She was in bed, holding court. She looked not ill but rather strained. Seated around the bed were several more New Orleans matrons. He was somewhat relieved to see Madame Amboy among them. But Héloise rose immediately, signaling her friends.

"Ah, M'sieu Armand, you have returned to be met with sad news. Do not grieve. You can be happy your wife will recover, *n'est-ce pas?"* She swept out of the room, ignoring his silent plea to stay. With fond adieus, her friends took leave of Amalie.

"In the name of the good Lord, what has happened?" Armand demanded when he and Amalie were alone.

She lay looking up at him with an expression in her clear young eyes which he found mystifying. In it were both unshed tears and laughter, but with an underlying anxiety that he could not understand. What did the child have to fear? He awaited her answer in some apprehension.

What she said was, "M'sieu, I have lost our baby."

FIFTEEN

AMALIE WAS watching him closely. What she saw first in his face was a baffled anger, then understanding and a quick alarm. "What is it? What has happened to Ma'm'selle Clotie?"

His instant comprehension and concern for Clotie were admirable —oh, admirable!—but they stabbed her. "She has gone—and taken our expected child with her."

"*Gone?*" A mask slid over his face. "And that, I assume, is the reason for the 'misfortune' for which I am so much pitied?"

"What else could we do? You would have been forced to make me truly *enceinte,*" she said, feeling quite contrary, "or be made the laughingstock of New Orleans when I could not deliver."

His head jerked up in surprise and his brilliant eyes narrowed on her. "And make *you* their laughingstock with a fourteen-month pregnancy? You had better stop trying to be clever, little Amalie, and tell me what your sister has done now." The dislike and scorn he had shown Clotie ever since their wedding were back in his voice, but Amalie knew she would not forget his first concern.

Yet a part of her welcomed it because she was so very worried herself. "I do not know what Clotie has done, M'sieu Armand. I know only that she has disappeared."

"Disappeared! But how can that be?"

"I do not know," Amalie repeated.

"How long has she been gone?"

"Over twenty-four hours, not longer than thirty. We discovered yesterday morning that her bed had not been slept in."

"And what has been done?"

"What could we do, m'sieu? Madame Amboy has offered to make discreet inquiries—"

"Madame Amboy! *She* knows?"

Amalie regarded him steadily. "I had no one else, m'sieu."

"And I suppose it is Madame Amboy who has been spreading the story of our 'misfortune'?"

"It was her idea. She has been bringing her friends to commiserate with me."

"So soon?" he said, with irony. "And if I find Ma'm'selle Claudine and bring her back?"

Amalie was silent. Of course she wanted Clotie back—*didn't she?* But—it was hardly the time to bring up her folly in trusting Madame Laval or to point out the risks they would run in bringing Clotie back into the house now.

"Tell me, what 'discreet inquiries' does Madame Héloise plan to make? You must have some idea of what your sister is about!"

"None, m'sieu. But I did have a call from a M'sieu Arouet who wanted permission to follow Clotie to Les Chênes and speak to Papa. Of course, I tried to discourage him."

"François Arouet?" the count exclaimed. "That puddinghead?"

Amalie bit back laughter. "I think Clotie shares your opinion, m'sieu. She refused to open the letters he had sent to Les Chênes and which Maman returned here. But it was all we had to go on. Madame Amboy said she could find out if M'sieu Arouet has also left New Orleans."

"So there were letters." His anger was like a rising wind, fanning her with its force. "Why was I not told of this?"

"Perhaps," Amalie said, lifting her chin, "if you had shown enough interest in your home to regard it as more than a place to sleep when there was nothing better to do—"

Monsieur Armand sent her a look of fury and went to her bellpull, giving it a vicious yank. Too impatient to wait, he strode out of her room to the galérie overlooking the court and shouted, "Callou!"

Amalie remained where she was, propped up against her hard pillows on the sweet-smelling moss mattress. She could hear Callou's answer from below, and the count's crisp order. "I want all of you in Madame's chamber, all except Jean-Baptiste. Immediately!"

One by one the servants filed into the room and lined up before the count. He looked down the row of apprehensive faces, his own dark as a thundercloud from the north. "Where is Madi?" he demanded of Dulcie, who stood tall in her dignity.

Dulcie looked askance at Amalie, then said, "She gone, too, *michie.*"

"*Tiens.* Tell me what you know. When did Ma'm'selle Claudine and her servant leave?"

"In the night, *michie*. Yesterday night."

"You heard them go?"

"*Non, michie!* We soun' asleep."

He made an angry sound. "All right. When did you miss them?"

"It was Callou. When he go to make kitchen fire, he pass Julie's room—"

Amalie caught her breath as Callou took up the story and said, "She gone. I tell Dulcie, and she come up to tell Madame, but Madame not here."

The count turned blazing eyes on Amalie, whose heart was beating like a drum. His straight black brows almost touched in the angry scowl he gave her. But before Amalie could speak, he had whirled on her servant. "Well, Julie? Where was your mistress? Don't lie to me!"

"It was the curfew, *michie,*" Julie said calmly. "We could not come home, so Madame Amboy kep' us."

"Madame Amboy!" he exclaimed again, in a peculiar tone.

"She has been very kind," Amalie told him, and thanked the Blessed Virgin for Julie. There were some advantages in being treated like a child with a nurse! She had been too frightened to think herself.

She was very relieved when Monsieur Armand turned back to Dulcie and let the cook finish telling how she had been "so a-fright" when Estée, sent to see why Madi did not come for M'selle's *café au lait,* came back screaming, to say the rooms had been "toss' by a hurricane, *michie!* An' no Madi, no M'selle!"

"Now think hard, all of you," Monsieur Armand commanded. "I want you to tell me of anything unusual that has happened in the last month."

They stared back at him, solemn and silent.

"Did Madi ever ask to visit friends?" he asked Dulcie.

"Why she do that? She have us. She an' Estée good friends."

"Were Ma'm'selle or Madi outside of their rooms at any time that you know about?"

"*Oui, michie.*" It was Callou. "Madi went to market for M'selle. Madame scol' her."

The count shot an accusing look at Amalie. "So! Madi could have met someone, or carried a message! Did anyone ever come here asking for her?"

"*Non, michie,*" Dulcie said.

But Callou spoke up again. "Don' you remember, Estée, that time a strange man come to the kitchen door an' you talk to him?"

"I tol' him Madi not here," Estée snapped.

"Oui, an' when you tol' Madi, she say she don' know somebody like that."

"Could he have been someone's servant, Callou?" the count asked.

"Oui, michie, but I never see him before."

"What did he look like?"

"He black-black. An' big."

A big black man! "Was he bald?" Amalie asked, from her bed.

"He wear a kerchief, madame."

"You may go now," the count told them. "If you remember anything else, come to me."

When they were alone, Monsieur Armand demanded of Amalie, "You know something about this big slave?"

"Only that a big bald negro was lounging down in the street opposite this house the day before Clotie left. He seemed to be watching—"

"I will inquire about him. If Arouet owns such a slave, we will have something to go on. Now I am going to try to discover whether she has booked passage on a ship, or hired a carriage. Had she any money?"

"Her jewel case is missing."

"Ah! I can be looking for a gift for my wife." But he was pacing the floor, not even looking at her. "Shipping agents and livery stable proprietors are not averse to turning a profit on the jewelry they sometimes take in for fares. You had better describe her more valuable pieces for me."

"There was a ring that belonged to Maman," Amalie said slowly. "I do not know its value." She was seeing again the look in Clotie's eyes when she displayed the stone Maman had paid the *yanqui* trader for their silks. Would Clotie part with that? Amalie did not think so. She described the other pieces she remembered.

The count left, his manner abstracted, and Amalie sank back on her pillows.

She felt as if she had walked through a treacherous swamp, only narrowly avoiding precipitating the duel Madame Amboy had warned her would take place if the count learned about her disastrous visit to Monsieur Peralta—a duel that he would fight not for her, but for his honor.

She was still in her bed that afternoon when Madame Amboy returned, alone. The older woman sat down beside the bed and motioned to Julie, who had brought her in, to leave them.

"I have some news for you, madame," she said. "That young scamp, François Arouet, has indeed left the city, telling no one where he was going. His mother is quite aware of his infatuation and believes he has gone to Les Chênes to offer for your sister. I suspect they are planning to face your parents with their marriage an accomplished fact."

But her words did not have the effect she expected on Amalie who, greatly depressed, said, "M'sieu Armand is out trying to discover if Clotie purchased transportation with her jewels. Madame, he married me, but it is Clotie he loves."

Madame Amboy's delicate eyebrows drew up in shock, making a little tent above her fine eyes. "M'sieu Armand is not the father of her child, surely!"

"Oh, *non,* madame! But he offered for her, and Clotie would have none of it. When she told me why, I—I took her place. It is my own fault, madame, for he never loved me. But I did so hope it would be all right. I was determined to be the best of wives, to—to bear his children and—and manage his household—but, madame, he locks his door against me!"

"*Ma foi!*" murmured Madame Amboy, who did not want these confidences at all. "Has it not occurred to you," she asked, after a moment, "that M'sieu Armand thinks you are still somewhat young to begin producing sons for him? You have time for that, you know."

Amalie shook her head, blowing her nose. "*Non,* madame, he married me for my dowry, which was Les Chênes itself. He told me so."

"*Mon Dieu!*" Her heart filled with compassion as she looked at the woebegone face. Armand's pride had been wounded, Madame Amboy realized—that arrogant aristocrat's pride that she knew so well. But to wound this child because of it—!

"It is just as Maman has always said." Amalie gave a final blow and wiped at her eyes. "Papa has spoiled me dreadfully, and now I must suffer for it."

"Spoiled?" Madame Amboy echoed briskly. "Nonsense! You are a loving, caring little person and Armand is stupid, indeed, if he does not love you. One day he will open those handsome eyes of his and see you for what you are, a very attractive young lady. And then, if you wish, you can lead him in a merry dance. *I* could show you how! Would you like that?"

Amalie laughed shakily. "It might be great fun, madame, but I do not think it will ever happen."

"Don't you? I do."

Amalie felt better. She was not quite aware of it, but Madame Amboy's words had stirred a small memory—the count saying, *I think someday you are going to break some hearts, Ma'm'selle Amalie.*

"After all," she said, with more spirit, "Clotie *is* a goose, and I don't doubt if he had married her, M'sieu Armand would be bored in three days!"

Madame Amboy laughed with her.

Amalie was sitting composedly in the salon when the count returned several hours later. He flung himself into a chair opposite her, looking extraordinarily vexed.

"No one has engaged a passage or hired a carriage with jewels in a fortnight. It means that Ma'm'selle Claudine must have had the help of a friend, if she had no money."

"I am certain she had none, m'sieu." Amalie rose and poured him a whiskey.

"Merci," he said, taking it.

"Madame Amboy has learned that M'sieu Arouet has also left New Orleans, and his mother thinks he may be heading for Les Chênes. Madame Amboy is of the opinion that he is taking Clotie with him."

The scowl on her husband's face deepened. "Such a thing is inconceivable to me."

Amalie seated herself opposite him again. "Is it so inconceivable? I confess I no longer understand Clotie."

"Have either of us ever understood her?" He swung one smartly booted leg irritably. "I have sent Jean-Baptiste out to make inquiries that it would be indiscreet of me to attempt. If he turns up no clues, I think your mother and father will have to be told that she has left this house."

"Oui," Amalie agreed. "It is a task I have been dreading."

They waited in some impatience for the return of Jean-Baptiste, going over and over what they knew of Clotie's flight, advancing theories and discarding them, feeling their hands quite tied by the need for secrecy.

Jean-Baptiste returned that evening with no clues except a vague story about a young gentleman hiring a carriage, in the livery stablehand's words "two-t'ree day ago" to take him to St. John's landing on the lake, an event memorable only because the stablehand had never seen the gentleman before or since, "an' *oui*, he mention a wife." Someone had been sent to return the carriage from St. John's landing where it had been left. He did not know more than that.

"It could not have been M'sieu Arouet," Amalie pointed out. "He is surely well known in the city, is he not? And the time does not exactly fit the time we know Clotie left."

It was so little that the count decided he must travel to Les Chênes, since they had all but exhausted their sources of information in the city. If Clotie were not at the plantation, he would break the sad news to her parents.

So she was to be left alone again, Amalie reflected, looking at her husband across the blaze of candles and the flowers Estée had brought from the market to try to cheer her mistress. Neither Amalie nor the count was tempted by the excellent dinner Dulcie had prepared for his homecoming.

"I have another reason to go to Les Chênes," Monsieur Armand told Amalie across the expanse of table between them. "The sugar mill I have purchased for the plantation is now on its way up Bayou Lafourche by barge. I should be at the upper end of the bayou on the river to receive the mill and see it carted across to our bayou so it can be floated down to Les Chênes."

"This is extraordinary," Amalie said, after a stunned moment. "Was the money you were carrying to Barataria used to purchase a sugar mill for Les Chênes, then?"

"*Mais, oui*. What did you think?"

Mon Dieu! What could she think? Why had she not been told? Anger sharpened her voice. "That you were sending money to the royal exiles in England by some roundabout way."

He looked surprised. "Why should you think that?"

"Because I know that Papa used to give you money for them— money we could ill afford to part with!"

"But I have long since detached myself from royalist plots. I no longer believe it is possible to put a Bourbon back on France's throne, and I have no desire to fall before Napoleon's firing squads as did Caudodal's men, and the duc d'Enghien."

"But Papa believes Louis XVIII will succeed—"

"And so he might, if Napoleon should fall. I cannot foresee that, and I am no longer willing to waste my means and my strength in so risky a venture when I have an opportunity to become a sugar planter. No, *ma petite,* I traveled to Barataria to purchase a mill from the privateers who said they took it from a Spanish ship bound for the West Indies. It is crude, but the money it makes for us will pay for a better one in a few years."

At least, he was telling her now. His expression was more animated than any she had seen on his face in some time. "You will like the harvest time, little Amalie. You can smell a sugar plantation from miles away on the river, for the air is sweet as molasses. And that fragrance is the sweet smell of money, for it is a crop that is bringing incredible riches to the men who harvest it."

"And that is why you married me."

"I married you because I could not bear the way your father is wasting his resources and impoverishing you all. Les Chênes needed me, did it not?"

It was the Creole way, after all, Amalie told herself. He had not loved her—but, then, he must not have loved Clotie, either! Was it only his pride Clotie had damaged?

"Will you like being rich, *chérie?*"

"I suppose so," Amalie said, her head in a whirl. He was no longer a royalist. He had not been in danger from Napoleon's secret agents. This was another thing Madame Laval had lied about. Had she lied, too, about the "hotbed" of royalists at Madame Amboy's salon? No, Amalie did not think so. But, surely, about that shocking murder on the levee road?

She said aloud, "Then there was no royalist plot against M'sieu Beaulieu."

"*Against M'sieu Beaulieu!*" The count straightened in his chair, his face darkening with passion. "Do you also think me a murderer, madame?"

"Oh, no, m'sieu—I didn't mean—" But it was too late.

He had risen, throwing down his serviette, and strode out of the dining room, not waiting to hear her agonized wail that it was *Clotie,* only Clotie, who thought so ill of him!

SIXTEEN

MADAME AMBOY had not just been comforting Amalie when she predicted the count would one day open his eyes and find her an attractive young woman. She was resolved to make it happen. With the count away, she took Amalie under her wing. She came to the house on Bourbon Street every morning. She begged Amalie to call her Héloise.

"The first thing we must do," she announced, "is to get your dressmaker here to refit all those gowns. I think something a little more sophisticated." She stood, tall and elegant, with her head tilted, her piquant face thoughtful. "Something to make you look taller. Perhaps the simple long style that is favored by the Empress Josephine?"

"My dressmaker has been told I am too shy to have a fitting," Amalie told her mischievously.

"But you have been married over five months and lost your first child, n'est-ce pas?" said Héloise, her eyes brilliant with laughter. "I think you have recovered from your shyness, by this time."

And so the dressmaker was summoned, and the dresses were taken out of the big armoire one by one and examined with great care to see what could be made of them.

"Let us see your figure, chère," suggested Héloise, and Julie skimmed the soft morning dress from her shoulders, leaving Amalie in her shift. The dressmaker whipped out her tape, her hands flying.

"Ma foi!" exclaimed Héloise, "but are you not growing taller?"

"Perhaps it is only that I am thinner. I have not much appetite since—"

"Your husband left?" Héloise interrupted, and Amalie was grateful for she had almost said, "—since Clotie ran away," forgetting that the dressmaker who, like Madame Laval, went from house to house, also had ears! Lying made everything so complicated!

"But it is a delicious figure, is it not?" Héloise appealed to the dressmaker.

"A pleasure to fit, madame," said that quick-fingered woman.

What she had longed for was here at last, Amalie saw, looking into her mirror. Her breasts were like small, round melons above her flat abdomen and slender hips. All the while Julie had been binding and swathing her, her body had continued growing and shaping itself into something that could be called a woman. When the first remodeled gowns were delivered for her trying-on, Amalie gasped in pleasure.

Madame Amboy began bringing her women friends when she came to call. As New Orleans matrons became aware that Amalie was once again accepting invitations, she was soon going everywhere, with Madame Amboy as her companion—to morning coffees with the ladies, to soirées and salons. Madame Claiborne, the American governor's charming Creole bride, was the toast of New Orleans and Amalie was astounded to learn that that poised young woman was barely four years older than she was.

"But the four years between sixteen and twenty are formidable, *n'est-ce pas?*" she sighed.

"Ah, but you are no longer *'la petite comtesse',*" Héloise told her gaily, "but *'la belle comtesse!'* That is making progress, *non?*"

Sometimes she and Madame Amboy attended a ball together, and neither lacked for dancing partners. Amalie found herself quite comfortable in society now, for she had an easy answer for those who asked about her husband's absences from the city.

"He is overseeing the delivery of a sugar mill to the plantation, m'sieu," she would say. "We shall be planting cane at Les Chênes."

The response was always animated, for rumors were flying about the fortunes being made in the tall, sweet grass. Sugar was on everyone's mind, now that talk about a war with Spain was dying down. The American army's General Wilkinson was still breathing fire about an attack on the city, but no one took him seriously now; the Creoles laughed at him as they went about their pleasures.

Her social activities kept Amalie from brooding over Clotie's disappearance, yet in her bed at night the questions swarmed into her mind to chase away sleep. Would the count find Clotie at Les Chênes? Was Monsieur Arouet with her? And if not, who had helped her leave the city, and where was she now? Was she in good health, with her time approaching? Would they even know when her child was born? There was a deep ache accompanying such thoughts.

The more Amalie thought about Clotie, the oftener their last con-

versation returned to haunt her. She remembered how Clotie had refused to be concerned about the count but how, when Amalie reproached her, Clotie had said, *Do not ever think me ungrateful.*
Amalie was convinced now that Clotie even then had been planning
to run away. It had been a deliberate, deceitful plan, with Madi
closely involved in the planning, Amalie was sure.

Oh, Clotie, whatever made you do it? Could you not trust us?

Life was such a muddle. She loved Monsieur Armand—oh, in spite
of everything she loved him more each day!—loved even his quick
anger that crackled about her, frightening and exciting her at the
same time. While he claimed only to love Les Chênes! And Clotie? It
was a chilling thought that Amalie immediately put away—had she
run away because she realized that she loved Monsieur Armand after
all?

Amalie was glad to see the morning come, with its fresh round of
calls and gossip over "small blacks" and sweet cakes with her new
circle of friends, to dispel such unhappy wonderings. In spite of the
sweet cakes, she grew thinner.

One morning, when she and Héloise called on Madame Turnbeau,
the wife of an officer of the battalion, that lady's servant said, "Madame is with her hairdresser. She begs you will join her in her boudoir, for she would like your advice on a new style she is adopting."

Amalie glanced at Héloise, who lifted her eyebrows, but they
could scarcely refuse Madame's request. It was, indeed, Madame
Laval who was with Madame Turnbeau in her private rooms. The
octoroon, exotic in a skyblue *tignon,* greeted them with her golden
eyes cast down in false humility.

Another servant brought orange blossom syrup and wafers, and
they sat and watched Madame Laval pile up glossy curls while Madame Turnbeau carried on a lively conversation with her callers.

"We miss your handsome husband at our soirées, *madame la
comtesse.* When does he return to New Orleans?"

"When his sugar mill is installed, madame. I do not know how
long that will occupy him."

"But he misses many fine balls, *non?* Ai, madame, more gently!"
she reproached the hairdresser. "Madame Laval has brought me the
most extraordinary news this morning. Héloise, you remember meeting M'sieu Aaron Burr, do you not?"

"*Oui,* a charming man. He spoke excellent French."

"He has been arrested again on the east coast, and charged with treason!"

"*Non!* Is your news reliable, then, Madame Laval?" Madame Amboy asked.

"Oh, yes, indeed, madame," the octoroon said. "I cannot reveal the source, but I heard it in the home of a very high official."

"Oh, and have you heard," Madame Turnbeau exclaimed, interrupting their protests, "that one of M'sieu Beaulieu's murderers has been arrested here in the city?"

"Indeed?" Amalie and Héloise exclaimed together.

"*Mais, oui.* Just as my husband thought, he is a 'kaintock,' one of those riverboatmen from upriver. He has confessed to the crime and claimed he and his companions meant only to rob M'sieu Beaulieu because they had dissipated their wages on gambling and drink and so had no money to buy horses and no desire to walk back to Kentucky. My husband thinks his accomplices will also be found."

Madame Laval placed a tiny wreath of small white jasmine buds atop Madame Turnbeau's pile of curls, and they all exclaimed over the effect.

"But have the murderers remained in the city all this time, then?" Héloise asked. "One would expect them to leave immediately they got their hands on Monsieur Beaulieu's purse."

"Apparently it was gambled away, as well."

Amalie was watching Madame Laval. Her smooth, brown face was expressionless as she twisted a curl now this way, now that, settling the dainty wreath in place. "So it was not a royalist plot, after all," Amalie observed.

"A *royalist*—" The hairdresser made a sound of protest as Madame Turnbeau jerked her head around to dart an anxious—and revealing—glance in the direction of Madame Amboy, and exclaimed, "Wherever did you hear that?"

"It is of no consequence," Amalie said lightly, "for I gave it no thought."

At these words Madame Laval lifted her eyes and looked straight at Amalie with such concentrated venom that Amalie could not control a shiver. It was a dark and malignant look that warned Amalie the woman was still dangerous.

From the deck of the flatboat he had hired to transport his sugar mill, Armand watched with mixed feelings as the whitewashed columns of Les Chênes slowly came into view around the bend in the quiet bayou. It was midafternoon. A soft winter rain that had been falling all morning was over, but a mist lay over the bayou. Steam seemed to be rising from the trees and, through it, their intertwined creepers glistened wetly. Drops of moisture ran down the twisted tendrils of moss hanging from the oaks, dripping into the tall, wet grass beneath them.

Looking at the lush and peaceful scene, Armand tried to imagine the sugar mill installed somewhere behind the slave quarters and beyond it, in those abandoned old indigo fields, a thick juicy stand of cane streaked with lavender, ready to be cut. He tried to recall the heady fragrance of boiling molasses, but instead caught a flowery whiff that brought back vividly his wedding day last summer—Claudine pale and distraught, little Amalie looking rapt and a bit dazed, he himself still inwardly raging at his humiliation and bent on avenging it.

Instantly, the painful discomfort of that day was back, warring with the elation he was feeling because Les Chênes was virtually his, an excellent plantation that he was certain he could induce to pour riches on them all. Adding to his present discomfort was his annoyance with Claudine—God knew what additional scandal she had loosed on them by her impulsiveness now!—and his awareness that he could be facing her in minutes. Was she here?

A few moments later, he thought his question was answered, for as he stepped ashore at the landing and began giving orders about his cargo to the slaves who had run down to meet him, a young man arose from a chair on the galérie and sauntered down the stair at the side of the house. Even at this distance he recognized the careless brown curls of François Arouet. The languid poet, he thought in disdain.

Nevertheless, he greeted the young man civilly.

"Ah, *m'sieu le comte,* I am glad to see you," Monsieur Arouet said, "for I hope to enlist you in my suit for your sister-in-law's hand." He glanced over his shoulder at the house where Monsieur and Madame de l'Ouvrier now stood awaiting the count on the galérie, as was their custom when visitors arrived. "If you will only intercede with M'sieu and Madame for me—"

"Does Mademoiselle favor your suit?" Armand asked bluntly.

"That is precisely where I need your help." A distraught look had come over his face. "I have not been able to see her."

"She is not here?" With an effort Armand kept the alarm he felt out of his voice. If she had not come to Les Chênes with Arouet, where in God's name had Claudine gone?

"She is at present visiting friends, but Madame will not reveal where. If you could prevail upon her—I will go anywhere to see Mademoiselle Claudine!"

"Perhaps Mademoiselle does not wish to see you," Armand suggested, his mind on the unpleasant task ahead, for it was apparent the de l'Ouvriers knew nothing about Claudine's departure from New Orleans. He must dissemble doubly, before this poor fool and before them until he could speak with them in private.

"I am sure that she does not wish to see me," the unhappy François was confiding. "If Ma'm'selle Claudine had only read my letters—Madame said she destroyed them unopened! A great pity, for I am an accomplished letter-writer. M'sieu, love like mine cannot fail to move her, if only I be allowed to make her aware of it. M'sieu and Madame do not seem to welcome my suit and I do not understand why. I am not poor, my family is without reproach—"

"We will talk later of this, m'sieu," Armand broke in.

"*Oui,* m'sieu. Forgive me, but I could not but seize this opportunity to enlist your help before we join M'sieu and Madame—"

"If you will excuse me." Armand strode swiftly toward the house and ran up the stair to embrace his handsome mother-in-law and then his father-in-law, who, stiffly formal in his old-fashioned attire, immediately asked in a trembling voice, "My Amalie? She is well?"

"Very well," Armand assured him. "She sends her love."

"And Clotie?" Madame dared, in an undertone.

Armand signaled her to silence with a jerk of his head toward Monsieur Arouet, now climbing the stair, and she made a moue of distaste before asking, in a sprightly voice, "What is that I see on the barge? Is it really a sugar mill you have brought us, m'sieu?"

"It is the heart around which we will construct our mill, madame. It comes to you at the end of an eventful journey, for I believe it was commissioned for some disappointed planter in the West Indies."

"You bought it from the privateers!" she exclaimed.

"*Oui,* madame. You must help me decide where it should be set up so we can go about removing it from the flatboat."

"Let me offer you refreshment from your journey," said Monsieur de l'Ouvrier, who had exhibited none of his wife's enthusiasm for the equipment.

"With pleasure, m'sieu. The removal may take several days, for we shall have to construct a contrivance on which we can drag it to a suitable site."

Monsieur de l'Ouvrier brightened. "And while we wait, perhaps we can make a little sortie into the swamp, you and I, eh?"

Unbidden, an image sprang to the count's mind: Amalie, in her pale short *jeune fille* dress, was leaning against a pillar, her eyes laughing at him. *I warn you, m'sieu, that you will come back sunburned and mosquito-bitten—*

They sat on the galérie with tall, cool drinks, listening to the news Armand brought them from New Orleans. There was a noticeable strain underlying the light talk; it was obvious the de l'Ouvriers were eager to talk privately with him—and so was Monsieur Arouet. Armand became loquacious about the possibilities in growing sugar cane, and since Madame was extremely interested in his plans for the plantation, she warmed to the subject.

Soon both Monsieur de l'Ouvrier and Monsieur Arouet were listening in sleepy boredom. It was then Armand suggested that since it was no longer raining, they should walk through the slave quarters and inspect a location he had in mind for the sugar mill.

Monsieur de l'Ouvrier observed that he would be damned if he would go walking in the wet grass, and the count smoothly suggested that Monsieur Arouet might wish to keep his host company on the galérie. Since he accompanied the suggestion with a significant look at Monsieur Arouet, the pale young poet assumed that the count planned to plead for him and, brightening, said he would prefer to remain with his host, who looked slightly alarmed at the prospect.

As soon as they were out of earshot, Madame de l'Ouvrier clutched the arm of her son-in-law and said, "That young man is driving us mad. He has announced that he cannot leave without hearing from Clotie's own lips that she despises him. He has no pride! But of course, he knows he is a good marriage prospect. We cannot fault him, either on family or wealth. I do not wish to discourage him, if there is any chance that Clotie would accept him, for I would like nothing better than to see her safely married, and I do not think we could get a better contract for her. But I do not know how long I can tolerate him as a houseguest, m'sieu!"

"If you cannot tolerate him as a houseguest, madame, I do not see how you can tolerate him as a son-in-law."

She made an impatient sound. "If he offers for Clotie, I shall manage."

He said quietly, "I am afraid there is no longer any question of making a contract for your daughter. She has run away, madame."

Madame de l'Ouvrier stopped and stared at him, her face going quite pale. "Run away? What are you saying? What do you mean?"

"Ma'm'selle Claudine has left our house, madame. We do not know where she is. When we found evidence that M'sieu Arouet was on his way here, we wondered if she might not be with him."

"*Mon Dieu!*" Madame de l'Ouvrier cried, clutching her head as if to hold it on. "And her time soon on her! It is all your fault, *m'sieu le comte!*" she cried, turning on him. "If you had not insisted that I stay on the plantation— Oh, if I had been with my poor Clotie in New Orleans, this would not have happened!"

"You would be well advised to keep your voice down, madame. You may be right, I do not know. We have made inquiries, of course, but you surely appreciate the fact that we must be very discreet, for her sake as well as our own."

"*Mais, oui.* Oh, my poor Clotie! Where can she have gone? How will she manage? She is lost to us, Armand! I am sure she is lost to us." She began weeping, and the count held out his arms.

She wept against his shoulder for a few minutes, then dried her eyes. "I cannot abide that simpering young man in my house," she declared with passion. "It has been a strain having him here pestering us when I thought I knew where Clotie was but could not reveal her hiding place. Now I shall not be able to face him. You must rid us of him, Armand."

"I will see what I can do, Madame de l'Ouvrier," he promised, "if you will convey my unhappy news to your husband. I do not think *I* can face *him*. Now, you must compose yourself. We will walk for half an hour and talk about the sugar mill, *non?*"

By the time the half hour was up, they had examined the site Armand had in mind for the mill and agreed that it was possibly the best place for it, and Madame, though her face had sagged, making her look suddenly older, declared she was ready to face her husband and her guest.

On the galérie they found Monsieur Arouet almost asleep with ennui. Monsieur de l'Ouvrier had set full sail on his favorite topic. The young man, who was obviously uninterested in the botany of the region, looked up hopefully, but when the count gave a barely perceptible shake of his head, Monsieur Arouet's face settled again into a disconsolate expression. But the conversation that had so bored Monsieur Arouet had given the count an idea. Why not bore the young lover, indeed?

That evening, when they met again around Madame's dining table, he set himself to draw Monsieur de l'Ouvrier out on his hobby until the old émigré, beaming, proposed a plant-collecting expedition on the morrow while the slaves were building a drag-sled on which to haul the mill equipment. He was taken off guard when the count turned to Monsieur Arouet and asked, "Has M'sieu taken you on a plant-hunting expedition? *Non?* But you are missing a rare treat if you do not come with us in the morning."

"M'sieu Arouet does not arise early enough to go out with us," that young man's reluctant host said, with a glare of displeasure for the count.

"I am sure he can make an exception," the count said, and Monsieur Arouet, who had watched in some wonderment as the count gradually thawed the old gentleman, quickly took the hint and assented.

Madame de l'Ouvrier sent a signal to her husband, who remained somewhat irritated, since he had hoped for one day to escape his unwelcome guest, but he made no further objection and it was decided that the three men would set off at dawn on a collecting jaunt.

Not surprisingly, before dinner was over Madame de l'Ouvrier developed an incapacitating headache which she foresaw would last for the remainder of Monsieur Arouet's stay. So she did not appear the next morning when the men gathered on the galérie to watch the final preparations for their trip and to try to forecast the weather. The sky was overcast and the air chill, but rain did not seem imminent. Accordingly, Monsieur de l'Ouvrier's small flatboat was provisioned and presently the three men set out, with two stalwart slaves to wield the poles.

They were rowed down the bayou to a shallow inlet through the grassy bank and into a nearly stagnant stream. Overshadowed by hanging branches, they moved through the leafy tunnel which widened and darkened as the water spread shallowly through the forest. In a short time they had entered a gloomy netherworld. No direct sunlight could penetrate the roof of massed leaves, and what light filtered down was absorbed by the still, black water through which they were being poled. The cypress trunks rose writhing all around them, ringed at their base by strange misshapen roots that pushed bony knees out of the water.

The air was heavy with the odors of decay. Strange fungoid plants attached themselves to the trees and in places a green iridescent scum grew on the black surface of the water. Sometimes the long snout and arched eyes of an alligator lay almost invisible in the scum. Birds shrieked as they moved deeper into the gloom and insects buzzed about their heads. Monsieur Arouet's eyes grew wide.

"You have never ventured deep into a cypress swamp before?" the count asked him.

"No, never, m'sieu. I was sent by my father to Paris at an early age, and only returned at his death to take up my position in New Orleans."

"Which is?"

"Why—why, as my father's heir," said Monsieur Arouet, floundering. He was obviously unnerved by the sight of a long alligator moving lazily out of their way just under the surface ahead of the flatboat.

Monsieur de l'Ouvrier had begun humming under his breath as he rummaged happily in a canvas bag in which he kept various hand tools, and rearranged the leaves of his temporary press. Now and then he pointed out a curious parasitic plant growing on a cypress knee or stopped to scoop up a floating water grass. He seemed oblivious to the bloodthirsty mosquitoes swarming around them, but young Arouet was constantly slapping himself and uttering little cries of irritation. The count, on whom the insects had little effect, presently took pity on the uncomfortable young man and tossed him a length of mosquito gauze and told him to drape himself in it.

They were approaching a *chenière* of higher ground, thickly covered with a variety of trees through which innumerable birds seemed to be darting, and here Monsieur de l'Ouvrier proposed they go ashore. The flatboat was poled in close and one of the slaves stuck his pole deep into the mud below the surface to hold the boat in place while the other threw down a plank between the boat and the shore. Monsieur de l'Ouvrier, carefully carrying his equipment, crossed first. The count stood and gestured to Arouet to follow Monsieur.

François Arouet rose from his chair, still swathed in gauze, and stepped gingerly to the plank. As he did, the count leaned ever so slightly against the standing pole. The flatboat moved, the plank parted from it as Monsieur Arouet stepped off the boat, and he fell on his face in the shallow water.

A curious apparition scrambled to its feet. The gauze was still draped over Arouet's head, black mud and dead leaves clinging to it. The unfortunate young man was wildly pawing at it, trying to get his hands to his face to wipe the muck from his eyes, succeeding only in smearing it. At the same time he was doing an improvised jig attempting to stay on his feet in the slippery mud. It was such an extraordinary sight that the count could not restrain a chuckle even as he reached out a hand to Arouet.

With the help of the slaves Armand hoisted the young man aboard, the flatboat was poled in again and the plank lifted in place. But the count could not restrain his amusement at the ludicrous sight the young man made with the gauze at last removed, two pale, unhappy eyes looking out of a black, dripping face. The two delighted slaves could contain themselves no longer and added their laughter to the count's.

In a fury, Monsieur Arouet swung around and struck at the nearest grinning black face. The slave clutched at the pole to save himself from going over and very nearly caused Monsieur de l'Ouvrier, who had turned back and stepped on the plank, the same dank fate.

Outraged, Monsieur de l'Ouvrier shouted, "No guest of mine strikes one of my servants!" He came aboard and confronted the dripping Arouet. "You are no longer welcome at Les Chênes, M'sieu Arouet! Pull in the plank," he ordered the slaves, "and take us back. I will arrange for your transportation immediately, m'sieu."

"I shall be happy to leave, m'sieu!" said the furious young man.

The count, hiding his amusement at this development, was seized by another quite irrational memory. He saw the *yanqui* trader racing for his little boat with Monsieur de l'Ouvrier's dogs at his heels, and little Amalie's eyes brimming with the laughter she was holding back, and he laughed aloud, quite unintentionally doubling Monsieur Arouet's fury.

But Armand did not notice. Amazed, he realized that he could now laugh at Claudine's hated seducer!

He was already somewhat ashamed of the way in which he had humiliated her new admirer, but the cleansing laughter Monsieur Arouet had inspired was washing out some corrosion in his soul. And now a queer thought slipped in—*how long since he had heard Amalie laugh?*

SEVENTEEN

IT WAS February, and spring had come to Louisiana while Armand floated down the river. The air was mild and sweet-scented at sundown when his flatboat tied up alongside others at the landing at New Orleans. The levee muted the sounds of the city, and the thickening dusk seemed to soften the cries of the boatmen and roustabouts. A ship's bell on a barque anchored behind them in the river sounded mellow across the deep-flowing water. Above the levee, where strollers were taking the air, Armand could see a faint luminosity in the windows overlooking the river where candles were already lit.

Leaving Jean-Baptiste to see to his trunks, Armand walked into the town and strolled the few blocks to the rue Bourbon and his house. Lent was close and the carnival season in full swing, so he was not surprised to learn from a grinning Callou that Madame was dining with friends with whom she would go to the ball after dinner. Julie, he was told, had not accompanied Madame, and he instructed Callou to send Amalie's *femme de chambre* to him.

Presently Julie appeared at the door of his chamber, her dark eyes filled with questions as she searched his face.

Armand shook his head. "Ma'm'selle Claudine is not at Les Chênes, Julie. *Madame la comtesse* has heard nothing of her?"

"*Non, michie,*" Julie said sadly. "And Madame and *le gran' michie?*"

He shrugged. "They grieve. But all else is well." He sensed the weight of her hunger for news. Had she left a child at the plantation? He was moved to say, "We shall return to the plantation one day, Julie, I promise you. Tell Dulcie I will dine at the Exchange. And when Jean-Baptiste arrives with my trunks, ask him to lay out my clothes for the ball."

"*Oui, michie.*"

Armand ran down the stair and walked over to the Merchants' Exchange for some oysters washed down with whiskey and a little conversation. He was immediately hailed by Monsieur Moreau, an acquaintance for whom the barman was also shucking fresh oysters.

"Comte de Valérun! I have not seen you in a while."

"I have only now returned to the city."

The barman raised his head from the oysters and regarded Armand curiously.

"Just in time for the ball," Monsieur Moreau said. "Are you attending?"

"Indeed. And you?"

"Me, *non!"*

"And what is new in the city?"

"Very little, my dear Count," Monsieur Moreau told him, wiping his beard and showing his teeth in a sardonic smile. "Our Creole legislators still battle with our American governor and with each other about anything and everything, our gutters still overflow with refuse, and the Americans still run in circles, mocking our indolent ways."

Armand laughed and accepted Monsieur Moreau's offer of another whiskey. The barman poured the two drinks, then moved down the counter, removing his apron. "I am going out for a smoke," he told his young assistant, taking a Cuban cigar from his shelf under the counter. But before he left he took a coin from his cashbox. Outside, he summoned a young boy and gave him the coin and a message.

When he returned to the oyster bar, Monsieur Moreau was saying, "Perhaps you have not heard that Beaulieu's *yanqui* murderers are now lodged in the jail."

"That is good news."

"And your journey? Was it for pleasure or for profit?"

"Both. I escorted my sugar mill equipment to the plantation and saw it partially assembled and placed under shelter. When I go back I shall see to the drainage of some fields to ready them for next season's planting."

For a few moments they discussed the problems and rewards of the sugar planter. Then Monsieur Moreau, who had not missed the barman's exit, lowered his voice so he could not be overheard and said, "I did hear something recently that will be of interest to you, *m'sieu le comte.* My nephew is employed by the governor. He told me in confidence that a certain M'sieu MacInerney of Philadelphia has written several letters to the governor about you."

"Ma-ka-nair—" Armand stumbled over the unfamiliar name. "I do not believe I know—"

"But assuredly you do! He has written to the governor pressing for the inquiry into his son's death on the river which has twice been postponed."

Armand struck his forehead. "The matter had dropped from my mind! It seemed merely something the Americans had seized upon to embarrass one of us. M'sieu, I had nothing to do with the young American's death. He leaped into the river to save his friend who had insulted me. True, it was a well-placed kick that tumbled the peasant overboard, but any gentleman would have struck the lout."

"*Mais, oui,* my friend. But they say the Creole merchant with whom the young American traded for his goods is also being pressed to urge that you be brought to trial."

"Will he?"

Monsieur Moreau hunched his shoulders expressively. "Who knows? I believe that he has business associates in Philadelphia, that one."

"That is very interesting. *Merci,* m'sieu." Armand soon took his leave.

At home he allowed Jean-Baptiste to help him into his formal attire, a sky blue coat over a creamy embroidered waistcoat and pale pantaloons, and once more left the house. Music spilled out of the windows of the Salle d'Orleans, echoing down the street. Armand entered the building and made his way slowly through the friends who pressed close to greet him. When he gained the ballroom floor, a spirited waltz was in swing.

He stood for a moment beguiled by the color and movement of the swirling couples. Soft light from hundreds of candles in the crystal chandeliers gleamed on silks and laces and glossy hair, and bathed the creamy shoulders of the women in a lustrous glow.

Armand's eyes were drawn to the figure of a young woman, small and perfectly formed, who danced with a delicate but spirited grace. Her back was turned to him; her well fitted white gown revealed the small hollow between her shoulders and a neck that rose like the stem of a flower to her high-piled dark hair. The way she held her head was poetry. He wondered who she was, then as her partner turned her, exclaimed, *"Mon Dieu!"* It was Amalie.

It was an Amalie he did not know. She was not the lively *jeune fille* who had been merely Claudine's young sister to him, dressing up in her sister's gown with stuffing in her bosom—he realized belatedly that he had continued to think of her as "dressing up" in her wedding gown and in her first ball gown to be presented to the governor and his lady, and felt somewhat ridiculous.

Nor was she the surprisingly efficient little manager of his household who had been wearing her sister's clothing again to carry on a charade that made him so uncomfortable he had no pleasure in his home. No, she was a woman. A woman of tender years, but nevertheless one poised and confident in her femininity. For the first time he was seeing Amalie as a person, distinct and separate from Claudine's little sister.

She was laughing up at her partner—a Creole gentleman's second son who was, Armand understood, something of a rake. Armand strode purposefully out on the floor, dodging the whirling dancers until he could clap a hand on the young man's shoulder. "I beg your pardon, m'sieu, but I should like to dance with my wife."

"M'sieu Armand!" Amalie gasped. She recovered herself quickly, gave her partner a beguiling smile, and said, "Please excuse us, m'sieu. My husband has only now returned from a journey."

Her partner bowed and withdrew, and Armand put his arm around his wife's waist. If he had touched her so before, he could not remember it, but he knew he would not forget this awareness of how like a feather she moved in his loose embrace. The natural way she had said "my husband" had stirred a new and strange possessiveness in him. He looked closely at her to see if she were stirred by its implications, but she was regarding him with cool self-possession.

"I did not know you danced the *valse*."

"It is one of the things I have learned during your absence," she said, with perfect composure.

While he pondered that reply, they dipped and whirled in the kaleidoscope of dancers. He had not noticed before that she had beautiful eyes, but now he saw how clear and translucent was the white around the dark iris, marveled at their black fringe of lashes and wondered what feminine thoughts lay concealed in their mysterious depths.

"Did you find Maman and Papa well?"

"They are well and send love."

"And my sister?" she asked, quite naturally, and he marveled again at her composure.

The music was ending, so he said just as casually, "She was away visiting friends. A pity! M'sieu Arouet, who had hoped to see her, could not await her return."

He thought some of the color left her face, but she concealed her feelings admirably, for they were immediately encircled by friends wishing to welcome Armand back to the city, and one who claimed Amalie for the promised next set. Armand was annoyed when she did not make excuses to remain with him, but walked away with the young man.

Making no move to seek a partner himself, Armand stood alone after his friends had joined the dancers. After a moment he became aware of a vaguely familiar scent and turned his head to see Madame Amboy standing beside him.

She regarded him with an enigmatic smile. "She is a charming girl, your wife. She has charmed half of New Orleans, including me."

"Indeed?"

"Indeed. It is time you took her to bed."

Armand's expression froze. Then he lifted one eyebrow high. "*You* say that, madame?"

"Who better?" Her eyes, level with his own, held a glint of humor. "Are you going to ask me to dance, Armand?"

The set had ended and another waltz was beginning. Wordlessly, he held out his arms. "So you think I have been neglecting my wife?"

"Shamefully!" She placed her hand on his shoulder and he whirled her out on the floor. "You have left her much alone for a bride. There was some excuse while she was a blind for her sister. But she is sixteen and ready for love."

"Has Madame complained to you, then?" His tone was sardonic, but his pulse had quickened.

"Not at all," she lied. "That is why I am warning you. There are many young Creole blades who would gladly relieve you of your marital duties if you find them distasteful."

"Indeed!" he said again, softly, his eyes seeking Amalie among the dancers. Once he had found her he followed her progress around the ballroom. He could not help seeing that she took no notice of where he was and with whom he was dancing.

Amalie was not as cool and unmoved as she appeared, but she had gained some experience in hiding her emotions. The unexpected sight of Armand standing at her elbow in the middle of her waltz with young Philippe Castellano had been a paralyzing shock. When her husband put his arm around her waist and led her into the first steps with him, she had leaned away so that he would not be aware of the shameful pounding of her heart.

"Amalie, little Amalie, you have grown up!"

"Have the scales fallen from your eyes, then?" *Do not make yourself too easily available to him if you wish to win his love,* Héloïse had counseled her.

Amalie did not know whether that was good advice or not, but she was sure of one thing: She would not bore him with an unwelcome passion. But her apparent coolness was more the result of emotional shock than of deliberate thought. She did not know what else to do but accept the invitations to dance that kept her occupied, since they were constantly being separated by friends who wished to greet Monsieur Armand, but she did not have to search among the dancers to know where he was at each moment. She seemed to have an unsuspected sixth sense that told her.

Toward midnight Armand claimed another dance and suggested that they leave, pleading fatigue from his journey. Amalie assented, trembling inside. She was eager to hear what he had found at Les Chênes, but she was very much aware that Clotie's disappearance had changed things between them. Even though her sister had remained secluded, not even appearing for meals, her presence in the house had made it a *ménage à trois.* Now Amalie would be alone with her husband, and there was no longer any reason why her marriage should not be consummated. It was what she ardently desired, but she knew she could not bear it if Armand took her in his arms with closed eyes to pretend she were Clotie!

As they descended the broad stair to the foyer, Armand suddenly called, "M'sieu Peralta, *bonsoir!*"

Amalie's heart stopped a full beat before it recovered and pumped raggedly on. The despised Monsieur Peralta was, indeed, standing just across the foyer from them with a small group also leaving the ball. His eyes flickered at Amalie and away before he answered, "M'sieu?"

"I hope to see you soon on a matter of business," Armand said in a pleasant voice.

Frozen with fear, Amalie heard Monsieur Peralta reply stiffly, "You can find me at the Exchange, m'sieu."

"Merci." Armand took Amalie's arm and guided her into the street. She could almost feel the heat of Monsieur Peralta's eyes boring through the thin stuff of her wrap as they left, and knew the

Spaniard was wondering frantically, as she was, what Armand had heard tonight. What should she say now?

Before she could say anything, Armand spoke. "I must find a worker who understands the process of making sugar and can teach his skills. I have been told M'sieu Peralta may have such a man, since he brought slaves from Saint Domingue. Perhaps I can avoid another trip to Barataria."

Amalie began to breathe normally again. She hoped Armand had not noticed that Monsieur Peralta, also, had gone quite pale.

They found Callou waiting outside with a lantern to light their way home. The night was warm and odorous with its distinctive aromas of roasting coffee and dank river, with a hint of rotting refuse beneath the scent of blossoms. Music in waltz rhythm followed them from the windows of the ballroom. Monsieur Armand's hand on her arm was a warm, living presence speaking to her blood.

"I am eager now to return to Les Chênes—" Armand began.

"Ah, yes, the plantation," Amalie interrupted, in a flat voice, reminded that he had married her for her dowry. "I, m'sieu, am eager to hear what you found—"

"The galéries have ears," he warned her, in an undertone, and continued normally, "There is much to do there before the next planting season." He continued discussing his plans for Les Chênes until they arrived at his house and she listened, impressed by his energy and enthusiasm, so different from Papa.

"Bring us wine to the salon," Amalie ordered Callou, after the servant had led them into the paneled room and lit the wall sconces and a candelabra that stood on a table between two chairs.

With hands that were not quite steady, she began removing the withered flowers from her hair. When Callou had left them, she said, "Now, m'sieu, if you are not too tired, I should like to hear about Maman and Papa. How did they take the news about Clotie?"

"It was not easy for them."

"Ah, *non*," she said sadly.

"And you found no clues here?"

"Nothing, m'sieu. I sometimes wake in the night from a dream of Clotie in the river—"

"No," he said swiftly. "She would not do that!"

"I do not think she would take her child's life, even if she cared nothing for her own," she agreed. "But still—" She shook off her depression to ask, "You said you found M'sieu Arouet at Les Chênes?"

"Oui, and your maman was at her wits' end, besides finding his importunities extremely boring."

"I am sure she did," Amalie said, amused.

Armand launched into the tale of how he had persuaded the love-sick young man to leave without seeing Clotie, but midway in his recital Callou returned with a tray bearing a carafe of wine and two glasses and handed the count a note which he said had been delivered earlier in the evening.

While Armand scanned it, Amalie dismissed Callou and rose to pour the wine herself.

"Mon Dieu!" Monsieur Armand exclaimed, so violently that she spilled the wine.

"Clotie?" she asked in fear.

But when Armand lifted his eyes from the note, what she saw in them made her curl up inside. "Have you no shame, madame?"

"M'sieu?" she faltered.

"Ma'm'selle Claudine was being forced into a marriage she did not want, but you offered yourself to me. I will not tolerate this from you!"

"I do not understand—"

He flung the note at her as if it were burning his fingers. She caught at it, dropped it and bent to pick it up with a dreadful premonition. Before she straightened, she had seen in a glance what it was.

Ask your wife about her assignation with M. Peralta. It was unsigned.

"Madame Laval," she gasped. The hairdresser had taken her revenge.

Armand had grasped her arms and was shaking her with such fury that she dropped the note again. The lightning of his anger crackled about her. "Did you go to Peralta? *Did* you?"

"N-no, m'sieu—"

"You are lying! I saw it in his face tonight. He is your lover!"

"He, my lover?" Amalie said in such revulsion that it rang with truth. "I wish Julie had killed him!"

"I myself will—*what did you say?"*

"I went to his house, *oui,* but not to an assignation. I went because I thought you were in danger."

"Me?" He was pale now and scornful, but he was listening. "Why would I be in danger, madame?"

"I was tricked." She was very frightened, for Héloise had warned her what would happen if the count learned about that horrible incident. Yet she read in Armand's stern and angry face that nothing but the truth would satisfy him. "I was told to go to his sister's soirée to receive a secret message from you. When I arrived, he was alone in the house. He would have taken me by force, but Julie felled him with his brass clock."

"Have you told me everything? You were not harmed?"

"*Non,* only terribly frightened." She did not dare to tell him how Monsieur Peralta had ripped her clothing, but he saw the reflection of her frightened thought in her eyes.

"I will kill him for this!" He reached for her again, and she braced herself for another shaking, but his arms went around her, crushing her soft breasts against his satin coat. He bent his head, and his mouth captured hers in an angry passion that seemed to flow into her body like liquid fire.

It was not the kiss she had dreamed about. It was brutally hard, and her response to it shocked her. Her breath grew short, her lips tingled, then a melting softness spread down through her body. Soon she was clinging to him, pressing herself against him, half swooning with the new and surprising sensations she was experiencing.

He lifted his head and said, "You are mine. Mine alone. Remember that."

He let her go and she swayed on her feet. "Where are you going?" she cried, when she realized that he was leaving her.

"To find Peralta."

"*No!*" she cried. "It was Madame Laval—she lied to me—"

But the door at the end of the hall had closed and she heard his hard, purposeful steps crossing the court to the street.

EIGHTEEN

AMALIE SANK into a chair. Her heart was pounding, her senses spinning wildly. Monsieur Armand was on his way to challenge Monsieur Peralta—of that she had no doubt. Héloise had warned her this would happen. Monsieur Peralta expected it—she had seen it in his expression when Monsieur Armand called to him across the foyer tonight.

They would duel. There was nothing she could do now but pray. *Holy Mary, Mother of God—*

But there was another reason for the trembling of her hand as she reached for the wine she had poured and left untouched when Monsieur Armand flung down the note she knew had come from Madame Laval. The duel would not take place before daylight, she was sure of that—and probably not on the morrow. Seconds would be chosen, rules agreed upon. For Monsieur Armand and Monsieur Peralta were not young hotbloods eager to put their fencing skills to the test who would repair immediately to the garden behind the church to settle a quarrel. *Non,* Monsieur Armand would return tonight—and when he returned he would take her to bed. Not because he loved her, but because she was his wife.

In all her fantasies in the past months, Amalie had imagined nothing resembling her completely melting capitulation to his passionate kiss. Her body had reacted quite independently of her control. A stray memory brought back Clotie's dreamy voice, saying, *When he touches me—here—there is nothing I would not do for him.*

She had not understood then, but now—*mon Dieu,* but she would be as besotted and tiresome in love as poor Clotie had been!

She was still in the salon when he returned, less than an hour later. His face was white and set. Amalie stood and walked toward him with the cold fear spreading through her. "You challenged him."

"Oui." He passed her, going to the table where his untouched wineglass still sat on the tray. He lifted it and drank, then said, "I challenged him, which gave him his choice of weapons. He must think me the better swordsman, for he chose pistols."

"Pistols!" Her fear congealed in icy terror. "He will kill you!"

"It is very possible that one of us will be killed." He took up the carafe and refilled his glass, but he did not pick it up. He turned to her and held out his arms, and she ran into them. "Amalie, little Amalie," he said, holding her close. "Our life together may be over before it has even begun."

"Non, ah, *non!"* she cried, clinging to him, completely forgetting her resolution not to bore him with excessive love. *"Mon Dieu,* it is all my fault! It is because I listened to Madame Laval. I should never have let that wicked woman into my house. She suspected we had secrets, m'sieu. I thought I could buy her silence, and when she threatened me—"

"Ma foi, she threatened you? What is this?" He picked her up and sat down with her on his lap. "I do not understand what you are telling me. Start at the beginning, *ma petite."*

Amalie did, confessing how she had allowed the hairdresser to divert her from her boredom by repeating the gossip of her patrons. She told him about the gifts Madame Laval had come to expect and finally to demand, and the woman's growing power over her with her hints about Clotie's secret and the danger to him from his royalist activities.

"I was naive," Amalie said, "as Madame Amboy has made me see. And for my mistakes you, m'sieu, must risk your life! I cannot forgive myself for that."

"But I am to blame," Monsieur Armand said, stroking her hair. "As Madame Héloise has also pointed out, I left you too much alone in a city you did not know, under difficult circumstances. My Amalie! I have waited long for you to grow up, perhaps too long."

Amalie raised her head. "Do not think to comfort me by telling me now that you wanted me," she said indignantly, "for I knew quite well you had asked for Clotie. You married me for my dowry, as you told me plainly." She grimaced. "That does not make my fault any less."

"It is true that I badly wanted Les Chênes. I still do. *Mon Dieu,* what your father is *not* doing with the plantation is such a waste!" Armand sighed. "But my heart was my own, although I thought Ma'm'selle Claudine would make me a wife whose beauty I could be proud of. For a long time I could not forgive her, indeed, I could not forgive any of you for the humiliation I suffered hearing the gossip aboard that flatboat!

"But in time I came to see that, beautiful as your sister is, in some ways, as you have often pointed out, she is a beautiful goose! While you, *ma petite,* have never bored me." He smiled at her incredulous look. "It is quite irresistible to be loved so uncritically."

"You *knew?*" she said, appalled.

"That is one of the reasons I stayed away from the house. You were dangerous, and I had promised your father."

Papa! She was sitting upright on his lap now. She said, choosing her words with care, "If you knew I loved you, m'sieu, why did you accuse me of taking that awful M'sieu Peralta as my lover? You had no reason to believe the octoroon's lies."

He said soberly, "Love is not reasonable, *chérie.*"

Her face held such a mixture of doubt and love that he took it between his hands and kissed her. His kiss, this time, was sweet and teasing, and as she abandoned herself to it, that deliciously melting sensation began spreading through her. For a time they pleasured themselves with kisses. Then his hand cupped her breast, as she had once imagined it long ago.

"You no longer need to stuff a handkerchief in your bodice, *eh?*" he teased her.

She was drowning in such delightful sensations that she was scarcely aware when he stood up with her in his arms and carried her into his chamber. What happened there was so naturally inevitable that Amalie murmured, much later, "Why was I frightened? Loving is as easy as breathing." And Armand, laughing, kissed her again.

She wakened alone in the count's bed, to find Julie standing beside it, holding her *café au lait.* The black woman's eyes were wise. "So!" she said, smiling.

But now Amalie remembered all of the events of the evening before, and she sat up in a panic. "Where is *m'sieu le comte?*"

"He say he go see his lawyer."

Amalie's heart fell like a stone dropped in the river. Her husband had gone out to set his affairs in order, preparing to meet his death. She set down the coffee Julie had brought her, untasted. The sensuous memories that even now surged through her body sharpened the edge of her pain. This day before her could be Armand's last—the last day on earth that she could look on his face, or lie in his arms— and if he died beneath the dueling oaks, she would have sent him to his death.

The irony of it! If she had not been persuaded to go to Madame

Chouinard's house to find Monsieur Peralta there waiting for her, she would now be the happiest woman in New Orleans.

Oh, Clotie, where are you? I wish I could tell you that I know at last what you were suffering.

"You goin' eat or not?" Julie demanded.

Amalie burst into tears.

Later in the morning, Madame Amboy came to call. "You've heard the news," Amalie greeted her, seeing that this morning there were no dimples showing in Héloise's heart-shaped face.

Héloise nodded. "It is all over New Orleans that Armand meets M'sieu Peralta at daylight tomorrow." She walked to the fireplace and stood looking down into the small fire Callou had laid against the winter morning's chill. "How did he learn of that night?" She swung around to face Amalie accusingly. *"You* did not tell him?"

"Madame Laval sent him a note—I am sure it must have come from her. Héloise, they are dueling with *pistols.*"

"Oui, with the silver dueling pistols of M'sieu Daubigny. They have been used before, and each time a man has died."

Her words fell like stones of ice on Amalie's heart. "Is there nothing we can do to prevent it?"

"We can only pray that he shoots M'sieu Peralta first. He should be meeting that Laval creature."

"But it is my fault for allowing her to send me to M'sieu Peralta." Héloise did not contradict her, as Armand had done, and that twisted the knife of Amalie's remorse. "Oh, if only I had it to do over—"

"You will be a famous beauty," Héloise told her bitterly. "Barely sixteen, and a man killed for you."

Amalie looked at her friend's pale and tense face and exclaimed, "But—but you love Armand, too."

"I love my husband," Madame Amboy corrected her, then hesitated. "But *oui,* there was a time—a brief time—when I loved Armand madly. It was over long ago, and now you are both my dear friends. And you love each other," she added, her sharp eyes going over Amalie as if she were seeing her for the first time since she arrived.

Amalie flushed scarlet, feeling as if her friend were looking in at her lovely memories. "I have not even offered you coffee!" she apologized, and went quickly to pull the bell.

She was glad, later, that she had learned from Héloise when the duel would take place, for she suspected that Armand would try to keep the actual time of meeting from her. Unable to bear her inaction while she awaited his return, she called Callou to her and instructed him to go to the livery stable and hire a carriage for her for the early morning.

"I intend to be there when M'sieu duels with M'sieu Peralta."

Callou looked shocked. "No ladies be there, madame."

"I will be there," she repeated. "You must say nothing about this to anyone, for if *m'sieu le comte* knows, he will forbid us to go."

"*Oui,* madame, he will!"

"He will take Jean-Baptiste with him, and I want you to go with me."

"He be angry."

"Callou, if he is hurt, he will need us. Tell the man you will come for the carriage an hour before daylight. And pray for fog."

She was glad she had had the forethought to make her plans before Armand returned toward evening, because he resisted all her efforts to learn more about his arrangements. "I leave that to our seconds," he told her impatiently. "I have been settling my affairs as any sane man would do. If I do not prevail against M'sieu Peralta, Madame Héloïse will come to you. You do not mind my asking her?"

"She has been a good friend to me," Amalie said steadily.

"*Bien.* She will help you do what must be done. You are to return immediately to Les Chênes. That is all you need know. Now let us forget the matter, and enjoy ourselves."

But in spite of their resolve, a constraint lay over the table that Dulcie had loaded with the count's favorite dishes, scarcely tasted. The hour after dinner was even worse for, although the count had steadfastly refused to admit that the duel was to take place at daylight, he called all the servants in and made them a little speech, charging them with the safety and well-being of their mistress if anything happened to him.

Since they knew everything, in that mysterious way slaves always did, Dulcie and Estée wept. But Jean-Baptiste said, "You be back, *michie.*"

"*Merci,* Jean-Baptiste."

That night Amalie lay in Armand's arms and their lovemaking had a desperate finality, as if each tried to lay by memories for a time of separation. When Armand slept at last, Amalie lay very still beside him, unwilling to sleep and lose the exquisite novelty of his body lying curved around her own, alternately wondering if she would conceive, and sending up silent supplications to the Holy Virgin for Armand's life. For a love so new to end so soon would be unendurable!

Sometime before dawn she wakened to find that Armand was very gently disengaging himself and sliding out of bed, obviously trying not to waken her. It took all of Amalie's resolve not to throw her arms around him and cling to him, but instinct told her that she must respect his need to be alone at this moment. He must have a steady eye and arm! So she lay quietly, pretending to sleep, wondering if Armand, too, were pretending not to be aware that she watched him beneath lowered lashes as he readied himself for his fateful encounter.

As soon as he left the chamber she arose. Quickly and silently she dressed in dark clothing, throwing a black veil over her head, and went to stand at her window. Down in the courtyard Jean-Baptiste was waiting with the count's carriage. The mists that rose from the river at night were thickest at dawn, and they gave the scene below her a ghostly quality as the count emerged from the house and Jean-Baptiste opened the carriage door. Amalie glimpsed Monsieur Moreau sitting inside. So he was Armand's second. Armand stepped in and Jean-Baptiste closed the door and mounted the driver's perch.

Amalie watched until the carriage passed through the porte cochère. Then she ran down the stair, through the courtyard and into the street. It was deserted except for the count's carriage, just disappearing into the fog. Amalie waited impatiently until Callou drove up in the hired conveyance. They took the direction the count had taken.

Dogs barked and sleepy voices scolded behind the shuttered windows. A woman stepped out on her dark balcony and watched them pass. The mists thinned as they left the river for the old Rope Walk along the canal, and they soon saw Armand's carriage.

Ahead of them two men on horseback followed by a servant on a third horse rode out of a dark street and followed the count. "*Bien*," Callou grunted, and kept a discreet distance behind the newcomers.

They were headed for a grassy clearing in a grove of large oaks half an hour's journey from the city, but still within the crescent curve of the river. It was a spot which had been used so often for resolving quarrels among young Creole men that the large trees marking the limits of the clearing had come to be known as "the dueling oaks."

Although a hint of the dawn lightened the horizon above the trees, the mists had thickened, for they had neared the river again. They could just see Armand's carriage. The horsemen had galloped past it and ridden into the forest a little distance beyond the dueling ground. When Armand's carriage stopped, Callou immediately pulled up in the shelter of a large moss-draped oak, but it was not possible that they were unseen by the four men who alighted. Yet none paid them any attention.

Armand and Monsieur Moreau were approaching the clearing from Armand's carriage; Monsieur Peralta, accompanied by his second, whom Amalie did not recognize, walked toward them, leaving their horses held by the groom. They were four dark figures obscured by the patchy mists.

But now a third carriage could be heard approaching, its horses' hooves muffled in the damp air. To Amalie's consternation, its driver turned his horses in beside her own and a strange man stepped down and walked over to her carriage.

He was startled when he looked in and saw her. "Madame! I had thought to find a colleague. I am Doctor LaMartine."

Amalie threw back her veil. "I am glad you are here, *m'sieu le docteur*. My husband, *m'sieu le comte de Valérun,* is one of the duelists, and I fear for his life."

The doctor's soft, brown eyes held compassion. "Ah, these hothead duelists! The practice should be outlawed here, as it has been in England. I was engaged by Madame Chouinard to attend her brother in the event that I am needed."

"I should be happy to engage you, also, m'sieu."

He pulled at his short beard. "It is possible that both men will need my attention. In that situation, I should have to attend M'sieu Peralta first."

"Then pray tell me what to do," she begged.

"If your husband is wounded, madame, the essential thing will be to stop the bleeding. When that is done, bring him to the hospital in New Orleans where I can care for him."

Her heart seemed to stop at the thought of Armand's strong body bleeding. "*Merci,* m'sieu, and how will I stop it?"

"I cannot make a nurse of you in a few minutes, madame, but I will tell you what I can. *M'sieu le comte's* second will assuredly be prepared to render assistance."

He stood beside the carriage and together they looked through the trees to the clearing where the four men were conferring. "Their seconds are asking them to apologize and avoid bloodshed," observed Doctor LaMartine, who must have attended many such meetings.

Amalie clenched her hands and sent up a desperate prayer. But, *non,* the matter had progressed too far. She saw the gleam of silver as the box was opened and the pistols offered, first to Monsieur Peralta and then to Armand, and each took one of the beautiful deadly weapons.

"They are an English pair of dueling pistols," Doctor LaMartine told her, "owned by a M'sieu Daubigny. They have been used before on this spot, not once—"

"I have heard the story," Amalie interrupted him, in a panic lest she hear again of the men the pistols had killed.

Armand and Monsieur Peralta now stood back to back. The seconds had stepped to one side, and Monsieur Peralta's second was counting, his voice a faint sound wafted without substance through the distance. Amalie's eyes followed Armand as the men paced. The light overhead had brightened, the mists were thinning. The two men halted.

"Abo-out!" came the ghostly cry.

"A-a-aim!"

Amalie held her breath. Faintly, she heard "Fir-r-re!" and almost immediately the sounds of a double explosion battered her ears. The horses jumped and strained against their harness. Birds rose from the trees with frightened squawks. Smoke from the gunpowder obscured her vision, but she was out of the carriage and running before she could see clearly that both men had fallen.

Doctor LaMartine pounded past her, his bag flapping against his longer legs. He stopped to bend over Monsieur Peralta, who was nearer, but Amalie had eyes only for Armand, lying on his back, and for the spreading dark stain the rising sun revealed.

NINETEEN

Monsieur Moreau reached Armand first and was already slashing his blood-soaked trousers to get at the wound. He gave Amalie a shocked look—*"Madame!"*—which she ignored to bend over her husband. Armand's eyes widened when he saw her, and he murmured weakly, *"Ma foi!"* then said no more.

Monsieur Moreau had exposed the wound, in the fleshy part of Armand's thigh, and was pressing a wad of cloth against it to staunch the bleeding. "I do not think the large artery is breached, thank God. If it were, we could not save him. The wound is too high to apply a tourniquet with any success."

"Doctor LaMartine is here—" Amalie ventured.

"Doctor La Martine will be occupied for some time with M'sieu Peralta, I fear." He raised his arm and signaled Jean-Baptiste to bring up the carriage, then gave Amalie a sharp look. "You will not faint, madame?"

"Non, m'sieu!"

"Then do you press on this bandage with all your strength while Jean-Baptiste and I place him in the carriage."

It was not accomplished without difficulty. When they were installed on the cushioned seats, with Monsieur Moreau holding Armand, and Amalie kneeling beside him to press his bandage firmly in place, Monsieur Moreau instructed Jean-Baptiste to drive them to the hospital.

"Do not drive recklessly, but go with all possible haste. See that you make no sudden turns, or jolt us more than is necessary." He looked at Amalie and added, "It will be up to us, madame, to see that the count loses no more blood. If I can hold him steady, and you can keep a continuous pressure on the wound, we may succeed."

"Oui," said Amalie, her heart quailing.

Armand was conscious but pale. His skin felt cold, although the sun was now up and they could already feel its warmth through the carriage window. Amalie carefully slipped the cloak from her shoulders and with one hand tucked it around Armand's legs. He did not seem to be aware of her, but stared up at the carriage top which had been closed for privacy.

"Peralta?" he asked.

"Wounded." Monsieur Moreau said no more, and presently Armand murmured, "Where?"

"The face."

"The *face!*" Armand started up and Amalie, pressing down on his bandage, cried, "Lie still, I beg you!"

"He discharged his pistol a fraction of a second before you did," Monsieur Moreau told him, "and when you were hit, it apparently deflected your shot upward."

Monsieur Armand seemed to be watching the light and shadow chasing each other across the carriage top as the horses galloped by the overhanging trees. "Will he live?"

"It is very possible that he would prefer to die."

"*Mon Dieu,*" Monsieur Armand muttered.

Nothing more was said until they reached the small hospital where nurses, free women of color, directed Jean-Baptiste and Monsieur Moreau where to lay the count, and immediately went to work cleaning and dressing the wound with gentle, skilled hands. Monsieur Moreau drew Amalie away from the cot, saying, "Perhaps you should go home and change your gown, madame."

Amalie looked down and saw that her gown was stained with Armand's blood, and for the first time felt quite faint.

The nurse nodded in agreement. "It is not a serious wound, madame. If we can ward off infection, he will live."

"I will stay and speak with the doctor when he arrives," Monsieur Moreau told Amalie. Jean-Baptiste took her arm, and she allowed him to lead her out to the carriage, for her knees were quite trembly. In fact, in her sudden relief from fear as she realized at last that Armand had survived the duel, she was so lightheaded that she failed to notice Monsieur Peralta being carried in from the doctor's carriage as she left in hers.

The sun was high now, and the sky blue with a few ballooning clouds being driven ahead of a whippy wind from the Gulf. The river behind the levee was filled near to overflowing with the winter rains falling in the north, making the barques at anchor appear to be floating above the city. Worshippers were streaming out of St. Louis church after mass, and the hawkers were out, offering them fruit and ginger beer and sweet cakes. Already soldiers of the Louisiana Battalion were drilling in the Place d'Armes. The ordinariness of the morning's activities made the scene in the mists under the dueling oaks something remembered out of a nightmare, and yet to Amalie it was the people moving past her carriage as they went about their usual tasks who seemed unreal.

When Jean-Baptiste drove through the porte cochère, all the servants ran out into the court, even Callou who had followed Amalie back to the city and delivered the hired carriage to the livery stable.

"*Michie* lives!" Jean-Baptiste called to them, jumping down from the driver's seat, and they cheered. But when he helped Amalie from the coach and they saw her bloodstained gown, their cries of joy turned to dismay.

"He will recover," she told them, with a confidence she wished she felt, then went up the stair with Julie following close behind her.

When Amalie passed the open door of the salon on the way to her chamber, a young man rose from the stiff little rosewood chair beside her desk, exclaiming, "Madame!" As Amalie paused in confusion, he came swiftly toward her. It was Monsieur Arouet.

"Forgive me, madame! I came—" he began, then stopped, his look appalled as he saw the condition of her gown.

Amalie collected her wits desperately. "Why did you come, M'sieu Arouet?"

"I came to inquire about Ma'm'selle Claudine, but—forgive me," the young man stammered again, "I fear I have arrived at an inopportune time. Have you met with an accident, *madame la comtesse?*"

"It is my husband. You will excuse me, M'sieu Arouet? I can give you no word from Ma'm'selle Claudine. You must put her out of your mind."

"Madame, I cannot eat, I cannot sleep—"

"I am sorry, m'sieu. You must excuse me. Julie, will you show M'sieu Arouet out?" She hurried along to her room, flung herself into a low chair and waited for Julie to come to her.

She felt a fleeting sympathy for the young poet who had conceived such a passion for Clotie—and a spasm of worry about her sister. Clotie's time must soon be on her. Was she receiving the care she needed now? Where was she? And if Monsieur Arouet had not helped her leave the count's house, who had? They knew no more about what had happened now than they had in the days after Clotie left them.

Amalie had scarcely finished a quick bath and change of clothing when Estée came to tell her Madame Amboy was calling. Amalie went quickly to the salon to greet her friend. Héloise looked pale and strained, as if from a sleepless night, but she was elegantly groomed, as always, and her smile was brilliant.

"Estée told me. I am so glad for your sake, Amalie, as well as Armand's."

Amalie began to tremble again. "When I think that he might now be lying cold—"

Héloise patted her hands. "You left him at the hospital? How is he?"

"His wound is not serious, unless it infects. I am going back now. I came only to change my gown."

"And M'sieu Peralta?"

"I do not know—only that if he lives, he will be disfigured." She added, "Poor man."

Héloise raised her eyebrows. "You can feel sympathy for him?"

"*Non,* never for what he did. But he is paying a high price for his —indiscretion. And much of the blame can be laid at Madame Laval's door, after all. Can nothing be done about her?"

"I am afraid not, *ma chère.* She knows too many secrets about men in high places! I will take my leave now, for I know you are anxious to return to your husband."

A few moments later Amalie was on her way back to the hospital. She found Armand sleeping, and a dusky nurse, smiling, signaled with her finger to her lips. Amalie quietly brought a chair to his cot, content to sit and watch him sleep, for she had not had another opportunity to study him so closely.

It was a proud face, even in sleep, with a hint in the flat planes of his cheeks of the hardness that had brought him to the point of dueling. Looking at him, she thought that what she had called love for him only a week ago was a pale emotion compared to what she felt now, and she closed her eyes and said a prayer of thanks for his life.

The colored nurse came on her rounds, and nodded approval. "See? He already gains some color. He will sleep for a long time, madame, for we gave him laudanum. It is necessary to keep him quiet, you understand, so that he cannot move around and in so doing reopen the wound."

Amalie nodded, watching the even rise and fall of his chest. "I understand."

"In a few days it will be safe to take him home."

When the hospital ward began to darken with the dusk that was gathering outside its windows, Armand opened his eyes and looked at her. "Are you real, Amalie?" he murmured.

She bent and kissed his lips, and he put his arms around her and held her against him with surprising strength.

"*Oui,* you are real. You came to me in a dream at the dueling oaks."

"That was real, too, *mon cher.*"

"*You* were there?" She thought she detected laughter in his weak voice. "You are an eccentric, *ma petite comtesse.*"

"Madame!" a nurse protested softly behind her, and Amalie raised her head reluctantly from the sound of Armand's strong heartbeat.

The little nurse had another draft for him, and a few minutes after drinking it, he drifted into sleep again. Shortly after that, Jean-Baptiste came. "Callou waits outside to take you home, madame. I will stay with *michie* tonight."

Amalie did not protest.

Back in her own chamber, Amalie let Julie remove her shoes and put her feet on a cushion. She felt desperately tired now, and it was comforting to let Julie cosset her as she had when Amalie was an adored child on the plantation.

"The nurses are all free women of color, Julie, but they are not like Madame Laval."

"They *good* womans," Julie soothed her. She left the chamber and presently returned with a tray. Lying on it beside the covered light meal was an impressive-looking official document.

"What is this?" Amalie asked, picking it up.

"*Un américain* bring it. A soldier."

Amalie broke the seal and unfolded it. "But this is in English!" she exclaimed, indignant. "I can't read it at all! What did the soldier who brought it say to you, Julie?"

"He no speak French."

"*Ma foi!*" Amalie flung the document aside.

She went to the hospital every day and sat beside Armand's cot, quietly when he was drugged, reading or talking to him when the drafts were taken away and the pain or his enforced inactivity made him restless. At such times they talked a great deal of Les Chênes and his plans for a sugar crop, and sometimes they talked of their love and of how their marriage had come about.

"It was destined, *ma petite*," Armand told her. "It was our Fate, conspiring to bring us together under the guise of a *mariage de convenance* inspired by your maman's need of me at Les Chênes."

"*Oui*," she said, her heart overflowing with love.

At last the day came when the doctor said Monsieur Armand could continue his convalescence at home. Jean-Baptiste was dispatched to find him a pair of crutches and, after some experimentation with them, Jean-Baptiste was allowed to dress him, and the carriage was brought.

They rode the few blocks to Bourbon Street in a gay mood, their spirits lifted by their release from the unhappy atmosphere of the hospital. Neither had referred to the duel since that fateful morning, although Amalie had ascertained from the nurses that Monsieur Peralta lived. But now, as they rode through the sunny streets, alive with color and noise, Armand looked about him with hungry eyes and said, "I am fortunate that M'sieu Peralta, although faster with his pistol, is not a good shot."

He added, "And M'sieu Peralta is fortunate that he is faster, for if he were not, my bullet would have found his heart instead of his jawbone."

Amalie shuddered. "Please, let us speak of that no more!"

When they turned in at the porte cochère on the rue Bourbon, an American soldier suddenly appeared at each side of the landau. "Mon—soo—er—ah—Valrun?" one of them asked.

"I am *le comte de Valérun*," Armand replied in French.

The soldier looked at a paper in his hand. "Guess you're the party," he said, in English.

Amalie, who understood no English, demanded, "What is it?" She turned to Armand, agitated. "M'sieu, there was an important English letter which I forgot. It arrived while you were in the hospital."

"What's she saying?" the soldier demanded, suspiciously.

"Speak slowly, please," Armand told him. "I understand a little English." He listened carefully, then told Amalie, "They have come to take me to the Cabildo. It seems that an inquiry has been scheduled into that flatboat incident, after all."

"Must you go today?" she exclaimed.

"Indeed I must, *chère*. They think I ignored their summons."

"But it was my fault!" Amalie exclaimed. She turned to the soldiers and said urgently, "It was I who ignored the summons because I cannot read English, and my husband was in the hospital—"

They looked at her with baffled admiration and she realized, frustrated, that they had not understood anything more than her gestures toward herself. "They are uneducated!" she exclaimed, in dismay.

"Do not worry, *ma petite,*" Armand told her. "Fortunately, I have proof enough of where I have been these past few days when I am supposed to have been evading the inquiry." He spoke to the soldiers again in halting English, then told her that they would allow Jean-Baptiste to drive him to the Cabildo, since he was on crutches.

"I must go with you, of course."

But Armand said firmly, *"Non, ma petite.* Jean-Baptiste can better assist me. I will not be long."

One of the soldiers held out his hand to assist her as she stepped from the landau, then they jumped up beside Armand. Jean-Baptiste turned the horse around and drove out into the street, and Armand was gone.

An hour later Madame Amboy was admitted and Amalie asked Julie to bring her to her boudoir. Héloïse came in with flags of excitement flying in her heart-shaped face. "My dear Amalie, I came as soon as I heard! Do you know that they have found a witness to that accident on the flatboat, at last?"

"Yes, indeed, I know," Amalie said. "Two soldiers came for M'sieu Armand not an hour ago. And he just released from the hospital!"

"Truly? I do not know what they hope to discover that they do not already know. It is this cursed duel that is behind it, of course."

"How can that be?" Amalie asked, feeling anxious. "The duel was a matter between gentlemen, and it was not fatal."

"The Creoles are making jests about poor M'sieu Peralta's former notorious success with the ladies, but the Americans profess to be shocked by his disfigurement. To my way of thinking, it is simply another example of the low esteem in which Creoles and Americans hold each other. A pity there is not more understanding! But," she said anxiously, "I fear the Americans will deal harshly with M'sieu Armand."

Amalie rose and paced the floor. "But this witness they have found —who is he?"

"I have heard that he is one of the boatmen on the flatboat who saw the incident. A curious thing—he is reported to be saying he saw *three* men go overboard."

"Three?"

"The 'Cadian trapper whom Armand kicked, his American friend and the American's servant, a big black who jumped in after him."

"A big slave." The words conjured up an almost forgotten picture in Amalie's mind. She was back at Les Chênes, sitting on one of Maman's delicate chairs on the lawn between Maman and Clotie, with Papa and the count standing beside them, watching as Papa's big dogs came tearing down from their pen behind the house and the Yankee ran for his pirogue. Sitting in the shallow boat had been a large black slave.

Slowly, another picture supplanted it—the big, bald black man who had lurked in the shadowed doorway across the street on the day before Clotie disappeared. Could they be the same man?

"Ma foi," Amalie said. Had the big black come for Clotie? "But would she go with the slave?" Amalie was not aware that she was speaking aloud. "Not unless he brought word that his master—"

"What are you talking about?" Héloïse demanded.

"I have just had the strangest thought," Amalie explained. "I wonder—" There could be no way of proving what she thought might be true—that if the big slave had survived, his master might also be alive!—and besides, Clotie's reputation must still be protected.

She did not have time to explain further, for there was a peal of the brass knocker at the head of the stair and soon Estée was hurrying to Amalie's chamber to announce a visitor.

"An American gentleman. He say he have a message for *madame la comtesse.* A sea captain." Estée giggled. "He speak funny, madame."

"Another man with a message?" Amalie sent an alarmed look at Héloïse. "Will you stay with me, *chère* Héloïse?"

"But of course. I am eaten with curiosity."

Together they went to the salon, where a young man in a resplendent naval uniform awaited them. In passable French, he asked, "Am I addressing *madame la comtesse de Valérun?"*

"I am *la comtesse de Valérun,"* Amalie said.

"Captain Ezra Taylor, of the brigantine *Excelsior,* at your service, madame. I have a letter which I was instructed to place in your own hands. It is from your sister, Madame Dennis MacInerney."

"Ma foi!" Amalie took the fat letter from him and sank, rather

breathless, into the nearest chair. "Pray be seated, m'sieu. Can—can I offer you coffee? I would so like to hear how you left my sister."

"*I* should like to hear how you left Madame MacInerney's husband!" Héloise said, rather sharply.

"Pardon, Héloise!" Amalie cried, aghast at her lapse of manners. "I am so excited! Madame Amboy, may I present *m'sieu le capitaine* Taylor?" Then Amalie realized what Héloise had said. She jumped up from her chair. "Captain Taylor, did you see my sister's husband? Is he alive, then?"

Looking startled, the captain said, "He was very much alive when I left him, madame. It was M'sieu MacInerney himself who brought his wife's letter and asked me to deliver it. I have also a letter to his former business associate here. Perhaps you can direct me—?"

"Captain Taylor," Amalie said breathlessly, "would you be so kind as to accompany us to the Cabildo immediately? There is in progress now an inquiry into the supposed death of M'sieu MacInerney by drowning in the Mississippi five months ago."

"Certainly, madame. I can testify that I left him in good health forty-five days ago. But first I should like to deliver his letter to a certain importer, his former—"

"I think you will find the gentleman you want at the inquiry," Amalie interrupted him. "It is he who is under the misapprehension that M'sieu MacInerney drowned."

"It will be faster if we go on foot," Héloise told them.

Amalie rang the bell for Julie and in a very short time a curious procession was hurrying toward the Place d'Armes and the imposing Cabildo facing it. First Amalie, her slippered feet twinkling, with Julie following her, and Héloise followed by her servant, with the rear brought up by Captain Taylor, magnificent in white and gold.

TWENTY

THEY SAT in Amalie's salon over a glass of wine and some of Dulcie's sweet cakes, Amalie and Armand and Héloise and the charming Captain Taylor—obviously an educated man, since he spoke French!

—and relived their triumph at the Cabildo where the captain had proved himself an able and sympathetic interpreter.

"But what of the man you kicked overboard, m'sieu?" the captain asked Armand. "Surely the inquiry is not closed if he drowned?"

"There is no proof that he, too, will not rise from the river to confront the judge."

"True," the American murmured.

"It was an affair of honor, m'sieu. I could not countenance the remarks he made publicly about my wife's family. Since he was not a gentleman—we Creoles understand—"

"Even an American understands an affair of honor, m'sieu."

"But of course! I beg your pardon, m'sieu. It was unfortunate that the 'Cadian became overbalanced, and even more unfortunate that M'sieu MacInerney so rashly followed him into the river. It was not something that I foresaw, certainly! How long will your barque remain at anchor, *m'sieu le capitaine?*"

"For several weeks." Captain Taylor turned to smile at Amalie. "We return to Baltimore, madame. I shall be happy to carry a letter to Madame MacInerney for you."

"You are very kind, *m'sieu le capitaine.* I shall prepare a lengthy journal for her. And you must allow us to make your stay as pleasant as possible. Would you not like an invitation to some of our balls while you are here?"

"It would give me the greatest pleasure, madame. I was wondering how I could meet some of your charming young Creole ladies, who are reputed to be the most beautiful in the nation. If I may say so," he added diplomatically, "I do not find your reputations overpraised."

"You will charm them, m'sieu," Héloise told him.

"Do you know M'sieu—my brother-in-law well?" Amalie asked.

"I know his family, madame. His father is a respected merchant in Philadelphia. Dennis has a bit of the adventurer in his blood, but now that he has acquired a lovely wife, he seems content to enter his father's business. But perhaps your sister has told you of that?"

"I have saved her letter, which is lengthy, as you saw, for reading when I am quite alone. Although I am anxious for her news, there has scarce been time for it this busy day."

"Then I will take my leave, madame, and with your permission call on you tomorrow."

Héloise rose from her chair. "And I will ask you to escort me and my servant to my door, *m'sieu le capitaine,* since I came away this morning on foot."

When their guests had departed, Amalie drew out the letter from Clotie. "Shall I read it aloud?" she asked, a little timidly.

"Pray do! I am curious to know how the *yanqui* took her from under your nose." But Armand no longer seemed so irate when speaking of Clotie, and so Amalie began reading with confidence.

" 'Dearest Amalie,

'At last I have an opportunity to send word to you by Captain Taylor, a friend of the MacInerney family, to tell you that Dennis and I arrived safely in Philadelphia after taking a small boat from St. John's landing to a barque at anchor in Lake Borgne. We were married by the captain soon after we sailed into the Gulf. It was a rough voyage with some storms, but I was seldom ill, perhaps because I was so happy. By the time you receive this, my child may already be born. I am feeling well, and Madame Mac-Inerney's doctor tells me I should have no trouble.

'You cannot imagine the joy I felt when I learned Dennis had not drowned in the river!' "

"Can I not!" Amalie exclaimed, in an aside.

" 'His servant saved him, for Dennis struck a submerged log and would surely have drowned had not 'Ti-Bo jumped in after him. By the time 'Ti-Bo had dragged him out of the current and into a shallow pool, poor Jacques had disappeared. Have you heard nothing of him?

'Some colored boys who were fishing nearby helped 'Ti-Bo bring Dennis out of the river. They took him to the plantation of a free man of color where he convalesced from the severe blow to his head. When he was fit again, he started back to Les Chênes, but on hearing by chance that a big wedding had been celebrated there between Monsieur de l'Ouvrier's daughter and *monsieur le comte de Valérun,* he assumed it was mine.

'So he reversed his steps, traveling to New Orleans. There he set about discovering where the count lived. He sent 'Ti-Bo, who learned the truth from Madi. From that moment, we planned our elopement.

'Forgive me for leaving as I did, but I dared not tell you

I had heard from Dennis for fear you would stop us. Admit that you would! Please believe that I am happy, dear Amalie, and try to reconcile dear Maman and Papa to my marriage. My husband is heir to a respectable business here in Philadelphia and I want for nothing.

> Your loving sister,
> Madame Dennis MacInerney.'"

Amalie wiped her eyes. "What a silly goose she is, to be sure."

Armand smiled. "And you, Amalie, are you not something of a goose, too? Racing out to the dueling oaks where no lady goes? Bursting in on a sober inquiry in the American court, babbling about a man five months in the Mississippi being seen in Philadelphia only a month and a half ago to a judge who understands no French?"

"Yes," Amalie admitted. "I am just as foolishly in love as poor Clotie."

He came to her chair and pulled her to her feet so he could take her in his arms. "I think it is time now for us to return to Les Chênes, where we will begin to grow rich while you give me thirteen sons."

"And why not thirteen daughters?" she teased.

"Mon Dieu!" exclaimed the count in mock horror. "Think of the difficulties in making *thirteen* marriage contracts!"

Innocent Deception

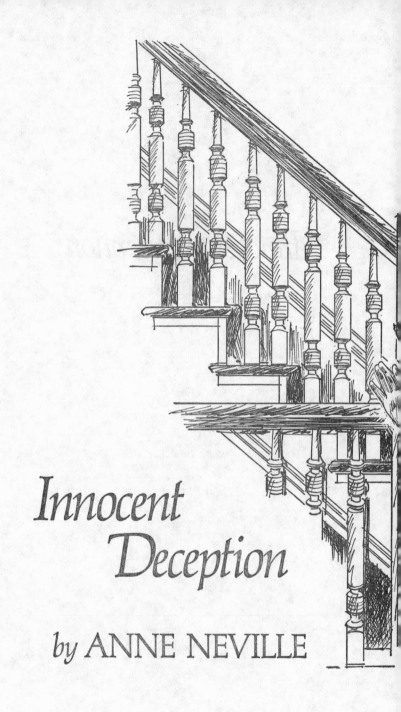

*Innocent
Deception*

by ANNE NEVILLE

For Carl and Jean

ONE

THE FACT that she was the only person at her father's funeral neither surprised nor distressed Laurel. Even when she watched the coffin being lowered into the ground and heard the openly curious vicar speak the well known, chilling words over it, her emotions were curiously detached. It was as though they had been so bludgeoned of late, since the moment three days earlier when the kind faced young police constable appeared at her doorstep with the unhappy news, that they were numbed. She had nursed her one remaining parent and cosseted him; she had tried to give him love. She had cried often for him when he lived, for the wreck of a man he had become, but she could find no tears to shed for him now that he was dead.

At length she turned away from the freshly dug grave and walked back through the large, sprawling cemetery, stepping on the gravelled path, her sensible brown Hush Puppies crunching a little on the stones, hardly hearing the vicar call out her name.

When the call was repeated she did halt and turned to look at the young man who hurried up to her. He was scarcely older than she and, being a perfectly normal young man, could not help but be intrigued by the events surrounding the funeral. He looked now into Laurel's face. She could, he was sure, be quite hauntingly beautiful. Her eyes were hazel, but more green than brown, and her hair auburn, but now the expression in those eyes was sombre and desperately tired and the thick, shoulder length hair hung lank and dull round her face. Nevertheless, her gaze was direct and slightly disconcerting because of it so that the vicar faltered in his prepared speech.

"Miss Anderson, I was just . . . I wondered if you . . . if you were all right," he managed to stutter. "I mean . . . you have no family—no one to comfort you?"

Something that might almost have been a smile flickered briefly across her pale, colourless lips. "I'm perfectly all right, thank you," she said, without answering his question. "I don't need any comfort." She turned and walked away, digging her hands into the pockets of her brown raincoat and leaving him standing there uncertainly, aware of having failed to provide the spiritual strength that she surely needed. He saw her turn left at the gate and walk off down the road.

It had been raining earlier but now the sun, pale and without heat, was beginning to fight its way through the clouds. Laurel walked on with her head down, her lower lip caught between her teeth as she finally faced the problems that seemed to beset her on all sides. This numbness would have to wear off sometime and circumstances would force her to face the reality of the situation she was in. The first thing, she supposed, was to find somewhere to live, somewhere cheap, because everyone these days demanded at least one month's rent in advance and she had very little. Then she must get a job . . . and there were his debts to be paid . . . momentary panic rushed through her on a hot wave and she clenched her hands into fists. God . . . it wasn't as though she was unused to coping. She had coped with him for years, hadn't she? She had paid the bills—those she knew about anyway—had hidden his bottles of whisky, persuaded, cajoled, threatened when he began to gamble . . . she had cooked and cleaned and made their money stretch because she dared not get a job and leave him alone all day. Surely now she ought to feel relief, because now she had only herself to think about.

If only she could have had some breathing space, time to get a job and then look for somewhere else to live. That would have made things easier. But she had only two days. No sooner had she returned from the harrowing task of identifying her father's body than Mr. Coleman, the landlord, had confronted her on the stairs. She could still hear the chilling words:

"Three weeks rent he owed," Coleman had said. "Seventy-five quid."

Laurel had paled. "But I paid you!" she cried out. "Every week I paid—you know I did. I have the rent book."

"Aye, and he borrowed it back. And *I've* got the IOUs to prove it."

She had thought then that she would faint yet knew she must show no weakness before this man with his lecherous stares and sly smile. Somehow she had managed to mutter that she would see that he was paid. There were other bills too, that came in with alarming speed as soon as the news of Frank Anderson's death got round: an account from the local betting shop for five hundred odd pounds; a bill from a tailor for the hand sewn mohair suit her father had been wearing when they fished him out of the river; another from a nearby off-license. Laurel shivered as she remembered. She had some savings and a few odd bits and pieces of jewellery left by her mother, so she would be able—just—to raise the necessary money to pay these bills and Coleman's seventy-five pounds. But Coleman had told her she must get out at the end of the week. She wasn't sure that he had the right to turn her out on to the street but was too beaten into the ground to try to find out. Besides, she had to get somewhere cheaper. Twenty-five pounds a week was not much by the day's standards but it was more than she could afford.

As she turned into Motton Street and regarded the tall, sombre buildings, mostly with shops at street level and two or three flats above, she knew she would not be sorry to leave. The place held too many awful memories: the night Lorraine walked out and their father fell all the way down three flights of stairs in a drunken stupor; the occasion Coleman had tried to lure Laurel into his rooms, just two days ago, saying that if she would "be nice to him" he might just let her stay on; the time Ben Lester had taken one look at Lorraine and decided she was a far better proposition altogether than her sister. . . .

She turned towards the front door of the house which Coleman had converted into flats and bedsitters, scrabbling in her bag for the key and failing to notice the yellow sports car parked outside, as incongruous in this street of dark buildings as an orchid in a patch of cabbages. She trudged upstairs, her shoulders slumped a little, only pausing with a sort of detached interest when she noticed that the door to her apartment was already on the latch. The door swung open at her push; it led straight into the square lounge, a room that had wall paper of green and yellow, rather bilious looking, flowers, and a thin, bottle green carpet. Laurel had always intended doing something to brighten it up but somehow there had always seemed more important things to do. She took off her raincoat and threw it over a chair, at the same time pushing one hand through her long straggling hair in a gesture that spoke eloquently of her despair.

"Oh, you're back at last, I see."

The voice, coming from the direction of her bedroom, caused Laurel to move more swiftly than she had done for days. She literally spun on her heels to stand, open mouthed, staring at the vision that stood framed attractively in the doorway.

Eyes of precisely the same colour as her own looked back at her, eyes that dropped to her feet and moved back again to her face, widening slightly as they took in every aspect of her appearance.

"God, you look a mess!" Lorraine said.

Laurel said nothing, but through her shot a great burst of pure, undiluted anger, anger followed almost immediately by bitterness as she, in turn, looked at her sister. It had once been like looking in a mirror—to look at Lorraine was to look at herself for they were identical twins, identical in every way. Of course, they had played the usual tricks when, as children, they were dressed alike. Sometimes even their parents had found themselves confused and at school they had been put in different classes to lessen the problem. There was no physical way of telling one from the other then. Their hair, eyes, complexions, were identical; they were of the same height and could wear each other's dresses, shoes and hats; even their voices had been so similar in pitch and intonation that speech had been no real test of identity. It was only later, when they reached their teens, that people had suddenly begun to be able to tell them apart without too much difficulty for they developed into very different girls. Lorraine was lively, her bubbling humour overflowing and enveloping everyone about her, her laughter so infectious that wherever she went she became the centre of a bright, laughing group of people of both sexes. Both sisters had always been beautiful but her lively personality made Lorraine seem suddenly more lovely than her quieter, more serious sister. Those who did not know there were two of them could still be fooled, but everyone else would take one look and think: "Ah, yes, that's Lorraine. She's the one with the extra something."

Now, thought Laurel bitterly, no one would believe they were even sisters let alone identical twins.

"What are you doing here?" she asked, recognising and despising the sullen quality that had entered her voice. Once she would have been delighted to see Lorraine but no more—oh, definitely no more! "Father's funeral was an hour ago. You're a bit late, aren't you?"

Lorraine shrugged her elegantly clothed shoulders. She wore a trouser suit of silk shot through with autumn colours, and over one arm hung a silver fox jacket lined with grey silk. "I'm not a hypocrite, sister. I hated him when he lived just as he hated me. Why should I pretend to mourn him?"

It was Laurel's turn to shrug. She walked past her sister into the kitchen where she put on the kettle and proceeded to make a pot of tea. She noticed then that her hands were shaking and made an effort to calm herself. Lorraine strolled over and stood behind her, watching her with that air of detached condescension that had always rankled.

"I wouldn't have thought you'd want to mourn him either," she drawled. "Look what he's done to you. My God, you look . . ."

"A mess. I heard you perfectly well the first time!" Laurel snapped. "And I wasn't aware that I asked for your opinion on my appearance. I haven't exactly had time to worry about such things. Do you want some tea?"

"Tea? Ugh, no, I don't. I'll have coffee."

"I only have instant."

"Then that will have to do, won't it?"

Laurel carried the two cups back into the living room and set one down beside Lorraine who had reclined in the only comfortable chair, one long slim leg crossed over the other. Her shoes, Laurel noticed, were crocodile skin, most certainly genuine. Having recently watched a documentary on television about the mindless slaughter of crocodiles and snakes for their skin, Laurel hoped her distaste was not caused by anything so petty as jealousy. She had no wish to wear crocodile skin shoes . . . but, oh, they were lovely, with high, narrow heels and straps across the instep, showing off Lorraine's slim pretty foot to perfection.

"How did you get in?" she asked tonelessly.

"That frightful, lecherous creature downstairs let me in. Is he the landlord?" Lorraine shuddered delicately as Laurel nodded. "He told me the old man chucked himself in the river."

"That isn't true!" Laurel flashed, the colour rushing to her previously pale face. "The police were satisfied that it was an accident."

"In other words, he was bombed out of his mind as usual. I thought you intended keeping him off the bottle."

"I tried. Most of the time he was all right but I couldn't watch him every minute." It was true of course. An almost empty bottle of whisky had been found in the pocket of his overcoat.

"It's probably just as well anyway," Lorraine said lazily. "The way you look now, you're well out of it. What are you going to do? Have you got a job?"

Laurel shook her head and wondered at this sudden burst of sisterly interest from a girl who had given no thought for her or their father for well over five years. She glanced at Lorraine, noticing everything about her with absolute clarity. Whatever she was doing now, she was obviously doing very well for herself. That trouser suit and the shoes, not to mention the fur coat, proclaimed a very large expense account. Not only that though, Lorraine looked sleek and well groomed and cared for. Her lovely face was made up with faultless skill, her auburn hair glowed like burnished copper, her smooth white hands were tipped with beautifully manicured, scarlet nails. As she glanced down at her own hands, with nails cut off square and sensibly, the skin rather rough because she had lost interest in them, Laurel also took time to notice that no wedding ring adorned Lorraine's left hand. She raised her eyes and met Lorraine's, surprising a look of keen speculation in them.

"You know I left Derek?" Lorraine asked abruptly, and Laurel nodded.

"I met Diane Blackburn in town and she told me. Are you divorced?"

"No. You remember I told you about his aunt Caroline, the manageress of Clairt's in Paris where I modelled for a while? It was through her that I met Derek and she was terribly upset when we separated. She brought Derek up, you see, and is more like his mother than his aunt. Anyway, soon after I walked out on him she suffered a stroke and Derek agreed not to divorce me for at least five years, really just to keep her happy because I would never go back to him, not in a million years!" Lorraine lit a cigarette and drew heavily upon it, at the same time smiling rather smugly. "I suppose she thinks there's hope as long as we are still married, and it makes no difference to me. There is no one else I want to marry. . . ." She hesitated fractionally as though to qualify this statement and then continued, her voice hardening . . . "No, there's no one . . . and he makes me a very generous allowance."

"Even though you left him?" It was incredible how certain people always fell so easily on their feet. Derek Clayton, Lorraine's husband, was a very wealthy man of course and obviously still so enamoured of his wife that he was willing to keep her as his wife despite her desertion, in the hope of one day winning her back. Laurel read all this into the smile that lurked round Lorraine's mouth. She did not know Derek Clayton; she had never met him and knew next to nothing about him, but it was really just a repeat pattern. Every man

Lorraine met went mad for her. Even, Laurel thought with a renewed burst of frustrated bitterness, even quiet Ben Lester who worked in the library and had nothing to recommend him to a girl like Lorraine. Ben, who was Laurel's first serious boyfriend . . . but Lorraine could never resist making every man she met fall in love with her.

"He naturally hopes I'll go back to him," Lorraine continued, having no idea of the thoughts that were flying through her sister's brain. "I won't, of course, but I intend getting what I can out of him before the five years are up." Laurel's face must have registered her disapproval. "Oh, stop looking so prudish, Laurel! You can have no notion what it's like living with someone like Derek. It nearly drove me mad. If I so much as looked at another man he would get jealous as hell, and I just can't live without the admiration of men . . . I don't mind admitting it either. It's what my work is all about."

"What is your work?" Laurel interrupted.

"Modelling of course, as always," Lorraine said, but Laurel was surprised to notice a dull flush spread over her cheeks. She was tempted to ask—what kind of modelling? but thought better of it.

"Besides," Lorraine went on, changing the subject rapidly, "I couldn't have stayed another minute in that place." In answer to Laurel's inquiring look, for she had no idea which place she referred to, she explained, "He lives on the Isle of Wight."

"Oh, lovely!" Laurel cried spontaneously.

"Lovely! Oh, very pretty I suppose, if you like that sort of thing, which I don't. There's nothing to do and no one worth knowing. God, I thought I would go mad." She stubbed out her cigarette and almost at once lit another with jerky, nervous movements. For the first time, Laurel noticed that Lorraine was definitely agitated about something. She saw that her hands were constantly on the move, fidgeting with her cigarette, her coffee cup, the arms of the chair. Finally she muttered, "This coffee is ghastly. Haven't you something else? Something stronger?"

"If you remember, I did my utmost to keep alcohol out of the house," Laurel reminded her. "And it is only three o'clock."

"Oh, God, you haven't changed much, have you? Just as narrow minded and old fashioned as ever." She pulled hard on the cigarette. "You never answered my question. What are you going to do now?"

"I don't know. Get a job I suppose. And as quickly as possible. And I'll need to get out of here. I can't stay in this flat any longer."

"Mmm, well, you can stop worrying about either thing. I can solve both problems at once."

"You can?" Since when have you been so altruistic? Laurel could have added but knew sarcasm would be lost on her self centred sister. "Why should you want to help me?" she did ask.

"Well, of course it will be helping me out too," Lorraine said, perhaps predictably. "In fact, things couldn't have worked out better. When I thought of this idea I reckoned there would be some problems with the old man who would have got in the way, but as it is, with him dead . . ."

"Lorraine!" Laurel cried out, horrified.

"As I said before, I'm not going to get all morbid and sentimental about an old soak like that. Anyway, he is dead so you are in the position to help me and I to help you. No," Lorraine stood up and draped her fur coat across her shoulders, "come on."

"Where?"

"To my place. It'll do you good to get out of this dump for a while. Pack an overnight bag. Naturally my apartment is in London."

"But I . . ." Laurel stared at her sister, feeling not a little bewildered. But she also felt tired, too tired to argue and certainly it would do her good to get out. Since her father's death she had not managed to get one full night's sleep .

"All right," she agreed softly. "Give me a few minutes."

"I'll wait down in the car," Lorraine announced. "I've just about had enough of this place."

Lorraine's apartment was situated in a quiet square very close to Kensington Gardens. Around the square were several Georgian houses, all now converted into flats but in the most expensive and luxurious way possible. There were, parked along the road, an assortment of the world's more prestigious cars, Rolls Royces and Cadillacs, Buicks and Aston Martins. Against her will, Laurel felt herself becoming impressed even before entering the apartment in Lorraine's wake.

The interior was even more impressive. Laurel's feet sank into Wilton carpet as she took in the elegance of the wide hall with its gold and white decor. Lorraine led her into the lounge, a huge room with wide bay windows hung with gold velvet drapes, that overlooked the quiet, tree edged square. The furnishing was antique and Laurel guessed it to be Regency. She had no idea whether or not it was genuine but knowing Lorraine, thought it most likely. Lorraine had never accepted second best in anything. Now, as Laurel stood in the doorway, both hands clasping her handbag, she walked in her usual lithe, graceful way, across the room to a door opposite, tossing her silver fox across a gold brocade covered chaise longue as she did so.

"Stop standing there like an idiot," she drawled, "and make yourself at home. Anyone would think you had never seen a place like this before."

"Outside a movie, I haven't," Laurel replied dryly. "Dad and I never actually moved in such circles."

The sarcasm was lost on Lorraine whose mind was singular, hearing and understanding only what she wished to apprehend. It was because she saw only what she wanted to see and felt only what she cared to feel that Lorraine could never be hurt by anyone or anything. Now she moved to a padded leather, marble topped bar that graced one corner of the lovely room and poured out a very generous tot of vodka.

"What about you?"

"Nothing thanks." In reply to the quizzical rise of Lorraine's well marked eyebrows, Laurel quietly added, "If you remember, I've seen only the worst alcohol can do." Again Lorraine shrugged her shoulders as she sank gracefully on to the chaise longue and crossed her legs at the ankles. She placed her drink on a small leather topped table and lit yet another cigarette.

"Sit down, for God's sake," she demanded. "You make me quite uncomfortable standing there looking so disapproving—and so accusing."

Laurel sat herself gingerly on what appeared to be a Hepplewhite sofa, beautiful and fragile looking with its lovely mahogany shield back. She felt sure the piece of furniture would never take the weight of an adult person, even one as slender as herself, but obviously it was stronger than it looked, for it did not collapse in a heap as she settled herself.

"You said you had some kind of proposition," she prompted uncertainly.

"That's right . . . actually, though, looking at you now, in a good light, I'm not so sure. You've changed so much . . . do you remember how we used to be so alike that even our parents couldn't tell us apart? Quite frankly, Laurel, there wouldn't be much danger of that anymore."

"I'm perfectly aware of that."

"Still . . . I daresay if you had your hair re-styled, and the rest of your appearance fixed up, and you were dressed in something decent, there might still be some resemblance."

"Look, what is all this? Why should I need to look like you? For heaven's sake, Lorraine . . ." The despair and wretchedness of the past few days burst out at last, like a dam giving way. Laurel got to her feet, her eyes flashing. "I didn't come here to be insulted by you. If you think just because you appear to have everything, while I have nothing, that gives you the right to say whatever you please to me, you couldn't be more wrong. Things haven't changed between us, have they, Lorraine? You always did seem to think you were superior in some way. Well, maybe I put up with it once, but no longer. I've just about had enough of you in the last hour or so and whatever plans you have concerning me, you can just forget them!"

She had reached the front door before Lorraine caught up with her. Rather unexpectedly, Lorraine's eyes were pleading. Even though she felt sure this was as much an act as the rest of it, Laurel halted her flight and made the mistake of listening.

"I'm sorry, Laurel, honestly. I didn't mean to be insulting. I know you've had a lot to put up with and that explains why you look . . . as you do look. I really do need your help, just for a little while." She took Laurel's arm, smiling the charming, ingratiating little smile that had always managed to get her her own way. "Come back into the lounge and let me explain. Please."

"Oh . . . very well," Laurel agreed resignedly.

"It's like this," Lorraine said. She was seated again on the chaise longue while Laurel sat opposite on the Hepplewhite sofa. But this time Lorraine did not recline in her usual casual, elegant manner but sat upright, her hands clasped tightly round her glass. She had been given a brief glimpse of the steel behind Laurel's apparently docile exterior and began to realise that her sister was not to be so easily manipulated. Lorraine needed Laurel's co-operation; without it her own plans could well go amiss. She felt she could afford to act the supplicant.

"As I told you before, I'm still married to Derek, and he is paying for . . . well, for all this." She eyed her luxurious surroundings as though "all this" was really very little. "The money I make modelling goes straight into the bank. I've quite a bit saved. Eventually, when I have enough, I'll be able to tell Derek what he can do with his allowance . . . then he'll go ahead with the divorce despite his aunt's feelings on the subject."

"If he knew how you felt about it . . ." Laurel began, biting down the flood of distaste at Lorraine's callous and even vulgar words.

"Oh, he'd divorce me now . . . he'd get a divorce with no trouble at all, as I deserted him. The thing is, I don't want him to, not until I've enough in the bank to . . . well, to keep up my standard of living. Understand?"

"Only too clearly," Laurel replied sarcastically.

"If Derek found out anything about me that he didn't like, he'd probably start divorce proceedings," Lorraine went on. "And that, Laurel, is where you come in."

This time, when she was offered a cigarette, Laurel took one. It was years since she had smoked but just now she felt in need of a little extra support. As Lorraine continued with her story, now speaking in a rapid, staccato voice as though determined to get it over with swiftly and before she could be interrupted, Laurel felt very glad she did have the slim king size cigarette between her fingers. She narrowed her eyes and said, as Lorraine's voice came to an abrupt halt and the meaning sank in, "Let me get this absolutely right. You want me to stay here in this flat and pretend I'm you."

"That's it in a nutshell."

"So that you can go gallivanting all over the world and your husband, if he should take the trouble to inquire, will believe you are still living a blameless life here."

Lorraine shrugged. "There's no call to be like that about it. You might not believe it, but Derek does keep an eye on me . . . oh, not personally, but he would soon know if I moved out for six months. And as for me gallivanting all over the world, this is a job, a marvellous job. Modelling the clothes of Jacques Remande himself in a dozen different exotic locations. I refuse to turn down such an opportunity."

"No one's saying you need refuse. Just tell Derek and then go. Surely he wouldn't object to a perfectly legitimate job."

Lorraine actually reddened slightly, a phenomenon so unusual that Laurel stared at her in wide eyed surprise. It took a very great deal to embarrass Lorraine. Eventually, after a long uncomfortable silence, which she filled by pouring herself another drink and lighting a further cigarette, Lorraine said, "He would object if he discovered that the photographer is Richard Benson."

Laurel refrained from comment. Richard Benson was a celebrated fashion photographer of whom even she had heard. He was very talented and she knew nothing to his detriment. But Lorraine made no attempt to explain her words.

"All you have to do is move out of that frightful place you're in now and into here," she said persuasively. "I've thought it out very carefully. I'll have so much money transferred to your bank account each month so that you'll be able to live well. Just think about it, Laurel. You told me yourself that you were at your wit's end, not knowing what to do or where to go. Well, here's an answer to both problems. Come and live here for six months. All you need do is answer the door to tradesmen, let everyone see that you are here. People only see what they expect to see. They'll expect to see me and so that's who they will see."

"I don't know, Lorraine," Laurel said at last, doubtful still. Yet she was only human and had had a hard time over the last few years. Lorraine's offer was more than just appealing, it was temptation itself. The objections she made, she made because they had to be put forward, yet Lorraine knocked them all down one by one with consummate ease.

"It's dishonest."

"How? What I do with my money is my own affair. I could go and give it all away to the first person I met in the street if I wanted to. So I give it to you instead."

"Why not just tell your husband? You want a divorce eventually. What difference can six months make?"

"Probably none. If the job goes well there'll be more offers of work. Richard is doing this assignment for Peter Blakeney. You know him? Well, he owns a string of fashion magazines all over the States. He's extremely wealthy and I rather believe he . . . admires me." The slightly acquisitive gleam that always appeared when Lorraine was out to trap a certain man, came into her eyes. Then she seemed to come sharply down to earth, saying, "But I don't want to burn my bridges. I want to leave an option open."

"That surely is unfair to him."

"To Derek? If anyone's unfair, it's him, expecting me to live like a nun or something. Don't worry about the money. He has pots of that. Far too much for one man *you* might say."

"I don't look a bit like you anymore, Lorraine. You know I don't.

Look at the difference between us. Even the milkman or postman would know I wasn't you."

"We'll soon solve *that* little problem," Lorraine said firmly.

And they did.

TWO

LAUREL STOOD in the bedroom staring in wondering fascination at her own reflection in the mirror. She blinked her eyes once, twice, three times, each time half expecting to see something entirely different staring back at her. But each time the girl in the mirror remained unchanged. Each time her hair was as glossy and waving as before, falling on her shoulders in heavy cascades of silk; each time her skin was as clear and glowing, her eyes as bright, her dress as elegant and expensive. She smiled then, putting up one hand so that the dress ring on her beautifully manicured fingers caught the light and glittered with a million spears of colour. It was all true. Only a few minutes ago Lorraine, laden with pig skin suitcases, had gone off in the taxi that was taking her to Heathrow. And now Laurel was alone.

The last week had left her head still spinning. Lorraine, when she did a thing, certainly did it thoroughly. She had dragged her still reluctant sister to an extremely exclusive and, in Laurel's eyes, ridiculously expensive, hair stylist where her hair was meticulously washed, conditioned, cut and set while her hands and nails were being transformed; to a beautician who administered face packs, massage and various other tortures that caused Laurel to shudder in remembrance; to boutiques and couturiers where the style of garment that Lorraine herself would wear was chosen.

"You can't wear my stuff," Lorraine had said, admiring her own reflection. "You're much thinner than I am. But I'll leave a lot of my clothes so that if you should fill out a bit, you'll have plenty to wear. I shall be getting a new wardrobe when I'm in New York."

And now it was all over. Lorraine had gone, leaving in her place a sister who could no longer feel any guilt at what she had allowed herself to be persuaded into. How could she feel guilty when she felt so . . . so good, so pampered, so sleek, so beautiful? And what harm was she doing anyway? No harm at all. It would be such bliss to stay here, to forget the past months of dreariness, poverty and misery. To convalesce, as it were, until her body and mind were strong enough to face the real world again.

For there was no doubt that this was not the real world. It was not real to have so much money in her bank account that she had no need to think twice about buying anything; it was not real to be living in this wonderful apartment rent free for six months, to sleep between silk sheets and be able to relax all day if she wished before the colour television set eating chocolates and drinking wine—not that she did, but it was wonderful to think that if she wanted to she could! Well, so she was Cinderella at the ball, but for her the ball would last not one short evening but for six months. She would enjoy every minute of it.

Inevitably, Laurel's ideas of enjoyment were not Lorraine's. Had any of Lorraine's friends seen her and greeted her, she might have been in a fix, but it was a certainty that she would never come across any of them for they were unlikely to visit the Natural History Museum, the National Gallery, the Tower of London or Westminster Abbey. But Laurel had never lived in London and apart from a school trip which took in Madame Tussauds and St. Paul's when she was eleven, had had no chance to see any of London's "sights". Now she did the whole tourist routine and revelled in every minute. It all culminated, one glorious night, in a visit to Covent Garden to see Fonteyn herself dancing in "Swan Lake".

She sat through the performance alone, which was surely the best way to find complete enjoyment. In order to live up to the splendour of the occasion she had put on a long, pale blue dress of crêpe de chine, an old fashioned material that was becoming popular again. The dress had tight fitting sleeves that came to points at the wrists, and a low, round neck line. With a velvet, satin lined cloak trimmed with mink that she had found in Lorraine's wardrobe, she looked both elegant and lovely. The last few weeks of luxurious living had filled out her figure a little, had taken the dark smudges from beneath her eyes and put the colour back into her cheeks so that more than one pair of eyes followed her as she finally left the theatre and went to her taxi.

It seemed as though she floated on the air. Tchaikovsky's lovely music echoed softly in her brain as she leaned back in the limousine's comfortable seat and closed her eyes. A smile curved her mouth. This, as the saying went, was the life! And to think that while she was slaving away trying to look after their poor father, Lorraine was living it. Momentarily, Laurel's happiness faded. It hadn't been fair. Lorraine could have shared a little of her good fortune. A decent diet, somewhere pleasanter to live, perhaps a short holiday by the sea, might have made all the difference to their father's attitude of mind. With more to look forward to, he may never have taken that final, drink fuddled walk by the river.

After a while she pushed these useless thoughts to the back of her mind; she had been over them so often and it did no good. She tried to remember the glorious fairytale of Fonteyn's dancing and a smile more quiet than the previous one touched her lips. The taxi drew up smoothly outside Elm Court and she slid out, her skirts swishing round her legs; she smiled at the driver and tipped over generously because she had begun to realise her own good fortune. In the light above the main entrance to the building her hair shone like highly polished copper and even the taxi driver, hardened cockney that he was, drew in his breath as he took in her loveliness.

Her high heeled silver sandals made little noise on the steps as she ran lightly up them. The ballet music still whirled in her head and she hummed it softly, hardly hearing the taxi draw away and certainly not hearing another car door slam or the harder tap of a man's footsteps striding purposely across the broad pavement and up the stairs after her. But suddenly, even as she reached out to swing open the glass panelled door that led into the entrance hall, the door was thrust open for her and her startled gaze met a pair of narrowed eyes as a cool masculine voice said, "Well, well, my lovely wife, your escort is remarkably careless to let you come home alone."

Derek Clayton! She had never seen him before in the flesh but knew him from a small snap shot she had found in Lorraine's bedside cabinet. Shock robbed Laurel of words as she gazed, open mouthed, at the terrifyingly good looking but fiercely intimidating man who stood before her. She had never seen anyone look so disdainful or so ruthless.

"I can't imagine why you're so surprised to see me," he said with icy calm that was in marked contrast to the way her own body was behaving, her hammering heart, her trapped, painful breathing, her pulses fluttering and jumping. "I said I would keep an eye on you, didn't I?"

This time she managed a feeble nod, because of course the whole purpose of her being here was that Derek Clayton intended "keeping an eye on" his errant wife. By now, though she still felt rather numb and sick with shock, Laurel's brain was beginning to turn over in a sluggish fashion. She wondered what he wanted—why should he hang about waiting for her at this time of night? Unless he really was doing some private spying on her—or rather, on Lorraine. Perhaps the hiring of a private detective was too undignified for a man like Derek Clayton. Perhaps he really believed she would come home with an escort who would then stay the night. Laurel, whose life had been so much narrower and more conventional than her sister's, blushed with mortification at the thought, but it was too dark for him to see this.

"You seem to have lost your voice, my sweet," he said with studied sarcasm. "You used never to be lost for words."

"I was . . . was surprised to see you," she managed to utter, thanking God that her voice was so similar to Lorraine's that after three years it was unlikely he would recognise the slight difference in tone and accent.

"I don't doubt your surprise," he said, and took her arm just below the elbow. His fingers were hard and warm. "Let's go in. I don't intend discussing our private affairs out here on the door step." Her feeble protests were wasted on him; she found herself being hustled across the entrance hall to the elevator which was open on the ground floor. During the ride up to the third floor, Laurel clutched her evening bag with both hands and stared pointedly at the floor while she wondered in a desperate way what on earth she was to do. Somehow she had to get rid of him before he realised . . . for surely he would realise . . . dear God, he was *married* to Lorraine . . . he must realise . . .

"Where have you been?" he demanded, abruptly breaking in on her bemused thoughts. "I didn't expect you so early. I thought a night club until two or three in the morning was the usual order of things."

"I . . . I've been to Covent Garden," she muttered to the floor. "Margot Fonteyn was dancing in 'Swan Lake'."

There was a moment's pause in which she dared not look up. She should have made a more evasive answer for surely he would know that Lorraine loathed anything even vaguely cultural and would never sit through a ballet. Instead of uttering disbelief however, Lorraine's husband merely laughed rather unpleasantly.

"My poor love. How bored you must have been! No wonder you're home early. Who is he? Someone very special I imagine, to have got you to Covent Garden. Special . . . or very rich."

Laurel merely shook her head and refused to look up. She realised she would have to be very careful if she was to get away with this deception. No more confessions of any sort. Let him think what he liked.

They stepped out of the elevator and crossed the corridor to the door of Lorraine's apartment. Laurel's evening bag was removed firmly from her lifeless fingers. She made a useless attempt to retain it but it was snatched from her reach.

"I'm just getting the key," Derek Clayton said smoothly. "What's the matter, darling? Something to hide?"

She looked up then, her eyes gravely meeting his. She experienced a little shock as she took in his appearance fully for the first time, for though he was dark haired and dark complexioned, with the tanned skin of someone accustomed to spending many hours out of doors, and with strongly marked black brows and lashes, his eyes were a clear, translucent green. The look he cast her before searching through the small, beaded bag for the key, was amused but cynical, as though he took some kind of sadistic pleasure from watching her discomfiture. She dropped her eyes from his and allowed him to push her ahead of him into the apartment. Her movements felt stiff and unnatural.

Once inside, she put as much space as possible between herself and him and only then turned round and asked in a small voice, "What do you want?"

He was casually dressed in a thick knit grey polo neck sweater and dark slacks, clothing that emphasized his height and the broad shoulders and narrow waist. Laurel supposed it had been his looks as much as his money that had first attracted Lorraine to him, for he was certainly excessively masculine and not a man to be passed over unnoticed. Despite his good looks, Laurel shivered; he looked, also, like a man capable of anything. Just now he was looking her over in a slow, thorough way that was completely unnerving, his glance assessing her every point, critically rather than admiringly.

"To see you, of course," he said, replying to her question at last.

"And I must admit, Lorraine, you're still well worth looking at. You've lost a bit of weight but it suits you. It makes your more . . . er . . . prominent features more noticeable." His eyes lingered on the low neck line of her dress but again there was no real desire or admiration there. Lorraine had said he still loved her but Laurel doubted that. He was behaving as a man would who wanted to humiliate a woman. At the same time, she was unable to cope with this the way Lorraine would have and the colour washed hotly over her face at the blatant insult that lurked behind his gaze. At this, he laughed incredulously.

"My God, you're actually blushing! Where did you learn that little trick, for heaven's sake?"

Laurel turned swiftly away from him so that her voice was muffled. "If you came here just to insult me, I wish you would go."

"Insult you, darling? As though I would. Besides, I seem to remember you as being insult-proof. You haven't changed that much in three years, I'm sure."

There was a little silence during which Laurel wondered desperately what she should do. Any minute now and surely he would guess her secret. But then, why should he? People do not normally assume that someone is being impersonated by an identical twin just because they behave out of character.

"I like that dress," he said, and she quite literally jumped with fright, for his voice, which a moment ago had come from across the room, now sounded close to her left ear. Even as she began to move away his arm went round her waist, pulling her against him so that she felt the hardness of his chest muscles against her breast. He was smiling but it wasn't a pleasant smile; it reminded Laurel of the way a tiger might smile just before it takes the first bone shattering crunch. She moved swiftly, pulling herself from his grasp so abruptly that he, obviously not expecting her evasive action, let her go. He made no move to follow her but his eyebrows rose quizzically.

"It's like that, is it? You used not to be so shy, Lorraine. In fact, I remember a time when you were only too eager for my embraces."

She flushed again. "That was . . ."

"What?"

"A long time ago," she managed to mutter. "People . . . people change."

"Obviously," he agreed dryly. "Anyway, it doesn't matter. I can't say I'm exactly turned on by you anymore. In fact, sweetheart, if it weren't for certain extenuating circumstances, you could go to hell as far as I'm concerned. Oh, you're still beautiful—I suppose you always will be, but I'd rather have a wife ugly as sin than put up with a cold blooded, mercenary little bitch like you."

This was all spoken in the same even, unconcerned tones as before and Laurel stared at him, puzzlement in her eyes, remembering again that Lorraine had said he still loved her, that he hoped she would eventually go back to him. He certainly didn't sound or behave like a man in love, and somehow she was sure his obvious distaste was not an act. Then she remembered that she was supposed to be Lorraine and therefore should be angry at being termed a "cold blooded, mercenary little bitch". She looked levelly at Derek Clayton who had his hands rammed into the pockets of his corduroy slacks, and a strange warmth shot through her which caused her to shudder. She decided that perhaps she really was angry.

"I think it's time you went," she said clearly. "I didn't ask you to come here and I really don't see what can be gained by you standing there calling me names. I want to go to bed so would you please let yourself out."

She turned away, but his laughing—or sneering—voice called her back. "Alone, Lorraine? You mean you are actually going to bed alone?"

This time her temper really did rise; it was no longer Lorraine to whom he was speaking but her, Laurel, and she reacted as she would have to any man who had said that to her. She turned on him in a fury, her eyes flashing, her hand slashing indiscriminately at him, the open palm contacting with his sardonic mouth so that, taken unawares, his head jerked back. Her victory, however, was brief. Before she had time to savour it, her wrist had been enclosed by steel hard fingers and a cry of real pain wrenched from her as he whipped her hand behind her back, twisting her round so that his mouth was against her ear.

"You ever do that again, my lovely, and you'll be very, very sorry," he hissed.

"You asked for it," she cried out, not daring to move for it seemed that he really was capable of bending her arm even further up her back until it snapped. She had thought on first seeing him that he was a man capable of anything. She bit her lip hard to stop herself crying out with the pain in her bent elbow.

"My God, Lorraine, you've picked a fine time to be bothered by insults. After all you and I have been through, to start getting uptight about that . . ."

She said nothing then, for of course for all she knew he and Lorraine had spent their married life hurling insults at each other. She stood still and after a moment he released her wrist so that she was able to straighten her arm and gingerly rub her sore elbow and shoulder. She walked away from him, trying to still her trembling body and repress the no doubt ridiculous and spineless urge to burst into tears. This was like a nightmare. It could not really be happening. It was unbelievable that half an hour ago she had been that happy, carefree girl in the taxi with nothing on her mind other than the music of "Swan Lake".

"Would you please go away," she said with desperation in her voice.

"Of course. I'll be leaving almost at once," he replied promptly. "Or rather, we shall be leaving. You're coming with me."

"I'm . . . what? You're crazy."

"Not at all. I was going to tell you. Caroline is home and very ill. As you know, she always had very romantic ideas about you and me. Remember how she used to say what an ideal couple we were?" Again his lips twisted into that little humourless smile that Laurel now recognised as holding bitterness as well as sarcasm. She found herself wondering just what his and Lorraine's married years had been like. "The thing is," he went on, "she is home and her one wish is to see us together. Her last wish, I might add, that I intend seeing fulfilled. It won't be for long. She suffered a second stroke two weeks ago, much worse than the first one, that paralysed her left side, and the doctors don't hold out much hope."

He spoke in a flat, emotionless manner, but Laurel was not fooled by this. Much more sensitive than her sister, she recognised that there was a deep sadness in him as he spoke these distressing facts; he was obviously a strong man both physically and emotionally but she did not doubt that he felt very deeply about this. She tried to recall what Lorraine had said about Caroline; she was his aunt who had brought him up; she was like a mother to him. Gently she said, "I'm sorry about that but . . . how can I go with you? What would be the point? She's bound to realise that things aren't right between us."

"No. Once she would have but no more. She can scarcely speak and her eyesight is failing. I doubt that she knows much about what is going on round her. Sometimes she rouses herself but . . ." he shrugged, "not often. If she sees you she'll believe you've come home to High Ridge. That's all I require of you. A bit of play acting. I shan't expect anything more than that." His voice hardened. "There's no point in argument, Lorraine. I was prepared to come here and ask in a civilised manner but I might have known nothing can ever be civilised between us. So I'll resort to threats. You'll come with me or I'll make sure you don't get another penny of my money. After the way you left, there's not a court in the country would uphold any claim you might care to make."

Not one word of this did she doubt. His looks, his voice, were impeccable. He was a very, very ruthless man and Laurel shivered. She could not, of course, go with him, but at the same time she had somehow to get in touch with Lorraine and tell her what had happened so that she could cope with the situation as she wished.

"All right," she said softly, hoping that by sounding reasonable he might relax and relent a little. "I understand your point, but you must give me a little time to think about it. I . . ."

"Goddamn you, Lorraine!" he snarled. "You'll bloody well come with me tonight whether you like it or not. I'm up to here with your prevarications!" As he spoke he strode across the room to wrench open the kitchen door, which he immediately slammed, going on opening doors till he came to her bedroom which he entered. After a moment of stunned inaction, Laurel rushed in to see that he had opened a suitcase on the bed and was even then throwing in to it a mass of frothy lace and nylon lingerie. She stared in amazement as he opened the wardrobe door and began tossing dresses and skirts on to the bed.

"What on earth are you doing?" she gasped. "Stop this at once!"

"I said you're coming with me and I meant it. You can go a little way towards making up for the misery you've caused in your life. Now," he straightened up and regarded her silk clad figure. "You can't travel like that so you'd better get changed into something more practical. Slacks would be best."

"No!" she cried out, unreasoning panic sweeping through her as the ground seemed almost to shift beneath her feet. "I won't! You can't make me go with you."

"Get changed," he said flatly. "You've got ten minutes. If you don't, I'll come in and get that dress off you. There's precious little of it so that shouldn't be too difficult."

There was no doubt that this was no idle threat. When the door slammed behind him Laurel stood uncertainly staring at the masses of clothes that surrounded her. She knew she was beaten for the moment and the only thing to do was to carry off this casual abduction with dignity. Feverishly she pulled off the clothes she wore and got into slacks of grey jersey that had a matching waist coat which she wore over a long sleeved cotton blouse. She was putting the other clothes more tidily into the suitcase when Derek Clayton came back into the room. It was typical of the man that he did not bother to knock, she thought, firmly closing the suitcase and facing him with an attempt at being dignified about the whole thing. He picked up the case from the bed.

"Is this all you need?"

"Yes."

"Good. Let's go."

"How . . . how are we going?" she asked with some trepidation as she watched him lock up the flat.

"We'll fly of course."

"At this time of night?" she asked incredulously. "Surely there isn't a plane at this time of night."

He looked up from the door lock and stared at her with obvious puzzlement. "What the hell's the matter with you, Lorraine? Have you taken leave of your senses or something? You know very well I can fly us over at first light. It'll take an hour or so to drive down to Hampshire so there won't be too long to hang about." When she continued to stare at him he frowned again, even more forbiddingly. "What's the matter now?"

"Nothing," she mumbled. "I . . . I never thought."

A few hours later Laurel was even more confused as she sat beside Derek Clayton when he sent the helicopter whisking swiftly through the early morning sky. They had driven several miles, his dark blue Jaguar eating up the road so that it was about one in the morning when they arrived at a small airport that seemed to be in the middle of nowhere. Laurel had guessed from the road signs that they must be somewhere near Southampton but really was unable to be certain about anything. It seemed they must be at a private flying club of some sort for she glimpsed several low, wide buildings that resembled hangars, and the building which Derek led her into was obviously a club house. At that time of night the place was deserted and in darkness but he had his own key and took her into the bar-lounge which had several large comfortable armchairs. Meekly Laurel followed Derek's orders, going to sit in one of these and eventually, when he said they would be there for some time, even managing to settle down into a shallow sleep. Waking, her brain fuddled and numbed as much by the turn of events as by the awkward sleep, she had followed him out into the cold morning air and now found herself seated in the helicopter with Derek himself at the controls.

The worst thing about the whole affair was knowing nothing and not daring to ask. Laurel had read several novels involving impersonations, the most recent being Josephine Tey's *Brat Farrar* and *The Ivy Tree* by Mary Stewart, and in these the person doing the impersonating was meticulously tutored in their new rôle. Whereas she knew nothing and could not ask. She dare not even exclaim at suddenly finding herself in a helicopter. After all, for all she knew, Lorraine may have been quite accustomed to this unusual form of transport. She could not ask Derek if he owned the helicopter—she did not even know what he did for a living. It was confusing, even bewildering, and not helped in the least by having to keep all words and thoughts to herself. She had soon discovered that the man beside her, after his earlier taunts, was totally uncommunicative.

It was a strange but exhilarating experience to fly in the helicopter, to be shot suddenly skywards in an almost vertical sweep, to feel the engine throb in every nerve and bone of her body. And to be so low that as they left Southampton docks behind and headed out across the Solent towards the Isle of Wight, she could look down and see the changing shades of water. Her one comment had taken the form of a gasp of delight as they passed close over the QE2 that was steering up the Solent to dock at Southampton, helped by many tiny, powerful tug boats. At Laurel's side, Derek Clayton had merely glanced in the direction of the beautiful liner and then his hard green eyes had gone to his supposed wife in a swift, enigmatical stare. Laurel was sure that for some reason she puzzled him, and equally she was uncertain of him. Earlier he had quite literally terrified her but she felt no sense of fear during this short journey. Though she could in no way like this man, she felt that he was completely dependable when it came to flying. There was something eminently safe about his strong, long fingered hands on the controls, and the cool, assessing way his eyes took in his surroundings.

She had never been to the Isle of Wight and was quite enchanted by her first view as they flew over it at a height of no more than five hundred feet. Again eager questions sprang to her lips, only to be hastily repressed. Was that Osborne House below them, where Queen Victoria had once lived, a jewel of Palladian architecture set in surroundings of greenery and woodland? And surely that had to be Carisbroke castle where Charles I had been imprisoned and where donkeys now worked the water wheel in the place of prisoners. Unselfconsciously she leaned forward against her seat belt, her eyes wide as she looked down at the massive castle atop its hill and bathed in early morning sunshine. She smiled because it was all so lovely, and looked up eagerly towards Derek only to have the smile dashed from her face as she met his eyes.

"You never fail to amaze me, Lorraine," he taunted softly. "How, leading the life you do, you still manage to keep that fresh faced, eager little girl look."

"How do you know what kind of life I lead?" Laurel flashed back.

He laughed. "Believe me, there's little about you I don't know. Tell me, how's Richard Benson these days? Has he taken any good photographs lately?"

The abrupt change of subject confused Laurel and there was something about the tone of his voice that again had her floundering in the dark. It was Richard Benson of course who Lorraine was with at that moment; it was he of whom Derek apparently disapproved so that he would not agree to Lorraine taking the modelling assignment if he knew Benson was the photographer. Laurel realised again that she was going to have to keep her wits about her every second of the time in the days to come. She would have to become a very master of evasion.

"I don't know what you mean," she replied loftily and Derek laughed again. Laurel steeled herself for further sneering remarks but no more came then for he had more important things on his mind as he brought the helicopter down to land. Below them Laurel glimpsed a concrete strip on which were parked two other helicopters similar in design to the one they were in and painted similarly in red and white. Derek set his helicopter down nearby, assisted by a young man who had run out from a nearby building and guided him down. To do this he made hand signals, using two things that looked like table tennis bats. When the vehicle had settled and the great rotors slowed a little, Derek undid his seat belt and removed the ear phones which were required to cut out some of the noise. Laurel copied these actions, shaking out her hair and taking the proffered hand of the young man who had run round to open the door on her side. She smiled her thanks and the youth looked admiringly at her, holding her hand for a long moment until Laurel had forcibly to pull away.

"This is my wife, Jack," Derek Clayton said with a certain acerbity in the voice that Laurel had already learned could most aptly portray any number of emotions. It was a pleasant voice, well pitched and deep with a faint trace of an accent that she thought may well have been Scottish. She had heard it biting and sarcastic, clipped and practical, and plain angry, and wondered how it would sound were he amused or gentle. Or did he ever experience such tender emotions? She smiled faintly at Jack who was regarding her with the same open admiration as before, and said, "Hello, Jack."

"Morning, Mrs. Clayton," the boy mumbled, glancing at Derek and then hurrying away, while a red hot blush swept over his face. He was very young, not more than eighteen.

Derek picked up Laurel's suitcase and with the other hand took her wool clad arm above the elbow, hurrying her across the flagging to a nearby building. He said, "For God's sake, Lorraine, must you try to flirt with every man in sight? Jack is just a kid and not up to coping with someone like you."

Astonishment robbed Laurel of coherent speech. She had intended only a friendly smile and certainly was too unaware of her own beauty to attempt to flirt with anyone. "But I didn't . . ." she gasped. "I wasn't . . ."

"Oh, save it," he said wearily. "Just remember that you are still my wife and while you're here you'll behave yourself. What you do in London is your own affair."

Laurel said nothing more, only shook her head in a little gesture of bemused wonder that her "husband" did not miss. She was hustled through a sort of reception building complete with a desk, several armchairs and coffee tables each with a neat pile of magazines. This time there came a thin ray of enlightenment. They walked outside again to the front of the building and, turning to glance back, Laurel saw the words "Clayton Air Ferry" in large letters above the front door. She looked up at the stern profile of the man beside her as questions came again to her lips, questions she could not ask. But then she did ask, "How's business?" reasoning that this was a fairly innocuous question. He did not look at her as he replied. He was busy putting her case into the boot of a car, a long, gleaming, flame red Jaguar XJS that was parked in the small car park.

"Obviously booming," he replied, opening the passenger door for her. She slid in and watched him walk round to get into the driver's seat. The car pulled away smoothly and with scarcely a sound from its powerful engine.

"Why obviously?" she inquired lightly.

"Because I can still afford to pay you a very large allowance each month. As long as that goes on being paid into your account you needn't trouble to make pointed enquiries into my affairs."

"They weren't pointed enquiries!" she replied indignantly. "I was interested. Why do you have to be so . . . so sarcastic about everything I say?"

He took a packet of cigarettes from the glove compartment and tossed it and a lighter to her. "Light one for me," he said, and then, "As I said before, I long since gave up acting in a civilised manner with you, Lorraine."

Laurel lit a cigarette and leaned across to place it between his lips. It was an intimate gesture made utterly prosaic by his attitude and his words. She wondered just what Lorraine had done to him to make him despise her so. Of course she herself knew how expert Lorraine was at ignoring other people's feelings and trampling over everyone who got between her and her desires. Nevertheless, she *wasn't* Lorraine and felt sure she would be unable to take this kind of treatment for long.

"You could make an effort," she reasoned quietly. "I mean, it is three years and people do change. I don't see how it's going to help your aunt if we spend the whole time rowing and being bitchy to each other."

He took one hand from the steering wheel in order to remove the cigarette from his mouth and unexpectedly said, "Though I don't think you can possibly have changed that much, I concede that you have a point. Besides, Lisa is especially sensitive to atmospheres and I don't want her upset in any way. I'd like to have got her out of the house while you're there but she's never been away and it would be too traumatic an experience." In the silence that followed, while Laurel wondered who Lisa was and why she should be affected by Lorraine's appearance, he added, his voice angry again, "While I wouldn't even contemplate you showing any affection towards her, I thought you might at least have asked how she is."

"I . . . I was going to," Laurel lied unconvincingly. "How is she?"

"Well, and happy. It took a long time but now she is perfectly contented. I'd appreciate it if you don't upset that state of affairs. In fact, to this end I don't intend her to know who you are. She will merely call you Lorraine. Mrs. Mackenzie and the rest of the staff have all agreed to keep up this minor deception."

By now Laurel's head was whirling with the effort of trying to make sense of this, and she felt a renewal of panic surging through her. God, she must be crazy! Why didn't she tell him at once who she really was? What, after all, had Lorraine ever done to help or protect her? But now, having got so far, she was more scared of backing out than of going on. Derek Clayton looked quite capable of becoming physically violent if he discovered how she had been deceiving him.

Her mind was taken off the problem then for at that moment he swung the wheel hard to the left and turned the car into the drive of a large white bungalow that was set back off the road. Until then Laurel had scarcely noticed her surroundings but now she saw that during the drive they had approached the coast and were high up on the cliffs overlooking the sea. The bungalow—she noticed a sign that read "High Ridge" on the gate post—was almost teetering on the edge of the cliffs and had a wonderful view. Below the cliffs the sea foamed on to dangerous looking rocks, but further away the coast curved into a gentle, sand lined bay. There was a town in the bay, sprawling along its curve, presumably one of the island's many resorts.

"Come on," Derek said irritably, opening the front door. "I'm sure you've seen enough of that view in the past."

"I was just admiring it," she replied. "It's easy to forget exactly how lovely a view is." She walked up to him, relieved that he had unknowingly informed her that she was supposed to know this house. He glanced strangely at her.

"That'll be the day when you start admiring natural beauty," he said cuttingly.

Laurel refused to jump at the bait, but walked past him into a long cool hall with ivory coloured walls and a magnificent terrazzo floor. The house was spacious and expensively furnished. It took her only a cursory glance to ascertain that much. She looked swiftly round, surreptitiously taking in as much as possible without this inspection being noticed by Derek's keen eyes. With luck she would have some time when he was absent to make a proper exploration, but it would be disastrous if he were to say, for example: "You're in your old room," and then leave her to find her own way there.

However, her luck, which had been conspicuously absent, seemed to have pity on her for this did not happen. The open plan staircase led straight into the hall and from up above Laurel heard two voices, the high shrill tones of a child and the deeper voice of a woman with a marked Scottish accent. Laurel did no more than glance enquiringly at Derek but he said, curtly, "Wait!" and set off up the stairs still carrying her suitcase. While Laurel waited uncertainly, he returned, this time holding a girl of about four or five in his arms. The child had one arm firmly about his neck and was saying: "But you always bring me something back."

"Not this time," he replied, with a smile such as Laurel had not previously seen from him. It changed him completely, taking away the sternness from his mouth, causing his eyes to seem a more brilliant, and warmer green. Laurel looked from him to the little girl, as they halted before her. Both pairs of eyes were of the same shade of green but the child's hair was auburn. As Laurel smiled uncertainly at her, she put out one hand and caught at a handful of Laurel's own hair that was almost exactly the same colour.

"Is this who you brought me, Daddy? This pretty lady?" the child asked.

And while Laurel stood paralysed, while horror and deep rooted fury aimed only at her sister, ran hotly through her veins, robbing her of speech, Derek Clayton said smoothly, "That's right, Lisa. Her name is Lorraine and you can call her that. Now, go into the kitchen and see if they can rustle us up some breakfast, there's a love." He straightened up and looked at Laurel's face, noticing how white she had become but totally failing to apprehend the reason. "What's the matter, Lorraine? Don't you recognise your own daughter?"

THREE

LAUREL SAT on the bed and buried her face in her hands. The tears were of anger and frustration and overwhelming sadness that she was unable to explain even to herself. She thought she would never forget or recover from the moment that she met Lorraine's daughter. It seemed that those few words Derek had spoken would be seared on her heart for ever. Yet all she could do was rage inwardly and wonder at the sheer, unbelievable callousness of Lorraine who could go off and leave, not only a husband, but a baby too. Of all the infamous things Lorraine had done, this calumny had to be the worst. No wonder Derek hated her.

And of course that meant that she, Laurel, had to bear the brunt of his hatred. Now that she understood so much, Laurel could forgive his taunts, his bitterness. She began to wonder what he had been like before Lorraine's desertion. Had he loved her as most men soon learned to love her? Surely he had, and it must have been torture for a man like that to discover how shallow and lacking in ordinary human feelings the loved one was.

After her first moment of stunned horror, Laurel could remember very little of what happened next, but she did recall the puzzlement that flickered over Derek's face at her reaction to his words. He was an alert, intelligent man and surely he must have realised that her strange attitude was caused by more than surprise at how big Lisa had grown.

The Scottish housekeeper, Mrs. Mackenzie, who obviously thoroughly disapproved of Lorraine, chose that moment to say: "If you'll come this way, madam, I'll take you to your room." Laurel thankfully left Derek standing there watching her and followed the woman upstairs and along a wide, carpeted corridor which was bathed in light from the east facing window at one end. Someone in the house evidently had a fondness for indoor plants for at intervals up the stairs and along the corridor was a variety of plant pot holders with a splendid array of ferns, a rubber plant and various more exotic blooms. Yet Laurel was not then able to appreciate these, or the pleasant south facing room into which Mrs. Mackenzie led her. The woman indicated Laurel's suitcase which now stood inside the door and said with a tight, prim expression on her face:

"The bathroom is next door, madam. I'm sure you won't be able to remember your way round seeing as you weren't living in the house that long before you left."

Although she was innocent of the unspoken charges being aimed at her, Laurel felt shrivelled by the venomous glare from the cold, grey eyes and would love to have made some equally daunting reply.

But though Lorraine would no doubt have held her own, Laurel could only stand silent, closing her eyes in thankful relief when she was alone. She sank on to the bed, burying her head in shaking hands as the full purport of her situation came to her.

It was much much later that she roused herself, unpacked the suit-case and went to have a bath. The house seemed to be deserted for it was absolutely silent, but later, after she had bathed and dressed her-self in a beige dress of crimplene with a full skirt and short sleeves, the door was pushed open and Lisa came in.

Laurel was momentarily unable to speak, but she managed a smile and turned round on the stool where she had been sitting before the dressing table brushing her hair. "Hello, Lisa," she said at last.

"Hello." Lisa was far from shy. She looked wide eyed and intelli-gent and lively, and at this moment distinctly conspiratorial. She closed the door softly behind her and tip toed across the room to Laurel.

"Mrs. Mac said I had to stay in the kitchen, and Daddy said you wouldn't want to see me, and you only came because Auntie Car-oline is ill, but I thought you would *really* like to see me." She grinned cheerfully, revealing a large gap where two of her milk teeth were missing. Laurel's heart warmed to her. She was, after all, her niece.

"Yes, Lisa. I would really like to see you."

"That's what I thought. Are you really my mummy? Mrs. Mac said you weren't fit to be anyone's mummy."

Laurel's eyes widened as she remembered Derek's edict. "Did she say that to you?"

"No. I heard her tell Jackie who works in the kitchen. But you are truly my mummy, aren't you?"

Remembering what Derek had stipulated, Laurel hesitated, for she was sure he would be furious that his subterfuge had failed. Besides, what Lisa had overheard was untrue anyway and though she had lied to Derek who was big enough and tough enough to take care of him-self, she could not bring herself to lie to Lisa. So she smiled and touched the child's auburn hair. "I don't think you should listen too much to what grown-ups say, Lisa. Let's just say that I would like to be a friend to you and I hope you'll be my friend."

"Okay," Lisa said equably. "But I know you are really my mummy because you look like the picture Daddy used to have in his bedroom." She sat on the bed and bounced on it as she made this statement. She was obviously a talkative child and, Laurel guessed, something of a little minx. She had, inevitably perhaps, been spoilt, probably in order to make up for her lack of a mother, but at least she wasn't a problem child. There was no difficulty in breaking the ice with her. She chatted happily about her school and her friends, and eventually suggested that she should take Laurel round the garden. Laurel readily agreed.

It was still not yet nine in the morning and though the sky was a clear, virtually cloudless blue, there was a nip in the air that was very un-July like. Slipping her hand into Laurel's, Lisa led the way downstairs, through the lounge, a long rectangular room furnished throughout in a very modern way with an Aubusson carpet on a polished wood parquet floor and Scandinavian furniture, and out of some french windows on to a wide flagged patio which over looked the lawn. The garden was large and very well cared for with a magnificent rockery in which was incorporated a small waterfall and ornamental fish pond. Lisa showed Laurel where the water was pumped up from a natural spring underground and how it ran away to fall eventually from the cliffs into the sea.

It was while they were standing near the pond watching the aimless meanderings of the dozen or so large goldfish among the water lilies, that Derek appeared, striding purposefully across the lawn. Laurel had relaxed so much during the short interval with Lisa that she greeted him with a welcoming smile that received no answering smile.

"Lisa, go into the house," he ordered peremptorily. "Mrs. Mac has been looking for you and I told you you weren't to bother Lorraine."

"I'm not bothering her, Daddy," Lisa insisted and a little impish and rather crafty smile crossed her face. "I was just showing Mummy the fish and the water and . . ."

To say Derek looked angry at this disclosure was a master piece of understatement, Laurel thought, cringing inside. He glared at her with the full force of his green eyes and snapped, "Go in at once, Lisa!" so harshly that tears brightened the little girl's eyes. Probably she had never been shouted at like that in the whole of her short life and was obviously very hurt. Perhaps Derek had provocation but it was no excuse. Laurel turned to face him when Lisa had run into the house, her chin held high and determined.

"There was no need to shout at her like that. She was doing no harm. And before you start yelling at me too, I didn't tell her. Honestly I didn't."

"Do you expect me to believe that?" he grated edgily, the sting taken off his anger. "You didn't want to come here, did you, so I suppose this is the way you intend getting your own back on me. Well, I'm warning you, Lorraine, if Lisa suffers in any way because of you, I won't answer for my actions!"

"Oh . . . oh, don't be so dramatic!" Laurel burst out, frightened by the deadly intensity in his low pitched voice. "I tell you, I said nothing to Lisa. She knew already when she came up to my room. Oh, I wouldn't expect you to believe me!"

"I can always ask her," he suggested.

"Of course you can. And I suggest you do ask her! And while you're at it, you might ask yourself what good this attitude is doing any of us. If you loathe and detest me that much, I can always go back to London." She turned on her heels, intending to get away from him as fast as possible, but he forestalled this movement. His arm shot out and he grasped her waist, pulling her jerkily round to face him. She would have stumbled then had he not put out his other arm to encircle her shoulders and hold her upright. Briefly she was aware of his arm around her, not hard but curiously pleasant in its strength. She glanced up at him through her lashes and he was staring at her, the expression on his face unreadable. But though it was impossible to tell what he was thinking she was unnerved by his closeness and thought she would rather see him angry for at least that would be safer. For a long moment their eyes held, unflickering, unwavering, and then Laurel gave a little twist of her body and moved from him, but he caught her back again, this time holding her by the upper arms with tight fingers, pulling upwards so that she was forced on to the tips of her toes.

"Not so fast. You aren't going anywhere. I'll soon find out the truth about Lisa and meantime the real purpose of your visit is still with us. Caroline wants to see you. She has had a very good night, the nurse tells me, and is overjoyed to hear that you have . . . come back to me. So we're going in to see her now, and I'm adding another warning to you. When you're with her you will prove to her that we are happy together. You will be a sweet, loving wife, compliant and obedient and . . . oh, so apologetic for causing so much misery."

"And what will you do if I don't?" she whispered, aware of the pain in her arms beneath his fingers and the throbbing blood in her ears. "You're full of threats, aren't you? Hasn't it occurred to you that you have only to ask?"

"No it hasn't. Threats of physical violence are the only way to get through to you, aren't they?" He released her and she moved away from him, rubbing her arms. She couldn't help thinking that if he had spoken to Lorraine like that, she would have retaliated in some equally physical and violent way. The thought made her very nearly smile though she had little enough to smile about. She walked with Derek into the house, too overwrought by the scene with him to be nervous about the coming interview.

The old lady, whom Lisa called Auntie Caroline, who had brought Derek up as her own son, was in a south facing room. She lay on top of the bed with a colourful crocheted blanket spread over her, and was propped up on many lace edged pillows. It was a beautiful, elegant room, light and airy, bathed in sunlight from the open casement and smelling of perfume from a bowl of roses atop the dressing table. Laurel's eyes went at once to the figure on the bed. She rather thought she had expected a little, white haired old lady with pink cheeks and tired eyes. Caroline Clayton, who had once been manageress of a fashion house in Paris, was none of these things. Undoubtedly she had been very ill for she looked pale as parchment and so thin there seemed very little of her beneath the quilt. But her hair that was still almost black and only flecked in parts with iron grey, had been expertly swept into a chignon and her face was carefully made up. The grey eyes that regarded Laurel steadily and with interest were shrewd and missed very little. For a moment Laurel stood away from the bed returning the steady, rather disconcerting look, and she smiled. She had no idea how Lorraine would have greeted the old lady but could only do as she saw fit. She crossed to the bed and took the thin hand that was held out to her. Suddenly she knew what to do, how to cope with this. And if it was the wrong way, that was too bad.

"So you really came back at last, eh? I hardly believed Derek when he said you had—and here you are as lovely as ever—or even lovelier." The voice was a mere croak, not easy to understand, and now that she was closer Laurel could see that the hair style, the make up, constituted a mere front. Really she was a very sick old lady hiding behind these things. The hand that lay in Laurel's was cold and painfully thin, the skin hung about her neck in wrinkles but was taut and yellowish round her mouth. Apparently the stroke had temporarily paralysed her left side and this had left a reminder in the slight slackness on that side of her face. An overwhelming pang of pity swept over Laurel so that without thought she leaned forward and kissed the withered cheek. It smelt of perfume, something musky and expensive. The hand that had lain in hers reached up and touched her face.

"Lovely girl. Stay here and talk to me. It seems so long since I talked about the world I know—about things that interest us women." Her eyes shifted to Derek who had been watching all this in speculative silence. "I'd like to talk to Lorraine alone, Derek. Do you mind?"

Obviously he was not sure of this. He still did not trust her to behave herself, Laurel realised, and some imp of mischief she had not known she possessed prompted her to take his hand in hers, squeezing it hard. She flashed him a wide, loving smile.

"Don't worry, darling. I won't let her get over tired."

Something flickered at the back of the remarkable green eyes and she knew he would not allow her to get away with that scot free. No one played the fool with him that easily. He said, coolly, "Very well, my love. But don't stay more than ten minutes." He moved forward to lay a light kiss upon his aunt's cheek and, before straightening up, turned to where Laurel was sitting. Before she could guess his intention he had claimed her lips with his own in a long kiss from which she was unable to escape because of his hand hard on the back of her head. When he pulled away and regarded her flushed face and outraged expression, he laughed softly and kissed her again on the cheek before going out of the room.

As Laurel had to turn straight back to Miss Clayton, she had no time to analyse the effect Derek's kiss had had on her, which was probably just as well. She had never had many boyfriends. Somehow there had never been time, or the right ones had not come her way. Even Ben Lester whom Lorraine had stolen, had never done more than bestow a vague kiss on her lips after an evening at the cinema. She was aware even at the moment that Derek's mouth had pressed on hers that it was illogical to feel so breathless and so filled with a strange sense of elation. After all, she hardly knew the man and he hadn't been exactly pleasant during their brief acquaintance. As the hot blood began to fade at last from her cheeks, she turned back to the bed and saw that Caroline, unmoved by this short, intimate scene, was smiling at her.

"You must love him very much, child, to blush like that when your man kisses you."

Such a remark merely caused Laurel to blush all over again and she had to give herself a moment or two to collect herself and her thoughts and think of something evasive to say. Instead she decided to ignore the subject altogether, merely smiling enigmatically and saying, "We aren't here to talk about me but about you. How are you?"

"Oh . . . me." This was said with a little Gallic shrug. "I'm all right. A little thing like a stroke and everyone seems to think I'm going to pop off at any moment. Derek especially fusses over me like an old mother hen."

"He cares about you," Laurel said with assurance.

"I know that, and I'm not ungrateful for his caring. But there are times when the subject of my own health gets somewhat wearing." The old lady tightened her hand over Laurel's as it lay beside her on the bed. "I am glad you and Derek made it up at last. It's what I always hoped for. If not for his sake, for the sake of the child you both made." Laurel's colour heightened at the intimacy of this statement but Caroline misinterpreted the reason for this. "It is not a good thing for a mother to desert her child . . . but I'm thinking you're beginning to realise that, eh?"

"Yes. It's not a good thing," Laurel agreed wholeheartedly. "But . . . but I'm back now."

"And for good, I don't doubt. I was always sure you would one day realise what you had thrown away. Three years is long enough to bring someone to their senses. I always told Derek there was no harm in you, my dear. Just youth, I said. She's too headstrong and too spoilt, but she'll come round." The lined, cool hand squeezed again but with considerably less strength. "He was very bitter against you for a long time, child."

"I don't doubt it. He had cause, hadn't he?"

It was strange, Laurel thought, that old people are always supposed to be clever and worldly wise, to be able to see through the veneer that another person can put up. In fact Caroline, who looked shrewd enough, had obviously been fooled right down the line by Lorraine. She wondered just how much about his married life Derek had kept from his aunt.

"You've been living in London, so I hear," Caroline was saying, her voice less strong now as though the last long speech had weak-ened her a great deal, so that Laurel realised she really must be very ill indeed. "How I used to enjoy life in London. The theatres . . . the concerts . . . not to mention the night clubs. I suppose it is all different now."

"In some ways," Laurel agreed. "But London theatre is still the best in the world and only two nights ago . . ." No, it had been last night. Dear God, only last night! . . . "I went to see 'Swan Lake' at Covent Garden."

"Ah, I read that there was to be a Gala performance. Fonteyn and Nureyev. And you were there. Tell me about it, child."

So the remainder of the short visit contained no hurdles because Laurel, kneeling on the floor now, with her head close to the old lady's as this seemed to aid her hearing, told her about the performance that had sent her into the throes of delight. She wondered afterwards if she had gone on too long, for the tired grey eyes were far away, and suddenly she realised she had stayed much longer than she should have for the door opened softly and Derek looked in. He seemed surprised to see Laurel actually kneeling beside the bed, one of Caroline's hands between hers, talking in a low voice while the old lady watched her face unwaveringly. Obeying his summons, Laurel kissed Caroline's cheek and got to her feet.

"Come again," Caroline bade her. "Tomorrow. You will come?"

"Of course I will."

She was thoughtful as she went outside, impressed and drawn to the old lady and almost forgetting her own awkward position. She turned to Derek and murmured, "I don't think I tired her. She seemed to like listening. Surely she isn't that ill. Her mind is in no way impaired. What did the doctors actually say?"

"I've already told you that," he replied. "I didn't exaggerate her illness in order to make you come here."

"N . . . o. Of course not. It's just that most of the time she seemed so alert."

She had been talking to him in a perfectly natural way, her eyes on his face, but now she became aware of the keen scrutiny in his gaze that wandered over her face in puzzlement and realised she was not behaving as Lorraine would have. She managed a sort of casual shrug that looked as contrived as it felt and said, "You told me to be nice to her."

"I did. But I never realised you were quite such a good actress."

"I wasn't acting!"

"Not at all? That's nice to know." He grinned then and Laurel knew he was referring to the fact that she had called him "darling" and been fairly compliant when he kissed her. Again the betraying colour threatened to wash over her face and she turned and walked swiftly away towards her own room, stopping at the door only because he had followed her. Obviously he had seen the rise of her colour. "Now that's something I really don't know how you do," he told her back. "How does a woman who's probably never blushed in the whole of her life, suddenly learn to do it at will?" When she made no reply but bit her lip uncertainly and looked pointedly at the floor, he moved closer so that he was standing right behind her. Laurel could actually feel the warmth emanating from his big, muscular body just inches from her own. "If you were any other woman I would almost think I was embarrassing you," he murmured. "But you don't know the meaning of the word embarrassment, do you, Lorraine? Any woman with a mite of decent human feeling would never have . . ." His voice had hardened though he still hadn't moved away and she could actually feel his breath on her hair. She was aware of his closeness in every nerve of her body and had become so tense that she felt her nerves had to snap if this lasted much longer. What had he stopped himself saying? What unnamed crimes was he silently accusing her of? She took a determined step forward and then, at a safe distance, turned to face him. "I thought I'd go for a walk. Do you mind?"

"Not in the least. So long as you don't go too far."

"I'm not going to run away!" she said spiritedly. "Don't you trust me that much?"

It was the wrong thing to say for a faintly incredulous smile touched his mouth. "Trust you?" he repeated in astonishment. "You can ask that? I made the mistake of trusting you once before and look what happened. No, Lorraine, I don't trust you. I don't trust your motives in behaving as you have been, so sweet and innocent as though you never did a bad thing in your life; I don't trust that beautiful face of yours or that equally beautiful body. I don't—most especially I don't—trust your morals. I'd say they were as bad as an alley cat's but that would definitely be unfair to all cats."

Every vestige of colour left Laurel's cheeks at these words. She felt as though she might actually be sick there and then, right in front of him, and certainly a hot stinging sensation in her eyes proclaimed that tears were not far away. She blinked hard as she opened her mouth to say something in her defence, but no words came out, just a peculiar little croak that might or might not have been a denial of his ruthless, harsh summing up of her character. She had completely forgotten that his words were actually about Lorraine who most likely deserved them. There was no escape except down the stairs and to get to them she had to push past him. He made no move to prevent her going, only stood immobile watching her as she ran down the stairs.

FOUR

BECAUSE EACH DAY Derek left the house early—Laurel had ascertained without actually asking, that he owned the small air ferry service that specialised in running business men and occasionally important or fragile freight between the island and Southampton or London, using a fleet of swift helicopters—her days were very much her own. On the second day of her stay at High Ridge, Laurel had written a long letter to Lorraine explaining in detail what had happened, but of course she had no address and so had sent the letter to the flat in the hope that Lorraine might return there early and find it. In the meantime, while she waited to be rescued from the situation, Laurel resolved to make the most of it. She ought, she knew, to be reasonably content. What more could she ask but to live in a luxurious house in a beautiful position, with the use of Derek's second best car, a lime green Ford Cortina that went like a dream, and comparative freedom each and every day. The flies in the ointment were Mrs. Mackenzie who persisted in regarding her with stubborn dislike, and Derek himself. Derek was an enigma that she soon gave up trying to understand. That he could be kind she knew, and often, when he didn't know she was looking at him, she would study him and get the impression of a man who laughed a lot, and who was thoughtful and considerate. She had seen him behave this way with Lisa and with his aunt; she guessed that once he had been like this with Lorraine. Yet Laurel had seen the other side of him and soon learned to dread his moods when he would lash her most effectively with a barbed tongue. It was disconcerting when he went with her into Caroline's room and he suddenly changed; to act the affectionate husband in front of his aunt he frequently hugged Laurel close to him or repeated that first kiss. She was sure he gained considerable amusement out of disconcerting her but at the same time was puzzled as to *why* she was disconcerted. The Lorraine he had known would have given as good as she got.

Heavy eye-lids drooped as Laurel enjoyed the warmth of the sun rippling over her bikini clad body and allowed the face of Derek to drift before her eyes. She didn't understand him and perhaps never would, not with her deception like a massive wall between them. She told herself she hated him but she could no longer think badly of him no matter what he said or did. Somehow, insiduously and against her will, the hatred had given way to liking and even to something warmer that she was reluctant to face up to or admit to herself. She had wondered once, when he had shown particular affection for her when they were with Caroline, how he would be as a lover. The thought had shocked her, sending, as it did, pangs of aching longing seering through her.

"Mummy, why don't you come and help me?"

The imperious, childish voice pushed aside such unwelcome thoughts. Remembering guiltily that it was unwise to allow a young child to play on the beach unwatched, she flicked open her eyes and looked down at Lisa. The little girl, wearing a two piece swimming costume of a gay multi-coloured material that showed off the smooth roundness of her suntanned limbs, was kneeling beside a huge pile of sand watching Laurel with her head on one side. They smiled at each other with a fondness that needed no words and Laurel thought for the thousandth time how beautiful Lisa was, and also that for the sake of modesty she should not say so for Lisa was the absolute image of what she and Lorraine were like at that age.

"You don't really need my help, do you?" she murmured. "I'm feeling lazy."

"Then can I have an ice cream instead, please?"

Laurel laughed as she reached for her handbag. "Blackmailer! Go on then. I'll watch you from here."

She turned in her deck chair and followed Lisa's progress as she threaded her way through the crowds that were spread out upon Shanklin beach to where the ice cream van was parked. That morning Laurel had decided the good weather was too perfect to be missed and on impulse had packed up a picnic and driven down to Shanklin which Mrs. Mac had reluctantly thawed enough to admit possessed one of the best beaches and safest bathing on the island. Jackie, who worked in the kitchen, volunteered the information that if they parked the car in the town and walked down through Shanklin Old Village, they could go to the sea through the chine which was well worth a visit. Laurel had no idea what a "chine" was but was more than delighted when she found it. With Lisa skipping at her side only too happy to be given this outing, they strolled through the old village, where thatched cottages with charming old fashioned gardens gave them the impression of being in the depths of the countryside, and turned to walk down the narrow way where Laurel had to pay to enter the chine. A chine, it appeared, was a deep, narrow ravine with one end opening at the coast, worn down over millions of years by a river or stream. The stream that ran through Shanklin Chine seemed little more than a trickle in places, yet in others it crashed magnificently over steep sided cliffs into deep, dark pools, sending up clouds of spray on to the surrounding rocks and vegetation. The paths were many, some teetering on the very edge of the steep edged ravine, though all safely fenced, and at varying heights above the river and all around grew a preponderance of plant life; trees had grown tall and spindly as they strained upwards towards the sunlight; long glossy ferns and thickly tangled briars and ivy all contrived to cut out much of the light so that the chine was cool and smelt strangely of damp and muskiness much as is sometimes found in a thick wood after a heavy storm. As the paths took the walkers nearer the sea the trees above spread a little and long shafts of sunlight streamed through, causing steam to rise wherever it fell. At last the narrow, deep valley spread itself and there was the sea, sparkling blue and bright, a marked contrast to the dim greens of the chine.

Jackie had said Blackgang and Alum Chines were more spectacular but Laurel had been impressed with this and pleased she had thought to take her camera so that she was able to get some shots of the unusual and beautiful scenery.

She watched now as Lisa picked her way back across the sand clutching a large, swiftly melting ice cream. She sat herself down at Laurel's feet and said nothing but watched the sea with its vast assortment of oddly shaped beach craft as well as the more conventional triangular sailed yachts. At the end of the pier a "round the island" ferry boat was just pulling away. It was all very pleasant and normal and for the first time since the moment that Derek erupted into her life, Laurel felt really happy.

When she had finished her ice cream and allowed herself to be mopped up, Lisa said, "Now help me with my sand castle."

Laughing, Laurel dropped from the deck chair on to the warm sand and began to dig and scrape and pat the sand into shape. It was over fifteen years since the last family holiday when she and Lorraine had been taken by their parents to Weymouth, yet the touch and feel and texture of the sand beneath her fingers felt curiously familiar and even soothing. Like this she could feel content and happy, able to live each day as it came and in that way value every moment of happiness. This had to be her motto and she was beginning to manage it. She knew how well she looked. Her own mirror told her that the sunny lazy days at High Ridge had completed the process of convalescence that the weeks in Lorraine's apartment had begun. Her body was smooth and suntanned and sleek as a cat's; her hair glowed with health and beauty; and in her eyes was an awareness that had not been there before, an awareness of herself as a woman, her power and vulnerability, the sensuousness that lay yet unaroused in her hazel eyes. She smiled faintly and stretched in the sun, enjoying the feeling of sheer physical well being. When she opened her eyes it was to look into the amused eyes of a woman, large and middle aged, who was sitting in a nearby deck chair. The woman was with her husband and, Laurel guessed, her three grandchildren. They had all spoken earlier when they were in the sea, the usual English comments about the weather and how cold the water was. Now the woman said, "There's no need to ask what the relationship is between you two, my dear. I never did see a mother and daughter so alike."

Laurel heard her own voice make polite, meaningless comment in reply, but it was almost as though the sun had gone in. It was nearly four anyway and she used the time as an excuse to get Lisa into her towelling beach dress; hastily she pulled on her own dress and packed up their things. But as they said "goodbye" to the couple with the children, Laurel thought with a cry that was almost audible in its intensity, "If only it were true! If only Lisa were my daughter! If only Derek. . . ."

But that thought she could not finish even in her mind, despite the desperate longing to belong, to be part of something and someone to whom she was important and by whom she was needed. She must never, never think of Derek that way. It would be bad enough having to leave Lisa, as she would some day, but to tear her heart out twice over . . . no, it must never be.

"What's the matter, Mummy?" Lisa asked, her voice coming from behind Laurel's back for she was safely strapped into the back seat. Derek had insisted that this safety device must always be used. "You've gone all funny and quiet."

"Have I, darling? I'm sorry. I was just thinking."

"I wish you wouldn't think then. Grown ups go all funny when they start thinking."

Despite her sadness, Laurel had to laugh at this succinct comment. "I expect it's the heat, love," she suggested and Lisa didn't argue with this for it had certainly got much hotter and closer over the last hour. Looking forward and to the right, Laurel noticed that the sky had become clouded though as yet the clouds were high and light. The car radio emitted loud crackles and she hoped there was no thunder about. Laurel disliked, even feared thunder, having once been close by when a tree was struck clear down the middle by a blinding flash of fork lightning. She could still vividly recall the noise and the way the earth had seemed to shake at the moment of impact; she could remember the smell of burning wood. Even now she sweated at the remembrance and her hands on the steering wheel felt slippery with moisture. She accelerated a little but by the time they reached High Ridge, though the clouds were building up over the sea in the awe inspiring, towering alto cumulus formation that so often heralded thunder, there was nothing else except the heat to indicate the coming storm.

Derek's Jaguar was in the drive and Laurel drew the Cortina carefully up beside it, then turned and helped Lisa to unclip her harness. As they entered the house hand in hand, Derek came from his study and stood in the doorway looking at them. He was wearing a dark grey lounge suit and looked elegant and handsome and somehow *sleek* with his tanned skin and the curious light green eyes. Laurel smiled uncertainly at him, unwilling to commit herself until she knew his mood, and only saying in a soft, slightly diffident voice, "We've been to the beach."

"So I can see." His voice was lazy and relaxed and she guessed that his mood was reasonably affable so that she allowed herself to relax. She saw that he looked slowly from her bare brown feet encased in raffia mules, up to her face. Her hair was damp and rather lank because of the sea water, but her skin glowed with health and she had never looked lovelier. He took his gaze from her as Lisa ran up to him, and bent to pick up his daughter who wrapped her arms firmly round his neck.

"Have a good day, love?" he asked in the loving voice he reserved strictly for Lisa and his aunt.

"Lovely. We went in the sea and I swam a bit with my arm bands, and then Mummy helped me build a super sand castle."

"Did she indeed?" Again his eyes dwelt penetratingly on Laurel's face and she felt herself redden beneath the curious scrutiny. "I wouldn't have thought that was exactly in your line, Lorraine." The dry sarcasm in his tone irked her so much that she longed to hit back, to make him suffer as he could her. She said instead, in a brisk voice, "Come on, Lisa. You need a hot bath before tea."

It was the usual arrangement for Laurel and Lisa to eat their evening meal, a high tea consisting of eggs or fish, or perhaps a toasted snack like Welsh Rarebit, followed by an assortment of cakes enough to gladden any child's heart, together in the play room. But today, Derek said as he put Lisa down, "I ate at lunch time today so if you've no objection, I'll share your meal."

Laurel smiled with quick, not to be disguised pleasure, and Lisa squeaked, "Yes, come and have tea with us, Daddy."

"If your mother has no objection," Derek said levelly, his eyes not once moving from Laurel's face. Daringly she brought her gaze up to meet his, experiencing a little shock of breathlessness at the expression in them. They were amused but also, in some inexplicable way, admiring.

"Of course I don't object," she said quietly. "We'll eat at six. Come on, Lisa, bath."

The meal, scrambled eggs on toast, with grilled bacon and tomato added by Mrs. Mac in honour of Derek's presence, was the pleasantest one Laurel had eaten at High Ridge. Dinner with Derek at the weekends was purgatory and tea in the play room was presided over by a Mrs. Mac who lost no opportunity to be thoroughly objectionable. Laurel knew that Lorraine would never have allowed the housekeeper to get away with her snide remarks but she felt unable to deal with them because she was, after all, only here temporarily and then under false pretences. Today with Derek, changed into an open neck shirt and slacks, sitting at the head of the table, Mrs. Mac was charm itself, giving the impression of a fussy but caring woman who went out of her way to make things easy for everyone. Laurel was so happy because of the friendly atmosphere between herself and Derek that she was unwilling to change things and quite content to pretend that this was a normal state of affairs, but Lisa had no such guile and was not easily hushed. As the meal ended and she finished off her last piece of chocolate cake, she announced brightly, "Mrs. Mac is much nicer today, isn't she, Mummy?"

Laurel frowned a quick warning but too late for Derek had heard and now *he* frowned as he asked Lisa what she meant.

"Oh, she's usually horrid to Mummy—she sort of goes on in a nasty way." Lisa struggled to find the correct adult words and, though not finding them, nevertheless managed to convey her meaning adequately. "She sort of *looks* like she doesn't like Mummy, and Mummy never said anything nasty to her."

Derek's black brows lowered frowningly over his green eyes as he turned to Laurel. "Is this true?" he asked in a low voice, and Laurel shrugged.

"I suppose so . . . in a way . . . I don't know. It doesn't matter."

"Doesn't matter?" he repeated. "Of course it matters. Your position in this house is second only to me while you're here, and Mrs. Mac is only an employee. For God's sake, Lorraine, why didn't you say or do something? Once you'd have been quick enough to tell her where to get off."

"It didn't seem worth it," she replied lamely, her voice pitched low and unhappy. "I mean, she'll be here after I've gone and she is obviously a good housekeeper. Why should your life be disrupted because I . . ."

Momentarily they had forgotten Lisa; the conversation had been spoken in soft, almost intimate voices. But Lisa was still there and, what was more, was listening to every word. She cried out, "Mummy, you're not going! You like it here with me—you know you do. You said so!"

Derek said, his voice more harsh than he had intended, "I've told you before, Lisa, that Lorraine isn't staying long. You know we talked about this before."

"Yes, but that was *then*," Lisa shouted, tears already starting from her eyes and running down her woebegone face. "That was before, when you didn't like each other and Mummy didn't want to come here. Now it's different."

"Lisa, darling, it's no different," Laurel tried to tell her, almost in tears herself at this show of affection. "I told you myself that I wouldn't be here always."

"But that was *before*," Lisa screeched, jumping up. "You like us now. You must stay. I never had a mummy before. You must stay."

She hurtled out of the room, slamming the door behind her. White faced, Laurel looked across at Derek, fully expecting his anger. She noticed that he too was looking fraught and upset but, strangely enough, not angry. She bit her lip and blinked back the tears, beginning to get to her feet but being beaten to it by Derek. He said abruptly, "I'll see to her."

"Yes . . . I'm sorry," she murmured, slipping back into her seat and putting her hands to her face. She felt in utter despair, blaming herself completely because of the way she had won Lisa's love through deception. Reaching her side, Derek rested one hand firmly on her shoulder. She expected him to be derisive of her sorrow but his expression was quite gentle.

"It's not your fault," he said softly. "Not this time. I don't know how we could have avoided it. It certainly isn't your problem. After all, you didn't want to come here and start all this again." His fingers squeezed her shoulder. "I'll see to her."

When he had gone Laurel remained seated at the table, her head resting on her hands. Derek's attitude had surprised her. She could have understood it if he had been angry, blaming her for upsetting Lisa. But the gentleness in his words, the light touch of his hand on her bare arm had set her heart hammering uncomfortably. She found herself wondering if the scene with Lisa would in any way alter the state of uneasy truce that had developed between herself and Derek over the last few days. She wanted things to change, to become friendlier and warmer, but at the same time was wary of what might result from a more intimate relationship.

Abruptly she got to her feet and went downstairs. As she passed Lisa's bedroom she paused and heard soft voices but she could not make out the words and made no attempt to eavesdrop. She had invaded quite enough on Derek's and Lisa's lives already. She passed on downstairs and out into the garden, breathing deeply to entrap some of the heavy, warm air. It still felt thundery. The air was still and close and filled with gnats. She walked to the rockery and sat on the rustic chair that was set there, listening to the sounds of the summer evening, the crash of the sea upon the rocks below the cliff, the occasional fluttering of a bird up late, the chirping of a cricket; her nostrils were filled with the heady sweet honeysuckle scent and the almost overpowering night scented stock. How anyone could want to live in a city when they had all this. . . .

She almost resented Derek's intrusion into her thoughts, but managed to greet him equably enough when he came across the lawn to her. He stood before her, hands in pockets, feet apart.

"Is she all right?" Laurel asked tentatively, and he nodded.

"She'll have to be, won't she? I mean, you wouldn't consider staying . . ."

There was something of a query in the soft spoken words but not enough to merit a direct answer. As she realised that in fact there was nothing more she would like in the whole world than to stay here with him and Lisa forever—as the thought hit her with the effect of a sledge hammer blow—Laurel licked dry lips and managed to murmur, "No more than you would wish me to stay."

"Exactly," he agreed shortly. "It's a bloody nuisance that she ever found out who you are . . ."

"I told you about that! I never mentioned . . ."

"I know," he interrupted peremptorily. "Lisa told me she overheard Mrs. Mac talking about you in the kitchen. That woman is becoming a menace." He hesitated as though finding it difficult to voice the words, and finally came out with an awkward, rather grudging apology for doubting her word. Laurel felt a warmth of genuine happiness at the apology and this was reflected in her voice.

"It doesn't matter, really. It was natural that you should think it, but I'm pleased you now realise that I wouldn't do such a thing."

"Does it matter, then, what I think about you?" he asked, a little surprised. "I mean, does it matter to you?" He put one foot on the seat near her and leaned with his elbows against his knee, a cigarette hanging from his long fingers. He sounded relaxed and contemplative, as though he too was affected by the night. A long, long way off the silence was broken by the soft stirring of thunder that seemed to echo the noise of Laurel's heart.

"Yes, it does matter. I wouldn't want Lisa hurt . . ." His head, silhouetted by the still light sky, turned sharply at her words and she said quickly, before he could speak, hearing the little catch of anxiety in her voice, "And please don't be sarcastic about that. It's true. I don't want her hurt. She's been hurt enough I know and I didn't want this to happen. But the damage has been done now and you haven't been able to persuade her that I'm not her mother."

"I haven't even tried . . . and neither have you, I'd guess. I thought it wouldn't matter much—that you'd see very little of her. I didn't expect these daily outings."

"Are you forbidding them?" she whispered, dreading such a prohibition.

"No. But you always said you had no time for kids."

"*I* always said . . ." Her voice was bitter. "It seems that I said a lot of things."

"And meant them."

". . . perhaps, but . . ."

"And don't tell me people change! I'm up to here with that one!" He turned on her with such a rush of violence that every nerve in her body leapt with fright, and his voice was loud enough to send some night bird screaming out of the undergrowth. He threw his cigarette away in a spasmodic, impatient movement. "Goddamn you, Lorraine. What game are you playing at? If I didn't know better I'd think I was the one who was wrong—that I'd been mistaken all these years about what you're really like. Or that *my* behaviour had somehow been the cause of yours. I almost think at times that you're not Lorraine at all!"

There was nothing to be said in reply to this shattering statement; she sat still, her eyes huge, while the light from the house glinted on her hair and picked out the pale blue dress she wore so that she seemed ethereal, not substance at all. Derek straightened up and moved towards her, so that his legs almost touched hers and she had to strain her neck to look up at him. He was breathing very unevenly. "Damn you," he repeated, snarling the words. "I'm not going to let you get under my skin again. Keep out of my way, Lorraine, or I won't be able to answer for the consequences."

Laurel watched him march away across the lawn and tears ran in a silent stream down her cheeks. She was not even sure why she was crying; she understood his uncertainty and a little of the physical and mental torture she was putting him through. Obviously he had deeply loved Lorraine, putting her on a pedestal from which she had most devastatingly tumbled. Had he thought—or hoped—to find some kind of monster of depravity that he could revile to his heart's content and enjoy doing it? And, finding someone ordinary, with normal human feelings and values, he was doubting his own judgement? Since coming to High Ridge Laurel had frequently despised herself for what she was doing, but never more so than at that moment. In a way it was for Derek that she allowed her tears to fall as much as for herself.

Later in the night the thunder broke. Laurel had fallen into a sleep made restless by her subconscious brain picking up and responding to the ever increasing rumbles and now one particularly loud bang caused her to leap into awareness, her skin clammy and cold despite the warmth of the surrounding air, her heart thumping. There was a moment or so of that almost deadly silence that sometimes falls between cracks of thunder, when the whole world seems to hold still in anticipation, and then the lightning came again, followed almost simultaneously by the thunder. Laurel was clenching her hands into fists, pressing them against her ears, but of course this made not the slightest difference. She heard the rain begin then, a few single drops at first and then a deluge that crashed against the windows and poured off gutterings. The rain made it seem a little better, less dangerous somehow, and she turned over in bed, forcibly relaxing her cramped limbs. She managed then to stop thinking about herself and to wonder if that loud crash had wakened anyone else, most especially Lisa. She recalled, as a child, always going into her parents' bedroom and crawling in between them when there was a storm. And often her mother would put on the light and go to make tea for them all. Since then Laurel invariably got up and made herself a pot of tea rather than lie in bed terrified out of her wits. Recalling this, she now knew she would never get back to sleep at least until the storm was over and that sounded as though it had set in for several hours to come. She got up and pulled on the green satin negligee that matched the nightdress she wore. This was one of the outfits Lorraine had chosen for her, beautiful, luxurious and expensive but highly impractical. Nevertheless, Laurel owned nothing more sensible and at least the material was not transparent. The negligee tied in a bow just on the bust line which, in negligee and nightdress plunged into a deep vee. She put on slippers, equally frivolous articles, scraps of fur and lace only, and softly opened her bedroom door.

At Lisa's door she paused, not liking to think that the child might be frightened of the storm that still crashed and banged and raged outside. She turned the handle and pressed her ear to the narrow gap but the only sounds, imperfectly heard above the elemental noises outside, were of deep breathing. Laurel smiled then at Lisa's ability to sleep through anything, and withdrew, closing the door again equally softly.

"Is anything wrong?"

FIVE

ALREADY TENSED UP because of the thunder, Laurel actually shrieked, clapping her hand to her mouth and spinning round, stark fear all over her face as she looked at the speaker. Derek was dressed in a navy blue dressing gown and was grinning in an infuriating way at her.

"Sorry. Did I frighten you?"

"Frighten me? You nearly gave me a heart attack!" Laurel gasped, completely natural in her behaviour towards him, perhaps for the first time in their acquaintanceship. "Do you have to go creeping about in that spooky manner?"

"I wasn't creeping. My footsteps were drowned by the thunder." He indicated Lisa's door. "I was checking on her. Obviously you were doing the same."

"Yes. She seems to be sound asleep. I . . . I wasn't sure if she was likely to be frightened of the thunder."

"You wouldn't, would you?" he said, but as one stating a fact rather than with his usual sarcasm. "Actually," he went on, "she isn't a bit frightened. Like you she enjoys a good storm and will probably be upset tomorrow at missing it."

Until that moment Laurel had forgotten that Lorraine had indeed always loved a thunderstorm. As a child she had never resorted to crawling into her parents' bed; she was generally to be found standing by a window, curtains flung wide, watching the lightning with delight. Involuntarily, Laurel shivered.

"How about a drop of liquid refreshment?" Derek suggested. "Since we're both up."

"I was just going to make some tea."

"I had thought of something stronger," he smiled. "But tea will be as good as anything.

"Have you turned teetotal, Lorraine?" he asked as he stood back so that she could precede him down the stairs. She glanced enquiringly at him. "You used to drink quite a lot. Since you've been here I've noticed you only have the occasional glass of wine."

Laurel went into the kitchen and busied herself putting on the kettle and setting out the tea things. She thought carefully about what to say and then said it quickly before she had time to change her mind.

"Look, do you have to keep harping back to what I used to be like? I get a bit fed up with it, if you really want to know. After all," she added, turning to face him, "I don't go on about what you used to be like . . ."

Her voice trailed to an uncertain halt. Turning towards him had been a mistake for now she could see the way he was regarding her. In the darkened hall and on the stairs he had failed to notice what she was wearing but now he was taking in her appearance fully, his eyes frankly and openly admiring as they travelled from the negligee's low neckline to the hem of its full skirts that swept softly round her feet.

"That is one hell of an outfit," he drawled softly. "I like the changes in your character, my sweet, but I'm very glad you haven't changed your style."

"We weren't discussing me!" she snapped, turning away and flushing miserably. She wanted him to admire her, but not like this . . . this was embarrassing and humiliating and her skin crawled because of the way he was looking at her.

"I was," he said, and then he laughed and the awkwardness had gone. He was suddenly nice and normal, very, very attractive but gentlemanly and polite. He took the tea pot from her nerveless fingers and made the tea quickly and competently while she watched him, her hands clasped nervously together. She followed him as he picked up the tray, loaded with cups, sugar and cream and the tea pot and headed for the lounge. Despite the fact that the atmosphere had eased a little, she still felt tense and on edge, and not too far off tears.

"It's better in here," he said cryptically. "Wait till you see the view. Look!" He pulled a cord and the curtains slid noiselessly back, revealing the dark night just at the moment that the sky was split in two by a streak of fork lightning that made the lounge momentarily light as day. Laurel bit back the sudden involuntary scream that rose to her throat and swiftly sat down, her back to the window. Fear swept over her so that she longed to screech at him to stop tormenting her.

"Come and look," he repeated. "Lorraine, what's the matter?"

"Nothing—nothing's the matter. I'm just . . . I don't want to look, that's all. Let's say I've outgrown the need to stare at thunderstorms." She wondered that he could not hear the tension and the distress in her voice. Surely he was not that insensitive; he must be able to see, to feel, her fear. He came over to her and reached for her arm.

"You used to stand here all night when there was a storm. Remember, my darling? You'd stand here like a wild thing, like part of the storm itself. And now you cower away like a frightened animal. For God's sake, Lorraine, what has happened to you?"

He shook her arm and she pulled away, jumping to her feet and flinching as another vivid streak of lightning played across the sky. "Nothing!" she cried out, knowing he would be satisfied only with the truth. "I saw a tree split by lightning . . . I . . . it frightened me . . . it was so close. I don't like thunder. I loathe it!"

There was a long silence broken by another rumble of thunder, then, with a muffled exclamation that may have been of irritation, Derek turned and pulled the curtains across the window, if not cutting off the storm's noise at least effectively removing the sight of it. He returned to Laurel's side and put one arm across her shaking shoulders. "Honey, I'm sorry. I didn't know. Why didn't you tell me at once?" His voice was soft, the words slightly slurred as though he were deeply affected by what had happened. "It must have been terrible," he said, "to have changed your feelings about thunder that much. When did it happen?"

"Oh . . . quite a long time ago," she murmured, not looking at him for fear he would sense that her words were only an impression of the truth. "It was pretty awful." Without realising it, she had leaned against him and suddenly he was stroking her hair and the atmosphere seemed to change, as though the air inside the room was charged with as much electricity as there was flashing about outside in the stormy sky. A stifled gasp escaped Laurel and she tried to pull away, but somehow he was keeping her from moving, gently but firmly pulling her back towards him. His arms were round her, holding her against his chest and she felt his lips against her hair. Even though everything in her screamed that she must get away, that it was against all human decency to let this go on, she felt her muscles go limp, refusing to fight any longer against the glorious feeling of being held like this. She felt the warmth of his breath on her hair and heard his voice, husky with gentle laughter.

"I suppose I should have known I couldn't escape from you forever. I always was lost where you're concerned. But I thought you'd become—I don't know—some kind of monster. Yet you haven't—you seem to be just as I always hoped you would be . . . as I always believed you could be if you gave yourself half the chance."

She stirred in his arms, unutterably moved by the words, yet still refusing to look up at him. ". . . Derek . . ."

"It's all right. The past is forgotten. I'm talking too much, aren't I?" He laughed and this time caught her chin in his hand and turned her face up towards him. For a long moment they looked at each other, deeply and silently, and then he brushed his mouth softly across hers. Her lips trembled a little in response and heavy lids shrouded her eyes as he slowly explored her face, letting his lips move with sensuous tenderness over every inch of it, as though in remembrance. Finally he returned again to her mouth, kissing her still softly but then less so as the kiss deepened. Almost without her realising she had even moved, Laurel's arms were round his neck. She clung there, her body, her arms, her mouth were somehow nothing to do with her—she was all fire and desire and sheer joy, clinging and kissing and laughing because she loved him and he loved her. . . .

"Lorraine," he whispered into her ear, his breathing uneven. "God, but you're beautiful. I must have been crazy to think I could ever forget you. I love you . . . I suppose I always have though I'm sure what I felt for you before was nothing like this. It's like falling in love all over again with someone the same and yet so very different . . ." His hand moved softly on her naked shoulder beneath the silken negligee, caressing as with remembrance, feeling the shudder that went right through her at his touch. He took the lobe of her ear between his teeth and bit gently.

"Let's go to bed," he murmured.

It took only this to drag Laurel out of the dream of delight in which she had been drifting. A spasm seemed to jab through her, stiffening the soft body that had been resting submissively against his. He looked at the expression of outrage on her face and laughed.

"What's the matter? Anyone would think I had made a really outrageous suggestion. Darling, we are still married." When she still made no effort to speak, but just looked at him, her eyes bleak, her lovely mouth soft from his kisses but drooping a little, he grew slightly irritable.

"For heaven's sake, what is it? I could have sworn a moment ago you were wanting me as much as I want you. Whatever else was wrong between us, Lorraine, we always made out pretty good in bed . . . Now what the hell have I said?" She had flinched at the outspokenness of the words and probably he had every right to feel irritated by her apparently inexplicable attitude.

"I take it from this rather odd behaviour that while you're willing enough to take my money, my hospitality . . . and a few kisses, that's as far as it goes. I've got to hand it to you, Lorraine, you sure as hell know how to let a man down with a thump."

"That's . . . that's not fair," she whispered through dry lips.

"Fair! Who's talking about fair? God, I must be some kind of imbecile to think you'd changed—"

"Don't!" Laurel cried out, tears spurting into her eyes. She brushed the back of one hand across them angrily. "It isn't like that—I didn't intend leading you on. But, don't you think you're rushing things? You made me come here and for one reason only, to convince your aunt of our happiness. You had no thought of me, of what I felt. You used nothing short of blackmail to make me come and . . . and now you try this on and expect me to go jumping eagerly into bed with you." How she said these things Laurel never knew, for she loved him and knew that she was wholly in the wrong, but things had gone too far and somehow she had to convince him that her momentary lapse in responding to his caresses was just that, a weak moment that meant nothing.

Her empassioned speech was followed by a silence broken only by Derek's angry breathing. He had never, Laurel thought wildly, looked better looking nor more dangerous. He looked capable of striking her, or breaking her neck or of taking from her by force that which, a few minutes earlier, he had expected her to give willingly. However, before her startled, frightened gaze he overcame the emotional onslaught and relaxed his clenched fists, flexing the fingers of both hands.

"Very well," he said quietly. "I think we now understand each other. I'll take my obviously unwelcome presence from out of your sight. Goodnight." He turned abruptly and went towards the door. Unhappy, hating what he obviously thought of her, Laurel called his name in a little, desperate voice. But when he turned back to her she could only shake her head despairingly. His mouth twisted into a little sardonic smile before he went out and only then did Laurel, crying bitterly even as she stood there, realise that the storm had stopped and outside the night had become still and quiet and peaceful. She pulled back the curtains and stood by the window looking out and thinking that the world, her world, could never be the same again. If only she hadn't agreed to go along with Lorraine's plans! If only she had admitted her deceit to Derek at once! She could not tell him now. He was angry enough with her and how much more furious would he be if he learned the trick she had played on him, that the woman he had held in his arms and admitted his love to was a complete stranger! She loved him too much to be willing to submit him to that kind of humiliation and was too frightened of the darker side of his nature to risk his wrath. No, she must stay as long as he wished, perhaps until poor Caroline did die or, less likely, get better, but she must keep a distance between herself and Derek. After the night's events she doubted that he would want to come too close to her anyway.

The morning dawned bright and fresh after the storm, with the sky clearing rapidly and the warmth of the air promising a fine day. Pale faced after an almost sleepless night, and with dark smudges beneath her eyes, Laurel breakfasted in the play room with Lisa, preferring to eat corn flakes and toast rather than share a more substantial cooked breakfast with Derek. She dreaded the moment when she would have to see Derek, feeling she could hardly bear to face him, but when he actually came into the play room she was given little choice in the matter.

He was wearing a thin white cotton tee shirt and light blue denim trousers, the most casual clothes Laurel had seen him in. The tee shirt emphasised the muscular appearance of his chest and upper arms, the whipcord litheness that proclaimed him a man who believed in physical fitness and Laurel felt a now familiar yearning for him, a longing to be permitted to be with him, to touch him and love him: ironic that she had been offered that opportunity and had refused it! As she looked away from him lest he should read the longing in her eyes, what little colour there was in her cheeks died away. Surprisingly he smiled, the smile deepening the attractive creases down his cheeks. He kissed Lisa and then said, "Have you finished your breakfast, love? I want to talk to Lorraine so just go out and play for a while. Okay?"

Laurel sat motionless, her hands clasped tightly together on the table. She was confused by the smile and nervous of what he had to say. It was almost as though he had come in peace, but surely not! She heard Lisa go out, softly closing the door behind her, and there was the scrape of a chair as Derek pulled out one and sat down. He filled the brief awkward pause by lighting a cigarette.

"I was wondering—it's such a nice day and perhaps we . . . you, Lisa and I, might go out somewhere," Derek said. "I haven't had a day off for a long time and I daresay it would do us all good." Laurel's head had jerked back. She stared open mouthed at him and he smiled again. "You look as though you expected little less than murder from me. Am I that bad?"

"N—no. But you . . ."

"I know—last night. I've been thinking about that—a lot—and . . . well, you were right."

"I was!" Laurel gasped and this time he laughed, throwing back his head and laughing loudly and completely without affectation. Laurel watched the difference this made to his appearance; he suddenly looked younger and somehow carefree. When he stopped laughing he became momentarily serious.

"I came to apologise, Lorraine. What you said last night made me realise that I was expecting too much, too soon. My only excuse is that I wanted you like hell and, masculine like, I was convinced you felt the same." He paused, as though expecting her to fill in the gap by telling him she had. But when she said nothing he sighed and continued. "I realised afterwards that we can't just take up where we left off. Too many things have happened between us—too many terrible things have been said and done. But maybe we can give ourselves some kind of chance if we take it slowly. No . . ." He placed the fingers of one hand gently against her protesting lips. "Leave it now. Let's have our day out and see how things go. You can give that much, can't you, Lorraine?"

And she knew she could, and had to. She nodded and tears rushed to her eyes, blinding her to his puzzlement. If it was just herself being hurt she knew she would go on willingly with his suggestions. But he would be hurt too when she finally left High Ridge, or when he discovered that the real Lorraine cared nothing for him. She raised her eyes to his and he saw the hunted, miserable look.

"Don't look like that, sweetheart. It's not the end of the world. I promise you I won't press you into anything you don't want or aren't ready for. But if you feel at any time that you want to put our relationship on a different footing, just give the word. Okay?"

"All right," she whispered, and then he smiled quite gaily as he stood up.

"Fine. Get yourself and Lisa ready and we'll be off in about half an hour. Bring your swimming gear. I know a quiet place where we can swim without being invaded by holiday makers."

If it hadn't been for the shadow of Lorraine that seemed to hang ominously over Laurel, she knew she would have thoroughly enjoyed that outing. Derek was in his very best mood, considerate, amusing, cheerful and relaxed, keeping right off any personal level of involvement with her. In fact he treated her as a man might well treat a wife of some years, a wife he still cared deeply for but had grown comfortable with so that there was no need for too many outward signs of affection. Only very occasionally, when she became aware of his eyes on her, did Laurel realise the depth of desire and love that lurked beneath that amiable surface. She could not help but be aware that it was she, Laurel, and not Lorraine, who had aroused those feelings in him, but this did not make things any easier for her. She was only too glad that Lisa was with them. The effort of entertaining and looking after the child took both their minds off more personal things.

True to his word, Derek did indeed know a small, secluded bay which they shared with half a dozen or so other people. For a while Derek helped Lisa with her sandcastle building and at lunch time Laurel unpacked the picnic basket provided by Mrs. Mac and laid out the various tempting delicacies for inspection. There was chicken salad, cold summer soup, followed by individual fruit salad and cream, and cheese and biscuits, all washed down with white wine for the adults and home made lemonade for Lisa. While this repast was being digested, Lisa, changed now into her bikini, played in the sand while Derek stretched out on the blanket, his hands behind his head, and dozed contentedly. Laurel, sitting near him on the blanket, watched him covertly and thought what a contented family group they must look to the others on the beach.

Derek opened one eye sleepily. "What was that in aid of? You sighed very dispiritedly."

"Did I? I didn't mean to. I expect it was just caused by too much food and wine."

"More than likely. Do you intend getting that delicious looking swim suit wet?"

"Yes. I'll take Lisa in as lunch will have gone down by now. Ready, Lisa?"

While they played together in the warm, shallow water, splashing and laughing, Derek propped himself up on his elbow and watched, the frown between his eyes not entirely caused by the sun shining into them. After a little while he got up and stripped off jeans and tee shirt, having swimming trunks beneath, and joined them, delighting Lisa by taking her up on his shoulders and plunging into deeper water. Laurel watched from the edge where small waves washed over her feet. She was actually a very strong swimmer, having taken to the water at a very early age and soon passing various swimming proficiency tests at school, but she remembered that Lorraine had never liked swimming, had always, in fact, detested it, and though it was likely that she might have, in three years, overcome her distaste enough to paddle, it would certainly make Derek suspicious if she suddenly became an excellent swimmer. So though she longed to plunge in after them, she remained on the shore line, a slender, pretty figure in her white one piece suit, and waited for them to come out. When they did approach her, Lisa still high on Derek's shoulders, he seemed to have forgotten for a moment that he was going to keep his distance for he smiled intimately at Laurel, taking her hand and kissing her firmly with soft, salt tasting lips.

"Pity you can't swim," he said. "Why don't you let me teach you?"

Laurel, while her body trembled with delight because of the kiss, managed to smile and shake her head. "No thanks. This is quite enough for me!"

They walked back up the beach, each holding Lisa by a hand and, while the little girl prattled on happily, there was a heavy almost embarrassed silence between the two adults. Once their eyes met briefly and almost shyly and Laurel, the feel of his kiss still upon her lips, reddened and looked swiftly away. By that simple gesture, the lightest and most circumspect of kisses, Derek had aroused her as all the passion in the world could not. They reached the place where they had left their things and she sat swiftly, her back half turned to Derek, suddenly breathless and scared to look at him. She could not have explained her feelings except that somehow things were rising to a crisis.

"Can I go and climb over on those rocks, Daddy?" Lisa asked in her bright, happy voice. "If I take my bucket I might be able to find some crabs."

"All right," Derek agreed equably. "But mind where you walk. Those rocks can be very sharp. Put your shoes on, and don't go out of sight."

They watched her go running across the beach towards the rocks that spread across the beach and out into the sea. No doubt there were numerous rock pools there. Laurel well remembered the delight of splashing about among rock pools, the treasures to be found, crabs, sea anemones, shrimps, limpets . . . it was only then, as she smiled at these memories, that she became aware of how close Derek had moved to her. She turned her head and looked directly into his eyes. He was smiling a little apologetically.

"I didn't keep my word, did I?"

"What?"

"I promised I'd keep away from you. I intended to, honestly, but, God, you looked so beautiful standing there waiting for us that I couldn't resist kissing you. I'm sorry." He didn't look particularly sorry, Laurel thought, turning her head to look out at sea, and he leaned forward, pushing her hair back from her face while the other hand rested lightly on her shoulder. As he spoke the fingers of that hand gently rubbed against the smooth flesh.

"I have to admit that I'm in a terrible muddle as far as you're concerned, Lorraine. I said before that I had begun to wonder whether something *I* said or did in the past made you behave badly. But when you went off with Benson . . ."

She did not hear the rest. Her eyes closed and a shudder went through her. So that was it! Lorraine had run off with Richard Benson, leaving her husband and child. Oh, no wonder Derek had been so bitter towards her, no wonder he had fought against this renewal of his affection towards the woman he thought was his wife. In her pity for him, a pity made all the more tender and painful because of her love for him, she turned tear filled eyes towards him. He saw the tears and smiled.

"Don't, love. It doesn't matter—the past. We said we'd forget it and so we shall. Darling, I've told you my feelings. I love you. And there's no need to consult Lisa about whether or not she wants you to stay with us. There's only you to say the word now . . . is it so difficult?"

"Derek . . . I . . ."

"At least admit you aren't completely indifferent to me." He touched her cheek, turning her face up to him, leaning forward and looking deep into her eyes. His voice was gentle but implacable. He *would* get his anwer. "If I thought there was a real chance of us re-making our lives, then I'd be patient, or at least I'd try to be. You can't look me in the eyes and tell me you don't care at all, can you?"

"No," she whispered, and flicked her tongue over dry lips.

He brushed her hair with his mouth. "Darling, you are a funny little thing. Anyone would think we were almost strangers to each other, or that we had never spoken of love before. Yet we have . . . in the early days." He stroked her arm, his movements rhythmical as he recalled some memory. "I could never understand why you had changed—yet now I wonder if you were really like this all the time and that something about *me* made you change."

"I don't understand," Laurel murmured helplessly, and as he leaned towards her she blindly lifted her head so that their lips met and clung, parting reluctantly. She was living dangerously but somehow, in the last few minutes, the point of no return had been reached. And, as she sat there listening to his calm, even voice, she also knew that no matter what, she had to tell him the truth. She could not let this go on. Not now, not when to tell him would certainly spoil their lovely day, but later, when Lisa was in bed and she and Derek could talk without interruption. She cringed at what she thought his reaction would be but she was, basically, too honest to let it go on now that it had become such a personal, intimate thing.

"I don't think I ever told you where I first saw you, did I?" Derek was saying. He had determinedly moved away from her and was lying back on the towel, eyes narrowed against the sun. Laurel indulged in the luxury of looking at him, her adoring eyes taking in every aspect of his appearance, the wisp of dark hair that flopped a little over his strong, broad forehead, the finely moulded mouth relaxed and mobile as he spoke. Her eyes dwelt lovingly on the smoothly tanned skin of his chest with its liberal covering of black hair. Round his neck he wore a thin gold chain on which hung some kind of small medallion. The impulse to reach out and touch the medallion, to touch him, was almost over powering. She clenched her hands into fists and wondered that someone like herself, someone inexperienced and really quite naïve, could feel such blatant physical desire just by looking at a man. She gasped as a sort of pain hit her, and tried to concentrate on his softly spoken words.

". . . Regent's Street," he said in a soft, slightly drawling voice. "Outside Selfridges. I was with Peter Johnson—you remember him? He has something to do with fashion photography. He wanted to use the helicopter for a series of photographs. Anyway, he suddenly said, 'There's someone I'd give my eye teeth to photograph. That's Lorraine Anderson.' And there you were coming out of the store. I thought at once that you were the loveliest creature I'd ever seen but the impact wasn't that special because, to be quite honest, I was more interested in building up the business then and women took a very secondary part in my life. But then something happened to make me realise you weren't just a pretty face." He smiled without opening his eyes. "Remember?"

"I . . . I'm not sure," Laurel said, puzzled.

"Surely you must. There was a woman standing near you, a very harassed looking female with three young children, and one of them went charging out into the road. And suddenly Lorraine Anderson, who was looking very cool and elegant, as though she didn't give a damn about anyone or anything, shot out into the road and grabbed the child literally from beneath the wheels of a bus. Peter and I were too far away to do anything, but I noticed that you just handed the child over to its mother and got out quickly. I knew nothing about you but your name but I was determined at that moment that I would marry you." He opened his eyes and smiled lazily at her, reaching out one hand and gently encircling her narrow wrist. "Crazy as it may sound, it's true. Remember now?"

"Yes," Laurel whispered and tears suddenly blinded her for she did remember, only too well. If Peter Johnson had been closer he would have known the girl dressed in chain store clothes could not possibly have been *The* Lorraine Anderson. And she longed to cry out: but it was me! Not Lorraine, me!

"Hey, why the tears?" Derek sat up laughing. He glanced over the sand to where Lisa was playing still, where Laurel had been keeping half an eye on her all the time. "You've grown into a real little cry baby, haven't you?" he teased softly. "Come off it, honey. I only told you to explain—well, that it seems to me that now you are the girl I

always thought you were. Come on, sweetheart. Turn off the tap."
He pulled her close and bent his head to find her mouth. Just for a
moment Laurel relented and their bodies, warm from the sun, clung
together in a long, hard embrace. She fell back on the towel and he
bent over her, no longer laughing but serious, whispering urgently, "I
love you. Damn it, I'll make you love me. You do love me, don't
you? Don't you?"

"Yes," she returned brokenly. "I love you." And the sun was
again blotted out by his head. This time he gently moved her hair
away and let his mouth explore her neck and the curves of her shoulders. Lost in delight, Laurel touched the hair at the back of his neck,
letting her fingers dig into it.

Lisa's happy shouts came simultaneously with Derek's stiffening
and moving away, so that Laurel, aware of his withdrawal, assumed
it was because of Lisa and he had remembered himself and pulled
back. She tried to meet his eyes but he was not looking at her
directly but rather at the long slender curve of her throat and neck.
A myriad of emotions seemed to flicker over his expressive face.
First faint puzzlement, then a long searching look that may have
been disbelief, and finally what she could only interpret as anger.
Equally bewildered, she looked back at him and at last his eyes met
hers. He completely ignored Lisa who was dancing round them with
her bucket held out for their inspection. He had paled beneath the
tan and looked like a man in deep shock.

"What's the matter?" Laurel asked, smiling prettily, still too up in
the clouds to find anything ominous in this lightning change of mood.
"You look as though you've seen a ghost."

His lips were dry. He wetted them with his tongue and swallowed
convulsively. "Perhaps I have," he said, so softly she only just caught
the words. Then abruptly he moved, standing up and pulling on his
trousers and tee shirt. "Get Lisa dressed," he ordered in an imperious manner. "It's time we got home."

"But, Daddy, you haven't looked at my crabs," Lisa objected.
"I've got five, look, and . . ."

Laurel could tell from the way he was behaving, inexplicable
though it was, that Derek would take little of his daughter's childish
chatter. Swiftly she took Lisa's hand and led her away. "They're
lovely, darling. But Daddy's right, it is late and we must put the
crabs back or they'll die. Come on and I'll help you. We'll wash your
feet in one of the pools and then I'll carry you back here so that they

won't get sandy again." She rushed Lisa away, pausing only to throw a searching, worried look in Derek's direction. He was tossing everything back into the picnic basket with speed as though his life depended on it. As though he could not bear to stay on the beach one moment longer than necessary.

Almost as if to emphasise the change in mood of the outing, the weather too decided to alter. Before they were half way home the sun had disappeared behind some nasty looking black clouds and one or two heavy drops splattered on the windscreen. Laurel shivered.

"Looks like we're in for a storm."

She received no reply from the stern, hard faced man by her side. Since leaving the beach he had spoken only a few words and these to Lisa. It was as though he had reverted to the man who had arrived at Lorraine's flat to drag her away to High Ridge, and Laurel just could not understand why. It was completely inexplicable, unless—had he suddenly realised he was being a fool, professing love to a wife who had already been unfaithful to him once, or even more than once? Could it be that he suddenly realised that a leopard really doesn't change its spots? This was the only explanation Laurel could find and because she was feeling lost, being plunged from the heights of delight that were to be found in his arms, to the very depths of fear and apprehension, she dared not speculate further.

It was still not quite five o'clock but High Ridge rose out of the gloom of the drizzly evening with lights shining welcomingly. Derek braked the car outside the front door so that Laurel and Lisa could go inside before he drove round to the garage. As she turned to slam the door behind her, Laurel looked once more at Derek. His eyes were cold and without expression. He said shortly, "Go to my office. I want to talk to you."

"All right," she agreed reluctantly, attempting a small, placatory smile that was not returned. "I'll take Lisa up and get her bathed then . . ."

"At once, I said!" he replied with a remorselessness that caused her to shiver. "We have staff quite capable of seeing to Lisa. You be in my study when I get there."

After this, naturally, she was. The study was where Derek did most of the work concerned with his business. It was a practical, quiet room, very orderly with a big desk, much used, and two locked metal filing cabinets. The only indication of Derek's interest came in the photographs of helicopters that were spread round the walls.

Laurel had never been in this room before. She sat herself rather gingerly on the only chair other than the one at the desk but when Derek came in she jumped nervously to her feet and stared, eyes wide with trepidation, at him. He closed the door very softly behind him and stood there a moment, still holding the door knob, while his eyes caught Laurel's and held them. She tried another smile but it was stiff and uncertain and again there was no lightening of his stern features.

When he moved it was abruptly and made her jump. He seemed to erupt from the door, striding towards her and grabbing her by one arm turning her so that she stood near to and facing the window. Wondering what on earth he was up to, she made a feeble attempt to struggle free but his grip on her arm merely tightened. "Stand still!" he ordered and grabbed a handful of her hair, pushing it back so that the left side of her neck was revealed. He stared for a long time at the skin thus laid bare, even touching it quite lightly, though not lovingly, and then a strange sort of shudder went through him.

"It's true then . . . I thought so but I couldn't believe it . . . I was sure I had made a mistake . . . it was like some crazy nightmare. And yet . . . my God, you're not Lorraine, are you?"

SIX

A LITTLE CRY of anguish escaped Laurel's lips and she clapped her hand over her mouth in a vain attempt to hold the cry back. She would have dragged herself away but he hauled her close to him, openly furious now that she was unable to deny his words. His face was dark browed, the green eyes narrow and vicious. "You're not, are you? Goddamn you, answer me, you bitch! I know you're not Lorraine. She had a scar on her neck. Even accounting for plastic surgery, it couldn't have been removed so completely. So don't try lying to me or bluffing your way out of it."

This was the last thing Laurel had thought of doing. Through all this he was shaking her, shaking her until she felt sick and confused and clutched his arms in an attempt to stop him. She could not have spoken because her teeth were rattling, so that though he continued to demand her name, she was unable to answer. Eventually he seemed to realise her predicament and stopped the shaking though he retained the painful grip on her upper arms.

"I . . . I'm Laurel," she whispered.

"Laurel? Laurel who?"

"Anderson. I'm Lorraine's sister."

"Lorraine's sister?" he repeated. "I didn't know she had a sister."

"She has . . . me. We're twin sisters. Identical twins."

"I . . . see." Slowly his fingers relaxed their steely grip and Laurel was able to move away, rubbing her arms. There would be the most terrible bruises there but that was the least of her worries. She cared about nothing now. He knew and he naturally despised her, and there was nothing left in her world. She watched him with stricken eyes. He was still angry and she could only guess at his hurt. And she did guess it from his pallor and the way he shook his head uncertainly and rubbed one hand through the thickness of his hair. But as she watched he seemed to shed the pain and the anger and became colder and more watchful; his voice when he finally spoke was completely without warmth or feeling. The very sound of the flat, even voice told Laurel how utterly and completely she had been tried, found guilty and condemned.

"Perhaps you might care to enlighten me as to the whereabouts of my wife," he said sarcastically.

"I don't know where she is."

"Oh, God!" he burst out. "You've done quite enough damage, you bitch, without telling me that kind of lie!"

"It isn't a lie, truly. I don't know. She went on a modelling assignment—all over the world. I have no idea where she is."

Evidently he decided to believe this for he did not immediately press the point. He picked up a packet of cigarettes from the desk and lit one with hands that were perfectly steady. Laurel marvelled at a man who could gain control of himself so completely and in such a short time. She realised he was looking at her, studying her face with curious detachment.

"You're very like," he said, in the same far away, almost polite voice. "I don't know why I didn't guess, yet the similarity really is surprising even in identical twins. I suppose most people would consider you to be 'nicer' but I'm not so sure. After all, you've played your part so well, haven't you . . . Laurel? I presume you must be even more immoral than Lorraine."

"No!" Laurel whispered. "It wasn't like that, Derek. Oh, please believe me. I know it must seem bad to you but . . ."

"Bad!" he interrupted loudly. "Bad? My God, that's a good one. Don't you realise what you've done? Not only to me, but to Lisa too, and to Caroline. What am I supposed to do now? Go and tell them that we've all been fooled by a scheming little bitch who's only after . . . God knows what it is you're after . . . money I suppose. I could break your neck, by God I could!"

"You made me come here!" Laurel cried out, stung into speech by this. "Have you forgotten that I didn't want to come? If you remember, you threatened me and made me come . . . you . . ."

"I didn't threaten *you*. I threatened Lorraine. Which brings up a very interesting point. What were you doing there in the first place? Why the need to pose as Lorraine? She couldn't possibly have known I was going to fetch her."

"No, she didn't." Laurel's mind ran wild as it searched through a maze of thoughts. Lies and deception had been given enough rein over the past weeks; she had to tell so much of the truth. But even then she found herself trying to defend Lorraine. Her one thought was that she must not let him know that Lorraine was with Richard Benson. Afterwards she despised herself for this but just then habit was very strong.

"You were already living in the apartment pretending to be Lorraine," he pointed out. "Why?"

"I . . . it was a sort of joke," Laurel lied desperately. "We used to do it when we were children, just for fun. We were . . . we thought we'd try fooling some of her friends. Then when you turned up I panicked and—well, I didn't know where she was to let her know, so I . . ." Her voice trailed away. It was hopeless. He had come close to her and was staring incredulously at her.

"Don't give me that rubbish. I'm beginning to see how it was. I think I know the workings of my beloved wife's mind quite well, certainly better than I thought. I suppose she knew I wouldn't go on paying her such a generous allowance if she went running round the world with—well, who is she with?"

"I—I don't know."

In a moment he had her wrist behind her back and was twisting it with ruthless fingers. Laurel cried out and tried to go limp against him, lessening the pain. She understood his anger and knew that, with only her to take it out on, he might well make her suffer to alleviate his own disillusionment. Tears forced their way between her closed lids as he hissed in her ear, "I don't suppose I actually would break your arm though I admit it's very tempting. But I'm warning you, sweetheart, I'm very nearly at the end of my tether, so you'd better tell me now who she's with."

"She's with Richard Benson," Laurel whispered. Immediately she was released and, just as quickly, she burst into tears, putting her hands over her face so that the water ran between her fingers. Unmoved by this, he watched as she struggled to regain control of herself, finally saying with a sneer in his voice, "Don't think you'll get round me like that, sweetie. All those tears have succeeded in doing is make you look red and blotchy, not a sight likely to turn any man's heart. So I should stop that particular strategy. It just won't work with me."

Laurel found her handkerchief at last and blew her nose hard, finally looking at him with red rimmed eyes—she was past caring what she looked like, saying with quiet dignity, "I wasn't crying for that reason. I know you won't believe me, but I didn't want to hurt anyone—Lisa, Caroline or—you. I didn't even know about Lisa when I came here. Really I didn't. And I didn't think much harm would come of it. I am sorry, Derek, really I am."

She turned away and had reached the door before he spoke again. "And where do you think you're going?"

"To pack. I'll leave as soon as possible."

"Oh, no you won't!" He moved as swiftly as he had previously, putting his large frame between her and the door, slamming it shut and turning to face her. Startled, Laurel stepped back, raising her tear stained face to his. He was still a little blurred and she blinked hard to clear her eyes of the last remaining tears.

"You aren't getting away with it that easily, my dear . . . sister-in-law," he said softly, his mouth quirking into a little cruel smile.

"What do you mean? It would be best if I left, then you . . ."

"And what do I explain to Caroline? That all the time she was being fooled not only by you but by me also? That the 'love' we had shown each other before her was no more than the humouring of an old sick woman? Oh, no, you aren't going to do that to her. I shall make an attempt to find out Lorraine's whereabouts but in the meantime you will stay here and no one—no one!—will know that you are not my wife. That will be our little secret." His eyes glinted with cold green lights and quite deliberately he walked towards Laurel. She backed away until she felt the hard ridge of his desk and had to stop walking, then he arched her back painfully over the desk. She shivered as his long hands encircled her neck.

"And if you give anyone cause to think otherwise, I shall have very little hesitation in making you very, very sorry. Do you understand me, Laurel?"

"Yes." It was no more than a mouthing of the word but he understood.

"Good. Then I suggest you go and get changed for dinner. If you remember, the Gregsons are coming." He smiled grimly. "I had, of course, been assuming you know them but I suppose I'd better help your deception by filling you in on a few details about them. Get dressed and come down to the lounge. And remember what I said." Briefly his hands tightened, the thumbs forcing her chin up so that she was unable to escape the cold implacability in his eyes. When he loosened his grip she tore away from him as though his touch had burned her.

Laurel's hands were shaking as she fastened a gold pendant round her neck and surveyed herself in the full length mirror in her bedroom. She knew, in some part of her mind, that despite, or perhaps because of, the paleness of her face that caused her eyes to stand out hugely, she had never looked lovelier. The dress she wore was of navy blue jersey silk with an empire style waist line, a low round neck and full sleeves falling to the elbow. She had chosen it because the sleeves hid the terrible looking bruises that Derek's fingers had left on her upper arms, but it was a good choice anyway. Her hair had been newly washed and shone red and gold in the artificial light. She made herself up carefully, knowing that she must somehow look and behave like Lorraine. This had never been easy to do and, knowing that Derek would be watching her every move, she was sure this evening it would be even harder. At the thought of Derek she closed her eyes as a spasm of pure misery shot through her. Despite his cruel and heartless treatment, his refusal to listen to explanations, she knew that her love for him was unaltered. It had crept up on her unawares and could not now be turned off easily. In no way could she blame him for his behaviour towards her. How could she? Her behaviour had been far more iniquitous and the least she could do was try to continue her deception for the sake of Lisa and Caroline.

It had become her usual practice to visit Caroline in the early evening so now, having ensured that her appearance was good enough to satisfy even Derek, she went along to the old lady's room. Over the weeks Laurel had become convinced that Caroline's health was steadily improving; she had seemed so much brighter and livelier lately, sitting right up in bed and showing an interest in life. She had asked to see Lisa and was so cheerful that the little girl was in no way disturbed by being in the sick room; she had asked to have her radiogram moved into the room so that she could listen to some of her favourite records. Tonight, when Laurel knocked softly and entered, although the lovely strains of a Chopin nocturne filled the room, Caroline seemed different. It was almost as though she had shrunk into the pillows, her face as pale as they, and the paralysed side of her face was noticeably worse. Laurel stayed for half an hour, more disturbed and anxious than she had ever been, straining to raise a smile to the old, lined face. Eventually Caroline summoned up her efforts and managed a faint smile as she patted Laurel's hand.

"I'm tired tonight, child, so tired. You go off and enjoy yourself. I'll be all right. I have the bell to call the nurse if I need anything." She managed another small smile, a travesty of her usual one. "You look lovely, Lorraine. No wonder Derek adores you."

Laurel's face was solemn as she left the room. For a moment her own troubles had faded into insignificance and even when she went into the lounge to be faced by a grim faced Derek, she could not immediately bring herself back to this particular reality.

"Where have you been?" he demanded abruptly. "I knocked on your door on the way down."

"I was with Caroline." Laurel accepted the sherry and cigarette he offered with the actions of an automaton. She vaguely realised that he was wearing a dinner jacket and looked superb, but even this failed to arouse her. "She isn't at all well," she murmured.

"I've told you before that she won't get any better." Derek's voice was strained. "Don't you think I haven't had all the specialists I could get to give their opinions? She's just an old old lady whose body is worn out."

"I know that! But she was looking much better. But tonight she seemed so frail and tiny."

Derek was struck with a sudden, vicious desire to hurt. There was an uncontrollable sneer in his voice. "Don't take your role too seriously, darling. Remember you don't have to pretend in front of me. I happen to know you don't give a damn about Caroline."

"That isn't true!" Laurel flashed at him, her mood of indifference to him shattered. "I do care! She's a wonderful old lady and I've become very fond of her. What do you think I am?"

"I don't know. What are you?" he muttered. "A cold hearted bitch, with the face and figure of an angel, I'd say. An interesting combination, my dear, yet in some ways quite a challenge."

She flinched at the words but held her ground. "What does that mean?"

"You'll see," he told her unpleasantly. "One of these days. But now, sit down. I'll tell you about the Gregsons."

Afterwards Laurel remembered very little about that particular dinner party. The Gregsons were a pleasant enough middle aged couple who had apparently known Derek several years and were actually present at his and Lorraine's wedding. They were in no way suspicious of "Lorraine's" true identity but were very pleased to hear that she and Derek were attempting to make a go of their marriage. Derek seemed to be enjoying himself tremendously. He took a great delight in playing the role of lover and lost no opportunity of touching Laurel, holding her hand, putting one arm round her, even kissing her in a light hearted way, and there was little she could do about it. By the time the Gregsons had departed her earlier temper had long since vanished to be replaced by a deep rooted despair. Her head ached and she remained downstairs only long enough to see the visitors off as politeness dictated before slipping away to her bedroom. She wondered in a moment of madness whether it might not be better just to go, to pack her suitcase there and then and slip away in the middle of the night. She could walk all night and in the morning catch a bus to Cowes and the ferry. But she felt so tired and dispirited that she doubted her ability to walk five hundred yards. Drearily she sank down on the bed, kicking off her sandals and tucking her feet up under her. She rested her head on the pillows and closed her eyes as she wondered in desperation how long it would be before Lorraine could be found. . . .

She must have slept but probably not for long. She awoke because she was a light sleeper and always woke if someone came into her bedroom. Derek was standing by the closed door watching her and as she scrambled inelegantly to her feet a slow, derisive smile touched his mouth. He had discarded his dinner jacket and undone the top two buttons of his shirt. His hair was slightly tousled and Laurel was inclined to think he had been drinking.

"What do you want?" she asked, still a little sleepy as she attempted to keep her voice firm.

"What do you think?" he murmured, and his voice was slightly slurred. "I was sure you'd be in bed by now."

"As you can see, I'm not. So if you'll go, I'll . . ."

"Oh, no," he said remorselessly, leaning against the door and folding his arms. "I'm not going anywhere. You go ahead and get ready for bed. After all, I'm your husband, aren't I?"

Now she was sure he must be drunk, completely drunk, though he certainly did not look it. Her father, who was frequently in an inebriated condition, was incoherent, staggering and pathetic; Derek looked cool, utterly in control of himself and all the more dangerous because of it. Yet only drink, she was sure, could make him behave so badly. She bit her lip uncertainly and wondered what to do. She had learned to cope with her father but Derek was a very different proposition.

"What's the matter?" he demanded to know. "I've come to my wife's bedroom, what's so terrible about that? I've had a wife some years now and precious little comfort I've got from the fact. Well, I think it's time I claimed my . . . conjugal rights. Don't you agree, Lorraine? Or should I say Laurel?"

"Derek, stop it," she said sharply, taking two or three uncertain steps towards him. "This is ridiculous and you know it. I know you're trying to punish me by frightening me like this, and believe me you're succeeding. But you'll regret it in the morning, you know you will."

"Regret it? No, I don't think so, beautiful. You see, you were playing with fire when you came here pretending to be my wife. What did Lorraine tell you about me, huh? That I stood by without lifting a finger when she ran off with her lover? Well, maybe I did, but I can assure you it wasn't because I'm the sort of man that would let a woman trample all over him. I wasn't too sorry to see the back of her."

"She didn't tell me anything much about you," Laurel murmured. By now he was standing only inches from her and her firmness turned to mesmerised horror as he began to undo his shirt. She knew that the only chance was to talk him out of it but doubted if she knew the right words. A fate worse than death? Well, perhaps not.

But she knew that to be made love to by him because of his anger and humiliation and hurt pride would be almost as bad as dying.

"Derek, if you'd only let me explain to you exactly what happened, I'm sure you'd . . ."

"Explain?" he interrupted harshly. "There's nothing to explain. You and Lorraine may have thought it would be a great joke to fool everyone, but I assure you the laugh is on you. You've been pretending for some weeks now that you're my wife, so now I think you owe me something. Right?"

He reached for her arms, already bruised by his earlier treatment of her and inexorably pulled her closer. She managed to get both hands flat against his chest but even by pushing with all her strength she could not prevent herself being drawn against him. She was aware of his heart thudding fiercely beneath her hands and that her own breathing was coming in harsh little sobs.

"Derek, stop this now. I'll scream if you don't let me go. I will. I'll scream the place down."

"No you won't. Lisa is sleeping next door. You wouldn't want to waken her and frighten her. Besides, you love me, you said so this afternoon. You should be quite willing to prove that love."

"I didn't mean it!" she gasped, pulling her mouth away before his could touch it. "I hate you! I don't blame Lorraine for leaving you if you behave like this. You're hateful and cruel and conceited and . . ." She was gasping these words in a weak, breathless voice and for all the notice he took of them she might as well not have spoken. With a particularly fierce effort he overcame her struggles, ignoring the hands that pushed at his chest and holding her hard against his body. With his mouth on hers, Laurel was unable to struggle further, was almost unable to breathe. Her body ached with the effort of holding him off, her brain swirled as she struggled to get some air. She felt as though she might faint and certainly waves of thick, dark clouds seemed to sweep over her. She hung limp in his arms, no longer able to prevent him doing anything he wished . . .

There was a soft, insistent tapping on the door. With a muffled oath, Derek released Laurel so that she staggered and fell back on to the bed. Their eyes met and held and the only sound in the room was of their breathing. Then the knocking came again and a voice said softly and urgently, "Mrs. Clayton, are you awake? Mrs. Clayton."

It was Mrs. Mac. Laurel got unsteadily to her feet but still hesitated, even when Derek told her to open the door. She stared doubtfully at him and he said with irritation, "For God's sake, I'm supposed to be your husband. Where else would I be at this time of night but in your bedroom?"

In silence Laurel walked past him and opened the door. Mrs. Mac took a couple of steps into the room. She looked agitated and worried but still took time to glance curiously at Laurel's tear smudged face and wild hair, and Derek's naked chest and dishevelled appearance. Laurel had thought for some time that Mrs. Mac guessed that the relationship between herself and Derek was not all that it seemed, and no doubt this little scene would give her much food for thought in the future. Just now, however, she had more important things on her mind. Seeing Derek, she turned to him, ignoring Laurel.

"It's Miss Caroline, sir, she's taken a bad turn. The nurse is doing what she can and I've called the doctor. But it looks bad, very bad."

From then on and for the rest of the night a sense of complete unreality crept over Laurel. Coming after the scene with Derek, the shocking news about Caroline hit harder than it might otherwise have done. Afterwards when she recalled the night—and never without a shudder—she remembered the darkened room lit only by a small lamp, and Caroline's laboured breathing as she held on to the tiny spark of life that kept a small pulse fluttering in her thin wrist; and Derek sitting beside the bed, dramatically sobered, harsh lines of unhappiness and remorse on his face; and finally the moment when the doctor straightened up and, glancing across at Derek, slowly shook his head. . . .

Laurel knew she should leave the room. Derek had the right to suffer his unhappiness alone. That he was quite distraught she knew though he gave no outward sign of it. But Laurel, loving him so that her senses towards him were most acutely attuned, felt the stiffness of his body, the unsteady breathing, the way his jaw line worked as though he were gritting his teeth. She noticed a little pulse beating in his temple. She longed to comfort him and thus herself be comforted and after a moment of looking sadly down at Caroline's still, lifeless body, nerved herself to whisper his name. Like a man in a trance he raised his head and stared, almost unseeing, at her. It must have been like losing his mother, she realised. After all, Caroline had been all the mother he ever had. Gently, infinitely compassionate, she reached out and touched his hand. He continued to stare and then, firmly and determinedly, moved his hand from hers. His eyes were cold.

"What are you doing here? You don't belong here."

Tears hotly filled Laurel's eyes, tears that she had, until then, held back. "I loved her too."

"Love? What do you know about love?" The question was softly spoken and meant very little. She doubted that he even knew he had said the words. He was staring at Caroline, his eyes far, far away. As Laurel watched, he reached out and gently tucked her hand beneath the covers. Softly Laurel got up and stole out of the room.

She discovered that now she had started crying she couldn't stop. It was, she supposed, nervous reaction of some sort. The best thing would be to go to her room and hide herself away, but she could not face the room with its ruffled bed and Derek's shirt flung across it. Instead she went to the lounge and sat with her back to the door, mopping up the tears as they appeared. They came silently, unaccompanied by the usual sobs and sniffles and the more she wiped her cheeks and eyes, the more they fell.

SEVEN

IT WAS very quiet in the lounge, quiet and rather chilly. Clothed still in the thin evening gown, Laurel had her arms crossed over her breasts and was clutching her bare arms. She was shivering a little but scarcely noticed it or the cold. At some time or other the sky had begun to lighten and she got up and switched off the light and pulled back the curtains. Over the sea dawn was breaking; the sky was a pale, greyish blue and as she watched, the sun slid up out of the sea. At the same moment a blackbird burst into a streaming, silver song that took Laurel's breath away. The silence that followed must have lasted at least a minute then suddenly it seemed as though every bird for miles around was singing. Laurel realised she was listening to the dawn chorus. Enthralled she stood before the window, her head thrown back as she listened, the tears drying on her face. A small sound from within the room broke into her consciousness and she turned, startled, to see that Derek had come in and was in the process of putting a tray laden with coffee pot and cups on the table. He said nothing but straightened up and walked over to where Laurel stood, his eyes going to the window and its glorious view of the sun streaked sea.

"It's beautiful, isn't it?" Laurel murmured, looking up at his profile. She thought he seemed different, quieter, more withdrawn and sombre, somehow more at peace with himself. At some time during the night he had put on another shirt and changed the trousers of his dinner suit for corduroy slacks. He lit a cigarette and the smoke curled past his narrowed eyes. The smell of the tobacco mingled in Laurel's nostrils with the delicious aroma of coffee. She discovered she was hungry.

"Is there plenty of coffee in the pot?" she inquired, her voice gentle as she feared spoiling the moment and bringing his wrath down upon her head once more. But he merely nodded and she went to pour out two cups. While she was doing this she glanced up and his eyes were on her.

"Why aren't you in bed?" he asked. "It's not five o'clock yet."

"I . . . wouldn't have been able to sleep. I just came in here and—and sort of stayed." Her voice trailed away into uncertainty. It sounded lame and stupid and no wonder he was looking faintly sceptical. She could not believe he cared one way or the other how she had spent the night but when she handed him the coffee he said in a strange, deep tone, "You stayed . . . and cried."

"What?"

"Evidence," he said dryly, bending over the settee and picking up a small white handkerchief, crumpled and damp. He held it up thoughtfully before dropping it into her outstretched palm.

"I was upset—about Caroline," she said shakily.

"Is that all that upset you?" he asked, his eyes searching her white face, and she, knowing what he meant, nodded vigorously. Not for all the world would she let him see how much *his* behaviour had contributed to her unhappiness.

"I know you don't believe me, but I had grown to love her. I've been with her a lot lately. We've talked about all sorts of things and I always hated deceiving her. Sometimes it seemed to me that she knew I wasn't Lorraine, but of course that's impossible. But I did care about her, honestly I did." Unexpectedly tears welled in her eyes. She had thought she was all cried out and quickly turned her head from him.

"Use this," he said, handing her his own large handkerchief. "It's a bit more substantial."

His voice was unexpectedly gentle and this, it seemed, was the final straw. Her strength completely drained away and Laurel simply howled. She sat on the settee and everything, all the emotions of weeks, came bursting forth. She had cried gently before when on her own but now, when she would most wish to be less histrionic, she could not stop the flood. She rested her head against the arm of the settee and her body lurched with painful sobs. For a while Derek watched impassively, his eyes still narrow and considering, his face blank as though he cared nothing about whether or not she cried herself into hysteria. But eventually, with a gesture almost of resignation, he stubbed out his cigarette and went to sit by her, grabbing her shoulders and shaking her.

"Stop it, Laurel. You'll make yourself ill and that won't help anyone. Laurel, stop it right now!" He shook her again, harder, and this, coupled with the harsher tone of his voice, seemed to calm her. She stopped sobbing and stared at him, the blood draining from her wet face.

"I'm sorry," she whispered. "I'm sorry. I didn't mean to . . . I couldn't . . ."

"Forget it," he said coolly. "I guess it's been a hellish night. You shouldn't have been left alone. Here, drink your coffee." He handed her the cup and lit a cigarette which he placed between her lips. These lips trembled a little as did her hands.

"Don't be nice to me," she whispered. "I can't stand it."

He smiled faintly at this rather silly remark and asked baldly, "Would you rather I behaved as I did when last we were alone?"

"No—but even that didn't make me cry!" she replied and his smile widened.

"No, it didn't, did it? And you would have fought me all the way, wouldn't you, Laurel? Despite the fact that earlier you seemed to enjoy my kisses."

"That was different!" she responded with as much spirit as she could muster after the long harrowing night. Tiredness was beginning to scratch little aches up and down her backbone and her eyes were suddenly desperately heavy.

"Yes, it was different," he agreed sombrely, his voice coming from a long way off. "In fact, I think we should have a talk, Laurel, a serious talk. What do you think?"

"Anything you say," she murmured, at last giving way to the temptation to let her lids close over her eyes. "You'll never believe me," she murmured. "That I only did it because Lorraine said . . . because I thought. . . ."

"What?" he demanded, his voice echoing in her head as he leaned forward, tense and anxious. "Why did you do it, Laurel?"

"I can't remember. I'm so tired. Just let me sleep. Please let me."

"All right," he agreed, giving in reluctantly. "But we will have that talk."

Through her sleepiness she was aware that he had lifted her in his arms and was carrying her up the stairs. As he walked into her bedroom she came to sufficiently to struggle feebly, opening her eyes and whispering, "No, no!"

"Don't be ridiculous," he said sternly. "I can assure you I have no intention of carrying on where I left off. That particular . . . demon has been well and truly exorcised." He laid her on the bed and for one moment, as she stared up at him, leaned over her, one hand either side of her head. "I'm sorry about that demon, Laurel. I'm not really such a monster . . . and I'll always hope and believe that if it had come to the point I wouldn't actually have harmed you. It would be too much to expect you to believe that but . . ."

"I do believe it," she said, opening her eyes wide and looking up at him. He stared down at her and suddenly his mouth was against her cheek, soft and sweet and brief, there and gone before she could do more than close her eyes for the kiss. When she opened them it was in time to see the door close softly behind him.

* * *

"Is it true that Auntie Caroline has gone to Jesus?" Lisa asked. "That's what Mrs. Mac told me, but if it's true, why is everyone so sad?" They were in the playroom having breakfast and Lisa touched Laurel's face. "Your cheeks are all puffy. Have you been crying?" she asked rather severely.

"Yes, dear. Even though Caroline will be happy, naturally I'm sad that we won't see her again." It was only a small white lie, Laurel thought. She could not possibly admit to Lisa the true cause of these particular tears.

"Shall I cry too?" Lisa demanded, and Laurel smiled and hugged her.

"No, Lisa. Auntie Caroline was old and ill. She's all right now and won't feel any more pain." It wasn't easy, she reflected, presenting death in an honest way to a child as intelligent as Lisa. Perhaps Mrs. Mac's stark "gone to Jesus" explanation was the best.

She poured herself some more tea and wondered what was going to happen today. Every day was a little like part of an obstacle race course but she never knew what particular obstacles were going to crop up until they did actually loom up before her. It was two days now since Caroline died and a state of truce had developed between herself and Derek. Sometimes she thought he wanted to make their relationship warmer, more as it had been for those brief moments the morning after Caroline's death, when he had carried her to bed and kissed her so sweetly. But then he would hold back and become aloof. Yesterday was the funeral, a dismal affair not improved by Mrs. Mac's morbid carrying on, or by Derek's obvious ill temper. Laurel assumed the temper was his way of keeping his mourning a secret and forgave him for it, but she thought it unreasonable that he should take it out on her.

Today the obstacle came in the form of a solicitor from Newport, Caroline's solicitor, a small, lively man named Jason Harcourt, whom Laurel had met before, just three weeks earlier when he visited Caroline and stayed the night at High Ridge. That morning before breakfast, Laurel was informed by Derek that she would be required at the reading of the will.

"Me? But I . . . what for? I can't imagine that . . ."

"Put it this way," he said coldly. "You're required in your rôle as Lorraine. Naturally you are not mentioned personally in the will since Caroline did not know of your existence."

"Well, since it's not me, I don't see why I have to attend," she objected, and was interrupted by one of his thankfully rare bursts of vicious temper.

"You'll damn well go and what's more you'll behave yourself! That threat I made before, when I found out who you are, still stands. Your lovely neck is no less breakable now than it was then."

It was this, of course, that had brought on the tears commented upon by Lisa. Laurel did not believe that Derek would actually carry out his threat but it hurt unbearably that he should still think so badly of her. She felt a little disgusted with her lack of backbone; she seemed to do nothing but cry lately. But she had hoped Derek would begin to realise she was not the deceitful gold digger he had first thought her, and she was quite sure he felt some sort of attraction for her. But she was also sure he would fight that attraction all the way, determined not to show any more warmth in relation to her.

The will began with the usual list of small bequests, to Mrs. Mac, to the nurse who had been with Caroline for several months, and finally to some of Caroline's pet charities. Derek, Laurel knew, was expecting little for he was a wealthy man in his own right and had mentioned long ago to his aunt that he would rather she left her money in trust to Lisa rather than to him. He looked satisfied and pleased to learn that Caroline had done as he wished; Lisa, on her eighteenth birthday, would be a very well off young lady without any help from her father. However, sheer incredulity broke over the faces of both he and Laurel when the solicitor read the final clause.

"To my nephew's wife, Lorraine Margaret Clayton, I leave the sum of twenty thousand pounds, conditional only on her remaining with my nephew in a state of marital bliss for a period of at least two years." Mr. Harcourt added, without looking up, "Miss Clayton added the rider that naturally she hopes this state of affairs will continue all your lives and not just for the stated two years."

Into the silence that followed broke a sound that caused Laurel to wince. Derek let out a shout of laughter, harsh laughter that echoed round the room and caused the solicitor to look up in astonishment and to open his mouth to question this strange reaction. But Derek was looking across at Laurel. "Well, well, my sweet, you and Lorr . . . and your sister are well and truly hoist with your own petard. You did very well indeed coming here and getting round Caroline in that manner but you'd have done better to stay away. Obviously you didn't know she had left you ten thousand unconditionally in her previous will. I would say that was better than twice the amount under such conditions." He laughed again.

"Mr. Clayton, I am not quite sure I understand you," Jason Harcourt put in tentatively. "Are you presuming your wife will be unwilling to abide by the conditions set out by the will?"

"I really don't know," Derek replied, still not taking his eyes off Laurel. "I suppose the persuasive powers of twenty thousand pounds is quite considerable. I shall just have to wait and ask my wife, won't I?"

At this point Laurel got up and walked out, stiffly but with dignity. She hardly knew what she was going to do; she simply walked and eventually found herself in the garden. She needed the fresh air after the things Derek had said. A few minutes after she had got outside she heard footsteps, his footsteps, behind her. Panic stirred in her and she contemplated running, but that was pointless. She could never run in her slender, high heeled sandals, and even with decent shoes she had no hope of outdistancing him. So she turned from the garden and walked instead through the french windows into the lounge where at least they could not be overlooked.

"What's the matter?" Derek asked, grasping her by the arm and turning her to face him. "Don't you think she'll go fifty-fifty with you? She ought to because I doubt if she'd have brought about such results. It was clever of you both to decide that you'd got more chance of getting round Caroline than Lorraine had. She would never have stayed the course as you have. I daresay she'll give you a fair hand out."

Laurel snatched her arm from his hand, beside herself with fury. "Don't touch me! Don't you dare come near me! How dare you say such things! Not only are they terrible things to accuse me of, but, if you'd only think, they're stupid as well. I didn't come here of my own free will, you practically forced me. Neither Lorraine nor I knew Caroline was ill and I certainly had no idea until today that she was so wealthy. You've got the lowest mind of anyone I've ever been unfortunate enough to meet. I suppose you think the twenty thousand pounds should be yours . . ."

"Not in the least. I'm just wondering whether Lorraine will think that much money is worth putting up with me for two years. Or will she try sending you as her deputy again?"

For the second time in her life, Laurel hit him across his mouth, this time with her clenched fist, an unladylike punch with all her strength behind it. His head snapped back and his hand went up to his face, the fingers coming away wet with blood. There was a small jagged cut near his mouth where her dress ring had struck. The sight of the blood horrified Laurel too much for her to worry about what he might do in retaliation. As he stared in bemused wonder at his bloody fingers she clapped her hand over her mouth and wailed, "Oh, Derek, I'm sorry. Oh, God, have I hurt you? I didn't mean to . . ."

"Of course you meant to," he said in a peculiar voice, staring at her stricken face not with anger but with a hint of amused respect. "And no doubt I deserved it."

"No," she gulped. "It was all understandable, what you said. It isn't true, but I can see why you thought it. Oh, Derek, I didn't. . . ."

"Shut up," he said, still in the same odd voice, a low voice with no inflection whatsoever. "You talk too much."

She found herself being taken firmly by the elbows and pulled close to him. She stared up at him, seeing tiny reflections of herself in the green of his eyes. "D—do I?" she whispered.

"Far too much. So I suggest you keep quiet for the next few minutes while I see if I can't sort out all the misunderstandings. Do you think you can manage it?"

"I'll try," she murmured, a second before his mouth contacted with hers. Her arms slid round him and her eyes closed. She was lost, drowning in the loveliness of this thing that was happening. Once she muttered his name, but immediately his mouth was firmly on hers again and there was no time for words. Later the explanations would come but just for the moment nothing mattered except this physical demonstration of their love.

"I still think I owe you some kind of explanation," Laurel murmured later. She was cradled on Derek's lap, the fingers of one hand in his hair while she dabbed at the small cut on his mouth with her handkerchief.

"You do, do you? I don't. It doesn't matter."

"Of course it does. I don't want you thinking badly of me."

"I don't." He smiled lazily at her, pulling her closer and nuzzling gently into her neck. "You told me you didn't get friendly with Caroline for her money and I believe you. That's all that matters. That and the fact that I'm crazy about you."

"But don't you want to know why I was pretending to be Lorraine in the first place?"

"I don't want to think about Lorraine at all. I want to think about you. I love you." He smiled again. "And you'd better damn well say you love me or I'll want to know the reason why."

Laurel kissed him. "I've loved you for ages, but I felt it was wrong. It *is* wrong. After all, you are still married to Lorraine and . . ."

"And you aren't the sort of girl to run round with married men. I know. It's a hell of a situation." He drew her head down on his shoulder and for a while they remained silent, thinking about what had happened to both of them. Derek's expression was grave as he lightly stroked one hand over Laurel's hair. Then he lifted Laurel to her feet and stood up, taking her immediately into his arms again. "I'll worry about that later. Hell, we've got to find the woman first. Personally I don't care if we never find her." He tightened his arms round Laurel and lowered his head towards hers. They were lost in their love and neither one heard the french windows swing open.

"Well, well, well," Lorraine drawled. "How very . . . touching. I do hope you realise, Derek darling, that that isn't your wife you're embracing."

It was Laurel who went white and jumped out of Derek's arms as though he had suddenly become charged with electricity. It was she who looked guilty, as though she had been caught out in some dreadful misdemeanour. Derek merely stood still, looking at his wife in silence, only his eyes alive in a face as still and cold as marble. His eyes then moved slowly over Lorraine's figure, taking in the elegant expense of her calf length silk dress, her beautiful legs clad in flesh coloured tights, the mink jacket slung carelessly over her shoulders. He looked at her lovely face and slowly smiled. "Oh, yes, Lorraine, I know. Personally I think I must have been out of my mind not to realise the deception weeks ago. I should have known you could never be so human or so beautiful in all ways as Laurel is."

Momentarily taken aback and angry, Lorraine recovered rapidly and smiled with about as much humour as Derek had smiled. "Now, now, darling, that's no way to talk about your long-lost wife." She looked coldly into her sister's pale face. "You certainly managed to entrench yourself well. I find it hard to believe that when I found you after the old man died, you looked like a down at heel tramp. It's amazing what money and know-how can do."

Before Laurel could even think of a reply, Derek had moved forward, his voice lashing at Lorraine. "That's quite enough of that! You will behave civilly in this house or leave. If you think you can just walk out and then come back again without a please or thank you, you're very much mistaken. You can just keep a still tongue in your head and leave Laurel out of this. What there is to be said is between you and me, and by Christ you won't find me quite such an easy proposition as before."

Laurel thought that if he had spoken to her in that tone of voice, not shouting, but softly and with deadly undertones, she would have shrivelled up and backed down, but Lorraine was too sure of her own worth to be thus intimidated. She merely raised her eyebrows quizzically and pouted a little.

"Oh, Derek, there's no need for you to defend my sister. But you must admit it's strange. I left her to live in my apartment because I felt sorry for her. I even gave her some of my money and clothes. And when I get back I discover she has come here deceiving you by pretending to be me."

"Lorraine!" Laurel cried out, horrified, but Derek raised one hand to her, admonishing her to be still.

"You can save your breath, Lorraine. I happen to know the whole story and, strange as it might seem to you, I find myself believing Laurel's version. So perhaps you'll tell me what you want and then take your very unwelcome presence out of my house."

"*Your* house? Darling, I am your wife and have certain rights. I've decided to come back to you. Isn't that lovely? And before you say anything, there's really very little you can do about it. You can't very well throw me out—that wouldn't be very good for your image, and you can't divorce me because there are no grounds."

"Divorce laws aren't quite what they were," Derek reminded her dryly. "And do you really think I give a damn about my image?"

They seemed to have forgotten Laurel was still there. She stood near the door watching, her heart surrounded by a curious, aching pain that she could not describe. She felt sick and ashamed and most of all desperately miserable. She didn't know anything at all about divorce laws but surely by coming back to Derek voluntarily Lorraine was making it very difficult. And besides, there was. . . .

"Lisa," Lorraine was saying coolly. "My daughter. I've been dying to see her. It wouldn't look very good, would it, if people knew you had allowed your daughter to believe that Laurel was her mother?"

"Do you think I care what other people think?" Derek demanded angrily.

"Perhaps not, but I'm sure you care what Lisa would think. Where is she, by the way? I'm longing to see her."

"Like hell you are! You never wanted to see her, not even after she was born."

Lorraine shrugged. "Maybe not, but I've seen the error of my ways. Where is she? In the playroom? I'll go and see her."

Both Derek and Laurel stood immobilised as she swung round and walked out. They listened to the tap of her heels on the marble hall floor, then Derek turned to Laurel.

"You'd better go with her," she said swiftly, before he could speak. "You don't know what she'll say."

He nodded. "Wait here," he said softly, giving her a ghostly smile. "Just . . . wait here, my love."

"Don't worry," she said, returning his smile. "I'll be all right. I've known Lorraine all my life, remember?"

After he had gone she allowed the smile to slip off her face. She hesitated there for a while and then, as though her feet had taken over her body, found herself following after Derek. Softly she crossed the hall and went upstairs. She could hear voices coming from the playroom—she had no compunction about eavesdropping. The door was ajar and she could see the reflection of Lisa and Lorraine in the mirror opposite the door, and Derek was standing near the open doorway, his back to it. Laurel held her breath and listened.

"Hello, Mummy," Lisa said in her bright, pretty voice. "Have you come to see me in my new dress?" She twirled round, obviously failing to notice any differences in the woman she called "Mummy". But Lorraine then proceeded to crouch down before her, saying in a cooing voice utterly unlike Laurel's warm, natural one: "It's quite lovely, darling." Lisa stopped twirling then and stared at her mother. A puzzled frown crossed her face and tentatively she reached out one hand and touched the fur draped round Lorraine's shoulders.

"You look different, Mummy," she said slowly and looked uncertainly at her father. Laurel noticed how his hands were clasped behind his back and how they tightened until the knuckles were white.

"I've had my hair done, darling. I expect that's it," Lorraine offered, patting her elaborate coiffuer. "Do you like it?"

"Yes, but . . . I liked it better the other way. Like that it'll get all messed up when we go in the sea. You are taking me to the beach today, aren't you? You said so."

"Well . . . I . . ." It was Lorraine's turn to look up at Derek but she received no help from him. He relaxed a little now, thrusting his hands into his trouser pockets. "Well, perhaps if I have time," Lorraine agreed reluctantly. "Now, give me a kiss, darling."

Lisa obeyed willingly, this time saying, in a warmer voice, "You do smell nice, Mummy, and I like your pretty fur."

Laurel waited to hear no more. It was as though, by this short statement, Lisa had become completely lost to her forever. She turned swiftly and went almost blindly to her bedroom. It surprised her that she didn't cry. Perhaps it was true that some things really were too bad for tears. But she was shaking, desperately and uncontrollably as she tossed her clothes into a suitcase. She had no idea how she could get away but knew she could not bear to stay and watch Lorraine charm her way into Lisa's heart. She felt reasonably certain that Derek would not succumb and that was some small comfort. He was wise to Lorraine and would probably attempt to get her unwanted presence out of his home. But what could he do? Lorraine was beautiful and a good actress. She could convince any court in the land that she was desperately regretting her erring ways and had come home to be a good mother to Lisa. It was possible that in a real fight she might even be granted custody of the child. One thing was certain. Derek would never submit Lisa to that kind of tug of war. No. She, Laurel, had to get out of their lives and leave them to work out their own salvation. No matter how painful it was to go; she had no choice.

Luck was with her in that, as she went out of the front door, she met no one, but outside on the forecourt, Jason Harcourt was just in the process of getting into his car. Laurel called his name in a breathless whisper and ran over to him.

"Are you leaving now?" she asked. "Could you please give me a lift to Newport?"

"Mrs. Clayton, I really don't . . ." The solicitor hesitated. "I think I should tell you, I saw the other lady—she told me. . . ." He halted again and frowned. "I'm sure I don't understand."

"I'll explain as we go," Laurel said drearily. "Only please take me to Newport. I can get a bus to Cowes from there, can't I?"

The tale was long and involved and the solicitor listened in silence, occasionally shaking his head in disapproval and even clicking his tongue, as though he wondered at anyone making their lives so complicated. Just before he dropped her off at the Newport bus station, Laurel ventured to ask him rather timidly where he thought they stood in the eyes of the law. He obviously disliked giving advice without knowing all the facts but ventured his opinion that though Lorraine probably would not have a leg to stand on in court due to her previous record, it was unlikely that Derek would bring it to that because of Lisa. This confirmation of her own thoughts on the matter did nothing to make Laurel feel less dispirited.

EIGHT

"HEY, MARGIE, have you seen that gorgeous looking feller sitting at number five?"

The high pitched, rather whining voice of Sally, one of her fellow waitresses, scarcely sank into Laurel's bemused brain. She had been on duty since breakfasts began at seven and it was now three-thirty; she felt tired in every bone and muscle. The other girls, cheerful, garrulous Margie who was pretty and bright and working her way through the summer holidays before going to college in the autumn, and rather slatternly Sally, never seemed to get tired. Laurel often wondered if her weeks of playing at being Lorraine had made her soft. Once, when her father was alive, she would have thought working in a café with no more problems than remembering the various orders and totting up the bills was some kind of rest cure. Now she felt old and worn out.

In the kitchen, as she loaded up two Welsh rarebits and some toasted cheese sandwiches on to a tray, she was joined by Margie. The young girl was eighteen, over-imaginative and convinced that there was some mystery about Laurel. Laurel just didn't seem the type, with her looks and voice, to work in a run down place like Rosie's, which catered mainly for truck drivers and the occasional band of rowdy students who couldn't afford anything better. Now she glanced at Laurel, nudging her gently and, lowering her voice so that Jack, who owned the café and did all the cooking, could not hear, said, "Listen to her. As though a bloke like that would look twice at her! Anyway, it's you he's been looking at. Have you noticed?"

Laurel pushed her hair back from her hot brow. "I haven't noticed anything."

"Well, you look when you go in. On number five he is."

But when Laurel glanced over to number five, which was one of Sally's tables, it was occupied by a beefy truck driver that no stretch of the imagination could describe as "gorgeous". Pulling a face at her, Sally said, "He's gone. Only gulped down half a cupper and just went. Smashing he was too.

"Never mind," Sally told her with a gurgling laugh. "P'raps he'll come back, unable to get your charms off his mind!"

The whole incident meant little to Laurel whose aching feet concerned her more than all the "gorgeous fellers" in the world. Yet somehow it was almost inevitable, and she was not even surprised when, as she left the café at six, Derek was standing there waiting for her. They stared uncertainly at each other, from about four feet apart, and Laurel noticed how very weary he looked, as tired as herself. She said at last, "How did you find me?"

"Does it matter? The thing is, I found you. Why the hell did you go off like that? Didn't you think I'd worry? I've been nearly out of my mind with wondering what had happened to you. You could have let me know you were all right."

Tears sprang to her eyes. "I'm sorry. It seemed best . . ."

"Best? Oh, God! And look at you, working in that disgusting place . . ."

"I had to eat, Derek, and I'm not trained for anything else." Mindful of the fact that Margie and Sally might be out at any moment, she turned and walked away, and he followed. The width of the pavement was still between them and it might have been miles. Nothing was said during the whole half mile or so to the place where Laurel lived but at the front door she halted and looked uncertainly at him.

"I'm coming in," he told her shortly. "We have things to talk about and I don't intend talking here."

"There's nothing for us to say, Derek." The words hurt to utter and she looked and felt so wretched that he must have realised what she was feeling. "Is Lorraine at High Ridge?" she asked.

"What do you think, with twenty thousand quid at stake?" he said roughly. "I don't make it particularly pleasant for her but with that kind of money, she's remarkably tough."

"Yes, I suppose so." She sighed and chewed on her lip, finally pushing open the door and leading him along the corridor with its rather threadbare carpet, and up two flights of stairs. She had hoped eventually to get somewhere better but when she arrived in London five weeks earlier, with only a few pounds in her bag, this had seemed like a haven. Her room was no more than a glorified bed sitter with a small kitchenette and shared bathroom. At the door she said softly, "It isn't much."

"I don't suppose it is," he said savagely. "Neither is that place you've been working in." His eyes raked the small room, taking in every detail. He was wearing a charcoal grey lounge suit and looked very distinguished and wealthy. Laurel watched him with eyes that were dull and tired but behind her weary exterior she was vibrating and her senses clamoured with excitement and delight at seeing him again. He turned and looked at her.

"Oh, God," he said, the words wrenched painfully from him. "Why did you go?"

"You know why. You must know."

"I don't know . . . I know nothing except that my life has been hell and I can't stand another day away from you." He came towards her, his arms held out, but as she backed away he stopped moving, startled and distressed. "Don't!" he said harshly. "Don't be frightened of me!"

"Frightened?" she whispered. "Oh, Derek." And then she was in his arms that went with ferocious intensity round her, crushing her to him. They didn't kiss at once. It was as though all their energy was used up in holding on to each other, in experiencing an easing of that ache of longing that had beset them both for weeks. Only later, when they were able to release this strangle hold, did their lips meet in a long, loving kiss.

It was later still that Derek finally lifted his mouth from Laurel's and released her. He said nothing, just dropped his arms, leaving her bereft and empty, and walked round the room in a prowling, restless manner. It was so small a room that only half a dozen of his long strides took him down its length.

"This is a terrible place," he said at last.

"I know. I didn't have much money to start with. Finding a job was the most important thing."

He turned and faced her, resisting the temptation to take her into his arms again. She looked thinner than when he last saw her and her eyes were heavy with fatigue. "Lorraine told me what you were doing when she came to you with that proposition, and all about your father. You had a pretty rotten life so no wonder you jumped at the chance to get out of it for a while. I'm sorry I behaved so badly to you when I found out."

"It doesn't matter," she said flatly, and was shocked at the surge of pain that might well have been jealousy that went through her at the mention of Lorraine. Had she expected that they would not even talk together?

He seemed to understand. "I had very nearly to knock that much information out of her," he told her with a little mirthless smile. "For the first few days after you'd gone I think I nearly lost my mind . . . if it hadn't been for Lisa—well, I guess Lorraine knew she was treading on thin ice and she kept clear of me. But later, when I'd cooled down a bit she tried turning on the charm full force. Needless to say, it had no effect. She turns me on about as much as a ten ton truck would." He stopped talking and looked at Laurel, his eyes hungry with longing. "I love you," he said unhappily. "And there's not one bloody thing I can do about it. I've thought of so many schemes—of taking you and Lisa and getting away, far, far away, even leaving the country. But if I did that, it's probable Lorraine would get some kind of court order slapped on us and, short of keeping on running for years, I'd have to hand Lisa over to her. I even—" he smiled faintly, the smile merely deepening the worried lines on his face—"I even thought of buying a small house for you to live in so that we could be together sometimes. But I don't think you'd agree to that."

"No," she agreed softly, "I wouldn't. Oh, not for the reasons you think. But that kind of impermanence wouldn't do either of us any good. Or Lisa."

"It all comes back to Lisa, doesn't it?"

"It has to."

He nodded and sank heavily down on the small sofa, rubbing his eyes wearily. Laurel, moving softly, made a pot of coffee and they sat side by side drinking it.

"The crazy thing is," Derek told her, "when she came back she didn't even know about the twenty thousand quid in Caroline's will."

"I wondered about that. Obviously she couldn't have known so soon. Why did she come then?" Laurel asked, surprised. "She told me she'd never go back to you. She said you wanted her back but that as far as she was concerned it was just not on."

"I never knew such a woman for twisting the facts to boost her own ego," he remarked, leaning back and letting his tired eyes close. "She's changed though—she's quieter and more thoughtful. I offered to pay her the twenty thousand out of my own pocket. God knows, that would leave a big enough hole but it seemed worth the effort. I thought if she left we could get a quick divorce—it doesn't take long nowadays if you can prove a break-down of the marriage. But she laughed at the idea. She said what she needed now was a home. I

have a feeling something happened—that she's been thwarted somewhere along the line and is resting her wounds."

"A man?"

"Most probably. Maybe she discovered that not everyone does fall
for her charms after all."

"Could it be this Richard Benson—the photographer she went on
the tour with?"

Derek laughed. "Never. Lorraine ran off with that little squirt in
the first place. He's crazy on her. No, it must be someone else."

"She did mention . . ." Laurel said slowly, frowning ". . . a man
called—what was it? Blakeney, Peter Blakeney. Does that ring a
bell?"

"Can't say it does."

"He has something to do with the fashion business. Wait a minute!
I remember. He owns the magazine that Benson was doing the photography assignment for."

"Well, whatever, it can't help us," Derek said quietly and reached
out his arms towards Laurel. He drew her close to him, kissing her
slowly as though savouring every moment for the lonely times to
come. Willingly Laurel yielded to him but it was he who disentangled
himself from her, though with reluctance, managing a smile that was
rueful.

"I suppose we must be incredibly old fashioned . . . I must go,
my love. It's hard enough to keep my hands off you as it is, without
this kind of encouragement."

She watched him walk to the door; despite his apparent light
heartedness, she sensed his despair that was, after all, a reflection of
her own. It was almost too much to bear, this tearing away from
each other. She spoke his name sharply and got to her feet, and he
looked silently at her as she approached him.

"You can stay if you like." The words came easily, bringing a sort
of relief that was increased by the lightening of his expression. She
knew he required no proof of her love but she was willing to offer it
anyway. He smiled, genuinely this time, and kissed her without
touching her with his hands or his body.

"No, my love. There's nothing in the world I would like better
than to make love to you, but it would only make things more
difficult afterwards." He took her hands between his. "There is one
thing you can do for me though, that would make me feel very much
better."

"What is it?" she asked eagerly, her love shining in the depths of her hazel eyes. "I'll do anything. You know that."

"The apartment Lorraine lived in—the lease is mine as you probably know. Here are the keys. Go and live in it—no, listen! It's standing empty and might as well be used. With me paying the rent you'll have time to look round and find a better job if you still want to retain your independence." His hands tightened over hers, the pressure hurting a little. "How do you think I'll feel living in comparative luxury at High Ridge and knowing you're stuck here in this place?"

"All right," she agreed quietly. "I will."

"You will!" He actually laughed. "I thought I'd have much more of a fight on my hands."

"And if you want me, you'll know where to find me," she said levelly, lifting her chin a little.

"I'll always want you," he insisted huskily. "And sometime soon, I hope, I'll be free to marry you. When that time comes, if you still feel the same, then I'll know where to find you."

NINE

IT DIDN'T TAKE Laurel long to settle down in the apartment again yet she knew she could never be happy there as she once had been. Often she wondered if she would ever be happy again, and if the pain of Derek's loss would ever ease. It certainly didn't as the days turned to weeks and then into a month and another month. She heard nothing from him and concluded that he was deciding to make the most of the situation. True, she had insisted that it would be best if they did not contact each other at least until the situation had resolved itself but sometimes, when her spirits were at their lowest, she thought unreasonably that he might not have taken her so literally at her word. She wondered if he was happy and it did not lessen her own loneliness to know that he couldn't possibly be.

She found a better job working as a receptionist in a small hotel out towards Wimbledon, a job which paid quite well, was interesting and frequently offered the chance of night work, something she jumped eagerly at every time. Nights were definitely the worst time.

One afternoon, just after she had finished washing and drying her hair, the door bell rang loudly and insistently. Frowning, Laurel put away the hair dryer and went to answer the summons. She was confronted by a complete stranger, a tall, well built man of, she guessed, about fifty years, with crinkly iron grey hair and sharp grey eyes. She regarded him gravely, with the usual blank expression with which a person generally greets a stranger. On the other hand, the eyes that returned her gaze were bright and suddenly filled with longing.

"Hiya, honey. See, I've given in at last. Did you think I'd hold out so long?"

Laurel opened her mouth to explain his mistake but before she could utter one word he had taken a step towards her, grasped her in a bear hug and was kissing her with a fierce intensity that knocked all the fight out of her. Next moment she was struggling desperately.

"Look, I'm not Lorraine! For goodness' sake, I'm not, really, I'm not!"

She was released as swiftly as she had been grasped, and swayed, catching at the door post for support. The man stared, horrified, at her.

"I'm Lorraine's sister," she explained hurriedly.

"Oh, my God," he said, his accent, which was American, very strong in his confusion. "I'm sorry, miss. Hell, what must you think of me? I just assumed . . . you're so like . . ."

"Identical twins," Laurel said and smiled shakily. "It doesn't matter. We've confused people before though never quite so dramatically."

"I do truly beg your pardon, ma'am. Let me introduce myself. I'm Peter Blakeney. You may have heard Lorraine mention me?"

"Peter Blakeney?" Laurel repeated. "Yes, she did talk about you. Please come in, Mr. Blakeney."

Half an hour later, as he drank the tea Laurel had provided, Peter Blakeney finished his explanation and said to Laurel, "Well, I seem to have done all the talking, Miss Anderson. What have you to say? You still haven't told me where Lorraine is."

"Suppose she doesn't want to see you," Laurel said slowly, feeling her way uncertainly. "You tell me that you and Lorraine were lovers but that you had a terrific row. You haven't seen her for several weeks and when she left you in Brazil she said she never wanted to see you again."

"She said it but I'm prepared to believe she didn't mean it. Like I said, it was a pretty hot affair that started very quickly. We had met a couple of years ago and had dinner together but it wasn't until I flew out to Rio to see how Benson was getting on with the assignment that I saw her again and really fell heavily for her. Miss Anderson, I am neither young nor foolish. I've knocked about the world a bit and had my share of women. I accept that maybe my money is half, or more than half, why she went for me. But I'm forty-seven and I've been divorced twice. Quite frankly, I want Lorraine and I'm quite prepared to marry her under any circumstances."

"I see." Laurel looked steadily at the man who sat opposite her. He looked what he was, a very hard, no nonsense, American business man. Probably he could be ruthless, certainly no one would be allowed to make a fool of him. She wasn't at all sure that she liked him one bit, but possibly he was the sort of man who would appeal strongly to Lorraine.

"You do know where she is?" he inquired.

"Yes. She's on the Isle of Wight."

"But . . . doesn't her husband live there? Surely to God she hasn't gone back to him! She told me she loathed him, that he was a cold fish who kept her short of money."

"That isn't true!" Laurel cried, springing hotly to Derek's defence. "Derek isn't a bit like that. He's . . ." She halted and coloured beneath the penetrative stare of the American. It was very doubtful if he ever missed much. She said with quiet dignity, "I don't know if Lorraine mentioned it to you, but while she was away I was living here pretending to be her. Presumably she didn't tell you since you obviously knew nothing of my existence. She didn't want Derek to know where she was going or with whom, and thought I could hold the fort. Things went wrong however and Derek turned up here. To . . . to cut a long story short, as you've probably guessed, I'm in love with Derek and he loves me. But there's nothing we can do about ourselves. You see, Derek's aunt died and left Lorraine twenty thousand pounds provided she and Derek stay together for at least two years."

Blakeney's eyebrows snapped together into almost a continuous line along his brow. "Clayton needs the money, does he?"

"No, of course not. *He* doesn't want it. But he can't just kick Lorraine out, and there's Lisa to think about."

"Hmmm, so that's how it is." He rubbed his jaw, a very stubborn, aggressive jaw that was deeply cleft, and looked at Laurel. She saw to her surprise that there was a glow of speculation in his eyes, and regarded him suspiciously. No, she definitely did not like Peter Blakeney though he looked and behaved perfectly civilised. There was that hint of steely ruthlessness about him that proclaimed that what he wanted he took and to hell with who got hurt or trampled on in the process. She didn't think she would like to get on the wrong side of him.

He moved suddenly, lifting his large frame off the settee with surprising speed, and striding across the room to Laurel. He took her hand and pulled her to her feet.

"What are you doing?" Laurel shrieked. "Let me go!"

Blakeney did so and chuckled. "Don't worry, Miss Anderson. I don't have any designs on you. Get your coat. You and I are going on a trip."

"Are we? To where?" Laurel asked suspiciously.

"Why, to the Isle of Wight, of course."

It was rather ironic, Laurel thought, that if, in normal circumstances, a man like Peter Blakeney wanted to get quickly to the island, he would probably hire one of Derek's helicopters. But Blakeney had no intention of letting Derek know he was going there. He refused even to tell Laurel his precise plans. So they crossed the Solent by hydro-foil, a relatively swift and comfortable means of travelling that Laurel had not previously experienced. It was raining slightly when they disembarked at Cowes. Laurel, wearing a light weight trouser suit of cream denim, tied a scarf round her hair and stood patiently waiting while Peter Blakeney arranged for a taxi. She felt curiously detached, almost uninterested, in the proceedings. To be swept out of London to the Isle of Wight, from despair to a glowing, glimmering hope, in the space of less than two hours, had left her feeling rather odd.

She asked, "Are you going to High Ridge now?"

Blakeney shook his head. "I want to see Lorraine alone, and probably Clayton will be there at this time of the day. We'll stay in an hotel tonight. At my expense of course." He smiled quite gaily and with rather less guile than usual but it was a smile Laurel found herself unable to return. "What is it, girl?" he demanded then. "You look kind of put out."

"I think I don't like being manipulated, Mr. Blakeney," she replied levelly and he laughed as he helped her into the taxi.

"I've done plenty of manipulating in my time, Laurel, but just now I can plead not guilty. In fact I'm the one willing to be manipulated. I'll go along with whatever your sister says. She thinks twenty thousand pounds is a lot of money. Well, to me that's peanuts. I can lay half a million at her feet."

The rain that had spoiled the hydrofoil trip across the Solent eased off during the night to be replaced in the morning by a light drizzle that reduced visibility to barely fifty feet and seemed to penetrate the warmest clothes. Laurel felt sick with nerves as she sat in the taxi that was taking herself and Peter Blakeney to High Ridge. It all seemed too easy, this solution to hers and Derek's problems. Impossible to believe that Lorraine would agree to go away with Blakeney. Laurel imagined so many things that could go wrong. Suppose, in the interim, Lorraine and Derek had fallen in love with each other again? It was impossible for Laurel to imagine that any woman could live in the close vicinity of Derek and not love him, and Lorraine was, after all, very nearly irresistible. Laurel tightened her hands in her lap and stared unseeingly at the cold, damp morning.

She looked outwardly calm. Her hair, hanging loose to her shoulders, was covered with a fine sprinkling of raindrops that had fallen as she crossed the hotel forecourt to the taxi; her face was rather pale but this merely accentuated the unblemished quality of her skin and the appeal of her large eyes. Once she caught Peter Blakeney's eyes and saw the curiosity there.

"I must have been crazy," she uttered. "To let myself be talked into this."

"If you remember, my dear, I didn't talk you into it. I bulldozed you. And you need feel no guilt at having given in. In the past I've pushed far tougher people than you into doing something they're doubtful about. And as on those other occasions, I have complete faith in my judgement."

"I wish I had," Laurel said flatly, and he grinned.

A moment later the taxi turned quite sharply to the left and she saw the low, orange roofed shape of High Ridge. Blakeney leaned across her to look.

"Hmm, this is it, is it?" he asked critically. "Not bad at all. But not to be compared to my villa on Ischia or my ranch back in Texas."

Suddenly Laurel laughed and turned her face towards him. There was a note of near hysteria in her laughter but her words were simple and honest. "I would rather be here than anywhere else in the world," she said softly. "Shall I wait here?"

"No, certainly not." Blakeney told the driver to wait for him. "I may be some time," he explained.

Mrs. Mac opened the door. In other circumstances Laurel felt sure she would have laughed out loud at the outraged expression on the housekeeper's face as Blakeney, in his loud, rather vulgar way, demanded to see Lorraine. It was a moment or two before the Scotswoman glanced towards Laurel. She hid her surprise admirably but her eyes narrowed as she asked, "Miss Anderson, isn't it?"

Presumably either Derek or Lorraine had explained at least part of the story to Mrs. Mac. Laurel could see she was uncertain whether or not to be welcoming and finally turned back to Blakeney.

"Mr. Clayton is not at home, sir."

"It was Mrs. Clayton I wanted to see," Blakeney told her in his harsh, no-nonsense voice. "Tell her we're here and let us come in, my good woman. It's deathly cold and Miss Anderson is getting wet."

He took a firm step forward as he spoke so that Mrs. Mac was forced into ignoble retreat. She looked utterly outraged and Laurel knew that before long a full scale row might ensue. She swiftly moved past the American, catching at Mrs. Mac's arm. "Please tell us where Lorraine is, Mrs. Mac. It's awfully important that Mr. Blakeney sees her. It's important for . . . all of us." Her eyes widened appealingly and the housekeeper visibly relented.

"She's in the morning room, miss, having breakfast." Her tone clearly indicated what she thought of someone who was still breakfasting at ten-thirty in the morning. "Through there," she told Blakeney, pointing down the hall.

"Right. I'll . . ." Uncharacteristically, Blakeney hesitated and looked uncertain. He turned to Laurel. "I'll see her first. I'm hoping to . . ."

"Sweep her off her feet?" Laurel inquired, and he ignored the sarcasm and laughed.

"Something like that. Make sure she doesn't have a chance to think anyway."

Laurel and Mrs. Mac, left alone, looked steadily at each other. Despite her obvious desire to wash her hands of the whole business, Mrs. Mac was beginning to look intrigued. It didn't take an imbecile to know what Peter Blakeney wanted of Lorraine and as far as Mrs.

Mac was concerned, it was good riddance to bad rubbish! It hadn't taken two days for Mrs. Mac and the staff to realise how ordered and peaceful had been the time when Laurel was mistress of High Ridge. Mrs. Mac had not approved of the double rôle Laurel had played even though Derek had told her it was for the sake of Caroline, but still less did she approve of Lorraine's sharp tongue and imperious manner.

"I may as well tell you, I know everything, Miss Anderson," she announced sternly. "And frankly, I don't like the idea of being deceived as to your identity."

"I know, and I'm sorry, Mrs. Mac. I didn't want to deceive you or anyone. Most of all not Lisa or Mr. Clayton. But things kind of ran away with me. It started as quite an innocent deception and suddenly became like a tidal wave. It soon got to the point where I couldn't say anything without hurting too many people." She bit her lower lip. "I didn't get away with it quite unscathed myself you know."

"Aye, I realise that. And who's *he,* may I ask?" Mrs. Mac grunted, jerking her head in the direction of the morning room.

"His name is Peter Blakeney. He's an American millionaire and he's in love with Lorraine." Laurel realised she should not be quite so open with the housekeeper but it seemed to her that now was the time to be completely honest. This seemed to have an effect with Mrs. Mac who became more expansive by the minute.

"She's going to run off, is she? Like last time. Well, it'll be no great loss and that's a fact. She may be your sister, miss, but I always say what I think. Mr. Clayton looks as miserable as sin and poor young Lisa hardly knows whether she's coming or going. She can't understand why her mother suddenly changed character overnight so to speak."

"Where is Lisa?" Laurel demanded. It would be dreadful if Lisa was confronted by both her and Lorraine at once.

"At school. Term started this week."

"Oh, of course." As they spoke, Mrs. Mac led Laurel into the kitchen but before leaving the hall she glanced once towards the closed door of the morning room. Apart from a single cry of "Peter!" from an astonished Lorraine when he first entered, there had been no sound at all coming from that direction. Laurel accepted a cup of coffee from Mrs. Mac and took it into the lounge where she sat down and listlessly flicked through a magazine. Something like twenty minutes passed before the door opened and Peter Blakeney came in with Lorraine.

To say Lorraine looked radiant would not have been strictly the truth. But she looked content, very pleased with herself and rather smug. It was an expression Laurel recognised from days gone by, the expression Lorraine wore when she had made herself a bigger, better or more wealthy conquest than anyone else had. The same look she wore when she had casually, and without giving a damn, taken some other girl's boyfriend. She gave Laurel a nod by way of greeting.

"Guess what? I'm off to Greece. Peter has a yacht, the . . . what is her name?" she asked Peter.

"The Ariadne. She's moored off Corfu." Blakeney too looked immensely pleased with the success of his strategy, though in a more pleasant way than did Lorraine. "She's all set for a good long cruise round the Mediterranean. We'll fly out to Athens this evening in my private jet. I reckon a year should see the divorce through and meantime we can just about see all the best parts of the world. What about it, sweetheart? The West Indies, Monte Carlo, Hawaii, you name it, we go there." He slid an arm round Lorraine who smiled prettily at him with wide open, acquisitive eyes.

"Of course. Lovely. I'd better go and pack my things, hadn't I?"

"Don't bother, honey. We'll stop off in Paris and buy you a whole new wardrobe. Now, let's get going."

Laurel reflected rather sourly as she pulled on her damp raincoat and followed them to the door, that when it came to pure, unadulterated vulgarity, they just about deserved each other. Private jets, yachts in Corfu and stopping "off in Paris"—no wonder Lorraine looked over the moon.

"Where do you think you're going?" Lorraine demanded, and Laurel blinked herself back into the present.

"To the taxi, of course."

"Don't be crazy. You're not coming with us," Blakeney said, surprised.

"I'm not? But I thought . . . I thought you'd give me a lift back to Cowes at least. I can sit in front and . . ."

"My dear Laurel, have my plans been so completely confusing? The idea was for you to stay here to explain to Clayton what has happened and to—well, to console him."

"Console him?" Laurel echoed on a gasp of disbelief.

"He's bound to be furious at me for leaving him again," Lorraine sighed, giving the impression that Derek would be heartbroken. "But quite frankly I'd have gone mad if I had stayed here much longer. You must stay, Laurel, and maybe he'll not be so angry."

"But I can't stay!" Laurel burst out. "You know I can't . . . I can't just throw myself at him! I thought you wanted me to come to help persuade Lorraine to go with you. I would never have come for this reason." She couldn't have explained exactly why she was behaving this way, and really didn't blame Blakeney for looking at her as though she were behaving very unreasonably. Obscurely, she felt that Derek must be allowed to make his own decisions, to do his own seeking.

"You're crazy, girl," Blakeney told her as he led Lorraine outside. "If you want something bad enough in this life, you gotta fight tooth and nail for it, like I've done for Lorraine. You want Clayton. Okay, so stay . . . and maybe we'll all live happily ever after."

Short of causing a commotion before the extremely curious taxi driver, there was little Laurel could do. But as she watched the vehicle depart, with Lorraine and Blakeney already entwined in a passionate embrace in the back seat, she thought it really didn't matter that much. She could always phone for another taxi and there was plenty of time before Derek got home. She walked back into the house where Mrs. Mac was standing in the kitchen doorway watching her.

"I thought you'd gone with them," she said in a neutral voice.

"I intended to, but they seemed to think I would be one too many. I'll order a taxi now." She moved to the phone.

"I'll do it," Mrs. Mac interrupted softly. "But why don't you stay for lunch? There's no rush that I can see and just look at the weather."

It was true that the drizzle of earlier had turned to a steady downpour and from the appearance of the sky it had set in for the day. Laurel shivered and was tempted to stay for a while. When Mrs. Mac told her she had made one of her famous and delicious steak and kidney pies she could not refuse.

"I'll get the taxi straight after lunch," she maintained firmly, and wondered why Mrs. Mac smiled rather secretly.

She was not kept wondering for long. Just after twelve when the kitchen was warm and smelt wonderfully of cooking pastry, and Laurel was setting the kitchen table, the door opened and Jackie came in with a dripping wet Lisa who was wearing a blue raincoat and hat. Laurel had not realised Lisa would be home to lunch; she would never have believed the way her love for the little girl twisted painfully inside her but as she saw her she longed to take her in her arms. It hurt terribly that Lisa virtually ignored her.

She turned to Mrs. Mac reproachfully. "You never told me Lisa would be home before I left."

"You never asked," Mrs. Mac asserted with a hint of triumph. "Lisa, get that wet raincoat off."

"Hello, Mummy," Lisa murmured in a subdued voice. She regarded the table with interest. "Am I having lunch in here?"

"We all are," Laurel told her. Lisa's lukewarm welcome had shown only too well how she got on with Lorraine. It would be as well to keep her own relationship with the child cool as she would be leaving after lunch, but it wasn't easy for she longed to kiss away that strangely grown up, rather sad look that was on Lisa's face. Instead she asked, "How was school?"

"All right," Lisa intoned, staring at Laurel across the bowl of soup Mrs. Mac had placed before her. "Mummy, you've had your hair done again."

"Have I?"

"It looks all nice, like it used to."

Laurel could not resist a broad, pleasurable smile. "Well, thank you, Lisa. I'm glad you approve."

Obviously Lisa was confused and Laurel felt very guilty at adding to this confusion. It seemed as though Lisa knew all was not as it should be but was too young to work out exactly what was amiss. All through the meal, which she ate with a healthy appetite and beautiful table manners, she threw Laurel the occasional, puzzled stare. But it was not until later, just before she was due to be taken back to school, that she relaxed completely and threw her arms round Laurel's neck. The unexpectedness of the gesture of love disarmed Laurel totally and before she knew it, her arms were round Lisa and she was holding her hard.

"You've come back again," Lisa whispered. "I knew you would. My lovely Mummy." But when Laurel questioned what she meant she merely shook her head and would not, or could not, explain. "You will be here when I get home, won't you?" Lisa asked.

"Well, Lisa, I . . ."

"Please!" Lisa cried, tears coming readily to her eyes. "You must be here. Please."

"All right, love, I'll be here."

"Promise?"

"I promise.

"You arranged that, didn't you?" Laurel asked Mrs. Mac who had listened to this interchange with an air of great satisfaction, as of a job well done.

"I suppose you might say so."

"You know nothing can come of it. It will only cause trouble and more heartache. No matter how we look at it, Derek and Lorraine are still married. I don't know much about divorce laws but it isn't that easy, not when there are children involved. And besides, neither of us knows how Derek will feel. He may think he's being manipulated, that his life is being organised for him."

"Pooh!" Mrs. Mac snorted scornfully. "I've known him since he was just a lad and I know him as well as anyone. Just you wait and see—there'll be no harm done."

"No harm done! Oh, Mrs. Mac! I'll be a nervous wreck by the time seven o'clock comes."

"No you won't. When Lisa comes home you can give her her tea and have her bathed and ready for bed. You won't have time to worry about anything else."

"Mrs. Mac, you didn't approve of me when I first came here, did you?" Laurel asked later. "Why have you changed your mind?"

"I thought you were her, didn't I? What else could I think? And I'd seen what she did. Running off with that soft, weak-kneed photographer chap and leaving Mr. Clayton and Lisa. Any woman that runs off and leaves her child, well, she deserves all she gets as far as I'm concerned. But you . . . you love them both, don't you?"

"With all my heart."

"Well then," said Mrs. Mac with satisfaction.

It was just after eight o'clock when Derek's Jaguar finally appeared in the drive. He dashed through the rain into the house, and Laurel, who had been standing partially hidden by the curtains by the window where she had been nervously waiting for over half an hour, saw him and quickly moved away to sit in a chair with her back to the door. He came into the lounge, shaking the rain off his wet hair and, as Laurel remained still, trying to calm her shattered, aching body, while every sense in her clamoured to run to him, to throw herself into his arms and experience the bliss of his embrace, his kiss, he crossed straight to the cocktail bar and poured himself a whisky. He scarcely even looked her way but stood there scouring the front page of the daily paper. Laurel glanced surreptitiously at him. His face was set in deep, unhappy lines and he glared at the paper as though it had personally affronted him. When he spoke it was in such sharp and harsh accents that she jumped.

"I thought you were going out."

"Wh—what?" she asked, her eyes wide. He had spoken without looking at her and his tone was distinctly unpleasant.

"I thought you were supposed to be going to some precious cocktail party. You've not even changed." So he had noticed her plain blouse and skirt.

"I . . . I didn't think I would," Laurel murmured, wondering why Mrs. Mac had overlooked this fact.

"Well, I don't give a damn," he said, tossing down the paper. "I don't suppose you were expecting me to come with you."

"Would you?" she asked softly.

"No. I've better things to do with my time than mix with that bunch of brainless idiots."

He had reached the door as he finished speaking and was in the process of leaving. This was just too much for Laurel. She stood up, saying his name uncertainly. He sighed with exasperation, obviously expecting recriminations, and turned reluctantly. "What now?"

"Look at me, can't you?" she cried out. "For heaven's sake, surely you can tell us apart!"

Only then, for the first time, did he raise his eyes and look directly at her. Slowly, wonderingly, his gaze took in the flawless perfection of her skin that was unmarred by make up, the casual prettiness of her hair style that fell in natural waves to her shoulders, the slim body clothed in its very ordinary skirt and blouse. His eyes came back to her face and saw there the anxiety and wariness, as though she were unsure of his reaction to her.

He said softly, "Laurel."

"Well, of course it is. Can't you see?" she cried out and then astonished them both by bursting into tears. He stepped forward then to start mopping up the tears, his voice and hands gentle as he soothed her. But this simply made the tears fall faster. He shook her a little then and decided drastic action was necessary, pulling her close and fastening his mouth on her wet, trembling lips. The tears stopped magically and she clung to him.

"And now will you stop crying, and tell me what you're doing here?" he demanded, and added, before she could tell him, "Oh God, I don't care what you're doing here. So long as you are here. I can't believe it. It's like a dream. Darling, what *are* you doing here?"

In his arms she could scarcely think straight. "Let's sit down," she suggested, blushing slightly at the love and longing she read in his eyes. "And I'll tell you."

Much later she continued, "So you see, it isn't that easy. It's not all finished. I don't even know if Lorraine will want to get a divorce. It all happened so quickly."

"Darling, now I can divorce *her,* and from the sound of this Blakeney character, he'll make sure she doesn't contest it," Derek murmured in a lazy, contented voice. "I'll marry you, my lovely girl, and soon. I don't know when, and it's going to be a strain keeping away from you . . ." He smiled again and put one hand over her mouth as she parted her lips to speak. "No, love. I know what you're going to say—that you'll come to live here with me even though we're not married. And I'll say no, for two reasons. First because I've waited so long for you that it won't kill me to wait longer—" He grinned. "Not quite anyway. And besides, it won't be so bad knowing that there will be you at the end of the waiting. Secondly, and more practically, it's possible that it may affect the divorce if we live together." He laughed softly. "If the waiting gets intolerable, darling, I'll let you know and we'll disappear for a weekend together."

"All right," she agreed promptly, and Derek let out a shout of laughter.

"I was only joking, sweetheart."

"I wasn't," Laurel said firmly, and joined in his laughter as he drew her into his arms.

*   *   *

Just over a year later, Laurel stood by the balcony of the third floor hotel suite where she and her husband were spending their honeymoon. The sea was immediately below her—for the hotel, built out of the towering cliffs of Capri, hung in an apparently precipitous position, over the rocky coastline. It was early morning and the heat haze had not yet begun to obscure the view. From where she stood Laurel could admire the mainland, the long, hilly and green peninsula of Sorrento and, much further away, strange and rather ominous even in broad daylight, Vesuvius rising above the city of Naples. She stretched lazily and luxuriously, lifting her heavy hair off her shoulders and shaking her head gently. She turned and looked at the bed where Derek was sleeping, on his back with one arm bent up behind his head. She shivered a little then, with the same kind of suppressed excitement that had beset her for many weeks now at the thought of being alone at last with him. The excitement was different now—the small element of fear had gone to be replaced by a deep sense of satisfaction with him and with herself. When she sat before the dressing table and looked at her reflection in the mirror, she surprised a look almost of smugness on her face.

"Why," said a sleepy voice from the bed, "do women always believe they look different after they have been made love to for the first time?"

Laurel caught his eye in the mirror and smiled. "Do they? Perhaps that's because they are different."

He propped himself upon one elbow. "You certainly look very pleased with yourself."

"So do you." She turned right round on the stool and looked directly at him. "You look positively smug."

"And why not?" He held out one hand towards her. "Come here."

A little sparkle of mischief lit her eyes as she shook her head and stood up. "I thought I'd go and have a bath. After all, there's a lot to see here. And we should do all the sight seeing we can."

"Laurel!" he said sternly, not altering his position. "Come here. Don't make me come and get you."

Hiding her quick smile, Laurel headed for the bathroom door. Next moment, before she had taken another step, she was seized from behind, lifted, legs kicking, clear of the floor. He dumped her, struggling—but not too much—on the bed and leaned over her.

"Disobedient wives I will not tolerate. Begin the way you mean to go on, that's my motto," he muttered, lying down beside her and stopping her half hearted protest with a kiss.

Some time later, Laurel wrapped her arms firmly round his neck and smiled with even greater smugness. "If that's the way you're going to behave every time I'm disobedient, I'm afraid you're stuck with the most disobedient wife in the world," she told him with extreme satisfaction.